One Good Crash

A Novel

SABRINA STARK

Copyright © 2018 Sabrina Stark

All rights reserved.

ISBN-13:

9781729032145

CHAPTER 1

Headlights.

Oh, shit. I stood frozen in the narrow street for what felt like forever. And yet, it was barely a split second. I knew this, because even in my addled state, I wasn't so stupid that I'd just stand around, waiting to be flattened like a pancake in a party dress.

And yet, here I was.

Tires squealed. Someone screamed. The vehicle swerved, missing me, but just barely – passing so close that it ruffled the fabric of my overpriced outfit.

A pounding heartbeat later, the sound of metal hitting metal echoed in the night. I whirled to look.

Oh, no.

I cringed, even as I tried to catch my breath. In the flickering streetlights, I saw an exotic sports car smashed up against a white delivery van – one of three that were parked along the opposite curb of the desolate city street.

The sports car's engine was still running, even if the car itself was now motionless. Its headlights were still on, illuminating the pavement ahead. From somewhere behind the car's dark tinted windows, its stereo was still playing, heavy metal if I wasn't mistaken.

The side facing me – the driver's side – looked absolutely pristine, with no damage whatsoever. But the other side? The side I *couldn't* see? Well, I didn't even want to think about it.

With my heart in my throat, I plunged forward, desperate to make sure they were okay.

I'd gotten barely two steps when a hand clamped onto my elbow. I felt a yank and turned to look. My mother was yelling again. "For God's sake, Cassidy, get back in the limo!"

If I weren't so worried, I might've laughed in her face. *Dream on, psycho.*

But I *didn't* laugh, and I didn't say what I was thinking. Worry aside, this was the woman who'd given me life twenty-two years ago. Unfortunately, this was *also* the woman who'd just suggested a three-way with her latest sugar-daddy.

I shuddered with revulsion, even as she gave my elbow another yank. "Come on!" she urged, as if oblivious to the accident.

But even my mother couldn't be *that* clueless. We'd caused that collision, plain and simple. And besides, wasn't it against the law to leave the scene of a crash?

I dug in my heels and refused to budge. "No."

My mother was petite and brunette, with stunning cheekbones and full, pouty lips. She looked barely thirty, even if she'd be forty-four next July.

She was dressed to kill in a burgundy chiffon cocktail dress and silver stiletto heels. The dress was stylish and expensive with a short, flared skirt and a neckline that plunged halfway to her navel. She looked good, fabulous actually. But then again, she always did, even now, when she was giving me that look – the one she *always* gave just before she popped.

But so what? She could pop all she wanted. There was no way on Earth I'd be getting back inside that limo – and not only because of the accident.

After all, I'd fled that thing for a reason.

"Forget it," I told her. "I'm not going anywhere."

Yes, it was a stupid thing to say. After all, I had to go *somewhere*. We weren't in the best part of town, and in my current outfit, I wouldn't exactly blend. Hell, I'd probably be robbed – or worse – within five minutes, ten tops.

The sad thing was, I had nothing worth stealing, even if my appearance suggested otherwise.

Still, I stiffened my spine and waited for the fireworks.

But for once, my mom *didn't* pop. Instead, she took a deep, calming breath and summoned up a fake smile. "Oh, come on," she said, "be reasonable."

I gave her a hard look. "Why?"

"Because Dominic's waiting."

Un-freaking-believable. My fingers clenched, and I fought a sudden urge to slap her. "Fuck Dominic."

My mother gasped. "What did you say?"

I gave a bark of laughter. "Oh, please. What, you're shocked by my language?" *To be honest, I was a little shocked myself.*

Her mouth tightened, but she made no reply.

I forced another laugh. "I mean, hey, that's what I'm supposed to be doing, isn't it? 'Fucking' Dominic?"

At this, my mother had the good grace to look embarrassed, but only for a split second before she lifted her chin and announced, "I suggested no such thing."

Liar.

I knew my mother, probably better than she knew herself. And I knew exactly what she'd been getting at, even if she was now trying to pretend otherwise.

Her hand was still on my elbow. Her fingers tightened, and she gave another yank. Her long nails dug into my skin, and I tried not to flinch.

That's when I heard it – the sound of an unfamiliar male voice, asking, "How's it goin'?"

I stifled a gasp. The way it sounded, the voice had come from directly behind me. I whirled to look, only to stop halfway when the hand on my arm prevented further movement.

Damn it.

With a sound of frustration, I whirled back to my mom and gave her a pleading look, not that it did a lick of good. Her gaze was firmly glued to the stranger.

From the way she was staring, she liked what she saw.

Well, this was just great.

I had no idea what the stranger looked like, but I could make some pretty good guesses. He was definitely tall. That much was obvious by the way my mom was craning her neck to stare up at him. He was also very rich or very good-looking – possibly both. My mom had an eye for life's finer things and even now, was probably cataloguing his clothes and assessing his net worth.

From the gleam in her eyes, it was impressively high.

Her lips curved into a slow, sultry smile. "It's going fabulous," she replied. "How's it going with you?"

Oh, for God's sake.

Again, I tried to look. Again, my mom held firm. Short of making a fool of myself, I didn't know what to do.

But soon, I didn't need to do anything because just then, the guy strode into my line of vision. He stopped within arm's reach, an equal distance between me and my mom. His cool gaze swept over both of us before it strayed to the limo, idling at the curb just a few feet away.

As for *my* gaze, it remained firmly on him.

He was no Dominic.

And for once, I could totally see why my mom was staring.

The guy was tall and perfectly proportioned with dark, wavy hair and dark, dangerous eyes. He was wearing a black tuxedo of all things. It fit him perfectly, showing off his wide shoulders, trim waist, and long, lean legs.

My silent inspection ended at his shoes. They looked expensive, but what did I know? My own shoes were borrowed, just like the rest of my stupid outfit.

I was still studying his shoes when it occurred to me that he hadn't answered my mom's question. I mimicked her voice in my head. *How's it going with you?*

I almost scoffed out loud. *Seriously?*

I was no mind-reader, but it wouldn't be hard to guess the guy's honest answer. *Terrible.*

The street was utterly deserted, which meant that he must've come from that exotic sports car – the one that had just crashed, thanks to the drama between me and my mom.

As I stared down at his shoes, I braced myself, waiting for him to start yelling, or at the very least, demand my name, or my insurance, or something.

But other than his oddly casual greeting, he'd been eerily silent.

Slowly, I looked up to study his face. Our eyes met for the briefest instant before his gaze drifted downward to my imprisoned elbow. He frowned. "Is there a problem?"

Oh yeah. Tonight, there were so many problems that if I started talking now, I'd still be yammering at sunrise – not that I'd ever subject a stranger to my list of complaints.

So instead, I gave my arm another yank. This time, my mom actually let go. Of course, she did it nice and smooth, as if she *hadn't* been holding me in a death grip. Her hand drifted to her hair, and she made a show of brushing a long tendril off her nearly bare shoulder. In response to the stranger's question, she practically purred, "No problem here. Just girl talk. You know how it is."

The guy's jaw tightened, and something in his eyes suggested that yes, he did know – and not the way she hoped.

The stranger looked back to me and asked, "You need a ride?"

Before I could even think of answering, my mom spoke up. "Actually, we have plans for tonight, but I'd just *love* to give you my number."

I couldn't help but cringe. One thing about my mom, she never wasted an opportunity, not even now, when she was literally on her way to meet someone else – a guy who happened to be a whole lot older and a lot less attractive.

But then again, my mom *did* like to trade up.

In the back of my mind, I gave it five minutes before she pulled out the old "I'm too tipsy to walk" routine. I *so* didn't want that to happen. Already, she was like two seconds away from tossing the guy her panties – assuming she was wearing any.

On that disturbing note, I took a deep breath and asked the awful question that I'd been dreading. "Was that your car?" I felt myself swallow. "I mean, the one that just crashed?"

Of course, it *had* to be. Pricey car, pricey guy, pricey shoes – well, as far as I could tell, anyway.

His gaze locked on mine. "Forget the car."

Across from us, my mom gave a little laugh. "As if we could." She glanced briefly toward the accident. "That *is* a Lamborghini, right?"

I tensed. *Oh, God. Was it?* With renewed dread, I turned to look. The car's engine was no longer running, and its stereo had gone utterly silent. As for the headlights, they were still on. But why? To illuminate the street ahead? Or because the crash had messed up something with the controls?

Either way, the car would surely need some serious repairs. I bit my lip. *How much would they cost? And who would be paying?*

I was still looking at the car when my mom told the guy, "You won't believe this, but that's my absolute dream car."

My stomach clenched. Her dream. *My* nightmare. I didn't bother pinching myself, because I was definitely awake – unfortunately.

The guy said, "It's not a Lambo."

It wasn't?

Was that good?

Or bad?

With *my* recent luck, the car was probably something *more* expensive.

I looked back just in time to see my mom reach out and place a flirty hand on the lapel of the guy's tuxedo jacket. She beamed up him and whispered, "Funny, I *still* love it. Crazy, huh?"

The stranger's gaze shifted to her hand. After a long, cold moment, he replied, "You said it. Not me."

Something in his tone – or maybe in his eyes – made my mom pull back. Still, she managed to say, "So…maybe you'll give me a ride sometime?"

Oh, she wanted a ride, alright.

I spoke up. "Would that be *before* or *after* it's repaired?"

Her gaze snapped in my direction. "Of course, I mean after." She tried for a laugh. "Obviously."

I was glaring now. "You *do* realize we caused that accident." I held her gaze and waited. For what, I didn't know. It's not like she was big on accepting responsibility.

After a long moment, she looked away and mumbled, "I wouldn't say *we*."

Well, that was nice.

Regardless, the guy deserved an apology and some sort of explanation. I looked back to him and said, "I'm *really* sorry about that. I swear, I didn't see you coming, and…um…" I paused. *And what?*

How could I explain without airing a whole bunch of dirty laundry?

I was still searching for the right thing to say when my mom tried for another laugh. "Oh, stop," she said with a breezy wave of her hand. "That was just a fender-bender. And besides, he already told us to forget the car." She gave the stranger her sexiest smile. "I mean, these things happen, right?"

In a weird, twisted way, my mom was surprisingly correct. These things *did* happen, every single time I was stupid enough to let her back into my life.

I should've known better.

If I weren't so used to this sort of thing, I might've cried. But I'd dried those years ago, back in Nashville, when I'd decided that I was done with her for good.

And yet, here I was, in Brentwood Beach, Florida – Ground Zero for what my best friend had dubbed Mama Drama. What *I* called it, I couldn't say – not without a lot of muttering and cursing.

Still, I tried to look on the bright side. At least I wasn't roadkill. That was something, right?

An electronic beep jolted me back to reality. I looked to see the stranger reach into his pocket and pull out a cell phone. He glanced at the display and made a half-scoff, half-chuckle before he began tapping at the screen, obviously texting back some sort of response.

I watched him in perplexed silence. Everything about him confused the heck out of me. Obviously, he'd been on his way to someplace important. And obviously, I'd just cost him a good chunk of money, not to mention the time and inconvenience.

Wasn't he supposed to be chewing me out or something?

So, why wasn't he?

He was still texting when my mom sidled closer to him and said, "When you're done, hand me your phone. I'll key in my number…" She smiled. "…just in case."

Oh, please. "In case what?" I snapped. "He wants to send someone the bill?"

My mom blinked. "The bill for what?"

"For the car, obviously."

Her brow wrinkled. "But he already said to forget it."

The guy finished texting and shoved the phone back into his pocket. He looked to the limo and said, "Your ride's waiting."

"Oh." My mom's shoulders slumped. "So you want us to leave?"

"No." He looked to my mom and said, "I want *you* to leave." He flicked his head in my direction. "But *she's* coming with me."

CHAPTER 2

I froze. "I am?"

True, he *had* offered me a ride, but I never said yes. Even now, I wasn't quite sure that I should.

Thanks to my mom, I'd seen more than my share of rich men, although not in the way she'd planned for tonight – thank God. Still, what I *had* seen had taught to me to be wary of guys with big wallets and even bigger expectations.

The guy looked to me and asked, "You need anything from the limo?"

Yeah. My sanity.

Stalling, I glanced around, taking in the empty buildings and deserted street. My gaze landed on his car, and I winced all over again. Feeling guiltier than ever, I looked back to him and asked, "Are you sure it's drivable? Your car, I mean."

He gave something like a laugh. "My car's fine. It's on the way."

Okay, that made zero sense. Again, I turned toward the accident. I couldn't see the damage, and yet, I did know that his car couldn't be fine. Drivable maybe. But fine? No way.

I was still thinking when the guy repeated the gist of his question. "The limo – you need to grab anything? Like a purse or phone?"

My mom gave a little stomp of her foot. "She's not grabbing anything. I already told you, we have plans."

Instantly, an image of those so-called plans flashed in my brain. Dominic was naked and – holy hell – so was my mom.

Eye bleach. I needed it fast, even more so because I just knew that any second now, I'd be making my own appearance.

I blurted out, "Yes!"

In unison, my mom and the stranger turned to look.

My mom's gaze narrowed. "Yes to what?"

I looked to the stranger and said, "A ride would be *really* great. Thanks."

"What?" my mom sputtered. "You're ditching me? Just like that?"

Technically, I'd ditched her the moment I'd run from the limo. But this wasn't the time to quibble, especially in front of an audience.

I gave the guy an apologetic look. "But I *do* need to grab my purse."

I'd been so distracted that I hadn't thought to snatch it on my way out. Score one for the stranger. At least *he* was thinking.

I turned away, intending to make a quick dash to the limo when my mom said, "Aren't you forgetting? It's not *your* purse."

Heat flooded my face. She was right, of course. The purse – some tiny silver thing – was only borrowed, just like the rest of my loathsome outfit.

Reluctantly, I turned back to face her. "Fine. I'll just take out my stuff."

She frowned. "But what about the dress? And the shoes? Those aren't yours either."

As if I needed the reminder.

My face was burning now. I snuck a quick glance at the stranger, expecting to see surprise or maybe contempt. But he wasn't even looking at us. He was looking toward the limo – no doubt, wondering why I wasn't there and back already.

I looked back to my mom and said, "I'll give them to you later."

"Oh, really?" She gave me a thin smile. "And where would that be?"

I wasn't following. "What?"

"If you think you can just waltz back into the penthouse like nothing happened, you're crazy."

I gave her a look. *"I'm* crazy? You're kidding, right?"

She stiffened. "What's that supposed to mean?"

I threw up my hands. "You know what? Forget it. We'll talk later." Once again, I turned away, only to nearly collide with the limo driver –

a big, beefy guy who'd apparently gotten tired of waiting behind the wheel.

He glowered down at me. "So, did you barf or what?"

I wanted to die of embarrassment. Still, I lifted my chin and said, "No."

"Are you gonna?"

Well, I suddenly felt like it. Did *that* count?

From behind me, my mom said, "No. She's not going to 'barf.' I told you she was lying."

Yes. That was me. A big barfy liar. "I'm fine," I told the guy. "I just need to grab my stuff." I made a move to sidestep around him. But he moved at the same time, effectively blocking my path.

He was still glowering. "What stuff?"

"My purse." I hesitated. "Well, I mean the things inside it."

My mom gave a derisive snort. "What are you planning to do? Put them in a paper sack?"

I turned to give her an annoyed look. "Do you *have* a paper sack?"

"No."

"Then I guess that's not an option now, is it?" I turned back toward the driver, intending to push my way past him. But something made me pause. It was the sight of the stranger, striding past, heading toward the limo.

I watched with the others as he yanked open the nearest back door, reached inside, and pulled out the purse.

The limo driver called out, "Hey! You can't do that."

But already, the stranger was heading back toward us, gripping the purse in one hand. He stopped beside me and held it out, saying, "You ready?"

Was I ever. Nodding, I took the purse from his outstretched hand and dug out my belongings – a cell phone, a mostly empty wallet, and – *oh, crap* – a slender tampon that I'd tucked away, just in case my monthly came early.

Damn it. Where was a nice paper sack when I needed it? Clutching my pitiful belongings in my right hand, I used my left hand to thrust the empty purse toward my mom. "There," I said. "It's all yours."

With a hard sigh, she snatched it away and said, "Terrific. Now, just give me the dress, and we'll call it good."

My jaw clenched. "I already told you, I'll give it to you later."

"No." She straightened. "I need it now."

What the hell? "For what?"

"Well, if *you're* not coming with me, I'll need to find someone else." She gave my dress the once-over. "It *is* part of a set, you know."

Oh yeah. I knew.

And I would've known a lot sooner if only she hadn't been hiding her own outfit under a long coat until we were already on the road.

From behind me, the limo driver said, "If you want, *I'll* get the dress."

Horrified, I whirled back to face him. "What?"

He gave a loose shrug. "I'm just saying, I'm here to help."

To help with what? Undressing me? I almost laughed in his face. "Yeah. I just bet."

From beside me, the stranger told the driver, "You wanna try? Go ahead. But you'll be flat on your ass."

The driver laughed. "You think so, huh?"

But the stranger wasn't laughing. His voice grew deadly quiet. "Try it and see."

Oh, crap. This wasn't what I wanted. Already, I'd caused more than enough trouble, and besides, the limo driver had surely been joking.

Right?

Hoping for the best, I said, "Let's just go, okay?" I turned away, only to feel a beefy tug on the shoulder strap of my dress.

With a gasp of surprise, I whirled back just in time to see the stranger haul back and clock the driver squarely on the jaw. My mom gave a little squeal, even as the driver staggered backward, blurting out, "What the fuck?"

Next to me, the stranger gave a quiet scoff. "Quit bitching," he told the guy. "That was just a tap."

I bit my lip. It hadn't looked like a tap to me. It hadn't *sounded* like one either.

But then again, what did I know? I'd never seen a fist-fight, at least not in person. I didn't *want* to see one, especially now. Desperate to smooth things over, I said, "Let's just forget it and move on, alright?"

Of course, my suggestion was promptly ignored by all of them, including the limo driver who looked ready to throttle someone. He lumbered forward until he was standing just outside swinging distance. He glowered at the stranger and said, "You sucker-punched me. Asshole."

In a near panic, I said, "It can't be a sucker punch if he warned you." I turned and gave the stranger a hopeful look. "Right?"

He grinned. "I like the way you think."

His smile – so darned cocky – did funny things to my insides, and I felt an obscenely warm glow settle somewhere south of my stomach.

It lasted for only a split second before the driver gave a guttural roar and plowed forward head-first toward the stranger.

In a fast, fluid motion, the stranger turned to the side, leaving the limo driver to skim past and tumble forward of his own momentum. His hands and knees hit the pavement a split second before his forehead, and I couldn't help but wince even as he yelped, "Son of a bitch!"

He pushed himself up and whirled toward the stranger. "You did that on purpose!"

The stranger shrugged. "You think?"

The driver made a noise that sounded suspiciously like a growl. If he started foaming at the mouth, I wouldn't have been surprised.

I yelled, "Just stop it, okay?" I gave the limo driver a pleading look. "We don't want any trouble." I looked to the stranger for confirmation. "Right?"

His gaze met mine, and I swear I saw the hint of a smile. "I don't mind a little trouble."

A nervous scoff escaped my lips. "Good thing, since I've caused you loads."

Behind us, my mom demanded, "But what about *me*?"

Huh?

I turned to look. "What about you?"

She gave me a frown. "You've caused *me* trouble, too, you know."

Right. Because it *had* to be about her.

What else was new?

From a few feet away, the limo driver was glaring at all three of us. I half expected him to charge again, but he didn't. Instead, he zoomed in on my mom and said, "Screw this. I'm leaving. Are you coming or not?"

She was still frowning. "But what about the dress?"

The driver muttered, "Hey, I tried."

Ignoring that disturbing tidbit, I turned to stare at her. "Seriously? You *still* want the dress?"

Her lips formed a pout. "I'm just saying, since you're not using it..."

"I *am* using it," I told her. "What do you expect? For me to run around naked?" As soon as the words left my mouth, I wanted to take them back. What was I? Some sort of glutton for humiliation?

My mom was saying, "I think there's a tablecloth in the limo. You could use that."

Well, I had to give her points for persistence.

But she could persist all she wanted. I was done arguing. "Forget it." With that, I turned away, intending to march to the stranger's car with my head held high.

I never made it.

Why? Because I'd gotten only half a step when the limo driver made his move. He charged forward, looking to take the stranger by surprise. That didn't happen. As if the stranger had anticipated this all along, he stepped to the side and lifted a clenched fist, which the driver promptly ran into, face first.

What a dumb-ass.

The guy staggered backward, lost his footing, and tripped in a pothole, sending him sprawling sideways on the darkened concrete.

All three of us stared down at the guy, groaning in the street. My mom scurried forward and said, "You're not hurt are you?" She glanced down at her watch. "Because we really do need to get going."

And this is when deja-vu hit like a ton of bricks – because what did I see rounding the nearby corner?

Headlights – all over again.

CHAPTER 3

I gave a little shriek even as the car roared closer. Without thinking, I plunged forward, wanting to alert the driver to the body in the road.

A hand on my elbow yanked me back. I whirled to look. It was the stranger, saying, "It's fine."

Tires squealed, someone screamed, and the headlights came to a screeching halt just a few feet away from where we all stood – well, except for the limo driver, who was still lying on the pavement.

In cheerier news, he wasn't groaning anymore. So that was good, right? The headlights were nearly blinding, and I shielded my eyes as I stared down at the guy. He looked perfectly fine – a little traumatized maybe, but weren't we all?

I gave him an encouraging smile. "You're okay, right?"

My mom said, "Of course he's okay." She gave him a little nudge with her foot. "But you'd better get up," she told him. "We don't want to be late."

In front of us, the headlights cut out, leaving spots dancing in my vision. I squinted in frustration, and the new vehicle finally came into focus. It was *another* exotic sports car.

What were the odds?

The driver's side door opened, and the driver emerged looking like – huh? – almost an exact replica of the first stranger, right down to the tuxedo.

I looked from guy to guy, wondering what on Earth was going on.

As if reading my confusion, the first guy said, "My brother."

"Oh."

"*And* my car."

I looked toward the first car, the one that had crashed however long ago. Just as I did, the guy's brother must've looked too, because he practically yelled, "My car – what the fuck?"

The first guy shrugged. "I told you there was a problem."

"But you didn't say you fuckin' crashed it."

"Hey," the first guy said, "watch your language, alright?"

"Fuck if I will," the brother said.

The first guy turned to give me an apologetic smile. "Sorry. He's an asshole."

The brother gave a hard scoff. "Yeah. And you'd be an asshole, too, if someone crashed *your* car."

"You *did* crash my car," the first guy said. "Last month. Remember?"

More confused than ever, I turned to look at the second sports car, the one that had just arrived. It looked perfectly fine to me.

The first guy explained, "A different car."

"Really?" I just had to ask, "How many cars to you have?"

"A few."

"How many is a few?"

He gave it some thought. "Seven. No. Eight."

I couldn't help but laugh. "What? You can't keep track?"

"Hang on," he said. "Are we counting trucks, too?"

"Uh, yes?"

"Then make it nine."

I had no idea what to say to that. I heard myself mumble, "Well, I hope you have a big garage."

While we'd been talking, my mom had been sidling ever closer to the new guy. When he turned to look at her, she batted her eyelashes up at him and asked, "How about you? How many cars do *you* have?"

The guy looked at her for a long, cold moment before saying, "None."

"But that can't be true." She pointed toward the crash. "I mean, you have at least one, right?" She edged a fraction closer and said in that breathy way of hers, "You won't believe this, but that's my absolute dream car."

"Oh, I believe it," the guy said.

My mom practically giggled. "I know, right?" She gazed up at him and said, "So maybe you'll give me a ride sometime?"

Well, this wasn't embarrassing or anything.

Reluctantly, I turned to look at the first guy, the one who'd been subjected to the same pickup line just minutes earlier.

He was watching their exchange with an expression that I couldn't quite make out. But soon, as if feeling my gaze, he turned his head in my direction and gave me the hint of a smile. From the look in his eyes, he was amused as hell.

Well, that made one of us.

Feeling suddenly self-conscious, I looked away just as my mom made another bid for a ride in the crashed car.

The brother was saying, "Forget it."

Her lips formed a pretty little pout. "Why? Because it has to be repaired?"

"No. Because you're scaring the shit out of me."

She gave him a playful swat to the arm. "Oh, please. A big, strong guy like you?"

I blurted out, "Aren't you running late?"

In unison, my mom and the brother turned to look. My mom's gaze narrowed. "Don't worry. We've got plenty of time."

While we'd been talking, the limo driver had pushed himself up to a standing position. Looking decidedly disgruntled, he said to my mom, "That's not what you said a minute ago."

My mom blinked. "What?"

His expression darkened. "Yeah. And thanks for the concern."

She gave him a perplexed look. "What do you mean?"

"I mean," he said, "you didn't care that I was almost run over."

"I did too care," my mom said. "If I didn't care, I wouldn't've screamed."

The brother said, "Dude, man up. I saw you a block away."

"Up yours," the driver muttered. And with that, he turned to go. Over his shoulder, he said to my mom, "I'm outta here. Get in. Or not. I'm done."

My mom's gaze darted between the limo driver and the brother. She took a tentative step toward the limo, but then hesitated as if feeling suddenly light-headed. Her hand flew to her mouth, and she breathed, "Oh, no."

I squeezed my eyes shut. *Don't say it. Pleeeease don't say it.*

She said, "I think I'm a little tipsy." She gave a light giggle. "Too much champagne, I think."

Damn it. I opened my eyes just in time to see the limo driver pause in his tracks. He turned to face her and said with a loud sigh, "Fine. I'll help you to the car."

My mom waved him off, saying, "Not *you*." She turned back to the brother and purred, "*You*."

He gave a low scoff. "Nice try, nut-job."

She froze. "What?"

I blurted out, "You know what?" I turned to my mom. "You really should get going."

The brother's gaze shifted from my mom to me and back again. "What are you supposed to be? Twins?"

Once again, heat flooded my face. In all the commotion, I'd practically forgotten that my mom and I were dressed in identical outfits, right down to the same style of shoes.

And yes, we *did* look alike, even aside from the clothes. It was freaky in a way. Every time I looked in the mirror, I saw my mom's face staring back at me. Maybe I should've felt lucky. My mom was undeniable beautiful. But in the back of my mind, I couldn't help but wonder if it was a blessing or a curse.

I mean, what had her looks ever gotten her except heartbreak and disappointment?

The brother's question hung in the air. *Were* we supposed to be twins?

My mom beamed up at the guy. "Do you want us to be?"

Mortified, I took a slow step backward and tried to fade into the darkness. Of course, this would've been a ton easier if I weren't wearing a burgundy party dress and silver shoes.

The brother looked at my mom for another long moment before

turning to the first guy and saying, "So, what the hell happened to my car?"

I spoke up. "Don't blame him. It was my fault, not his."

The brother gave me a dubious look. "What, you were driving it?"

"No." I hesitated. "I was—"

"It's done," the first guy said, turning to his brother. "So forget it. You ready?"

The brother scowled. "But what about my car?"

"I called Maurice. He's on his way."

The sound of the limo's horn made us all turn to look. The driver leaned his head out of the window and called out to my mom. "Are you coming or not?"

Her gaze shifted to the brothers, and she pursed her lips. I could practically see the wheels turning. If she left now, she might never have another shot with either one of them. But the clock *was* ticking, and neither guy had given her any encouragement whatsoever.

Hoping to nudge her in the right direction, I said, "He sounds like he means it. And isn't Dominic waiting?"

"I guess," she muttered. "And then, with a sigh, she finally turned and began walking toward the limo. As she moved, she called out to the driver, "You *are* going to get the door, aren't you?"

I half-expected him to tell her to get it herself. But he didn't. Instead, looking more disgruntled than ever, he got out and opened the rear door, and then waited while she climbed inside.

A minute later, the limo squealed away, leaving me alone with the two brothers.

Was I crazy?

Probably.

But as it turned out, I wasn't half as crazy as they were.

CHAPTER 4

The limo had just disappeared around the corner when the brother turned to me and asked, "So where's *your* ride?"

I tensed. So he didn't know? "Um…"

The first guy said, "*We're* her ride."

The brother frowned. "In what?"

The first guy pointed toward the car that had just arrived. "My car. What else?"

The brother made a scoffing sound. "That's what *you* think."

Beyond humiliated, I asked, "Is there some sort of problem?"

The first guy shot his brother a warning look. "No."

"The hell there isn't," the brother said. "The car's a two-seater."

The first guy gave a tight shrug. "Then you should've brought the Benz."

"Yeah, but I didn't."

"I know," the first guy said, "so you'll need to go on your own."

The brother was glaring now. "In what?"

The first guy pointed vaguely toward the wreck. "I dunno. Grab a van."

"I'm not driving a fucking van," the brother said.

I glanced around. There were three vans parked along the desolate city street. Two were fine. The third had been sideswiped by the brother's car. I said, "Don't tell me, you own the vans, too?"

The brother said, "Does it matter?"

I wasn't sure how to answer. Hell, I wasn't even sure if that was a serious question.

Luckily, the first guy replied on my behalf. "Hey, I already told you, stop being a dick."

"You did not." The brother looked back to me and said, "You were here. You hear him say that?"

I froze. "Um…" I hadn't. But I hated the idea of saying so. Going for some sort of compromise, I stammered out, "Well…he told you to watch your language, so that's sort of implied, right?"

The brother shook his head. "Wrong." He looked back at the first guy and said, "And I'm not gonna watch my fucking language either."

The first guy smiled. "Then it's a good thing you're driving separately, isn't it?"

"In what?" the brother asked for the second time. "And don't say a van, because that's not happening."

"Alright," the first guy said, glancing toward the crash. "Then drive your own."

"I would," the brother replied, "if you hadn't smashed it."

"Oh, quit bitching," the first guy said. "It's still in one piece."

Was it? I turned to look. Just as I did, something on the far side of the car clattered to the pavement. What it was, I had no idea. Maybe a side-view mirror?

After a long pause, the first guy said, "Make that *two* pieces."

I wanted to snicker. And I wanted to cry. The mental whiplash aside, I hated that they were arguing, especially because this was mostly my fault. Hoping to broker some sort of peace, I said, "But you have other cars, right?"

Both guys turned to look. The brother said, "So?"

"So, couldn't you use one of them?"

"Sure," the brother said, "if I want to drive an hour round-trip, and we're already late."

At this, a new wave of guilt washed over me. It was a Saturday night, and they were both wearing tuxes. Probably, they were on their way to a wedding or something. Cripes, for all I knew, I could be talking to the groom and his best man.

I summoned up what I hoped was a smile. "You know what? I'll just call a cab." I forced a laugh. "I don't know why I didn't think of it sooner." *Aside from the fact I had no money.*

Now both guys were frowning.

The first guy said, "You're not calling a cab."

"Why not?" I asked.

"Because, as the dickhead already mentioned, we've gotta go. And we're not leaving you here alone."

I looked to his brother, expecting him to say something dickish, like I deserved to wait alone for all the trouble I'd caused – or that I'd be perfectly fine and no one needed to worry.

But the brother didn't say any of those things. To my infinite surprise, he said, "No shit. If you think we'd just leave, you're nuts."

Huh. Imagine that. There *was* something they agreed on. Unfortunately, it appeared to be the only thing, at least when it came to vans and crashed cars – which is how I ended up sitting on the first guy's lap as the three of us crammed ourselves into a car designed for only two.

CHAPTER 5

"My name's Jax," he said. "What's yours?"

I should've been blushing. Who knows, maybe I *was* blushing. Here I was, sitting on the guy's lap, and I knew nearly nothing about him.

My mom would be *so* proud, well, if she weren't so angry, that is. But hell, she'd be even prouder if I could talk Jax or his brother into buying me dinner and a beachfront condo.

But I wasn't my mom – thank goodness. With my gaze straight ahead, I said, "My name's Cassidy, and um…it's nice to meet you."

Talk about a massive understatement. The guy had rescued me, plain and simple. And he hadn't asked for a single thing in return, at least not yet.

I felt like I should turn around and shake his hand or at least look him in the eye as I gave him my name. But I didn't dare. Already, my ass was shifting dangerously tight against his pelvis – not because I was grinding into him on purpose, but because his brother was driving like a maniac, and every corner and curve sent me shifting against my rescuer's lap.

And it felt embarrassingly good.

Damn it.

But I wasn't that kind of girl – the kind who'd throw myself at him, just because he'd done me a favor *or* because he was the hottest, most intriguing person I'd ever met.

Looking to silence my inner floozy, I kept my body rigid and my gaze firmly on the road, even as I prayed for the brother to slow down, at least while taking the corners.

It wasn't even because of the danger. It was because I was pretty sure that I was one good grind away from whimpering out loud.

From behind me, Jax said, "Hey Jaden, slow down, will ya?"

The brother laughed. "Why?"

"Because you're scaring Cassidy."

I couldn't help but smile. The sentiment aside, I liked the sound of my name on his lips. And I loved the feel of his arms, holding me just a little bit tighter when his brother – as if looking to make a point – hit the gas and rounded the next corner so fast, it was a wonder that all four wheels stayed on the ground.

The brother – whose name was apparently Jaden – said, "She doesn't look scared to me."

He was only half-right. I wasn't scared for my safety, although heaven knows I should've been. But I *was* scared because my inner floozy was growing more obnoxious with every block.

Even now, I could practically hear her whispering, *Go on, live a little. You know you want to.*

I stiffened. *Shut up.*

But she *didn't* shut up. *And you just know that's not his cell phone pressing against your ass-cheek, right? Feels good, doesn't it?*

Desperately, I looked to Jaden. "Maybe you *could* slow down a little."

"Sorry," he said, sounding anything but sincere. "But if we don't get there by nine, it'll be *my* ass in the hot seat."

Ass?

Hot seat?

Holy hell, don't remind me.

Seeking a distraction, I glanced at the car's digital clock. The time was 8:48. I frowned. "You mean nine o'clock? But that's only twelve minutes away. Why didn't you say something?"

"Because I'm *doing* something," Jaden said. "Screw talking." He gave me a sideways glance. "And if you want to be dropped someplace on the way, forget it. There's no time."

I tensed and not because of his rudeness. It was because I suddenly realized that I wasn't quite sure where they *could* drop me. Was I now homeless? I bit my lip. *Oh, crap.* I probably was.

Jax was saying to his brother, "Hey, I already told ya, stop being a dick."

"I'm not being a dick," Jaden replied. "I'm just telling her."

"Well don't," Jax said. "She doesn't need the grief."

"You mean *you* don't need the grief."

As they argued back and forth, I sat in stupefied silence while my mom's words of warning played in my head. *If you think you can just waltz back into the penthouse like nothing happened, you're crazy.*

At the time, I'd figured that was just anger talking. But now that I had some distance, it was dawning on me that things were a lot more complicated than I'd considered at the time.

We'd been arguing about Dominic. He owned the place my mom called home – which happened to be the same place I'd been living for the past week. In spite of what my mom liked to call it, it was no penthouse, even if it *was* on the top floor.

This might've been impressive, if only the building were taller than three stories or contained more than four apartments. The building didn't even have an elevator, which was fine by me. Still, it couldn't be a penthouse without an elevator, could it?

Jax's voice, softer now, interrupted my thoughts. "Don't listen to him. If there's someplace you need to be, say the word. I'll make it happen."

Jaden said, "Only if you're calling her a cab, because if *I'm* going, *you're* going."

In spite of my worry, I just had to ask, "Going where?"

It was Jax who answered. "Nowhere. It's not a big deal."

I didn't believe *that* for one minute. You didn't wear a tux unless it was *some* sort of big deal. I hadn't wanted to pry, but now, I couldn't resist asking, "Are you on your way to a wedding or something?"

From the driver's seat, Jaden laughed like I'd just said something funny. "Hell no. What makes you say that?"

I gave him an annoyed look. "Well, you *are* wearing a tux." His laughter grated on me, and I couldn't resist tweaking him at least a little. "Are you *sure* you're not the groom?"

He stopped laughing. "God no. Jesus."

Behind me, I heard a low chuckle, almost too quiet to hear. I felt it, too – Jax's body vibrating against mine, like we were sharing a secret joke.

I liked that feeling, and I let myself relax against him, even as the seatbelt dug into my hip and Jaden muttered something about marriage being for suckers.

Still, I *was* curious. "Okay, so if it's not a wedding, what is it?"

Jax said, "Just a party."

Funny, my mom had mentioned a party, too – something fancy with dancing and champagne. It had sounded surprisingly nice until she'd mentioned going someplace private afterward with Dominic.

But I refused to think about that now. "It must be some party if you're all dressed up. Who's throwing it?"

From the driver's seat, Jaden said, "A couple of assholes. We're only going because we have to."

I gave him a sideways glance. From what I'd seen so far, neither guy seemed the type to do anything they didn't want to, and I had the distinct impression that I was missing something important.

From behind me, Jax said, "Make that *one* asshole. And we're going because we promised a friend."

"*You* promised," Jaden said, "not me."

In a low voice, obviously intended for my ears only, Jax said, "…which explains why he's in such a sorry mood."

Before I could even think to reply, Jaden shot back, "No. I'm in a sorry mood because you crashed my car."

Jax said, "Yeah, well, I wouldn't've been driving the thing if you hadn't blocked me in."

"Oh, shut up."

"And that'll teach ya for leaving the keys under the seat."

Jaden was still grumbling. "You could've asked me to move it."

"While you were boning Phoebe?" Jax said. "I don't think so."

Phoebe? I had no idea who she was, but I was embarrassingly glad that she'd been with Jaden and not Jax, whose arms, even now, were holding me in a nice protective cocoon.

Still, I hated that they were arguing over something that never would've happened if not for me and my mom. Silently, I mulled this over, even as I noticed that with every passing block, our surroundings were growing noticeable nicer.

If I wasn't mistaken, we were heading toward the ocean – or more accurately, toward the gulf, with its calm waters and sandy beaches.

I loved the beach, but right now, it was the last thing on my mind.

At the next red light, I looked to Jaden and said, "I'm really sorry about the car."

"Yeah, me, too," he said. "If the dickhead had waited five more minutes, he could've crashed his own instead of mine."

I felt my gaze narrow. The so-called dickhead was my rescuer, my hero, and yes, my newfound fantasy. Even now, that inner voice was whispering something terribly obscene about dick and head, and a whole bunch of other naked stuff that I'd never consider with a stranger.

Pushing those thoughts aside, I gave Jaden a sarcastic smile. "Wow, five whole minutes, huh?"

His jaw tightened. "Meaning?"

"I'm just saying, Phoebe sounds like a lucky girl."

"Hey," he said. "We'd been at it since six, so it's not like I left her high and dry, if that's what you're getting at."

I rolled my eyes. "Good to know."

And that's when I felt it – the sweet vibration of Jax's silent laughter. The only problem was, I felt it everywhere – and I mean, *everywhere* – thanks to that latest turn, which had planted my ass more firmly against his pelvis, not to mention the thing that definitely wasn't his cell phone.

I felt myself swallow. Was Jax a five-minute man? *No. He wasn't.* I don't know how I knew, but I just did. He was the kind of guy who wouldn't stop until I was a quivering mass of pure satisfaction.

When the light turned green, Jaden floored it, sending me rocking backward into Jax, whose grip tightened further even as he told Jaden, "You're just pissed she got the better of you."

"No," Jaden said, "I'm pissed because we're gonna be late, and if I get one more speeding ticket, I'm gonna lose my license."

"So, slow down," Jax said. "We'll get there when we get there."

"Easy for you to say," Jaden said. "You're not the one who's gonna hear it from Darla."

Jax laughed. "Don't tell me you're scared."

"Hell yes, I'm scared," Jaden replied, glancing in my direction. "And you wanna know why?"

"Why?" I asked.

"Because she's fucking scary."

As he said this, it wasn't lost on me that he'd said basically the same thing about my mom. Was my mom scary? In a way, yes, she definitely was.

But less than fifteen minutes later, my mom was the furthest thing from my mind. And why?

Because we'd arrived in the land of money and mansions and who knows what else.

CHAPTER 6

It was a few minutes after nine when the car finally screeched to a stop behind a long line of expensive-looking vehicles that were inching along on an otherwise quiet street.

The street ran along the coastline and was lined with houses that could only be described as estates – big, glorious estates, the kind you never saw in real life, especially if you happened to be the kind of girl who'd been counting pennies for way too long.

Jaden cut the engine and shoved open the driver's side door, telling Jax, "Park it, will ya?" He took a single step away and then turned back to add, "And I swear to God, if you're not in there in ten minutes, I'm telling Darla what you did last October."

Jax's body stiffened. "You wouldn't."

"Oh yeah?" Jaden said. "Watch me." And with that, he turned away, crossed in front of our vehicle, and began striding forward along the sidewalk, heading in the same direction as the line of cars.

He hadn't even bothered to close the driver's side door.

Idiot.

Suddenly, I felt incredibly awkward, sitting on Jax's lap with the car's overhead light blazing down like some sort of spotlight, giving everyone around us a clear view of our distinctly unsafe and totally illegal position – a position that also happened to feel incredibly good.

I cleared my throat. "I guess I should get off, huh?" As soon as the words left my lips, a wave of warmth crept across my face and – *damn it* – settled southward, thanks to my ass pressing against his pelvis.

Get off? Seriously?

I tried again. "I mean, get out. Yes. Get out. Right."

I was reaching for the door handle when Jax said, "Hang on."

He shifted beneath me, and I heard a click, followed by the sensation of him releasing the seatbelt, doing it slowly, probably so it didn't whack me in the face or something.

How embarrassing. Now, he probably thought I was stupid. I should've remembered the seatbelt. I mean, I always wore one when I *wasn't* on someone's lap. But in truth, it was hard to remember anything with him was so achingly near.

Like seriously, what was my name again?

Oh yeah. Cassidy. Cassidy McAllister.

That settled, I reached again for the door handle, only to stop in mid-motion when he said, "Wait."

I dropped my hand. "For what?"

"A question. What happened back there?"

I didn't bother asking where or what he meant. I knew exactly what he'd seen – a girl fleeing a limo on a street where limos didn't belong. But none of this was his problem, and already, I'd inconvenienced him beyond all reason.

I forced a smile into my voice. "Nothing."

"Are you in some sort of trouble?"

Oh, boy. Was I ever. I had no job, no money, and no idea where I'd be sleeping tonight. Cripes, when I put it that way, even in my own head, I felt like a total loser.

But it wasn't always this way. Until just a week ago, I had a decent apartment, a wonderful roommate, and a job that actually paid the bills – as long as I wasn't too extravagant, anyway.

Luckily for me, I was almost never extravagant, probably because I'd seen firsthand the dangers of loving things more than people.

Still, his question hit a little too close to home, and I shifted in my seat, only to remember – belatedly, stupidly – that it wasn't a seat I was shifting on. It was the lap of a complete stranger.

What must he think of me? I didn't even want to speculate. "Everything's fine," I said, even as I pushed open the car door, scrambled off his lap, and found my footing near the curb of the street.

And then, standing there like a complete idiot, I glanced around. *What now?*

Already, the traffic ahead of us had moved forward at least two car lengths, which meant that Jax's car was stopped in the middle of the road for no good reason – with both doors open, no less.

And yet, the cars behind us weren't passing.

Why?

Searching for some clue, I looked to Jax. Taking his sweet time, he eased out of the passenger's seat and joined me on the street. He gave me a long, penetrating look before asking, "Is there someplace you've gotta be?"

This was a very good question. Unfortunately, I had no good answer, or at least none that wouldn't sound totally pathetic.

In reality, I had no place I *could* go.

I tried to think. I had maybe ten whole dollars in my wallet. Was that enough for cab fare? A hotel? Anything?

Not hardly.

At the recollection of my wallet, I stifled a gasp. "Oh, shoot."

Jax frowned. "What is it?"

I gave a nervous laugh. "I almost forgot my stuff."

Earlier, I'd placed my things underneath the passenger's seat, intending to swoop them up on my way out.

I glanced toward his car only to feel myself cringe all over again. My cell phone and wallet were nowhere in sight, which meant that they were probably still safely under the seat. But the tampon? *That* had rolled out into the open. *Of course.*

And there it was, sitting there in the middle of the floor-mat like some sort of tiny pink neon sign, announcing to everyone – well, to Jax, anyway – that I was on my freaking period, even though I wasn't.

Right then and there, I vowed I'd toss that stupid thing into the very next waste-basket I came across. The vow lasted only a split second before I considered how awful it would be to not have if I needed it.

I heard myself mumble, "I don't suppose you have a paper bag."

"For what?" he asked.

I was dying of embarrassment. "My stuff, actually."

"Do me a favor," he said. "Get back in the car. We'll figure it out."

From somewhere down the street, a car horn sounded, making me practically jump out of my skin. I turned to look and realized that the line of cars behind us had grown considerably. Meanwhile, the line of cars ahead of us had moved further forward.

I gave Jax's car a worried glance. "You should probably get moving, huh?"

He flicked his head toward the passenger's seat. "Get in, and we will."

We? I glanced around. "But don't you have someplace to be?"

"Yeah. I do," he said. "But I'm not moving 'til your ass is in that seat."

I stiffened. "What?"

"I'm not leaving you here," he said. "So get in." He paused. "Please."

Was it the "please" that did it? I had no idea. I didn't like bossy guys, but I *did* like him, probably more than I cared to admit.

Plus, I'd caused him more than enough trouble for one night – so without any further comment, I did what he asked and even fastened my seatbelt as he climbed behind the wheel, fired up the engine, and drove forward until we'd caught up with the other cars.

And that's when he made me the strangest offer.

CHAPTER 7

I stared at him from the passenger's seat. "Excuse me?"

"I'll pay you," he said. "A thousand bucks."

I felt myself swallow. *A thousand dollars?* In my world, that was a ton of money. And yet, I *so* didn't want to contemplate what he expected in return.

We were still in traffic, inching along behind the other vehicles. At the same time, my mind was racing a million miles a minute. He'd just asked me to be – in his own words – his "girlfriend" for the night.

What the hell?

It didn't take a genius to figure out what he was getting at. I considered how we met and what kind of impression he'd obviously gotten from that whole sordid scene.

I squeezed my eyes shut and counted to five. Part of me wanted to slap him. The other part reminded myself that he'd already done me a huge favor, several favors actually, including assaulting someone on my behalf.

Could I honestly blame him if he thought the worst of me?

No. I couldn't.

And yet, I did.

My eyes were still shut when he said, "Is there a problem?"

I opened my eyes and turned my head in his direction. Traffic had stopped, and he was looking at me with that penetrating gaze of his.

His eyes were amazing, and I couldn't help but think that if he hadn't just offered to buy me – or was it rent me? – for the night, I'd probably be falling under his spell, even now.

But I wasn't. "Thanks for the offer," I said, trying not to sound as insulted as I felt. "But I'm not for sale, actually."

He frowned. "I didn't think you were."

"Well, obviously you did, or you wouldn't've asked me that."

He leaned back against his seat. "Listen, I did a sorry job of phrasing it, but it's not what you think."

I gave him a dubious look. "Oh, really? Then what is it?"

He gave it some thought. "Protection."

I felt my eyebrows furrow. He was tall and muscular. And, as I'd seen firsthand, he could handle himself just fine. I asked, "Protection from what?"

"Say yes, and you'll see."

Now, *that* made me curious. But it wouldn't change my decision. Even if I believed what he was saying – and I still wasn't sure that I did – I wasn't going to be anyone's date for money.

No. That was the kind of thing my mom did. And, as I constantly reminded myself, I wasn't my mom.

I said, "I can't take your money."

"Why not?" he asked.

How to explain? "Well," I began, "it sounds like you need a favor more than anything."

"And what if I do?"

"Then I can't charge you for it." I tried to smile. "I mean, you've already done me a ton of favors tonight, so I'm sure I owe *you*, not the other way around."

"No," he said. "You don't owe me anything."

I didn't bother hiding my disbelief. Thanks to me, he'd crashed a car, gotten into a fight, *and* had been nearly molested by my mom.

Of all these things, it was the crash that worried me the most. I was no car expert, but I did know that the damage would cost a lot more than a thousand dollars.

As if reading something in my expression, he said, "Stop thinking about it."

"About what?"

"Everything." His voice became deadly serious. "You don't owe me."

I sighed. "How can you say that?"

The car ahead of us started moving again, and he turned his attention back to the road.

As we inched forward, I gave our surroundings a worried glance. "What do you think the holdup is? I hope it's not an accident."

"Trust me, it's no accident."

"How can you be sure?"

"Because I know what's ahead."

"What?" I asked.

"You'll see." He gave me a sideways glance. "Assuming you say yes."

"To what? Pretending to be your girlfriend?"

He gave a half-shrug. "Psycho-jealous girlfriend would be better."

In spite of everything, I had to laugh. "Okay, now I *know* you're joking."

"You think so, huh?"

"Honestly, I don't know what to think."

"What don't you get?"

He was still focused on the road, and I gave his profile a good, long look. He was beyond gorgeous and obviously rich. On top of that, he didn't look much older than I was. If I had to guess, I'd put his age at no older than thirty.

What was he? A trust fund baby or something?

When it came to female attention, he wouldn't need anyone to pretend anything. Probably girls would pay *him*, and not only with money.

I asked, "What's the catch?"

"It's complicated."

Yes. It definitely was – as I soon discovered for myself.

CHAPTER 8

The music was loud and jazzy, like something out of the 1920s. Around us, the place was jam-packed with expensive looking people. Some appeared to be around my own age while the vast majority looked at least a decade or two older.

Even before we walked in through the ornate front door, Jax had wrapped a protective arm around my waist and was now guiding us through the mass of society-types who were drinking and talking.

The whole scene was entirely surreal. Nearly all of the men wore tuxes, while the women wore a stunning array of cocktail dresses – some long, some short, but all fabulous in their own way.

I glanced down at my own outfit – the burgundy cocktail dress that I'd refused to give up. Thank goodness I had, or I'd be feeling seriously outclassed right about now.

I gave a silent scoff. Who was I kidding? I *still* felt outclassed. I was a fake girlfriend in a borrowed dress. I *so* didn't belong here, and stupid or not, I couldn't help but wonder if everyone knew.

As if reading my mind, Jax said in a low voice, "Hey, you're my girlfriend, remember?"

I tried to laugh. "So?"

"So if anyone gives you grief, I'll toss 'em out on their ass."

I gave him a sideways glance. "You wouldn't really."

"Hell, I'd have to."

"Oh yeah?" I couldn't help but smile. "Why?"

"Matter of honor." He gave me a sly wink. "Can't let them think I'm a pussy."

He was either joking or crazy. Aside from his impressive physique, there was something about the way he moved – so cocky and sure – that practically screamed he was no pushover.

And heaven help me, I liked it.

Around us, everyone seemed to know him. As we waded through the crowd, he exchanged quick greetings with at least a dozen people, all without stopping for anything resembling an actual conversation.

That was fine by me. I was so blown away by the mansion itself that I was nearly speechless. The place was three stories tall with big, elaborate windows and lights glittering from nearly every room.

Even before we'd entered, I'd realized that this wasn't your average house – and not only because of its size and beach-front location. Outside, uniformed parking attendants had been waiting to whisk away the car. To where, I had no idea. I didn't ask, and neither did my pretend boyfriend.

Instead, he'd led us straight into the mansion like he knew exactly where he was going. Once inside, we'd been greeted by a butler who surely would've taken our coats, if only we'd been wearing any.

But we weren't, and we had nothing to hand over. I didn't even have a purse, which meant that Jax was carrying my wallet and cell phone inside the front pocket of his pants.

As we moved, I gave him yet another sideways glance. Whenever *I* tucked several things into a single pocket, I looked lumpy and awkward.

But *he* didn't. No. He looked like a movie star or secret agent, all smooth and tailored in spite of a car crash, a fist fight *and* a pocketful of things that weren't his own.

How was this even possible?

Stupidly, I thought of that tampon. Like a total coward, I'd shoved it further under the car seat and made a mental note to grab it after the party.

I just prayed I didn't need it sooner.

Jax leaned his head close to mine and said, "Keep an eye out, will ya?"

"For what?" I asked.

"My brother." He paused. "Or a tiny redhead."

Okaaaaay. The brother, I got. The redhead, not so much. "I'm guessing you mean a specific redhead?" I tried to laugh. "I mean, this isn't like some sort of scavenger hunt, is it?"

After everything else tonight, I could practically see it. *Find a can of corn, something fluffy, and one tiny red-head.*

"No," he said. "It's more like a save-my-ass type of thing."

"Ohhhh, right." I gave him an apologetic smile. "Sorry, I should've remembered. This is about that ten-minute deadline, isn't it?"

Earlier, Jaden had threatened to tell Darla – whoever that was – some horrible thing if Jax didn't show up within ten minutes. I wasn't wearing a watch, but I *did* know that we were surely beyond the ten-minute mark.

Jax gave me a silent nod and kept on going.

As we moved forward, I glanced around. I saw no sign of his brother. As far as redheads were concerned, I spotted at least three, but none of them could be called tiny. Rather, they were all tall and statuesque with legs that went on forever.

The nearest redhead – the one who happened to be heading straight toward us – was wearing a very tiny dress. Did that count?

Probably not.

I looked to Jax and said, "The tiny redhead – I'm guessing that would be Darla?"

"Right." As he said it, he lifted a glass of champagne off a passing tray. Without breaking stride, he handed me the glass. "Here. You'll need this."

"Why?"

"Trust me."

A moment later, we nearly collided with the tall redhead in the microdress. Or, more accurately, *she* nearly collided with *us*.

Ignoring me entirely, she gazed up at Jax and practically cooed, "There you are."

I stiffened. *Yes. There he was.*

Funny though, he didn't look nearly as happy to see *her* as she was to see him.

Her dress was a shade of deep emerald that showed off her stunning green eyes – eyes that were molesting my fake boyfriend, even as he looked past her, still scanning the crowd for his brother or Darla.

Undaunted, the redhead reached for his unclaimed arm and gave it a squeeze. With a flirty smile, she said, "You're late."

"Am I?" he said, still looking past her.

"Totally," she said. "And you promised me a dance."

"No," he replied, "I promised to toss you out if you made a scene."

She drew back. "I'm not going to make a scene."

"Good to know," he said.

Silently, I looked from the redhead to Jax. *Was I supposed to be doing something?* Their conversation had reminded me that I wasn't *just* a girlfriend. I was supposed to be – how had Jax put it? – a *psycho jealous* girlfriend.

But he hadn't been serious.

Had he?

I bit my lip. Even if he *had* been, I wasn't one to play games. I didn't like lying *or* pretending.

This begged the question, why on Earth was I here?

But the reason for that was obvious. I had nowhere else to go, and he'd asked me for a favor.

I owed him, plain and simple. Unfortunately, this also meant that I couldn't accept any payment – not without feeling like a total ingrate. Already, I'd told him flat-out that no money would be changing hands.

Stupid? Probably. But I had my own code of ethics. So, here I was, wondering what to do.

As I watched, the redhead leaned closer to Jax and whispered loud enough for me to hear, "We don't *have* to dance standing up, you know."

What the hell?

Surely, she could see the girl on his arm – *me*, his supposed girlfriend – or, at the very least, his date. How would a normal girlfriend react?

I spoke up. "If you're talking about the horizontal hokey pokey, forget it."

Slowly, she turned her gaze in my direction. As if noticing me for the first time, she gave me a quick once-over and a little smirk. "And you are…?"

Stalling, I took a nervous gulp of my champagne. "His, um,

girlfriend?"

God, I totally sucked at this. I looked to Jax for any sort of guidance. I received none. He was still scanning the crowd, as if determined to not be distracted.

The redhead gave a little laugh. "Oh, please. You can't be his girlfriend."

I tried for a little laugh of my own. "Oh really? Why not?"

"Because," she said, "*I'm* his girlfriend."

Suddenly, I wasn't laughing anymore. *Wait, what?*

CHAPTER 9

Her announcement hung in the air, and I didn't know what to say.

His girlfriend? Seriously?

I was still trying to form a reply when Jax told her, "No. You're not." As he said it, he didn't even look at her, like she wasn't worth the effort.

It was so cold, I stifled a shiver.

Ignoring his denial, she looked to me and announced, "We're on a break. That's all."

"Yeah," Jax said, "And like I told you, the break's permanent, so stop bothering Cassidy, alright?"

"Who's Cassidy?" She fluttered her hands vaguely in my direction. "You can't mean *her*."

"I can," he said. "And I do. So cut the crap. I'm looking for Jaden. Have you seen him?"

She gave Jax a sly smile. "Maybe."

The smile was a total waste. He was still scanning the crowd. "I'll take that as a no." Finally, he looked to me and said, "Come on. Let's get you a drink."

I blinked. I already had a drink. I looked down and paused. My glass was nearly empty.

Had I been guzzling? No wonder she'd given me such a look.

I was a total lush.

But in my own defense, I'd been more than a little nervous. Plus, the champagne was the best I'd ever had. True, I was no expert, given the fact that my previous experience was limited to cheap bottles on New Year's Eve. Still, even *I* could taste the difference.

In a show of defiance, I lifted my glass and drained it dry, savoring the sweetness of the bubbles as they danced across my tongue. *Nope. Definitely not cheap.*

When I lowered the glass, the redhead gave me another smirk. "You might want to pace yourself, chickie."

Chickie? I gave her a smirk right back. "You too, snookems."

Her gaze narrowed. "In case you haven't noticed, *I'm* perfectly sober."

Jax gave her a look. "Yeah. Well, give it time." And with that, he guided me around her, leading us deeper into the mansion. As we moved, I swear I could feel her eyes shooting daggers into my back.

Was *she* the reason I was here? Was I some sort of proof that Jax had moved on? I could see the logic, and yet, he didn't seem like the game-playing type.

I liked him. And I *loved* the feel of his arm, wrapped around my waist. It felt good, like we fit together just right.

Right on cue, my inner floozy whispered that we'd fit just right in other ways, too. I told her to shut up and tried to ignore the warmth that was, even now, creeping across my cheeks.

It was just the champagne. That's all.

Jax had just snagged me another glass when we spotted his brother, standing near a pair of French doors that led to an outdoor patio. The patio was lit with sparkling candles floating across – I felt my eyebrows furrow – a swimming pool?

The pool itself wouldn't've surprised me if I didn't know that we weren't on the ground floor. To reach the mansion's front entrance, we'd climbed an impressive amount of steps, skipping the lower level entirely. This meant that the pool wasn't your basic in-ground variety.

But of course, there was nothing basic about any of this.

From what I could see through the glass doors, the patio was absolutely stunning – all granite and marble with a raised hot tub, Grecian columns, and even a couple of massive palm trees.

How was that even possible? I squinted past the pool into the space beyond. But all I saw was darkness, like we were perched on the end of the world – which, in a way, I guess we were.

Pushing aside the distraction, I looked back to Jax's brother. He was talking with a petite redhead who could only be Darla. I knew this, because she was, in fact, very tiny – probably no more than five feet tall.

Other than that, she wasn't what I'd been expecting. For some reason, I'd been expecting someone younger – maybe in her twenties or thirties, around the same age as the two brothers.

But Darla looked old enough to be their grandmother – or maybe even their great-grandmother.

Earlier, Jaden had called her scary. But she didn't look scary to me. She looked fun and festive in a classic flapper dress that would've been the latest fashion sometime in the 1920s.

The dress was silver and black with lots of fringes. Completing the look were long, lacy gloves and a sassy feather headband.

As I watched, she threw back her head and laughed at something Jaden had just said. As for Jaden himself, he looked far from terrified. Instead, he looked perfectly at ease.

Next to me, Jax said, "I'll be back in a minute. Wait here, alright?"

Without waiting for a response, he let go of my waist and began striding toward them. I took a nervous gulp of my champagne. It went down far too easily, and I had to remind myself to slow down.

When it came to drinking, I was a total lightweight *and* on the petite side myself. If I wasn't careful, I'd soon be staggering – or worse, hunched over some toilet, watching the champagne come right back up again.

With a little shudder, I lowered the glass and reminded myself that no one liked a toilet-hugger – or to hug a toilet for that matter.

Jax had just reached his brother when I felt a tap on my shoulder. I turned to look and stifled a groan.

It was the redhead.

Of course.

With a little smile, she said, "I like your dress."

Her smile was fake, just like her compliment. Oh, I knew the dress was likeable enough. It was expensive and stylish. And, I knew that I looked good in it – not because I was overly sure of myself, but rather, because I so strongly resembled my mom, and *she* had looked fabulous in this exact same outfit.

Still, I knew insincerity when I heard it, and I had the distinct impression that I'd just been insulted. Refusing to show it, I stiffly replied, "Thank you. I like your dress, too."

I didn't bother sounding sincere. Whatever game she was playing, I wanted no part of it, and I saw no reason to encourage her.

She smiled again. This time, it was a real smile, with lots of teeth. For some reason, it made me just a little bit nervous, and I took a nervous sip of champagne.

The glass was still at my lips when she said, "But here's something funny... *You're* not the only one wearing it."

I lowered the glass. "What?"

"Oh yeah. You didn't know?" With a little laugh, she glanced down at my feet. "And talk about hilarious. You're even wearing the same shoes."

I felt the color drain from my face.

Oh, shit.

I glanced around. She couldn't mean who I thought she meant?

Could she?

CHAPTER 10

Desperately, I scanned the crowd. Next to me, the redhead was saying, "If you want to leave, I'm sure he'd understand."

She didn't say who "he" was, but it was beyond easy to guess. She meant Jax, of course.

I snuck a nervous glance in his direction, only to feel myself pause.

He was gone.

And so was his brother.

But that wasn't the thing that had me reeling. It was the fact that Darla was talking to someone new. He was big and portly, with slick dark hair and sharp, wandering eyes.

I stared in stunned disbelief. I knew him. And, if my mom had gotten her way, I would've known him a lot better before the night was through.

It was Dominic – my mom's, well, whatever he was.

A whispered word escaped my lips. "Shit."

The redhead gave a cheerful little laugh. "I know. Embarrassing, huh?"

I whirled to look. Obviously, she thought I was traumatized by the news that a different guest was wearing the same outfit.

She couldn't've been more wrong.

Oh, I was traumatized alright, but not in the way she thought.

The sight of Dominic only confirmed what I'd already begun to suspect – that the person in the matching dress was my mom. She was here. With *him*.

Damn it. What were the odds? I glanced around, searching for something – I didn't know what. A place to hide? A place to run? A bathroom to barf in?

Suddenly, the champagne wasn't sitting so great, and I couldn't help but wonder if I'd be hugging some toilet after all.

I said, "I've gotta go."

Suddenly, the redhead was all smiles. "If you want, I'll call you a cab."

Obviously, she didn't get it. I wasn't going to hop in some cab. I had no money and nowhere to go. Plus, Jax had my phone and wallet, so even if I *did* want to run, I couldn't do it now, not without first retrieving my things.

This left only one option – hiding.

I told the redhead, "I don't need a cab. I just need some fresh air, that's all."

She frowned. "What? You're not leaving?"

I knew why she wanted me to leave, and it had nothing to do with the dress.

It was strange, really, because if the person in the matching dress had been anyone other than my mom, I would've simply laughed it off.

Seriously, it wasn't that big of a deal.

But this was.

So without another word, I turned and headed in the opposite direction, hoping to get lost in the crowd. As I moved, I glanced over my shoulder to make sure the redhead wasn't following.

She wasn't. But she *was* staring, as if she couldn't quite figure me out. I knew the feeling. I couldn't figure myself out either.

Why, oh why, had I ever listened to my mom at all?

In the back of my mind, I could still hear my best friend telling me just one week ago, "You're crazy for trusting her. You know that, right?"

One thing had led to another, and we'd gotten into a huge argument. Now, here I was, looking for a closet to hide in.

If only I had my phone, I swear, I would've called Allie right then and there and told her just how right she'd been all along. And then, I might've begged for her to come and get me.

If I knew Allie, she'd do it, too.

The only problem was, she was halfway across the country. Even if she left Nashville this instant, she wouldn't be here until sometime tomorrow morning.

Talk about painting myself into a corner.

I didn't find a closet, but I *did* find a small powder room off a side hallway. Surprised to find it empty, I ducked inside and slammed the door shut behind me.

I didn't mean to slam it, but my nerves had gotten the better of me. Obviously, I was losing it, and for no good reason.

I mean, I'd been in situations a lot worse than this. And really, it wasn't *that* bad. After all, it wasn't like my mom could drag me off by my hair. For one thing, she'd never behave like that in front of a crowd. And for another, I wasn't a kid anymore.

Even as I thought it, a little voice in my head whispered that if I was *so* brave and capable, why was I hiding in a bathroom?

But I knew the answer. I didn't want a scene, and not only for my own sake. I thought of Jax. Already, he'd rescued me more than once – and at considerable cost to himself.

Now, I was supposed to be doing *him* a favor. Causing a scene in front of his friends – or whoever these people were – would be a sorry way to repay him. So I hunkered down and tried to think.

Assuming that my mom hadn't spotted me, everything might still be okay. I'd just need to avoid her – and Dominic, too, while I was at it.

I'd only met the guy one time, but something in his eyes told me that he'd found *me* a lot more interesting than I'd found him.

Then again, I *had* been wearing a bikini at the time.

Stupid pool.

A knock at the door jolted me out of my thoughts.

Damn it. I gave the door a worried glance, wishing the knocker would just go away. But that was selfishness talking. This *was* a party, after all. Even in such a huge place, bathrooms would always be in short supply.

I was a girl. I knew this firsthand. And already, I'd been hogging the place for far too long.

Forcing some cheer into my voice, I called out, "I'll be out in a minute."

I used that minute to smooth my hair and practice smiling in front of the mirror. *See, everything's fine.*

Except it wasn't.

Because as soon as I opened the door, I wanted to slam it shut again.

And why? Because it was *her*. And I didn't mean my mom *or* the redhead.

CHAPTER 11

At the sight of her, I tried not to cringe – and not only because she was dressed like a hooker at Mardi-Gras. "Aunt Tabitha?"

From the look on her face, she was just as delighted to see me as I was to see her. "Cassidy." She glanced downward. "Nice dress."

Funny to think, it was the exact same thing I'd heard from the redhead. This time, I didn't bother returning the compliment. Knowing Aunt Tabitha, she was here for a reason, and it *wasn't* to exchange niceties.

Besides, her dress was definitely on the nasty side.

When I made no reply, she gave my dress a longer look. "You *do* know I picked it out, don't you?"

I *didn't* know. But I wasn't terribly surprised. Aunt Tabitha had been a clothing designer back in the day – or so she claimed.

Honestly, I didn't quite believe her – just like I didn't quite believe my rotten luck of seeing her *here* of all places. Then again, luck probably had little to do with it.

I glanced down at my outfit. Praying for some sort of peaceful resolution, I said, "Well, you did a nice job, of picking it out, I mean."

"I know." She gave me a thin smile. "And I need it back."

I tensed. "What?"

"The dress," she said. "I need it."

"You're joking, right?"

Her mouth tightened. "I never joke about clothes."

This much was true. I'd known Aunt Tabitha my whole life. She didn't joke about a lot of things.

It was really strange, too. Everyone always said she had a great sense of humor. But I'd never seen it, or rather, she'd never wasted the effort on *me*.

Aunt Tabitha looked a lot like my mom. Her hair was long, dark and luscious. Her lips were very full – naturally and with a little help from her cosmetologist. I knew this, because she and my mom went to the same place.

I crossed my arms. "Sorry, but you can't have the dress."

"Why not?" she demanded.

Wasn't it obvious? "Because I'm wearing it."

"So?" she said. "You can have mine."

I gave her dress a long, horrified look. No doubt, the thing cost a fortune. One thing about Aunt Tabitha, she never wore anything cheap.

But the truth was, when it came to the dress she was wearing now, there simply wasn't enough of it.

It was red and sparkly with nothing to keep it up on top *or* down on the bottom. It was like a big, festive bandage, cut so low on her chest and so high on her thighs that she was one good sneeze away from flashing whatever body part happened to pop out first.

If I were a betting gal, I'd put *my* money on a nipple. And just like that, another unwanted image flashed in my brain.

I stifled a shudder.

Stop thinking about your aunt's nipple.

Her gaze narrowed. "Don't give me that look. This dress was two-thousand dollars." She cocked a hip and announced, "You should feel lucky I'd let you wear it at all."

I almost laughed in her face. "Lucky, huh?"

"Yes. Lucky." She glanced at my feet. "And I'll be needing the shoes, too."

The implication of this was obvious. Apparently, I'd be trading my silver heels for her thigh-high red boots. I gave them a closer look. *Were they leather? Or latex?* Honestly, I had no idea. I mean, it's not like I was an expert in either one.

I shook my head. "Forget it."

She edged closer and said, "Listen here, you little snot. I'll have you know, I was in the middle of something when your mom called. And unlike *you*, I dropped everything to help her out. So excuse me if I'm a little miffed."

I recalled my mom saying that she'd have to find someone else to take my place. Apparently, that someone was Aunt Tabitha, which wasn't terribly surprising, given their history.

From the way they used to talk, they just *loved* threesomes, especially with rich, famous guys.

I heard myself say, "I'm surprised she didn't ask you first."

"She did," Aunt Tabitha said, "but I had plans, which I had to break, thanks to you."

I *so* didn't want to speculate what those plans were. But it was pretty obvious that she'd been smack-dab in the middle of them when she'd gotten the call.

Was I supposed to feel guilty?

Probably.

But I didn't.

Did that make me a bad person?

No. Definitely not.

"Look," I said, "I didn't realize what my mom had in mind until we were halfway there, so *you'll* have to excuse *me* if I don't jump at the chance to give up my clothes."

"Except they're *not* yours. They're mine." She gave me a cold smirk. "And I need them back."

"Why?" I demanded. "Your outfit is…" I cleared my throat. "…well, perfect."

Or at least it was perfect for whatever they were planning. I just thanked my lucky stars that those plans no longer included me.

"Perfect, my ass," she said. "Your mom? She was going for a twin thing. Hello? Matching dresses? What are you, stupid?"

I wasn't stupid, and she darn well knew it. In fact, I was a lot smarter than she ever gave me credit for.

"No, I'm *not* stupid," I said. "And you know what? I'm not your niece either, so give it up already."

She frowned. "What?"

"I'm just saying, you're not even my aunt."

At this, she had the nerve to look insulted. "I am, too."

"No. You're not." By now, I was so angry that I was shaking. "You and my mom? You're not *really* sisters. You're just friends. So stop acting like you have some hold over me. You don't." With an effort, I lowered my voice. "So fuck off."

She drew back and stared at me for a long moment. Obviously, she was beyond surprised.

Funny, me too.

It had been years since I'd last seen her, and I'd never been great at sticking up for myself. And even when I did, I'd always done it as politely as possible.

But tonight, I'd had more than enough. And I was definitely on a roll. After all, I'd cursed at my mom, too.

Who knows, maybe Allie was rubbing off on me. Or maybe, I'd grown a spine during my time away. Either way, I couldn't afford to back down now.

Tabitha was still staring. "What the hell's wrong with you?"

"What's wrong with *me*?" I gave a bitter laugh. "What's wrong with *you*? You're the one trying to take my clothes."

"Hey, I asked nicely." She stepped closer. "But if you want, we can do this the hard way." She bared her teeth to say, "Because one way or another, I'm getting that dress."

Part of me – the child I'd been – wanted to run. But I was no longer a kid, and I had nowhere to run. So I lifted my chin and said, "Oh, please. What are you gonna do? Rip it off me?"

Her eyes narrowed to slits. "You think I wouldn't?"

Yikes.

She looked like she meant it.

Still, I summoned up the bravest smile I could muster. "Oh, I think you would. But try it now, and you'll be sorry."

"Oh yeah? Why's that?"

I opened my mouth, planning for a sharp reply. But it never came, not because words failed me, but rather because a new voice – Jax's voice, low and dangerous – replied on my behalf. "Because if you try," he said, "you'll be looking at a broken arm."

CHAPTER 12

In unison, we whirled to look. And there he was, standing just a few paces away. His eyes were dark, and his mouth was grim as he looked from me to my so-called aunt.

I wanted to die of embarrassment. He wasn't even alone. Apparently, our little argument had attracted a small crowd. And of course, this *had* to include the redhead, who looked beyond amused.

Damn it.

I'd been so distracted, I hadn't noticed any of them.

Maybe I *was* stupid.

I straightened. *No. I wasn't.* It was just that between the noise of the party and the general mayhem, not to mention my own roiling emotions, I hadn't been paying nearly close enough attention.

Jax strode closer until he was standing within arm's reach. After the briefest glance at me, he turned his cool gaze on my aunt.

No, I reminded myself. She *wasn't* my aunt. She was Tabitha – just plain Tabitha.

Old habits might die hard, but I was determined to kick *this* habit for good. She was no aunt of mine – or even a friend for that matter. And I needed to remember that.

In that same low voice, Jax told her, "Get out."

Her brow wrinkled in a show of confusion. "But I was invited."

"Not by me." He flicked his head toward the front of the mansion. "You've got two minutes. Grab your shit and go."

Tabitha gave a shaky laugh. "Or what?" In a valiant effort, she batted her eyelashes up at him and tried for a purr. "You wouldn't *really* break my arm, would you?"

I held my breath as a wave of conflicting emotions washed over me – gratitude that he was rescuing me yet again, humiliation that it was even necessary, and yes, a twinge of fear that he'd actually make good on his threat.

After all, he'd threatened the limo driver, too. And he hadn't been bluffing *that* time.

Desperately, I looked to Tabitha and said, "Well, obviously, he was speaking metaphorically." I forced a nervous laugh. "I mean, he wouldn't *really* break your arm."

I looked to Jax and waited. For what, I wasn't sure. For him to say that I was right? Or to inform me that I was wrong?

If Jax were a normal guy, he'd simply explain that his threat was mere hyperbole, like, *"I'll kill you if you eat that last cupcake."*

But he didn't say anything remotely like that. In fact, he didn't say anything at all, even as he turned the full force of his gaze on me. Under his intense scrutiny, I felt myself squirm, and I had to ask myself a very disturbing question.

What if he *wasn't* joking? What if he *would* do such a thing?

What kind of person would he be? A hero? Or a villain?

I had no good answer, which of course, had me questioning my own ethics. They must be seriously slipping because the answer should've been easy. Nobody but a villain would make good on that threat.

Finally, it was Tabitha who broke the uneasy silence by telling Jax, "I know who you are."

With his gaze still locked on mine, he replied, "No. You don't."

Undaunted, she insisted, "Sure, I do. You're Jax Bishop." Her voice became nearly breathless. "And this is *your* house. Am I right?"

My gaze snapped in her direction. This couldn't be his house. Oh, sure, he was obviously wealthy. I'd guessed *that* already. But *this* wealthy? I couldn't even imagine.

When he made no reply, Tabitha sidled closer to him and whispered, "I hear the bedrooms are fabulous."

Oh, God. She wasn't going to –

And then, she did.

In a voice filled with all kinds of innuendo, she said, "If you wanted to show me one, I wouldn't say no."

And with that, my humiliation was complete.

I glanced around and was mortified to see the redhead watching with obvious satisfaction. When she saw me looking, she gave me a smug smile before turning to whisper something to the socialite standing next to her. The woman's only reply was a loud snicker.

Well, at least someone was having a jolly good time.

When I looked back to Jax, he was staring straight at my aunt. If nothing else, she had his full attention.

With a sultry smile, she gave a little shimmy. "Well?"

He didn't smile back. "One minute."

I felt my eyebrows furrow. *One minute for what?*

My aunt giggled. "Oh yeah?"

"Yeah," he said. "You heard me before."

She blinked. "Sorry, what?"

"I gave you two minutes," he said. "And one of them's gone."

She glanced around. "But wait—"

"Which means," he interrupted, "you've got about sixty seconds to get the hell out."

"But I can't leave," she said. "I don't have a ride."

Jax gave her a long, rude look, starting at the top of her head and ending at the toes of her shiny red boots. "In that getup?" he said. "You'll find one easy enough."

She gave a little gasp. "Just what are you implying?"

"If you don't know, I'm not gonna explain." With that, he reached into his pocket and pulled out his cell phone. He tapped something onto the screen and shoved the phone back into his pocket.

He then looked to me and said, "You ready?"

I gave a confused shake of my head. "For what?"

"You owe me."

He was right. I did owe him. But the reminder did nothing to ease my embarrassment. I glanced around, unsure how to respond.

And then, he reached for my hand. "A dance, remember?"

CHAPTER 13

I remembered no such thing, but I knew an escape route when I saw it. With a grateful smile, I let him lead me toward the front of the house and tried – not terribly hard, I'll admit – to *not* take any satisfaction from the look on the redhead's face as we passed.

She didn't look smug *now*, and no one was snickering.

Jax and I were halfway to the front when my steps faltered. "Oh, no."

He stopped moving. "What?"

"My champagne." I glanced back over my shoulder. "I must've left it near the powder room."

He smiled. "Don't worry. There's plenty more."

"I know. I'm not worried about *that*," I said. "I just don't want to leave a mess. Like, what if someone spills it?"

"Then someone'll clean it up," he said. "Not a big deal." He gave a gentle tug on my hand. "Now come on. It's our song."

We had no song, at least not yet. Still, I listened. The song was purely instrumental and probably a hundred years old. But I liked it. It was slow and sultry, like the prelude to a kiss.

As we moved through the crowd, I glanced around. "Where's the music coming from, anyway?"

"When we get there, you'll see."

He was right. I *did* see as soon as we entered a sizeable room off to the side. Here, the crowd was noticeably older, but that wasn't the thing that surprised me. It was the presence of a full band – meaning at least a dozen musicians, all decked out in formal attire. Like something out of the movies, they were playing atop a raised platform on the room's far side.

Silently, Jax led me to the middle of the dance floor and gathered me close like he knew exactly what he was doing.

And just like that, we were dancing. For a long, lingering moment, I let myself savor the feel of him as we swayed in time with the music.

None of this felt real. None of this looked real either, and part of me wanted to check for hidden cameras or to listen for a movie director to suddenly holler out, "Cut!"

But all I saw were other couples, and all I heard was music blended with the muted sounds of glasses clinking and laughter coming from the other room.

I felt like I could do this all night, sway in his arms like this was the only reality that mattered. But this wasn't the case, and there was something I needed to say. "Thanks." I laughed awkwardly against his shoulder. "Again."

"For what?" he asked.

"You know. For rescuing me. And what was that? The millionth time?"

With a hint of humor, he said, "How do you know you weren't rescuing *me*?"

I pulled back and gave him a playful eye-roll. "Oh, please. We both know that's not true."

"Yeah? That's what *you* think."

As thankful was I was, there was still something I needed to know. "You wouldn't't've *really* broken her arm, would you?"

"I never said I would."

I didn't want to contradict him, especially considering that he'd threatened her on *my* behalf. Still, I couldn't let it go. Trying to keep my tone light, I said, "Are you sure about that?"

"I know what I said."

"Right." I hesitated. "And so do I."

"Do you?"

"You, um, threatened to break her arm."

He shook his head. "Nope."

"Sorry, what?"

"I never said that."

At something in my expression, he added, "I told her she'd be *looking* at a broken arm. Big difference."

I tried not to scoff. "How is that different?"

"I didn't say *I'd* break it."

"So what *were* you saying?" I asked. "You'd have someone else break it?"

He looked at me for a long moment before saying, "I don't beat up on girls, if that's what you're asking."

Funny, it *was* what I'd been asking, but I was too embarrassed to admit it. On top of *that*, his logic was shady at best, and I wasn't blind to the fact that he still hadn't answered my question. Not really.

Would he have someone else break her arm? If so, that seemed like a distinction without a difference.

Before I could try for a better answer, he posed a question of his own. "Who was she?"

"You mean the woman in the red boots?"

"Yeah." He frowned. "Her."

"Well…" I sighed. "She's sort of my aunt, but not really."

"Not really," he repeated, as if wanting more information.

"The thing is," I explained, "she and my mom are really close – like sisters in a way – so I've always had to call her 'aunt,' even though I don't anymore."

"Since when?" he asked.

I gave a nervous laugh. "Since about five minutes ago, actually."

"Good," he said. "And your mom, what's *she* doing?"

"What do you mean?"

"I mean, she lets her friend treat you like that?" His voice grew just a shade colder. "Why?"

I *so* didn't want to say, but he'd done so much for me already that I felt compelled to be honest. "If I had to guess, I think it's probably because she…" I hesitated. "…sort of treats me the same way." I summoned up a tentative smile. "You've met her actually."

"The chick in the limo?" He paused. "That's your mom?"

Just like too many other times tonight, I felt my face burn with raw embarrassment. I gave a silent nod before saying, "So I guess I should apologize, huh?"

"For what?"

"Well, for the way she was acting, I guess."

"Why should *you* apologize?" A distinct edge crept into his voice. "She's the skank, not you."

I didn't like him calling her a skank. Maybe it was true, and it was definitely justified. But who wants to be the daughter of a skank? What if skankiness ran in the family?

If so, I was totally doomed.

From the little I knew of my grandmother, the trend was definitely there.

His voice softened. "Listen, I don't mean to insult you, but a woman like that? She's not fit to be called mom."

Probably, he was right. But emotionally, he had no idea what I was going through. How could he? Obviously, he'd grown up under very different circumstances.

Probably, *his* mom was some sort of socialite who never felt compelled to use her charms – or whatever you called it – to make ends meet.

Trying not to sound as low as I felt, I said, "Well, she's the only mom I have, so…" I gave a tight shrug and didn't bother continuing.

"So…?" he prompted.

"So, it's not like I can get a replacement."

At this, he actually smiled. "You'd be surprised."

I should've smiled back. But I couldn't. Not now. The whole sordid conversation was a grim reminder that my mom was *here* of all places. So instead, I leaned into Jax and tried not to think about it.

But no matter how hard I tried, I couldn't seem to make myself stop. Probably, my mom was looking for me right now. I wasn't so naive as to think that Tabitha had been the *only* one to spot me. Cripes, for all *I* knew, my mom was the one who'd sent her to get the dress.

Even as Jax held me so blissfully close, I found myself scanning our surroundings, dreading yet another ugly confrontation.

I tried to tell myself that probably wouldn't be nearly as dreadful as I feared. After all, Dominic was here, and she'd surely want to impress him, right?

Of course, that didn't mean I wouldn't *still* be humiliated in some way or another. No matter what, my mom always found a way.

In a fit of frustration, I squeezed my eyes shut and tried for once in my life to live in the moment. It shouldn't have been so hard. Here I was, dancing with the hottest guy I'd ever met, and he'd been so amazingly wonderful.

Still, a little voice whispered that the dance wouldn't go on forever, and eventually I'd be facing a different kind of music. For the millionth time, I wondered, where on Earth would I be sleeping tonight?

Jax's voice, low and soothing, brought me back to the present. "You're trembling."

"Am I?"

His voice was very quiet in my ear. "What's wrong?"

"Nothing."

Damn it. This was such a magical moment, and I was ruining it by worrying what might happen later. I didn't want to ruin anything, especially this dance. It might be our only one.

Desperate for a distraction, I asked, "Is this really your house?"

He pulled back to study my face. "I'll tell *you* if you tell *me*."

"Sorry, I'm not following."

"*Something's* wrong," he said. "Tell me."

I didn't *want* to tell him. I'd known him for less than two hours, but I'd seen enough of him to know that if he learned that my mom was here, he'd probably feel obligated to do something about it – as if he *hadn't* done enough for me already.

Skirting the issue, I said, "I was just thinking about my mom. That's all." I summoned up an apologetic smile. "Sorry."

"Don't be."

Suddenly curious, I said, "Earlier, you didn't notice the resemblance? Between me and my mom, I mean?"

"I noticed," he said. "But I had her pegged for a sister, or maybe a cousin. Your eyes are very different."

Now *that* surprised me. Our eyes were the exactly same color and shape. "Really?" I said. "Are you sure?"

His gaze locked on mine, and for the briefest instant, I felt like he was peering straight into my soul. "I'm sure," he said, "just like I'm sure you're not telling me the whole story."

Busted.

Again.

I bit my lip. "Well, I guess I'm just wondering…" I gave our surroundings a nervous glance. "What would you do if you saw her again?"

"Your mom? I *did* see her again, maybe ten minutes ago."

I stopped moving. "So you know she's here."

"*Was* here," he said. "At least as far as you're concerned."

I gave a little shake of my head. "What do you mean?"

"They're gone."

"Who?"

"Your mom and Dominic Jones."

I should've been relieved, but this posed a whole new set of worries. "You didn't kick them out or anything, did you?"

His gaze probed mine. "If I did, is that a problem?"

"No." I paused. "And yes. Maybe." I winced. "I just didn't want to cause you any more trouble. Or a scene." Silently, I considered the mansion, the guests, the music, the champagne, hell, even the valet parkers. "I mean, this is a really nice party."

Jax grinned. "It's no party without a scene."

I tried to laugh, but didn't quite succeed. I just had to say, "I bet you're sorry you met me, huh?"

"I'm *something*," he said, "but it's not sorry. And about your mom?"

"Yeah?"

"Don't worry. Leaving was their idea."

I felt my brow wrinkle in confusion. "I don't get it. Why would they want to go?"

"Because," he said, "a waiter pitched a tray of champagne onto his lap."

"*His* lap? When?"

The question had barely left my lips when I heard a crash in the neighboring room. Jax gave me a secret smile. "Now."

I blinked. "What?"

"The champagne thing," he said. "It just happened."

I stared stupidly up at him. "Huh?"

I was still in his arms, and around us, people were still dancing. And right here in the middle, Jax and I stood, utterly motionless in the crowd. If he was embarrassed, he didn't show it.

Oddly enough, I didn't feel it. In truth, I felt shockingly at home.

He shrugged. "Eh, what are you gonna do? These things happen."

I should've been horrified. And yet, I wasn't. "You mean the champagne thing?" I almost wanted to snicker. Was I being awful? Probably. "You made that happen, didn't you?"

"Me?" He gave me a look of mock innocence. "Nah. I've got better things to do."

"Like what?"

"Like this." And with that, he pulled me closer in his arms and began moving in time with the music. As he did, I felt my worries drift away like rainclouds after a storm.

His arms felt strong, and his movements felt sure and steady. I leaned my face against his chest and let my eyes drift, getting lost in the music and the feel of his body moving against mine.

It was like a dream, and for once, I let myself get lost in it. The music changed, drifting from one song to the next. But he didn't pull away, and neither did I.

I swear, we might've stayed like that forever if a stranger hadn't broken the spell.

CHAPTER 14

The stranger was a big, broad-shouldered man in a dark business suit. He was telling Jax, "I'm sorry, but you said to let you know."

Around us, plenty of people were still dancing, and I tried not to look as awkward as I felt. Jax and I would still be dancing, too, if only the stranger hadn't just tapped him on the shoulder and whispered something too low for me to make out.

So now, here we were, the three of us, standing motionless among the crowd. In a low voice, Jax told the guy, "Tell him to get the car. I'll meet him out front."

With a tight nod, the guy turned and strode away. I watched in silence as he made his way through the crowd and disappeared into the neighboring room. More confused than ever, I turned to Jax.

His posture was stiff, and yet, he gave me a smile. "Sorry, but there's something I've gotta handle."

Obviously.

Pushing aside my disappointment, I forced a smile, too. "Sure, I understand. And um, thanks for the dance." Stupidly, I wondered if I should've thanked him for the *dances*, as in plural, because we'd been out here for quite some time.

Reaching for my hand, Jax started guiding us toward the neighboring room. As he moved, he snagged another glass of champagne and handed it to me, saying, "Here. A replacement."

I knew what he meant. It was a replacement for the glass I'd abandoned earlier. I took a tiny sip as we moved closer to the front entrance.

When we reached the door, he turned to face me. "Listen, don't go anywhere, okay?"

I glanced around. The party was in full-swing and showed no signs of ending any time soon. Still, I dreaded the thought of staying on my own, even if had nowhere else to go.

I gave the door a nervous glance. *Maybe I could catch a cab?*

But to where?

And with what?

Jax said, "You can't leave. You know that, right?"

I was still thinking. "I can't? Why not?"

"Because you're my girlfriend, remember? If you ditch me now, what'll they say?"

I almost laughed. One thing I knew for certain. This *wasn't* a guy who obsessed over the opinions of others. I saw his argument for what it was – a way for me to stay under the happy illusion that I was doing this for him and not for myself.

Just then, Jaden appeared out of nowhere and said to Jax, "You ready?"

Jax looked to me and said, "You're staying, right?"

Unsure what else to do, I gave him a short nod and then watched as the brothers turned and disappeared out the front door.

I stood there for a long moment, sipping my champagne and wondering what on Earth was going on. I still hadn't moved when a female voice said, "So he ditched you, huh?"

I turned to look and stifled a groan. It was the redhead. *Of course.*

She was eying me with obvious satisfaction. "Wanna know what *I* think?"

Not particularly. But I didn't say it, mostly because it was pretty obvious that she'd be sharing her opinion no matter what.

Sure enough, she said, "I think he's tired of you already."

When I made no reply, she added, "And just so you know, I didn't buy that whole 'girlfriend' story. And you wanna know why?"

I sighed. "Not really."

Sure enough, she told me anyway. "Because I don't know you." She smiled. "And *I* know everyone."

"Well, goodie for you," I said, turning away. Before I could take a single step, a hand clamped onto my elbow.

When I whirled to look, she said, "You're not gonna land him, you know."

I almost laughed in her face. "Land him? What, like he's a fish or something?"

"If he is," she said, "he's the biggest fish of all, and I've been dangling *my* fine hook for a long time, chickie."

Again with the chickie?

I forced a smile. "Really? Where do you keep it?"

"Keep what?"

"The hook."

"Oh, shut up," she said. "You know what I meant."

Yes. I did. But I was so tired of this. Her hand was still on my elbow, and for some reason, it reminded me of my mom.

She was still talking. "And I'll tell you one thing for *damn* sure, I'm *not* going to be pushed aside by some nobody in a fake dress."

I looked down. *Was* my dress a fake? It *could* be, not that I cared. I hadn't checked the label, and even if I had, odds were pretty good that I wouldn't've recognized it, anyway.

Still, her words found their mark – not because of the dress, but because it was a grim reminder that I didn't belong here.

Belatedly, it hit me that Jax had never answered my question.

Was this his house? I *thought* it was. But if not, I was crashing someone else's party.

What if I was about to be tossed out on my ass?

As if sensing my uncertainty, the redhead said, "I'm right. Aren't I?"

I *so* hated this. I yanked my arm out of her grasp and said, "Listen, *snookems—*"

She stiffened. "Stop calling me that."

Well, that was rich. Ignoring her protest, I finished what I'd been about to say. "I don't know what's going on between the two of you, but I'm not involved, and I don't want to be."

"Oh, but you are," she said, "because you're playing where you don't belong." She made a show of looking around. "Just answer me one question. Who do you know?"

"What do you mean?"

She said it again, slower this time. "*Who* do you know? Here. At this party." Her voice hardened. "Name one person."

I lifted my chin. "I know Jax. *And* his brother."

"That's a little convenient."

"Oh yeah? Why?"

"Because they're both gone."

Yes. They were. I gave a tight shrug and said nothing else.

But apparently, she wasn't done. "Give me another name, someone who's here right now who can vouch for you."

There *was* no one.

It was like she'd found my weak spot and was kicking it for all she was worth.

Somehow, I stiffened my spine and said, "I'm vouching for myself, so take your 'fine hook' and shove it."

Escape time.

With that, I turned away. To my infinite relief, she didn't try to stop me as I stalked off, heading toward the rear of the house.

I didn't know where exactly I was going, but I *did* know that I'd be smart to put some distance between us. As the party went on, I tried to blend with the crowd, even as I kept a sharp eye out for the redhead.

From time to time, I spotted her, watching me with open malice, and I couldn't help but wonder what awful things she was planning behind those green eyes of hers.

The whole situation was beyond nerve-wracking, and I kept asking myself the same question. *What if she called my bluff? What then?*

I thought of my ex-aunt Tabitha. She'd been kicked out. Had she walked out on her own accord?

Or had she been dragged out, kicking and screaming? It wasn't lost on me that Jax had led me to a different part of the house, just as that one-minute deadline had expired.

I envisioned Tabitha being hauled out by a bouncer or something. *Would I be next?*

As the minutes turned to hours, I tried not to panic. But when Jax never did return, that's when I knew, I was in serious trouble.

CHAPTER 15

Around me, the party had thinned considerably. I wasn't sure how many hours had passed, but it was at least three or four.

You know how time flies when you're having fun? Well, it doesn't fly at all when you're dodging a redheaded psycho *or* trying to pretend that you belong someplace when you don't.

It didn't help that I'd realized – far too late, of course – that Jax still had my phone and wallet. I considered the ten measly dollars I had to my name. Back when I'd actually had it in my possession, it had seemed like nothing at all.

Now, it was everything, because without it, I was even more doomed than before. On top of that, the wallet contained my driver's license and debit card, not that any funds were available. Still, I did need it back.

I watched with increasing desperation as one guest drifted away after another. By now, even the band had packed up and left.

Oh sure, music was still wafting through the house, but this music was a lot quieter, coming from some unseen source, probably a central sound system or something.

I didn't know, and I didn't care. All *I* cared about was finding some way out of this mess.

I had to face facts. He definitely wasn't coming back, which meant that I had to leave. Cripes, I should've left hours ago.

Idiot. Meaning *me* of course.

As I drifted from room to room, trying to get lost in the small pockets of people who remained, I tried to think.

I had no money, no phone, and I didn't even know where I was.

Oh yeah. I was an idiot, alright.

I glanced around, searching for a friendly face – someone who might loan me their cellphone or give me a ride. I didn't know why I bothered. I had no one to call and nowhere to go – which, of course, was how I'd ended up here in the first place.

I was so lost in my worries that I didn't notice someone creeping up behind me until I felt a hard tap on my shoulder.

I whirled to look and wanted to scream in frustration. It was *her*, the redhead. I tried not to cringe. *Again?*

She said, "He's not coming back, you know."

Oh yeah. I knew.

She smiled. "Wanna know what *I* think?"

I was *so* tired of that question. "No."

"I think he met someone else."

I stiffened, but made no reply.

Unfortunately, she was on a roll. "A guy like Jax? He's hit on wherever he goes. You think you're the first girl to waltz in and think you're something special?" She laughed. "You're so cute."

I gave her a tight smile. "Thanks."

She blinked. "What?"

"You called me cute."

"Yeah, but I didn't mean it."

I forced a shrug. "Oh well. Too late now."

I didn't even know why I was tweaking her. It wouldn't solve any of my problems. If anything, it would make them worse.

Silently, I looked toward the main entrance, wondering if I should just slink away now, before things got really ugly.

I envisioned myself walking out through the front door and then down the front steps. Unfortunately, that's where the vision ended. I didn't even know if I'd be turning right or left.

Plus, it was *very* late, past midnight for sure. *What on Earth was I supposed to do?*

Damn it. I *should've* called Allie. If only I'd called her right away, she might've been halfway here by now.

The redhead gave a little laugh. "If you're waiting for him to walk through that door, you'll be waiting a long time."

I'd *already* been waiting a long time. *Stupid me.* I wanted to say something clever, but nothing came to mind. My only response was a tight shrug.

Into my silence she said, "You *do* know, he's probably fucking someone else by now."

The image sliced through me. That was stupid, too. I mean, it's not like I was his *real* girlfriend or anything.

"Or maybe," she continued, "he's onto his *second* girl. He likes to do that, you know, one girl after another – sometimes, two at once."

I didn't believe her.

And yet, her words burrowed under my skin. I had to remind myself that it wasn't like *I'd* planned on having sex with him tonight or anything.

After all, we'd just met, and I wasn't one to pounce on somebody just because they were hot. And chivalrous. And thrilling beyond all reason.

Suddenly, I wanted to cry. Stupid or not, I *had* felt like there was some sort of connection between us. And he'd been so wonderful, right up until the moment he'd left me stranded in a house full of strangers.

Aside from ditching me, what kind of guy takes off with someone's cell phone and wallet?

Thanks to this, I was totally screwed. And now, my eyes were stinging with tears that I refused to shed.

Damn it. I had to do it, the thing I'd been dreading. I looked to the redhead and said, "Can I borrow your phone?"

"Why?"

"To make a call." *Obviously.*

Her gaze narrowed. "To call whom?"

I was tired and stressed, and so ready for all of this to end. "I don't think that's any of your business."

"It is if you're using my phone."

I made a sound of frustration. "Oh come on. Jax has *my* phone, so…" I gave a little shrug, as if no further explanation should be needed.

She made a forwarding motion with her hand. "So…?"

"So…" I sighed. "I can't call anyone without it."

She smirked. "Bummer for you."

Yes. It was.

Even worse, any second now, I just knew I was going to burst out crying.

Shit.

Why here? Why now?

Trying to get a grip, I clamped my lips shut and looked away.

The redhead said, "So, are you gonna answer my question or not?"

I didn't even look as I muttered, "What question?"

"*Who* are you going to call?"

I looked back to her and snapped, "Well, it's not Jax if that's what you're worried about."

"I'm not worried." She gave me a slow, deliberate smile. "In fact, I'm enjoying myself immensely."

No kidding. I could see it in the curve of her lips and in the gleam of her eyes. She *was* enjoying this. And if I actually broke down and sobbed, she'd probably have an organism right here and now.

Whatever. I looked around, wondering who else I could ask. Probably, I should've asked one of the waiters while they'd been still circulating. If nothing else, the house surely had a landline *somewhere*, right?

But the waiters had disappeared to who-knows-where at least an hour ago. And, as if that weren't bad enough, while I'd been talking to the redhead, at least half of the remaining guests had drifted out the front door.

Just then, the music cut out entirely, making the massive space seem ten times emptier.

My stomach sank. *Oh, crap.* The party was officially over.

And I was totally screwed.

CHAPTER 16

Desperately, I looked back to the redhead and said, "Fine. The person I want to call is my roommate."

Technically, Allie was my *ex*-roommate, but she was still my best friend. Or, at least I sure hoped she was, even if we hadn't parted on the best of terms.

The redhead asked, "Why her?"

God, was this really necessary? Through gritted teeth, I replied, "Because, I'm going to ask her to pick me up."

This was true, but it wasn't the full story. Allie was at least ten hours away in Nashville. Unless she hijacked a plane, she wouldn't be here until long past sunrise.

This meant I was looking at a long dreadful night followed by a long uncertain morning. And this was assuming that Allie would be able to come at all.

But then, I suddenly perked up. "But wait, you probably have Jax's number, right?"

"Yeah. So?"

"So maybe you could call and ask him to bring me my phone."

She laughed. "Nice try, chickie."

"What do you mean?"

"If you think I'm falling for that, you're crazy."

Oh, I was crazy, alright, but not in the way she thought. I was crazy for coming here in the first place – not just to the party, but to the whole stupid state. Florida had *not* been kind to me.

I gave the redhead an annoyed look. "You know, he has my wallet, too."

"Bummer for you," she said for the second time in five minutes.

For the briefest instant, I almost debated calling my mom. She was local, *and* she knew my location, even if *I* didn't.

Maybe *she* could come and get me?

I considered that idea for like two whole seconds before rejecting it outright. Knowing my mom, she was still with Dominic, probably at the so-called penthouse, where I'd been living for the past week.

So I *couldn't* go there. After all, what kind of favors would be expected in return?

I gave a little shudder and tried not to think about it.

The redhead gave a long-suffering sigh. "Alright, fine."

I turned to face her. "What?"

"I *guess* you can use my phone." Her gaze narrowed. "But *I'm* dialing."

"Why?"

"Because I don't want you snooping through my contacts, that's why."

Boy, she didn't take any chances, did she?

I told her, "Fine, whatever."

"Whatever?" she repeated. "Don't you mean to say thank you? I'm doing you a big favor, you know."

If I had any other option, I might've told her where she could shove the phone *and* the favor. But I didn't, so I gritted out the two words she wanted to hear. "Thank you."

"You don't sound very grateful," she grumbled, reaching into her tiny black purse. She pulled out a cellphone and said, "What's the number?"

I froze. *Oh, crap.* I didn't know it, not by heart. I never dialed Allie's number. Mostly, I just hit her name in my contacts and let the phone dial itself.

I tried to think. I definitely knew the area code, but the rest of it was hazy at best.

The redhead said, "I don't have all night, you know."

Thankfully, I *did* know the number to our apartment, the one we'd shared until just a week ago. These days, Allie was living there with someone new, but the number was still good.

With sudden relief, I rattled off the digits and watched as the redhead tapped them out on the screen. When she finally handed the phone over, I turned away, seeking some semblance of privacy.

She demanded, "Where do you think you're going?"

I glanced back over my shoulder. "Nowhere."

"Yeah, well, see that you don't." She edged closer. "And I swear to God, if you start scrolling through my contacts, I'm calling the police."

Knowing her, she'd actually do it. I could practically hear it now. *Hello Officer, I'm calling to report phone-snooping.*

But this was no joke. For all I knew, she'd also report me as a trespasser and claim that I'd raided the safe or something. A place like this surely had one, right?

Trying to ignore her, I listened intently as the apartment's number rang once, and then twice. I held my breath. On the third ring, it went to voicemail.

Shit.

Probably, Allie was just sleeping, that's all. Praying that she'd get the message sooner rather than later, I said in a rush, "Hey, Allie, it's me. Um, Cassidy."

I gave a mental eye-roll. *As if she didn't know.*

I continued. "Anyway, I'm in a bit of a bind, but you probably knew that already, huh?" I tried to laugh. "After all, you *did* tell me I was making a huge mistake. But the thing is, I'm hoping – praying actually – that you might be able to come down here and get me." I paused. "Like now."

I took a deep, shuddering breath. "And just so you know, I'm *really* sorry to ask, and I swear I'll pay you back – for the time and the gas and everything. Just call me as soon as you get this, okay?"

These final words made me realize something, and I felt the color drain from my face. *Oh, crap.*

She couldn't call me.

I blurted out, "Wait, forget that. I don't have my phone, so just come here and we'll talk then, okay? I'm at..." I looked to the redhead and asked, "Do you have the address? To this house, I mean?"

She gave an irritated sigh. "It's 432 Beachview." Frowning, she demanded, "And just how long will it take for your ride to get here?"

Oh, about ten hours.

I held up a finger and returned my attention to the phone. "In case you didn't hear that, I'm at 432 Beachview. Well, technically, I won't be here-here, because I need to get going, but I'll be around." In a burst of inspiration, I added, "I think there's a public beach nearby. I'll just hang out there 'til you get here."

If you get here.

I might've said more, but a familiar beep informed me that I was out of time. And I didn't dare ask the redhead for a second call, especially because I needed another favor.

As I handed back the phone, I said, "If you see Jax, could you please tell him to call that number, the one I just called?"

She gave me a good, long look. "Why?"

"Because I still need my phone and wallet. And my roommate can give him our address." I bit my lip. "I mean, he'll probably have to mail me the stuff, but I really *do* need it back."

She held up a hand. "Don't bore me with the details, alright?"

I wanted to throttle her. But that wouldn't help me get my stuff, so instead, I persisted, "But you'll tell him?"

"I guess." She looked toward the front door. "So, are you done?"

Oh, I was done alright.

With as much dignity as I could muster – which, granted, wasn't much – I turned and strode toward the front door. And then, heaven help me, I walked out.

And where was I going?

I had no idea.

CHAPTER 17

The sand was cold, and I was shivering. Turns out, I'd been wrong about a public beach.

But the house *was* beach-front, so like a thief in the night, I'd sidled around the estate and found a patch of private sand to call my own.

I was facing the water and hugging my knees tight against my chest. I'd been sitting in the same spot for at least an hour, maybe longer. Probably, my dress was already ruined, but I couldn't bring myself to care. I just prayed that no one spotted me as I waited – for what, I wasn't even sure.

Even if Allie was already on her way, she wouldn't be here for at least several hours. And what if she *wasn't* on her way? In *that* case, I didn't even want to think about it.

Desperately, I tried to look on the bright side. Sure, the night was cold and damp, but at least I was hidden from sight – for now, anyway.

The morning, when it came, would bring warmth, but with it, a whole new set of problems, like the chance of being spotted.

Until then, I was hunkered down just beyond the mansion's rear patio – the second-story one that I'd spotted through the glass, back when I'd been on the inside looking out.

Already, that seemed like a lifetime ago.

Behind me, the house had grown dark and utterly silent, which was fine by me, because it lowered my odds of getting caught.

I leaned back against the cold sand and squeezed my eyes shut, trying to get some sleep – as if that were possible. My shoes were off, and I was using my own hands as a pillow, which meant that my bare shoulders and arms rested directly on the sand.

At that moment, I would've given almost anything for a blanket or beach towel. Hell, even a washcloth would've been better than nothing.

I was still lying there, praying for sleep, when I was startled by the sound of a door slamming shut. I tensed. The way it sounded, the noise had come from the second-story patio.

I held my breath and tried not to move. Was someone standing out there right now? And if so, could they see me through the shadows?

Silently, I waited, for what, I didn't know.

Soon, I heard voices – and not just *any* voices, the voices of Jax and his brother.

They were back.

Finally.

And yet, I still didn't move. It was true that I needed my things. But the thought of marching up to the front door, looking like a sandy street urchin was beyond mortifying.

Plus I didn't want to see either of those guys, Jax in particular.

Sometime in the last hour, I decided that I really didn't like him at all. I mean seriously, what kind of guy just takes off like that? Even if he'd gotten tied up or delayed, surely he could've sent me *some* sort of message.

But he hadn't.

He hadn't even thought to return my stuff.

No. Instead, he'd let me linger there, alone and uninvited, for hours, all the while being hounded by the Ginger from Hell.

I was so lost in my own anger and indecision that it took me a moment to realize they were talking about *me*.

"Oh yeah?" Jax was saying. "Then where the hell is she?"

Jaden's voice, sounding annoyingly calm, replied, "Why are you asking *me*? I was with *you*."

"Fuck."

"Dude, what did you expect? You were gone like six hours."

Yes. Exactly.

"What do I expect?" Jax made a hard, scoffing sound. "I expect people to do their fucking jobs."

"Yeah? Well, if you're talking about Morgan, good luck with that."

"Meaning?"

"Meaning she's not worth the trouble. Why'd you fuck her?"

I felt my jaw clench. *Morgan? Morgan who?* Was *that* where he'd been? Screwing someone named Morgan?

Jax replied, "Because I'm a dumb-ass. That's why."

"Hey, you said it, not me."

"Forget Morgan," Jax said. "Where the hell is Cassidy?"

"I don't know. Just like I didn't know the other ten times you asked."

"Shit. She was supposed to wait."

"Yeah. And you were supposed to be right back. Looks to me like you're even."

If I were sitting up, I might've nodded. *Yeah, you tell him, Jaden.* Suddenly, the guy was making a lot of sense. *Go figure.*

When Jax made no reply, Jaden continued. "My guess? She's fucking someone else."

I sat up. *What?*

No wonder I didn't like him.

Jax replied. "No. That's not her."

"Yeah?" Jaden's tone grew sarcastic. "Well, it's adorable you think so."

"Hey, I know what I know."

"Oh come on, you heard what Morgan said. She left with a better offer."

At this, my mouth fell open. *A better offer? What did that mean?*

Jax was saying, "Or *maybe* Morgan's full of shit."

"Well, there is *that*. But that doesn't mean she's lying."

"Oh, she's lying alright."

"How do you know?"

"Because I have Cassidy's phone."

"So?"

"So she wouldn't leave without it."

"Maybe it was a burner. You know, her hooker phone."

What the hell?

My hooker phone?

I knew there was a reason I hated that guy.

Jaden was still talking. "She probably goes through ten a week."

"For the last fucking time," Jax said, "she's no hooker."

Jaden laughed. "Sure. That's why she was decked out like twins with another working girl. My guess? That was her sister."

"No. It wasn't."

"How do you know?"

After a long pause, Jax said, "Because it was her mom."

"No fucking way." Jaden laughed like he'd just heard the funniest joke ever. "You're shitting me, right?"

"Oh, fuck off."

"Dude, she's gone. Forget it."

As I listened, my emotions bounced all over the place. I felt pathetically grateful that Jax was sticking up for me. Unfortunately, my gratitude was offset by the fact that he'd *still* ditched me and that his brother was a giant douchebag.

And now, I didn't know what to do. I definitely needed my stuff. And if I knocked on their door – or maybe even just hollered out to them – they might let me wait inside for Allie. But the thought of being seen in my bedraggled state was almost too humiliating to consider.

I was still trying to decide what to do when Jaden said something that made my heart sink to my stomach. "Holy fuck. Is that her?"

CHAPTER 18

I held myself very still, praying that he didn't mean what I thought he meant.

From somewhere above, Jax replied, "Where?"

"Down there."

A moment ago, I was freezing. Now, I was burning with raw embarrassment. Like a child, trying to hide from the monster in the closet, I squeezed my eyes shut and tried to pretend this wasn't happening.

Oh, but it was.

I knew this, because a moment later, even with my eyes tightly shut, I could still tell the difference between darkness and light as some sort of spotlight burned down on me from above.

It was funny in a way, because until then, I'd been absolutely certain that I'd been humiliated enough for one night.

Apparently not.

Reluctantly, I opened my eyes, only to feel the need to shield them with my hand. From what I could guess, those idiots were shining a flashlight – a very bright flashlight – straight at me.

I hollered out, "Will you shut that thing off?"

They didn't.

Instead, Jaden called back, "What are you doing?"

I could *hear* him, but I couldn't *see* him. Cripes, I couldn't see anything through the glaring light. I yelled back, "I'm not doing anything." *Damn it.* The stupid flashlight was *still* on. "Didn't you hear me?"

"Hell, everyone heard you," he said.

Terrific. And no doubt, everyone could also *see* me, thanks to the Spotlight of Shame.

I stumbled to my feet and glared up at him. Or rather, I tried to. But it was hard to glare while that light was roasting my eyeballs alive.

With a muttered curse, I crouched down and yanked my shoes out of the sand. Without bothering to put them on, I began stalking away from the light, planning to head back the way I'd come. But there was no escape. As I moved toward the side of the house, the light moved with me until, at last, the house itself was between me and Freddie Flashlight.

I welcomed the darkness, just like I welcomed a surge of hatred for both brothers. Obviously, Jaden was manning the light. But what was Jax doing?

Was he watching silently from above, like this was some sort of show for his amusement?

No. He wasn't.

I knew this, because a moment later, while stalking through the shadows, I ran straight into him, literally, and almost lost my footing. In fact, the only reason I *didn't* topple over was because his arms closed tight around me, pulling me close, even as he said, "Hey, are you alright?"

I gave a bark of laughter. "Oh, sure, I'm perfect. How are you?"

His voice was very quiet. "You're cold."

"No," I snapped. "I'm not. I'm roasting alive. Can't you tell?"

Yes, I realized I was being incredibly rude, but I couldn't bring myself to care. Tonight had been one of the worst nights of my life, and I saw no reason to pretend otherwise.

Pathetically, it wasn't even because tonight had delivered more bad stuff than I could handle. Rather, it was because the *best* parts of the night had been so very wonderful, which perversely, only made the awful parts seem ten times worse.

I yanked myself out of his grasp and demanded, "Where's my phone?"

His voice was low and soothing. "In the house. If you need it, just say the word."

"Fine," I snapped. "I'm saying it. And I need my wallet, too."

As my eyes adjusted to the darkness, I could see Jax more clearly now. He was still wearing the tux, but it looked slightly rumpled, like he'd slept in it or something. And yet, he still looked incredibly sexy.

The bastard.

He eyed me with obvious concern. "What happened?"

You left. That's what happened. I made a scoffing sound. "As if you don't know."

"I *don't* know," he said. "Why'd you leave?"

Now, that was a lovely question. In fact, it was *so* lovely that I tossed it right back at him. "I dunno. Why'd *you* leave?"

"Because I had to."

"Fine. Whatever. Just get me my stuff, alright?" I crossed my arms. "I'll wait here."

"The hell you will."

"What?"

"You think I'm gonna go inside and leave you standing here? Like *this*?"

Through gritted teeth, I said, "Like what?"

Dirty and disheveled? Half-crazed? Freezing? And sweating too?

I could only imagine what I looked like.

Even more maddening, I couldn't help but notice that I'd felt a whole lot better when I'd been in his arms. Now, I felt cold and lost – rudderless in a storm of my own roiling emotions.

He never *did* answer my question. Instead, he reached for my hand and said, "Come on, let's get you inside, and we'll talk there, okay?"

His hand was warm, and his voice was a soothing balm to my jangled nerves. Like an idiot, I might've melted right then and there if it weren't for the sudden appearance of that cursed light, coming from somewhere behind me now.

I gave a silent curse and tried not to scream in frustration. I just prayed that flashlight was nice and huge, because I swear to God, I was going to shove that thing up Jaden's ass.

Jax glared past me to say, "Shut that thing off, will ya?"

Jaden replied, "But you told me to keep it on her."

I gave Jax an annoyed look. "So that was *your* idea?"

He gave my hand a reassuring squeeze. "I didn't want to lose you."

The stupid light was still on, and I turned around to yell, "Are you gonna shut that thing off or not?"

"I dunno," Jaden said, sounding almost amused. "You're looking a little crazy. I'm not sure I should."

I wanted to strangle him. If he thought I was crazy now, just wait 'til I got ahold of that flashlight.

From behind me, Jax said, "Shut that fucking thing off before I shove it up your ass."

Well, at least we agreed on something.

And yet, the light was still on.

With my free hand, I shielded my eyes, trying to get a sense of what Jaden was doing. Under the glare, I could barely make out his silhouette as he said, "Gee, you try to do someone a favor…"

Obviously, the "someone" wasn't me. It wasn't hard to guess what they'd done. From what I could tell, Jaden had watched from the rear of the house while Jax had approached from the front.

It was way too devious, and I didn't like it.

Not one bit.

I looked back to Jax and said, "Did it ever occur to you to just call out my name or something?"

His voice remained calm in the face of my wrath. "I didn't want you to run off."

What a joke. Where would I run? I had nowhere to go. And yet, I *had* been running – or stalking or stumbling, anyway. By now, everything was a blur, and I had no good reply to what he'd just said.

So I said nothing. And this time, I didn't argue as he led me toward the front of the house. Together, we mounted the front steps and then walked inside, using the very same front door we'd used however many hours ago.

Unlike earlier, the house was mostly dark and utterly devoid of people. Even Jaden had melted away to somewhere in the night.

Whether Jaden had used a back door or left entirely, I didn't know, and I didn't care. I was just glad he wasn't here, because I just knew he'd be mocking me, and I wasn't sure I could take it.

Plus, the guy thought I was a hooker.

Jerk.

This only served to remind me of the other things I'd overheard while listening from below. None of them brought me any pleasure – in particular that bit about Jax screwing someone named Morgan.

It shouldn't have mattered. After all, I barely knew the guy. And I was determined not to pry, no matter how curious I might be. If nothing else, I refused to give him the satisfaction.

Unfortunately, he wasn't nearly as respectful of *my* privacy as I was of *his*.

CHAPTER 19

For what felt like the millionth time, he asked, "What happened?"

We were sitting in a side room, and I was wrapped in a soft flannel blanket that he'd grabbed from a nearby chest. Like the sap I was, I'd protested that I shouldn't be using the blanket at all, given the fact that I was so grubby with sand and who-knows-what-else.

Ignoring my protests, he'd tucked the blanket around me anyway, and then *also* ignored my claim that I wasn't thirsty. So here I was, wrapped up and sipping hot cocoa in the middle of the night. On the nearby side table sat an ice-cold bottle of water, which I'd yet to open.

Whether I was too hot or too cold, I'd have the perfect beverage either way. I hadn't asked for either one, and yet, I couldn't help but appreciate all of it – which only made it that much harder to be angry with him.

Damn it.

His question hung in the air, and I repeated the same answer that I'd already given. "Nothing happened. I just left, that's all."

"But why? You didn't get my message?"

Now *that* made me pause. "What message?"

His jaw tightened. "So, you didn't."

"No," I said. "I didn't even know you left one."

We were sitting in matching arm chairs with the side table between us. He abruptly stood. "I should've known."

I stared up at him. "You should've known what?"

"That it wasn't true." He shoved a hand through his hair. "Hell, I *did* know."

I wasn't following. "Sorry, but what are you talking about?"

He looked away and muttered, "Nothing."

I asked, "Are you doing that in retaliation?"

His gaze returned to mine. "Doing what?"

"Saying 'nothing,' because that's what I've been saying, like you're throwing the same word back at me to make a point?"

For a moment, he looked almost ready to smile. "That's not it," he said. "I just mean it's nothing I want you to worry about." His mouth tightened. "But I can promise you this. I'm gonna handle it."

"Handle what?"

"Forget it," he said. "It's my problem, not yours. And we're gonna keep it that way, alright?"

I was just about to object when his expression softened. He moved closer and crouched down in front of me. We were nearly at eye-level, with him close enough to touch.

He was still wearing his tuxedo, and I was still wearing my dress. But it was painfully obvious that both of us looked a lot rougher than we had earlier in the evening.

I was a total mess from head to toe. Even now, I could feel the sand in my hair and grittiness between my toes. I never did put my shoes back on, which was just as well, unless I wanted them ruined, assuming they weren't already.

As for Jax, his appearance was more complicated. He still looked amazing. But his tux? Not so much.

It wasn't just rumpled either. I gave it a closer look and noticed a tear in the jacket and a smattering of reddish-brown spots on his formerly pristine white shirt.

I felt my eyebrows furrow. "What happened to your tux?"

"Nothing you need to worry about."

I couldn't tell if he was being rude or trying to spare me. I zoomed in on his shirt. "That isn't blood, is it?"

He shrugged. "I dunno. Maybe."

I stared at him. "Maybe? What, you don't know?"

"Forget that," he said. "I want you to know something."

I was still looking at the shirt. Absently, I murmured, "What?"

"Tonight..." His voice grew very quiet. "It wasn't supposed to happen that way."

I looked up to study his face. His eyes were dark and troubled as he added, "I'm sorry."

Now, I felt almost guilty. Yes, it was true that he'd abandoned me at a party where I didn't know a soul. And it *had* totally sucked. But I was only here at all because he'd rescued me from a different sucky situation.

I sighed. "Don't be sorry. Probably, I shouldn't have been here in the first place."

But already, he was shaking his head. "You're wrong. It was me. I shouldn't've left."

I just had to ask, "So, where'd you go anyway? Was there a fire or something?"

He grew very still. "What makes you say that?"

"When I ran into you, I thought I smelled smoke." My nose wrinkled. "And I think I still smell it."

He glanced down at his tux. "Yeah, well, it's been one of those nights."

"What happened?"

"Nothing. Just family stuff."

And I thought *my* family stuff was weird. I asked, "Do you want to talk about it?"

He smiled. "Hell no. What I *want* is to make it up to you."

I shook my head. "There's nothing to make up. But you said you left me a message? What was it?"

"It was just letting you know I'd be late." He gave a humorless laugh. "*And* a reminder for you not to go anywhere."

I tried to smile. "Not even to the beach?"

His gaze met mine. "That shouldn't have happened."

I didn't know what to say, mostly because I wasn't sure what *should've* happened. I'd spent the whole night in limbo – not just because I'd been waiting for Jax, but also, because I had nowhere else to go.

I'd been trying not to obsess over it, but now, in the quiet of the house – *his* house, apparently – I couldn't stop thinking about it.

What now?

Earlier, he'd offered me a thousand dollars to pretend to be his girlfriend. Maybe I should've jumped at the money. But I wasn't *that* clueless. By now, I was nearly certain that the whole thing had been a ruse for my sake.

And if it wasn't? Well, I *still* couldn't accept the money. I mean, jeez, his brother *already* thought I was hooker. Accepting cash for a date seemed the perfect way to prove him right, especially if I fell into Jax's arms, and then into his bed.

But that wasn't going to happen, and not only because he hadn't asked. I wasn't big into one-night stands *or* jumping into bed with a guy I'd just met.

And this meant what, exactly?

I turned and looked vaguely toward the front door. I couldn't see it from here, but I did know where it was.

Jax said, "If you think you're leaving, forget it."

"Actually," I admitted, "I don't know what I'm thinking."

"You never answered my question," he said. "What happened?"

"It was just that the party was over and..." I gave a useless shrug. "Well, I had to leave eventually, right?"

He studied my face. "There's something you're not telling me."

There was a lot I wasn't telling him. But unless I was ready to dump a bucketful of problems on his doorstep, I was determined to keep it that way. Lamely, I murmured, "It's just late. That's all."

"You're right," he said. "It is. So why don't you stay here tonight. We'll figure it out tomorrow, okay?"

I bit my lip. It was a really nice thought, and yet, I wasn't quite sure what he was offering me.

When I made no reply, he added, "I've got a guest room."

Relief – and the barest twinge of disappointment – coursed through me. I gave a nervous laugh. "Only one, huh? In a place like this? I'm surprised you don't have ten."

"Yeah, well." He glanced around. "There's not ten. But you're right, there's a few."

Stalling, I asked, "How many is a few?"

"If you want, I'll give you a tour." He smiled. "Tomorrow." And with that, he reached for my hand and gently tugged me from the chair. The blanket fell onto the floor, and I glanced back, wondering if I should fold it up or something.

After all, it felt pretty rude not to.

"Leave it," Jax said. "The cleaning crew will get it tomorrow."

"But—"

"And," he said, "there's fresh blankets in the bedroom. Now c'mon."

CHAPTER 20

He was right. There *were* fresh blankets, along with a queen size bed, a private bathroom, and huge windows that faced the rear of the house.

In the bathroom, I found fresh towels along with a basket of toiletries. The way it looked, the room had been pre-stocked with anything a surprise guest might need, well, except for clothes.

And Jax solved that problem, too.

After showing me to the room, he told me that he'd be returning in a few minutes with some clothes that I could borrow. True to his word, he returned five minutes later with a neat stack of folded clothing.

Burning with new embarrassment, I took the stack from his hands and thanked him yet again.

"Not a problem," he said. "If there's anything you need, just holler, alright?"

It was a funny thing to say, because with the size of the house, I probably would need to holler. And loudly, too. For all I knew, he'd be on a different floor entirely.

"Actually," I said, "I really do need my phone. You said it's here in the house?"

Silently, he reached into his pocket and pulled out my phone, along with my wallet. He placed both of them on the stack of clothing and asked, "Anything else?"

I shook my head. "Thanks for everything. And sorry for all the trouble."

He smiled. "Like I said before, I don't mind a little trouble."

I'd caused him a lot more than a little, but this time, I didn't argue.

Instead, I said goodnight and watched as he turned away, only to stop in mid-step. He turned back and said, "Do me a favor. Lock the door, alright?"

I gave the bedroom door a nervous glance. I would've locked it anyway, out of habit if nothing else. But his warning wasn't exactly comforting. "Why?" I asked.

"Better safe than sorry." And with that, he turned and strode off, leaving me watching from the open doorway.

When he disappeared around the corner, I shut the bedroom door and locked it behind me. And then, I ran a hot bath and washed the grit out of my hair.

I emerged after a long soak feeling a lot warmer and nearly human. Wrapped in an oversized towel, I began sifting through the stack of clothing, which I'd placed on the bathroom countertop.

Rifling through the pile, I found several pairs of shorts, black yoga pants, a Michigan State sweatshirt, a bunch of socks, and a few cotton T-shirts in varying colors and sizes.

Tucked within the folds of the largest T-shirt, I discovered a wad of lacy undergarments with the tags still attached.

Feeling incredibly self-conscious, I lifted a pair of pink panties and glanced at the tag. I couldn't help but swallow. They cost more than my best pair of jeans.

Whose panties were these, anyway?

Obviously, they'd never been worn, but they surely belonged to *someone* – unless Jax kept a supply on-hand, just in case.

On that disturbing note, I dropped the panties onto the stack and stared at the whole pile. There was enough clothing for several nights.

It was incredibly thoughtful and just a little bit unnerving.

Wrapping the towel tighter around my chest, I looked up to study my reflection in the bathroom mirror. Just like always, my mom's face stared back at me.

My hair was still dripping, and any makeup was long washed away. But the face was all too familiar, and I tried to smile at my reflection. Why, I wasn't sure. To reassure myself that everything would be okay? Or to remind myself that I *wasn't* my mom?

If she'd gotten *her* way, it would be *her* inside this house, not me. And one thing was for darn sure – she *wouldn't* be staying in the guest room.

In the end, I dressed in the cheapest of the undergarments along with pink running shorts and a little gray T-shirt. And then, I dried my hair and wandered into the bedroom area.

With my cellphone in-hand, I sat on the edge of the bed to check my messages.

As I listened to one after another, I felt my stomach twist into knots. None of the messages were good, particularly the ones from Allie. They made me feel – and rightfully so – that I was the most thoughtless person in the universe.

When I finished listening, I blew out a long, shaky breath. Somehow, I had to reach her.

CHAPTER 21

With growing desperation, I clutched my cellphone tight against my ear and listened to the ringing on the other end. Silently, I repeated the same prayer over and over. *Please answer, please answer, please answer...*

But my prayers, like the phone in Allie's apartment, went unanswered as the call went eventually to voicemail.

Damn it.

I disconnected and tried her cellphone. This time, there was no ringing at all. Instead, it went *straight* to voicemail, like her phone was dead or turned off.

Double damn it.

I listened with growing impatience as her cheerful greeting told me to leave a message.

After the beep, I said in a rush, "Hey, it's me. Listen, I'm *so* sorry that I didn't call you sooner, but things are okay, so don't worry, alright?" I hesitated. "I mean, they're not a hundred percent okay, but it's nothing I can't handle. And..."

I tried to think. *And what?*

I took a deep breath and admitted, "Honestly, I'm not sure what I'm going to do, but it's not like I need you to drive through the night or anything." I forced a nervous laugh. "Not that you could, thank goodness, huh?"

I finished by saying, "Anyway, I'm really sorry for worrying you, and could you please call me when you get this? I have my cellphone back, so I'll be waiting, okay?"

With that, I disconnected the call and sank backward onto the bed.

In my mind, I could practically see Allie's reaction to my earlier call. No doubt, she'd cussed up a storm. She did that sometimes when she was upset, and the way it sounded, my call had rattled her, bigtime.

I knew this because during the last couple of hours, she'd left me at least a dozen messages, each more frantic than the last.

I couldn't blame her, especially when I considered my desperate call from the redhead's phone. To think, I'd practically begged Allie to drive all the way down here to get me. And then, like a total dumb-ass, I'd neglected to call her again when Jax returned.

I still didn't know what I was going to do about my living situation, but at least I had a few hours to figure things out. After all, it's not like I was sleeping outside or anything.

As far as the situation with Allie, there was at least *one* lucky break. Her car was in the shop, as she'd informed in her very first voicemail.

Thank God.

I wasn't happy that her car needed repairs, but I *was* thankful for the timing. If her car weren't out of commission, she might be driving through Alabama by now.

Just to be safe, I dialed the number to the apartment and left a message there, too. It was the middle of the night, and if she was asleep – which I hoped she was – she'd get at least *one* of the messages first thing in the morning.

It wasn't much of a comfort, but it was the best I could do.

I stayed awake for another hour just in case she called me back. And then, when she didn't, I crawled under the covers and closed my eyes.

The mattress was pure perfection, and the sheets smelled fresh and clean. They weren't cotton. They were something else – something softer and smoother. Silk maybe? I didn't know, and I didn't have the energy to speculate.

I fell into a deep, blissful sleep, only to wake far too soon to the sounds of yelling.

And it was coming from *inside* the house.

CHAPTER 22

My eyes flew open, and I bolted upright in the bed. My gaze darted around the room as I struggled to remember where I was.

And then, in a rush, I recalled everything – the car crash, the party, and most of all, Jax.

Pale light was creeping in through the windows, lending a dreamlike quality to my surroundings. I wasn't sure what time it was, but judging from the light, it had to be very early.

From somewhere inside the house, a woman yelled, "She called me a cunt!"

Woah. That was bigtime name-calling. In my whole life, I'd never even *said* the word, even if I *had* thought it a time or two.

Jax replied, "So?"

I froze at the sound of his voice. He sounded a lot closer than I might've expected. Unless I was mistaken, the argument was taking place just down the hall or maybe in a neighboring bedroom.

After all, *he* hadn't yelled, and I could hear *him* just fine.

The woman hollered, "This *wasn't* part of the deal!"

Sounding almost bored, Jax replied, "What deal?"

"My employment deal, that's what! Because if you think I signed on to be verbally abused, you've got another thing coming."

"So, you're gonna quit?"

After a long pause, she said, "You'd like that, wouldn't you?"

"Yeah. I would. So go on, get it over with."

"Get it over with?" she scoffed. "I can't believe you just said that. After all our history?"

"Hell, I've got more to say than that."

"Oh, really? What?"

"Later."

"What do you mean later?"

With a distinct edge, he replied, "We'll talk later."

"Why not now?" she demanded.

"Is that a serious question?"

"What, because you're in bed? Big freaking deal. It's not like I haven't seen it all before."

I frowned. *His bed? That's* where they were arguing?

Jax said, "Yeah, well you're not seeing it now."

In a disturbingly flirty voice, she replied, "I could if you'd ditch the blanket."

Oh, for God's sake.

"Forget it," Jax told her. "And who the fuck let you in?"

She gave a sarcastic laugh. "Oh, this is just great. So now *you're* cussing me out, too? What is this? Abuse Morgan Day?"

I sucked in a breath. *Morgan?*

I recalled snippets of that conversation I'd overheard between Jax and his brother. Assuming that this was the same Morgan, Jax had been – in Jaden's words – fucking her.

And yet, the way it sounded now, that sort of thing was firmly in the past.

I was obnoxiously glad, even if I did feel slimy for listening in. But in my own defense, it's not like was doing it on purpose.

She *was* yelling, after all. And what was I supposed to do? Run out there and announce that I could hear them? I could only imagine.

I glanced toward the bathroom. *Should I take a shower?* That would drown out the noise, right?

That's what a decent person would do, and I always *tried* to be decent.

I was still debating this when Jax said, "You never answered my question."

"What question?"

"*Who* let you in?"

"Oh, fine," she said. "If it's soooo important, it was Jaden. I caught him on the way out."

Jax replied with something too low for me to catch. Still, I was able to get the gist of it because a moment later, Morgan said, "No kidding. The guy's a total tool."

With that same edge, Jax replied, "Yeah. But he's my brother. So lay off, alright?"

"Oh, so you can insult him, but I can't?"

"Pretty much."

"I'll never get you guys."

"You're right," he said. "You won't. So stop trying. And I meant what I said."

"About what?" she asked.

"About you and me talking." His voice hardened. "Later."

She paused. "Maybe over dinner?"

"No," he said. "At the office. Eight o'clock."

"Tonight?"

"No. Tomorrow morning."

In a tone of pure temptation, she said, "We could meet for breakfast."

"Forget it."

"I don't know why *you're* so crabby," she said. "No one called *you* a cunt."

"Hey, I've been called worse," he said. "Now, shut the door on your way out, will ya?"

A moment later, I heard a slam followed by the tip-tap of heels across a hardwood floor.

Listening, I breathed a sigh of relief. Unfortunately, the relief was short-lived. The footsteps *weren't* receding. They were growing louder.

Oh, crap.

My room was at the end of the hall, which made it impossible to believe that the footsteps would simply pass by and keep on going. Sure enough, I soon heard the rattle of a doorknob. *My* doorknob.

Sitting upright in the bed, I watched in horrified silence as the knob turned back and forth, again and again. The rattling grew louder and more ferocious, even as I heard new footsteps thundering down the hall.

They ended just outside my door. In a quiet voice, Jax demanded, "What the fuck are you doing?"

The doorknob gave a final rattle as she asked, "Why is this locked?"

"Because it is. Now, get out."

"Is someone in there?"

I was holding my breath. *Yes. There was. And the someone was me.*

Stupidly, I couldn't help but wonder what Jax was wearing. What did he sleep in, anyway? Was he standing out there, naked?

No, I decided. Because if he were, Morgan surely would've commented on it by now.

Right on cue, she said, "Nice boxers."

"Screw this," he said. "Let's go."

With a smile in her voice, she replied, "Oh yeah? Where?"

"To the office. You wanna talk? Great." He definitely wasn't smiling. "Me, too."

They went back and forth a few more times before their footsteps receded down the hall. And then, I heard absolutely nothing.

Well, that was strange.

As quietly as I could, I settled myself back under the covers and stared up at the ceiling. It was pretty, with ornate trim all around the edges.

It looked expensive, just like everything else in the room. I *so* didn't belong here. And I'd caused Jax nothing but trouble.

On top of that, it was weird to think that I was in *his* house, wearing clothes that *he* provided, and yet, I knew nearly nothing about him.

But soon, all of that changed, courtesy of who?

My mom.

CHAPTER 23

It was still early, and I was huddled with my cell phone under the covers.

My mom had just asked, "Why are you whispering?"

"Because," I said, "it's early, and I don't want to wake anyone."

This was only partly true. Mostly, I had no idea who was in the house, and I dreaded the thought of yet another ugly scene.

Already, I'd double checked the bedroom door to make sure it was still locked after all that rattling.

Was I paranoid?

Definitely.

But, as Jax had said last night, better safe than sorry. Still, this made me wonder, had he known all along that something would happen?

Either he was totally psychic or even more paranoid than I was.

On the phone, my mom asked, "So, where are you, anyway?"

I couldn't help but scoff. "Do you care?"

"Of course I care. I'm your mother."

I recalled the voicemail that she'd left for me late last night. It was one of the rudest things I'd ever heard. Sadly, it wasn't nearly as rude as the message from Tabitha, who'd called me every name in the book, including the c-word.

Funny, I hadn't realized the word was so popular.

Last night, I hadn't called either one of them back. But this morning, my mom had called *me*, and I'd felt compelled to answer – not out of family loyalty, but rather because a bunch of my stuff was still at her place, and I wasn't ready to give it up.

I told her, "I'm staying with a friend."

"Oh, please," she said. "You don't have any friends."

"Gee, thanks."

"I meant *here*, in town. You don't know anyone."

I did *now*. And he was by far the most intriguing person I'd ever met. I replied, "I know *some* people."

"You're with *him*, aren't you?"

She didn't say who she meant, but it wasn't hard to guess. Looking to change the subject, I said, "Is there a reason you called?"

"Well, you *are* my daughter. Can't I call just to say, 'hi'?"

She never called without a reason. In fact, she seldom called at all, not unless she could benefit in some way.

I said, "Alright, what do you want?"

"Who says I want anything?"

"So, you don't?"

"No. I don't. In fact, I'm calling to give *you* something."

The idea was laughable. "Oh, yeah? What?"

"Some advice."

I stifled a groan. Over the years, my mom had given me plenty of advice. If I'd followed even half of it, I wouldn't be in a stranger's guest room. I'd be in some women's prison, stamping out license plates – assuming that was really a thing.

Bracing myself, I said, "Okaaaaay. What's the advice?"

"Don't leave."

This was so unexpected, I almost didn't know what to say. "What do you mean?" I asked. "You want me to keep living with you?"

"With *me*?" She laughed. "Sorry. That's not gonna happen."

I muttered, "Well that's nice."

"Oh, don't be insulted," she said. "We both know it wasn't working out."

She was right. It wasn't, especially last night when she tried to hook me up with her meal ticket. Still, her breezy dismissal hurt to hear.

How pathetic was that?

Now, I couldn't help but sigh. "I've just gotta ask, why'd you beg me to come down here in the first place?"

"I wasn't begging."

"You were, too," I said. "You were crying and everything."

Now, it was *her* turn to sigh. "It was just one of those days. You know how it goes."

I wanted to kick myself. Like a dumb-ass, I'd moved ten hours south just because my mom was having "one of those days".

From experience, I knew exactly what kind of day she meant. "Let me guess. Dominic was gonna kick you out."

"What? No." She paused. "Well, we might've had a little fight, but we worked it out. So see. You're worried for nothing."

I wasn't worried. I was tired of her games. As far as my stuff, I decided to think about *that* later. After all, it's not like I knew where I'd be moving it. I said, "I've gotta go."

"Wait," she said. "You haven't heard my advice."

"Fine," I snapped. "What is it?"

"When I told you not to leave, I meant don't leave *his* place."

I blinked. "Sorry, what?"

"You're with Jax Bishop, right?"

For a whole host of reasons, I didn't want to answer. In a carefully neutral tone, I said, "What makes you say that?"

"Because I saw the way he was looking at you."

At this, my heart gave an embarrassing little flutter. "He was?"

"Oh sure," she said. "But it won't last, you know."

Well, that took care of that ol' fluttering problem. "Good to know."

"Oh, stop being a snot," she said. "You know what I mean."

Sadly, I did. My mom had a long history of transient relationships. As far as I could tell, it was usually the guys who ended it – well, unless she was trading up, that is.

She was still talking. "So like I said, whatever you do, don't go anywhere."

"What does that even mean?"

"Oh, you know," she said. "Make yourself at home, like you live there. And then, if he asks you to leave, act all surprised and kind of insulted." Her voice picked up steam. "And don't be afraid to cry. That's your ace in the hole, you know."

With my free hand, I reached up to rub my forehead. And *this* was why I never took her advice.

She wasn't even done. "And if he tells you to leave anyway, don't do it – at least, not without first getting a check."

My head was pounding now. "A check?"

"Oh yeah," she said. "And make sure it's a cashier's check, not a regular check."

Against my better judgment, I asked, "Why?"

"Because with a *cashier's* check, it's a lot harder for them to stop payment." She made a sound of disgust. "I won't be making *that* mistake again."

I rolled my eyes. "Good to know."

Now, *she* sounded insulted. "You're not even taking this seriously."

"You're right," I told her. "I'm not."

"See?" she said. "This is why you won't get anywhere. You never think big."

My mom had been "thinking big" for as long as I could remember. But me? I wasn't like that. Oh sure, I liked nice things as much as the next person, but I wasn't willing to sell my soul – or anything else – to get them.

And now, my mom was on a roll. "I mean, he's got loads of money, so he might as well spend it on you, right?"

Already, I'd heard more than enough. "Just stop, okay?"

"No," she said. "I won't stop. You're my daughter, and I'm trying to look out for you."

If so, that would be a first. More likely, she was looking out for herself. I said, "Sure you are."

"I am," she insisted. "I mean, if I can't have him, you might as well give it a shot, right?"

"Wrong."

It wasn't just wrong. It was so *very* wrong.

She continued as if I hadn't spoken. "And you're *so* lucky he's hot. A guy like that? If I had the money, I'd pay *him*." She gave a husky laugh. "I bet he fucks like a rock star."

Good Lord.

What on Earth could I say to that?

When it came to fucking rock stars, my mom was an expert, which sadly, was the only reason I'd been born.

But that was a topic for another day. Right now, I was dealing with a different kind of trauma.

It was the mental image of Jax and my mom. Inexplicably, he was holding an electric guitar. *Damn it.* I squeezed my eyes shut and made a mental order for a bucket of eye bleach, industrial strength.

She said, "Are you listening?"

"No."

"Why not?"

"Because I don't want to hear it."

I didn't want to *see* it either. And yet, she went on painting the picture, making sly innuendos about the size of his feet and the fullness of his lips.

I was debating simply hanging up when she abruptly switched gears. "And you know how he made his money, don't you?"

I paused. "No." But suddenly, I *was* curious. "Do you?"

"Sure," she said. "I knew last night. I recognized him right away, you know."

Now *that* surprised me. "Really?"

"Oh yeah," she said. "And I mean right there on the street. You really didn't know who he was?"

"Why would I?" I asked. "I'm not even from around here."

"God, you're so provincial," she said. "He's national, worldwide even. It shouldn't matter *where* you live. He's major bigtime."

I made a sound of impatience. "So, who is he?"

"Well, you know he has that brother, right?"

"Right."

"I wouldn't mind taking *him* for a spin."

Oh, God. Just shut up. But I didn't say it, because for once, I was dying to hear what she'd tell me. Correction – I was dying to hear what she'd tell me *after* she verbally molested Jax's brother.

Finally, when I felt like I couldn't stand it another minute, she announced, "They're the Bishop Brothers."

"Huh?" This, I already knew. I tried to think. His last name was Bishop. He had a brother whose last name was probably Bishop, too. So of course, they were the Bishop Brothers. What was I missing?

"Oh, come on," she said. "You work in a sports bar. This isn't ringing a bell?"

I didn't bother pointing out that I didn't work there anymore – thanks to *her*, no less. Instead, I tried to think. *What would the bar have to do with it?*

And then, it hit me. "Wait a minute. You're not talking about that brand of beer, are you?"

"That's exactly what I'm talking about."

I felt my eyebrows furrow. "Oh."

"Oh?" she repeated. "Is that all you have to say?"

It was all I *could* say, because for once, my mom was right. He *was* bigtime, even bigger than I might've guessed – and that was saying something.

CHAPTER 24

Over the next ten minutes, I listened as my mom gave me a full rundown on Jax and his brother. I had to admit, their story was pretty incredible, assuming all of it was true.

A few years earlier – at least according to my mom – they'd picked up a regional brewing company that had seen better days. Within a year, they'd completely rebranded it, fine-tuned the operation, and then kept on expanding until they'd gotten a foothold in nearly every market across the globe.

And they hadn't stopped with beer. By now, they owned a whole slew of brands including several that I'd that served personally. In fact, when my mom rattled off a few of their top names, I'd been completely blown away.

And yet, I still couldn't quite believe it.

I was twenty-two years old. Jax was definitely older, but not *that* much older. If I had to guess, I'd put his age at thirty, give or take a couple of years. And his brother might be even younger.

For guys so relatively young, their level of success was hard to fathom.

My mom finished by saying, "So anyway, he's worth at least a billion."

I almost swallowed my tongue. "A billion? With a 'b'?"

"Oh yeah," she said. "So when you get that check, make sure it's a nice big one."

Good grief. "I already told you, I'm not getting a check."

"Well, don't count on getting cash," she warned, "because he might not have that much on-hand. That's *another* mistake I won't be making twice."

If this weren't so sad, I might've laughed.

Seriously, who even thought that way?
She did.
That's who.
Did I need to repeat it? *I wasn't my mom.*
And, I didn't plan on becoming her any time soon.

When our call ended, I remained under the covers for a long silent moment, trying to process everything she'd just told me.

In search of more reliable information, I pulled up the browser on my phone and did a quick Web search. For once, all of the details checked out.

One of the news articles actually had a photo of the mansion, *his* mansion, where I was currently staying. More accurately, it was *their* mansion, because the two brothers apparently owned it together.

Jax and Jaden.
The Bishop Brothers.
Who knew?
Not me, that's for sure.

But now that I *had* the information, what was I supposed to do with it? The answer came almost immediately.

Nothing.

As impressed as I was, it didn't change anything. Probably, it just put him that much further out of my league.

But who was I kidding? I'd never been in his league in the first place. I was a college drop-out with no clear plans for the future. In contrast, he was beyond rich and apparently famous, too.

I felt a wistful smile tug at my lips. At least I'd gotten to dance with him. That was pretty amazing, right?

I stayed in the room for several more hours, not because I was taking my mom's advice, but rather because from somewhere downstairs, I could hear the sounds of voices and vacuuming, and I didn't want to get in anyone's way.

Plus, it seemed rude to wander around by myself.

But I couldn't hide away forever, so just before noon, I ventured out of the guest room, only to stop dead in my tracks.

Jax was there, waiting.

For me?

It sure looked that way.

CHAPTER 25

Before I could catch myself, I'd already asked, "What are you doing?"

He was dressed in jeans and a black T-shirt. If my bluntness startled him, he didn't show it. "Thinking," he said.

I felt my eyebrows furrow. He was sitting in a sturdy wooden chair with his long legs stretched out in front of him.

I tried to recall. *Had the chair been there last night?*

I didn't think so.

In fact, I was almost sure of it.

Weird.

I gave a nervous laugh. "Thinking, huh? About what?"

"Right now? Breakfast."

Probably, he shouldn't've said that. I hadn't eaten since yesterday's lunch. Oh, sure, there'd been plenty of finger foods at last night's party, but I'd been far too unsettled to eat a single thing.

And now, I was utterly famished.

He stood. "In case you're wondering, that's an invitation."

Funny, it didn't sound like an invitation. It sounded more like a summons.

I glanced down at my clothes, or rather *somebody's* clothes. Who they belonged to, I still didn't know.

After splurging on a long shower, I'd dressed in the black yoga pants and a pale pink T-shirt, along with fresh underwear – just because it seemed grubby not to.

Still, I couldn't help but tally up the cost. I'd deliberately picked out the cheapest stuff, but it wasn't cheap to *me*, and I couldn't help but wonder if I owed some unseen person more than I could afford.

He looked to my feet. "You need shoes? We'll grab some on the way out."

Out? So he was inviting me *out* to breakfast?

I looked down. I was wearing somebody's socks, but no shoes at all. All I had were the silver pumps, which would've look utterly ridiculous with what I was now wearing.

Still, I hesitated. "Won't someone be mad? I mean, I've borrowed a lot already."

"Trust me, it's not a problem. You like pancakes?"

I *loved* pancakes. In fact, I was pretty sure I'd kill for a pancake right about now. And today was Sunday, my favorite day for a big breakfast.

Still, I *was* curious. I glanced toward the chair. "How long were you waiting?"

"Not long."

I considered the time. It had been hours since his argument with Morgan. Surely, he hadn't been sitting there the whole time?

No. Definitely not. From what I'd overheard earlier, he'd hustled Morgan off to some sort of meeting, which meant that he'd been away for at least *some* portion of the morning.

He flicked his head toward the stairway. "You ready?"

I was too distracted to be ready. And why? Because he looked so darn appealing.

Last night, he'd looked amazing in his tux, but now I realized that its formal lines had been hiding a physique that was even more impressive than I'd imagined.

And I'd been imagining plenty.

Now, with him wearing a basic black T-shirt, I could see his bulging biceps and perfectly defined pecs. His stomach was flat, and even through the dark cotton of his shirt, I could see the vague outlines of the tight ab muscles underneath.

He gave the stairway another glance. "Ladies first."

I hadn't said yes to his invitation, but who was I kidding? This might be my last decent meal for a while, and I'd be stupid to refuse.

Plus, breakfast with Jax? I couldn't say no to *that* even I were stuffed, which I definitely wasn't.

And yet, an hour later, I was wondering if I'd made a huge mistake – not because the pancakes hadn't been wonderful, but rather because it became glaringly obvious that he'd invited me out for a reason.

And what *was* that reason?

To grill me like a slab of bacon.

CHAPTER 26

The waitress had just cleared away our dirty dishes when he said, "So, what was your plan?"

I wasn't following. "What do you mean?"

"Last night," he said, "were you waiting for someone?"

My cheeks grew warm as I considered where he'd found me – stranded outside like some sort of vagrant. I glanced away. "Well, I did call my roommate."

"Yeah? And where was she?"

I really didn't want to say, so I gave a half-hearted shrug. "I had some trouble reaching her, that's all."

"But why didn't you wait inside?"

Hadn't we been through this already? "Because, the party was over."

"And...?"

"And nothing." I made a sound of frustration. "Actually, I'm not sure what you're getting at. I didn't know it was your house, okay? And I didn't want to intrude."

"On who?"

"Whoever."

His gaze locked on mine. "Were you *asked* to leave?"

I bit my lip, but made no reply.

His mouth tightened. "So you were."

Funny, he hadn't phrased it as a question. Speaking very clearly now, he said, "*Who* asked you to leave?"

I stifled a shiver. His voice, normally so rich and warm, had grown ice-cold.

Suddenly, I didn't want to tell him. Or at least, the *nice* part of me didn't want to. The nastier part wanted to give him a blow-by-blow of the redhead's rudeness. But that really wasn't my style.

When the silence stretched out, he said, "You can tell me now or tell me later."

"What does *that* mean?" I asked.

"It means," he said, "I'm gonna find out. If not from you, then from someone." His voice grew a few degrees colder. "And then, we're gonna have a talk."

I hesitated. "Who? You and me? Or you and the person who kicked me out?"

"That depends."

"On what?"

"On who did it." Almost to himself, he added, "If it's a guy, the conversation's gonna be a short one."

Listening, I recalled the stains on his tuxedo shirt. Had *those* been the result of a "short conversation?" I was almost afraid to speculate.

But I did know one thing for certain. I didn't want any violence on my behalf. I said, "It wasn't a guy."

Slowly, he leaned back in the booth. "Right. It was Morgan."

I felt my brow wrinkle. "Actually, she never told me her name."

"It doesn't matter. I know who it is."

"You do? Then why'd you ask?"

He smiled. "Better safe than sorry."

The smile caught me off guard. A moment ago, he looked ready to murder someone. And now, he was fine?

I just had to ask, "Why are you smiling?"

"Because I got what I wanted."

"Which is...?"

"A job vacancy."

"Sorry, but..." I gave a little shake of my head. "What?"

"You want a job?"

The question surprised me. "What kind of job?"

"A personal assistant job."

For who? Him? It sure sounded that way. Probably, I should've been happy. But I saw this for what it was. It was a pity job – or worse, something to keep me from walking the streets or something.

Before I could catch myself, I'd already announced, "I'm not a hooker."

He frowned. "I never said you were."

"I know."

And I did. Just last night, I'd heard him telling his brother pretty much the same thing. But sometimes, what people thought and what they said were two very different things.

Obviously, he thought *something* was going on, or he wouldn't be making such an offer.

His voice, deadly serious, interrupted my thoughts. "In case it wasn't clear, that's not part of the job description."

"Sorry, what?"

His jaw tightened. "I'm not hiring you for a good time."

Now, I couldn't help but cringe. Apparently, my statement had come out all wrong. *But how to explain?* Everything was so complicated, and my thoughts were a jumbled mess.

His gaze bored to mine. "And, as long as we're tossing our cards on the table, I don't pay for it."

It.

Meaning sex of course.

No doubt, he *didn't* pay for it. A guy like that? I recalled what my mom had said just this morning. She'd be willing to pay *him*. And she never paid for anything.

But there was no way on Earth I'd be sharing that little nugget.

Looking to make a point, I repeated something he'd said to me. "I never said you did."

When his only response was a long silent look, I felt compelled to explain. "I mean, look at you. I bet you've got girls lined up. Probably they'd pay *you,* I mean, like if you actually needed the money."

Damn it. I hadn't meant to say any of that. Going for a recovery, I added, "Not that I think you're some kind of gigolo."

The corners of his mouth lifted. "Good to know."

I sighed. "Look, I know I'm making an idiot of myself. It's just that your offer caught me off guard. I mean, you don't even know my last name, much less my qualifications. So, I've gotta ask, why would you want to hire me?"

"I've got my reasons."

"Yeah, and that's exactly what I'm worried about. I don't want a job out of pity." I hesitated. "Or because you think I'll do something worse if I don't get an 'honest' job."

Let's get one thing straight," he said. "Whatever you think I believe, you're wrong."

I muttered, "And I'm not homeless either."

He gave me a dubious look. "Alright."

Obviously, he didn't believe me. And in truth, I didn't quite believe myself.

I started to squirm under his penetrating gaze. Apparently, it wasn't lost on either of us that last night, I'd been only a few steps away from sleeping in the gutter.

I cleared my throat. "I was just waiting for a ride, that's all."

He looked far from convinced. "From your roommate."

"Right."

"Who lives *where*?"

"What?"

"*Where* does she live?"

I glanced away. "Um, Nashville, actually."

"Right."

Right? Again? I gave a confused shake of my head. "What do you mean by that?"

"I mean, I know more than you think."

I was almost afraid to ask. "Like what?"

He leaned forward. "I know you've been living in Nashville. I know you used to work in Bestie's Pub. I know you were employee of the month five times and that your boss cried when you quit."

My jaw almost hit the table. "How do you know all that?"

"I've got my sources."

"Yeah. I just bet." I straightened in the booth. "But maybe they're not as good as you think."

"How so?"

Actually, his recitation had been pretty spot-on. Grasping at straws, I said, "Well, like my boss, she didn't *really* cry. There might've been a sniffle or two but…" And then, way too late, my thoughts caught up with my emotions. "Wait a minute. You pried into my business?"

"No," he said, "I checked your references. Big difference."

"Not to me."

He shrugged. "Hey, it was all public."

"It was not," I insisted. "It was private."

"You want some advice?"

"No."

He continued as if I hadn't spoken. "If you want something private, keep it off the internet."

I stared at him from the other side of the booth. "That's a sorry defense, and you know it."

"I'm not defending anything," he said. "If you ask me, you should be more careful."

"Except I *didn't* ask you, did I?"

"Yeah, well you should've."

My gaze narrowed. "You went through my wallet, didn't you?"

He *had* to. I mean, how else would he know my last name? Or where I'd been living?

He didn't deny it, and by now, I was almost quivering with righteous indignation. "Is *that* why you agreed to hold it last night? Because you wanted to snoop?"

"No," he said in a tone of infinite patience. "I went through it because you were missing, and I wanted a place to start."

"To start what?"

"Looking." His gaze didn't waver. "For you."

I wasn't sure I believed him. "What else did you do? Go through my phone?"

"No."

Just as I breathed a sigh of relief, he added, "You've got a password, remember?"

"What?" I sputtered. "So you actually tried it?"

"Hell yeah," he said. "And I'd do it again."

I was glaring now. "Oh, really?"

"Yeah. Really. The way you disappeared? Without your stuff? What, you think I wouldn't?"

"But—"

He held up a finger. "Hold that thought."

I didn't want to hold anything. But like the sap I was, I waited while he reached into his pocket and pulled out his phone. He looked at the screen and frowned. After a long moment, he looked up and said, "We'll talk more later."

"Why later?"

He set his phone on the table and picked up the check. "Because we're leaving." He pulled out his wallet and peeled off several bills while I stared in growing disbelief.

Okay, I realized that he'd just treated me to breakfast and yes, he'd done me a ton of other favors, too. But it seemed pretty darn cruel of him to drop that bombshell – hell, *multiple* bombshells – and then leave when the questioning got tough.

And besides, there was something else I wanted to know. "Morgan – that's the redhead, right? The one who claimed to be your girlfriend?"

It *had* to be her. This morning, the voice had sounded eerily familiar.

Jax nodded. "Yeah. That's her."

I didn't like her. And yet, as the pieces fell into place, I realized something awful. The way it sounded, she was about to be fired because of me.

She and Jax had a history. She wasn't over him. That much was obvious. No wonder she was a little crazy. Hell, I'd be crazy, too.

Jax said, "Is something wrong?"

"That job you mentioned, does she have it now?"

"Yeah. But not for long."

I rubbed at my wrist under the table. "She's not getting fired because of me, is she?"

"No. She's getting fired because of herself. And if you decide to feel guilty, I've got something for you to remember."

"What?"

"Last night, *she's* the one who didn't give you the message."

I sat back in the booth. "Wait, you left the message with *her?*"

When Jax nodded, I felt my teeth grinding together. To think, while I'd been standing there, begging Allie for a ride, Morgan – who'd listened to the whole conversation – had *known* that Jax was coming back *and* that he didn't want me to leave.

Talk about cold.

I was just about to ask for more details when his phone vibrated on the table. He picked it up and took a look. After the briefest glance at me, he gave a half-scoff, half-laugh and then shoved the phone into his pocket.

I asked, "What's so funny?"

"Jaden – he's having it out with someone at the house."

"Really?" In truth, I wasn't *that* surprised. The guy really *was* a tool.

"Oh, yeah." Jax gave a low laugh. "And the way it sounds, he's getting his ass handed to him."

I didn't get it. "And why is that funny?"

"Because," he said, "it's your friend doing it."

CHAPTER 27

When we pulled into the driveway, I could hear the yelling as soon as I opened the car door.

I had to give Jax some credit. The drive *to* the restaurant had taken us twenty minutes. But the drive back? Thanks to some creative maneuvering on his part, it had taken only ten.

Ten terrifying minutes.

But I couldn't complain. It was, after all, at my urging.

I slammed the car door and practically sprinted up the front steps. I had no key, but that didn't even matter. The front door was wide open, which explained why they'd been so easy to hear.

Somewhere in the house, Allie was yelling, "Where the fuck is she?"

Jaden replied, "I already told you. Out."

"Liar!" she yelled. "What have you done with her?"

"Me?" Jaden said. "Shit, I haven't done anything. But my brother? Eh, I can't promise you anything there."

Standing just inside the front door, I glanced wildly around. I could hear them, but I couldn't see them. Where *were* they? *Upstairs?* In a house so big, it was hard to tell.

Allie was saying, "I'm not afraid of you, you know."

"Yeah? I wish I could say the same."

As they bickered back and forth, I heard the sounds of doors slamming one after another. I listened more closely. *Yup, they were definitely upstairs.* I made for the stairway and took the stairs two at a time.

Somewhere down the hall, Jaden was saying, "If you think she can fit in that dresser, you're nuts." He paused. "Well, unless we chopped her up or something."

"I swear to God," Allie said, "if you did *anything* to her, I will kill you. Slowly."

"Hell, you're killing me now."

I found them in the second bedroom on the right. Allie was in the closet, shoving aside bunches of clothes that were hanging inside.

From the open doorway, I stopped to stare. What on Earth was she doing? Looking for a secret passageway or something?

Searching for some clue, I looked to Jaden. He was wearing jeans, but no shirt, and his torso was covered in tattoos. I hadn't seen a hint of them last night, but then again, he *had* been wearing a tux.

Now, he was leaning against the nearest wall, eyeing Allie with open contempt. "Hey Velma," he told her, "you wanna check the bookcases, too?"

Velma?

Allie didn't even pause. "You don't *have* any bookcases, dumb-ass. I checked for those first."

At this, Jaden looked nearly insulted. "That's not true," he told her. "We've got a whole library downstairs." He gave her a smug smile. "So who's the dumb-ass now?"

The smile was a total waste. Allie didn't even look. She was still focused on the clothes. She shoved aside a row of hangers and muttered something about shoving a Scooby Snack up his ass.

A Scooby Snack?

Oh. Of course.

Obviously, they'd been referencing that classic cartoon. Probably, I should've figured that out at "Velma." I heard myself mutter, "Ruh-roh."

Jaden's head swiveled in my direction. Unsure what else to do, I gave him a little wave. He didn't wave back. No surprise there. Instead, he looked to Allie and said, "Found her."

"Oh shut up," Allie said. "I'm not falling for that again."

Jaden shrugged. "Suit yourself. If you want me, I'll be in the library." And with that, he sauntered out, walking past me without so much as a hello, not that I could blame him, all things considered.

From inside the closet, Allie yelled, "As if you can read!" Under her breath, she added, "Idiot."

I wanted to say something soothing, but words utterly failed me. The room was a total mess, with drawers pulled out and clothes falling off the hangers. Plus, at this point, what *could* I say?

Even for Allie, this was a bit much. But I knew who was to blame. It wasn't Jaden. And it wasn't Jax.

It was me.

Damn it.

Trying not to startle her, I tiptoed toward the closet until I was standing just outside its door. In the most soothing voice I could muster, I said, "Allie?"

With a little yelp, she whirled around. Her eyes widened at the sight of me. But then, a split second later, they narrowed to slits as she demanded, "Where were you?"

I bit my lip. "Um, out?"

From somewhere down the hall, Jaden yelled, "Told ya!"

Allie turned toward the sound and hollered back, "Oh, fuck off!" She looked back to me and said, "You weren't here."

"I know. I was getting..." I cleared my throat. "...uh, pancakes, actually."

She was staring now. "Pancakes? Are you freaking kidding me?"

It wasn't *just* pancakes. It was bacon, too. But I'd be stupid to mention it. And besides, I felt so awful, I could hardly speak at all.

Allie's long blond hair was tied in a messy ponytail, and there were dark circles under her eyes. She was on the petite side, but today, she looked even smaller than usual in clothes that appeared to be a few sizes too big.

Confused, I looked down at her shorts. They were long, black and loose, the kind that tied with a drawstring at the waist – not that I could see the drawstring now, since she was wearing an oversized grey sweatshirt that fell well past her hips.

Were those clothes even her own?

I didn't think so.

And why was she wearing a sweatshirt? It was a sunny afternoon, in Florida no less. Unlike last night, the temperature right now was definitely on the balmy side.

I didn't know what exactly was going on, but I did know who was to blame. I looked up to meet her gaze. "Gosh, Allie. I'm *so* sorry."

Her voice was barely a whisper. "You're okay?"

"Uh, yeah," I stammered. "I called. Didn't you get my message?"

"Of course I did." She made a sound of frustration. "Why do you think I'm here?"

I cringed. "Actually, I meant the *second* message, the one telling you that I was alright."

She gave a confused shake of her head. "What?"

"Yeah. In fact, I left *two* second messages – one at the apartment, and then another on your cellphone. You didn't get either one of them?"

She made a scoffing sound. "Do I *look* like I did?"

No. In truth, she looked like hell. Oh sure, she was still as cute as a button, but now, the button looked like it had gone through the wash cycle a million times too many.

I asked, "But how did you get here?"

"How do you think?" she said. "I drove."

"But I thought your car was in the shop."

"Yeah. It is." She looked away and mumbled something that I couldn't quite make out.

I shook my head. "Sorry, could you repeat that?"

She looked back to me and sighed. "I borrowed a pickup. You didn't see it when you came in?"

I didn't recall seeing a pickup. "In the driveway?"

"No. On the street."

"Honestly," I said, "I was pretty focused on the house."

She gave me a look. "Yeah. Me, too."

A noise near the bedroom door made me turn to look. It was Jax, standing in the open doorway. He was eying us with an expression that I couldn't quite decipher.

I tried to smile. "Oh, hi."

His voice was flat. "Hi."

I glanced around. The room was totally trashed, with open drawers and clothes scattered across the floor. I didn't even know whose room this was, but I was pretty sure that it wasn't the private domain of either brother.

After all, the clothes in the closet, not to mention the things littered across the carpet, included plenty of things that were decidedly feminine.

I zoomed in on an open drawer, overflowing lacy undergarments. Some of them still had the tags attached, which made me wonder something. Was *this* where Jax had gotten the clothes that I was currently wearing?

If so, whose clothes were they?

But that was a question for another time.

I gave Jax an apologetic smile. "Don't worry," I told him. "I'm gonna clean everything up. You won't even know we were here, honest."

He didn't smile back. But he didn't frown either. He replied, "I wouldn't count on it." He looked to Allie and asked, "You need anything?"

She glanced around, as if noticing the destruction for the very first time. After a long awkward pause, she replied, "No. I'm fine." Under her breath, she added, "*Now*, anyway."

But Jax looked unconvinced. "You sure about that?"

"Sure." She cleared her throat. "I mean, what would I need?"

"I dunno. A shower, breakfast, clean clothes?"

Allie looked down at the ill-fitting clothes that she was currently wearing. As I watched, a slow blush crept across her cheeks.

My heart went out to her. If anyone should be embarrassed, it was me. This was all my fault, and I was determined to make it right somehow.

I asked Allie, "Are you sure? There's a private bathroom, and…" I hesitated. "I have some things you can borrow."

Technically, these things belonged to someone else, and I felt a little awkward to be offering them up when they weren't even mine. But this was Allie, and she'd come so very far for a rescue that, as it turned out, wasn't even necessary.

Allie murmured, "I, um. No. But thanks." She looked to Jax and said, "And I guess I should apologize for barging in." She winced. "And I might've been a little rude."

"Forget it," he said. "Knowing my brother, he had it coming."

From somewhere down the hall, Jaden called. "I heard that!"

Jax turned his head and called back, "You were meant to hear it, jackass, so quit your bitching."

Allie and I exchanged a look. I whispered, "They're brothers."

"I know," she replied. "He just said so."

"Oh. Right." I'd heard him with my own ears. But I was so surprised by all of this, I hardly knew what I was saying.

From the doorway, Jax told Allie, "Let me know when you change your mind."

When? Not if?

I might've asked what he meant, but already, he'd turned and disappeared to who-knows-where. I looked back to Allie and said, "Come on. Let's talk in my room, okay?"

She frowned. "*Your* room?"

"Just for last night. But it'll give us someplace to talk." I reached for her hand and gave it a gentle tug. "Now, come on."

With a sigh, she let me lead her away from the closet. As we picked our way through the mess, I tried not to cringe. I meant what I'd told Jax earlier. I'd definitely clean it up. Just not right now.

First, I had a friend to take care of, and not just because she was the closest thing I had to a sister. *I owed her, bigtime.*

She'd just driven through the night *and* borrowed a vehicle to do it. This was a lot more than I deserved, especially after we'd parted on such awful terms just a week earlier.

But when I finally got the full story out of her, I almost wanted to cry. Apparently, things were a lot worse than I realized.

CHAPTER 28

I was still staring. "You stole it?"

"No," she said. "I borrowed it, just like I told you."

I almost didn't know what to say. We were sitting in the same bedroom where I'd slept last night. Before leaving for breakfast, I'd made the bed and straightened up as best I could. Now, Allie was sitting in a small armchair facing me, as I perched on the edge of the bed wondering if she'd lost her mind.

She muttered, "Hey, I left a note."

I tried to laugh. "Well, that's good. What did it say? 'I'm taking your vintage truck to Florida'?"

As I'd just learned, the truck belonged to Allie's ex-boyfriend. They'd been together for nearly six months until their breakup just a few weeks ago. Correction – their *bad* breakup.

Unless something had changed, they weren't even on speaking terms.

For this, I was glad. The guy really *was* a douchebag. Still, he didn't deserve to have his truck stolen, especially on my behalf.

Allie still hadn't answered my question, and I had a pretty good idea why. I gave her a no-nonsense look. "He doesn't know the truck's here, does he?"

"Not *exactly*." Her chin lifted. "I mean, I didn't tell him *specifically* where I was going, just that it was an emergency." She glanced away. "And besides, he was sleeping. I didn't want to wake him."

I rolled my eyes. "How thoughtful of you."

"Oh, shut up."

"Alright, forget last night." I gave her a hopeful look. "Did you at least call him this morning?"

"Are you kidding?" she said. "He'd just tell me to bring it back."

"Well, obviously."

"And besides, my phone died in Alabama. I couldn't call him even if I wanted to."

And she *hadn't* wanted to. That much was obvious. But if nothing else, this explained why she'd never answered my second call.

Allie sighed. "But what did you expect? You sounded scared. And I *know* how your mom is. You think I'd just give up because I couldn't drive my own car?"

I felt my eyes grow misty at the thought of everything she'd done. "I knew you'd come if you could, but God, Allie, I'm so sorry. I shouldn't've asked you in the first place."

Now, I was literally wringing my hands. "It was incredibly stupid, and now, I'm worried you're gonna get in trouble."

She gave me a weak smile. "Did you just call me stupid?"

"No. I called *me* stupid. For leaving that message, the first one, I mean."

"That wasn't stupid," she said. "Now, moving down here? *That* was stupid."

I blew out a long, unsteady breath. *Well there was that.*

Her voice grew quiet. "But calling me to take you home? That was smart, like the smartest thing you've done all month."

I tried to smile. *Home.*

It was a funny word. Growing up, my mom was always moving from city to city, following this guy or that. Wherever she went, she took me with her – New York, L.A., Houston, and lastly, Nashville, where I'd met Allie.

Probably, I was lucky that my mom hadn't ditched me somewhere else along the way. After all, it's not like I had any other family to speak of.

No, the closest thing *I* had to family was the amazing person sitting across from me. I'd known Allie for four years now – ever since that fateful day I'd walked out of my mom's Nashville apartment, never to return.

Since then, I'd barely seen my mom at all, not until just recently, after she'd begged for a second chance in a whole new city – this city, in fact.

I sighed at my own stupidity. I'd made a huge mess of everything.

But I didn't want to dwell it, not now, when there was at least *something* I could do for Allie. Regardless of what she'd told Jax earlier, she'd surely love a shower and a change of clothes.

But we'd need to hurry – and not only because of the truck. I glanced at my cell phone. It was two in the afternoon, and the drive would take at least ten hours. Plus, I'd need to swing by my mom's place to pick my stuff, assuming, of course, that she'd give it up.

I added up the hours. Even if we left by three, we wouldn't reach Nashville until very early tomorrow morning.

Tomorrow was a Monday. I looked to Allie and asked, "When do you need to be back to work?"

She hesitated. "I, uh, don't."

"What?"

She sighed. "I was fired actually."

My stomach sank. "What, why?"

She waved away the question. "Long story. It's not important."

"It is, too," I insisted. "You were so excited to get that job. And you've only had it for what? A month?"

Allie was a huge country music fan, and had recently been hired as the personal assistant to some bigtime music producer. At the time, she'd been so excited that she could hardly contain herself.

And now, she was acting like it didn't matter?

I studied her face. I knew Allie. This mattered a lot more than she was letting on.

In a very soft voice, I asked, "What happened?"

She gave a loose shrug. "Nothing. The job sucked anyway."

Yes. It had.

But Allie hadn't thought so, or at the very least, she'd been determined to stick it out, in spite of the fact that her boss was, in Allie's own words, a total monster.

But Allie handled monstrous people just fine. And she'd been planning to keep the job for at least a year, if only for her resume. This was in spite of the fact that the guy had her working nearly every day – and every evening, too, including weekends.

Hell, *especially* weekends.

I felt the color drain from face. "Don't tell me...." I tried not to cringe. "You were supposed to work today?"

"You know how that guy was." She gave a weak laugh. "I was supposed to work *every* day."

Now, I wanted to cry. "Oh, Allie. I'm *so* sorry."

"Do you realize that's like the tenth time you've said that?"

"So what?" I said. "If I said it a hundred times, it still wouldn't make it right." As I spoke, I tallied up everything that this little adventure had cost her.

It was way too much, and that was assuming she *wouldn't* be arrested for grand theft auto.

Somehow, I had to make this right. And wringing my hands wouldn't solve anything.

Right now, the most important thing was getting Allie a shower and fresh clothes, so we could leave right away. I'd do the driving so she could sleep. And then, back in Nashville, I'd get her job back somehow.

My mind was already whirling. Maybe I could talk to the producer and explain? If that didn't work, I could always beg.

Allie would *never* beg. And normally, I wouldn't be so fond of the idea myself. But it was the least I could do, considering that it was me who'd gotten her fired.

But first things first. As Allie watched from the armchair, I dug through the stack of clothes that I'd borrowed from Jax. I pulled out a pair of shorts, a little yellow T-shirt, and more undergarments with the tags still attached.

I handed the items to Allie and hustled her toward the bathroom. And then, I left to give her some privacy.

Plus, I had something I had to do. While she showered, I hustled to that *other* bedroom – the one that Allie had ransacked earlier. I'd simply clean up the mess so we could be on our way.

Easy enough, right?

Not hardly.

Because when I walked in through the bedroom door, a certain someone was sitting in an armchair by the bed, waiting like he'd been expecting me all along.

It was Jax.

And from the look on his face, I had some serious explaining to do.

CHAPTER 29

I stopped to stare. He definitely didn't look happy.

I glanced around, taking in the scattered clothes and open dresser drawers. Hell, I'd be unhappy, too, if a total stranger had trashed *my* place, well, if I had a place, that is.

I tensed at a sudden realization. This might not be the only room she'd ransacked. *Oh, God.* What if there were a dozen rooms just like this, all torn apart by a pint-sized blond tornado?

I looked to Jax and said, "I'm *really* sorry—"

"Stop."

I felt myself swallow. "Stop what?"

"Stop apologizing."

"Oh come on," I said, making a useless gesture toward the destruction. "How could I not be sorry? I mean, jeez, look at this place." As I spoke, I crouched down to pick up some of the scattered clothing.

"Stop," Jax repeated. "Please."

With the clothes in-hand, I stood and gave him a perplexed look. "Stop what?"

He stood and pointed toward the stuff in my hands. "That."

"You mean stop cleaning? But why?"

"I told you, I have a service."

"Yeah, but they're already gone."

"So they'll come back."

"But won't that cost extra?"

"So I'll pay it. Not a big deal."

Okay, I was fully aware that he could afford it just fine. But I hated the thought of costing him any more money or trouble. Already, I owed him a small fortune for the undergarments alone.

Plus, unlike my mom, I was the kind of person who cleaned up my own messes. But why would Jax care, anyway? And then it hit me. "Oh, sorry. Is it because you don't want me pawing through your stuff?"

"No."

I tried to think. "Are you worried the butler will get mad?" Yes, it seemed far-fetched, but I was running out of theories.

He gave me a look. "I don't have a butler."

"But last night—"

"He was a temp. And it wasn't my idea."

"Oh." If nothing else, this explained why I hadn't seen the guy after the party. "So then why can't I clean this up?"

"Because I want to talk to you. And I want your full attention."

Well, that wasn't ominous or anything.

I looked around, wondering where I should set the clothes that I'd gathered already. Finally, I walked to the nearest dresser and placed them on top in a jumbled pile.

I'd wanted to fold them, but I didn't dare, not with Jax glowering from the sidelines.

He looked to the doorway and said, "We'll talk in my office."

Once again, this sounded more like a summons than an invitation. But this time, I had to decline. "I can't leave, not with Allie here."

Plus, I simply didn't have the time.

"I meant my home office," he clarified. "It's just downstairs."

"Oh." Still, I wasn't terribly enthused. The way it looked, he wanted to chew me out, not that I could blame him.

I sighed. *Oh well, I might as well get it over with.*

But as it turned out, I was only half-correct. Oh sure, he wanted to have a serious discussion, but it wasn't because of the mess.

It was because while I'd been huddled in the bedroom with Allie, he'd received a visitor of the gun and badge variety.

And why?
Because of the truck.
Of course.

CHAPTER 30

We were secluded in his office, with him sitting behind his desk and me sitting directly across from him in a visitor's chair. The chair was brown leather and quite comfy. Still, I was anything but relaxed.

So far, Jax had told me just enough to scare the crap out of me.

Apparently, around a half-hour earlier, the police had knocked on the front door in search of Allie. It wasn't even because someone had spotted the truck – although the fact that it was parked out front certainly hadn't helped.

Rather, the police had shown up because Allie's ex-boyfriend had known exactly where to look.

Apparently, she'd written the address to Jax's place on a little message pad she kept next to the apartment's phone. And although she'd ripped out the sheet containing her actual handwriting, the impression of the address had remained in the notebook itself.

Knowing Allie, this made a ton of sense. When she got agitated, she wrote very hard. I knew this, because I'd seen firsthand the broken pencils along with a shocking number of slightly mangled pens.

Anyway, her ex-boyfriend, who was normally as dumb as a bag of hammers, had somehow been smart enough to notice the impression in the notebook. This had happened just today, when he'd barged into the apartment looking for Allie and his beloved truck.

Now, as Jax relayed what he knew, I mentally filled in the details that I could guess on my own.

I knew Stuart. He was a notoriously late sleeper. Probably, he hadn't even realized that his truck was missing until well after noon, which no doubt explained why the police hadn't shown up earlier.

Still, the whole thing was a giant mess, and I'd be willing to bet my last ten dollars that it was far from over. With my heart racing, I turned in my seat to look in the general direction of the front door. From here, I couldn't see it, but I could imagine plenty.

Were the police outside right now, waiting for Allie to make an appearance? Or – *oh, God* – what if they were *inside* the house? What if Jax had pulled me into this secluded room so they could drag away my friend with minimal drama?

Screw that. I jumped to my feet and gave Jax a desperate look. "Where are they?"

He leaned back in his chair. "Who? The police?" He gave a loose shrug that told me exactly nothing.

Well, that was helpful.

I said, "I've gotta warn her."

"No. You don't."

"But—"

"Trust me, she's fine." Almost as an afterthought, he added, "For now."

I made a sound of frustration. "What does *that* mean?"

He motioned to my chair. "If you sit, I'll tell you."

But I didn't sit. I couldn't. I was too busy listening, not that it did any good. There was nothing to hear. No yelling. No dragging. No commotion at all.

That was a *good* sign, right?

Jax said, "Cassidy."

Absently, I mumbled, "What?"

"No one's hauling your friend away, if that's what you're worried about."

I *was* worried and with good reason. I turned my attention back to Jax. "But you don't know Stuart – I mean the guy who owns the truck. He's *such* a jackass."

"I know."

I froze. "Wait, how would you know?"

Again, he motioned to the chair. "Because I know more than you think. Now come on. It's handled. So don't worry about it."

Handled? How?

I studied his face. He didn't look like he was lying, but how could I be sure? I'd known the guy for less than twenty-four hours.

And yet, during that timeframe, he'd been rescuing me non-stop. Already, he'd done a lot more to look out for me than my mom ever had.

If I didn't trust *him*, who *could* I trust?

Not my mom – and not Stuart, that's for sure.

I heard myself say, "You know what's funny? I *never* trusted him, just like Allie never trusted my mom. It's strange to think…" Remembering myself, I let my words fade to silence.

After all, Jax surely had better things to do than listen to me analyze my own glorious mistakes.

But already, he was saying, "It's strange to think what?"

I waved away the question. "Never mind."

"No." His gaze locked on mine. "Tell me."

His eyes were dark and probing, with the barest hint of danger. And yet, I wasn't afraid. I was stupidly hypnotized by the sight of him, the sound of him, and even the feel of him.

It was true that we weren't touching *now*, but I'd known what it was like to be held in his arms, to have him pull me close, to feel his breath in my ear and have his hand on my back.

In spite of everything, I couldn't help but wonder, what would it be like to be even closer? Not dancing, but…

With a start, I shook off the distraction. *Damn it. Focus, Cassidy.*

He'd asked me a question. *It's strange to think what?*

I replied, "It's just funny that both of us were right."

"Meaning you and Allie."

"Yeah. I mean, I never liked Stuart, and *she* never liked my mom."

I tried to smile. "You should've seen her when I announced that I was moving. I swear, I thought she was gonna clobber me." I gave a nervous laugh. "Or maybe tie me to a chair or something, anything to keep me from going."

Was I rambling? I felt like I was rambling. I clamped my lips shut and tried to ignore the warmth creeping up my cheeks.

It wasn't only because I was sharing far more than I normally would with a stranger. It was because on that day, Allie and I had caused such a ruckus that the neighbors had come in to gawk.

It was our first and only big argument, but it had been a doozie.

Jax said, "But you came anyway."

"Well, yeah," I said. "My mom was so nice – I mean on the phone – and I hadn't seen her in forever. Plus, Allie's cousin needed a place to stay, so I figured I'd just, you know, get out of the way and let them have some time to catch up."

I couldn't help but sigh. "And, well, I figured I could catch up with my mom."

Jax gave me a long, penetrating look. "Yeah? And how'd that work out?"

My spine grew twitchy at the memory of how Jax and I had met. I gave a self-deprecating eye-roll. "I think you know the answer to that."

"Yeah. I do." His tone grew a shade darker. "And you're not going back. You know that, right?"

"What do you mean? Back with my mom? " I stiffened. "I wasn't planning on it."

"Good to know," he said. "And if anyone gives you grief, let me know. I'll handle it."

"Grief from who? My mom?" I forced a laugh. "Thanks, but I can handle her just fine."

He gave me another look. He didn't need to say what he was thinking, because it was written all over his face. He didn't believe me one bit.

I gave him a look right back. "I can," I insisted. "And besides, why would you want to get involved?"

He smiled. "Why not?"

In spite of his smile, I felt just a little bit uneasy. It's not that his smile was evil exactly, but there was something there, a ruthlessness that he wasn't bothering to hide.

Or maybe that was just my imagination.

I cleared my throat. "Back to Allie...you *would* tell me if they were in the house, right?"

"The police?" He gave a low laugh. "Trust me, they're not coming in the house."

It was the second time he'd told me to trust him. I *wanted* to trust him. But we were talking about Allie's safety, not my own, and I didn't want to take any chances.

Already, this trip had cost her far too much.

I lifted my gaze to the ceiling. Somewhere above, Allie was blissfully ignorant of her impending doom.

Even if the police didn't come *in*, she'd have to go *out* eventually, right?

Jax's voice interrupted my thoughts. "If you want, I'll have Jaden guard the door."

I was still looking upward. "What door? The bedroom door?"

A hint of humor crept into his voice. "If that's what you want."

I pulled my gaze from the ceiling and gave Jax a long, perplexed look. *Was he kidding?* I couldn't tell. His eyes were serious, but his mouth had a slight upturn at the corners, as if he might laugh at any moment.

I was pretty sure I knew why. Even *I* wanted to laugh at the idea of Jaden guarding the bedroom door – as if Allie would let him

"No thanks," I said. "I mean, I'm pretty sure they'd kill each other."

"Nah. Allie might do *him* in, but..." With a shrug, he let the sentence trail off before glancing at his visitor's chair. "So, are you gonna be sitting any time soon?"

I didn't feel like sitting. I felt like dashing upstairs to warn Allie. And yet, I wouldn't be doing her any favors by delivering bad news in the middle of her shower.

For all I knew, this might be her only moment of peace before the you-know-what hit the fan.

Reluctantly, I sank back into the chair. "Well, I suppose I should hear the rest."

"Yeah," he said. "You should. But it's not about Allie. It's about you."

CHAPTER 31

I stared at him from the other side of the desk. I didn't want to talk about me. *I* wasn't the one in trouble, at least not at the moment. I said, "But what about Allie?"

He looked annoyingly unconcerned. "It's handled, just like I said."

"But for how long?" I asked. "I mean, she's not gonna get arrested when she leaves, is she?"

"That depends."

My stomach clenched. "On what?"

"If she goes for another truck."

I gave a little shake of my head. "What?"

"The thing with the *first* truck, it's handled." He paused. "No telling what'll happen if she goes for another."

Another truck?

Was that a joke? If so, it wasn't funny. "She's not gonna do it again," I told him. "She wouldn't have done it at all if I hadn't worried her for nothing."

His eyebrows lifted. "For nothing."

"Yes," I insisted. "For nothing."

He looked at me for a long silent moment, and I swear, I could tell exactly what he was thinking.

It was the same thing I was thinking. Last night, I'd been on the verge of sleeping outdoors because I had nowhere else to go. Maybe that was cause for a *little* worry.

Under his steady gaze, I shifted in my seat and mumbled something about it all working out in the end.

It was a stupid thing to say, of course, because the only reason it *had* worked out was because Jax had given me a place to stay.

Had I even thanked him? I thought so, but I couldn't be sure. "I guess I should thank you–"

"If you want to thank me," he said, "give me an answer."

I wasn't following. "About what?"

"The job."

Oh. Right. The job.

I wasn't naïve. Even when he'd first mentioned it, I'd seen that job for what it was. It was a pity job, something to keep me off the streets or wherever.

I didn't want anyone's pity. I summoned up a smile. "Look, that's really nice of you–"

"I'm not nice."

I felt my eyebrows furrow. "You are, too. I mean, look at all the favors you've done for me already."

When he made no reply, I began rattling them off. "You gave me a ride, invited me to your party, and even put me up in your guest room. If that's not nice, I don't know what is."

He gave me another long, penetrating gaze. This time, I had no idea what he was thinking. But as the silence stretched out between us, I would've given almost anything to know.

Finally, he said, "With you, it's different."

Now *that* surprised me. "It is? Why?"

"When I figure it out, I'll let you know."

As an answer, this was hardly satisfying, but I didn't want to dwell on it, not now, with that crazy job offer hanging between us. "About the job," I said, "I can't take it."

He frowned. "Why not?"

"Because I'm not qualified."

"It's not that hard," he said. "You've just got to be organized." He paused as if thinking. "And your boss? Eh, he's a bit of an ass." A ghost of a smile crossed his features. "But I think you can handle him."

I felt myself swallow. *Oh, boy.* I'd *like* to handle him in more ways than one. At the mere thought, I felt a rush of warmth flash across my cheeks and, like too many times already, settle southward to places best left unmentioned.

Damn it. I should be laughing, not lusting. After all, he'd just called himself an ass. In spite of my own jangled nerves, I was charmed by his self-deprecating humor. And – *holy hell* – he had a very nice ass, at least from what I'd seen.

Oh, for God's sake.

I gave myself a mental slap in the face. What the hell was wrong with me? It was like every thought led to his body and the things I wanted to do with it – and yeah, the things I'd like done to *me* in return.

Suddenly, I blurted out, "I can't take it."

As my statement echoed off the walls, I tried not to cringe. I wasn't even sure what I meant. That I couldn't take the job? Or that I couldn't take any more thoughts of Jax that were decidedly unprofessional.

Probably, I meant both, because let's face it, working for a guy who made your panties combust was a recipe for guaranteed disaster.

Plus, Allie and I were leaving, and that's all there was to it.

Jax replied, "You can. And you should." His gaze hardened. "And if it gets too tough, let me know. I'll rein it in."

Reining it in – that sounded like a terrific idea. I took a deep steadying breath and forced myself to say what needed saying. "Honestly, thanks. But I see this for what it is."

"Yeah? And what's that?"

"A pity job, like you're only offering it because you think I'm desperate."

In a quiet voice, he said, "And you're not?"

"No. I'm not. In fact, I'm leaving for Nashville as soon as Allie's ready. And maybe, if I'm lucky, I can get my old job back, and…" I hesitated. "…a new place to live, unless Allie and her cousin don't mind me crashing with them for a while…"

As I spoke, I considered all of the logistics. The apartment was a two-bedroom, and Allie's cousin was a little on the prickly side.

But so what? I'd dealt with difficult people before, and besides, it wouldn't take me *that* long to save up for my own place. *Would it?*

And yet, the longer my thoughts churned, the more I started to wonder. What if I *couldn't* get my old job back?

And what about Allie?

Thanks to me, she was unemployed, too. The apartment's lease was in her name. But how could she afford even a portion of the rent with no income?

And then, there was the matter of the truck. We'd been planning to drive it home. Was that still an option?

Doubtful.

For all I knew, the truck was already gone, towed away to some police impound lot or something.

And if that weren't bad enough, I just knew that Allie's decision to borrow that stupid thing would be haunting her forever.

I hadn't been lying about her ex. Stuart really *was* a jackass. And, as long as he owned that truck, he'd be lording it over Allie every chance he got. It would be pathetically easy, too. Even if he didn't press charges *now*, he could threaten them nonstop back home, just for kicks.

The more I sat thinking, the more my head pounded with new uncertainties. Everything was a total mess, and it was all my fault – first for stupidly moving down here and then for calling Allie to rescue me.

In a million years, I'd never be able to make it right – my breath caught – unless…

I sat up straighter in the chair. "This job, how much does it pay?"

As an answer, Jax reached into his top desk drawer and pulled out a typewritten sheet of paper. He slid it toward me, face down across the desktop.

I snatched it up and felt my eyes widen. The answer to my question was shockingly clear, right there in nice big digits. *The job paid very well.*

With growing excitement, I scanned the description. From listening to Allie talk in Nashville, I was familiar with the duties she'd performed for that music producer. Compared to *that* job, this one would be a cakewalk.

I leaned forward. "What are the hours? Like, is this a Monday-to-Friday thing? Or is it weekends, too?"

"That depends," Jax said. "Yeah, there's a few weekends, and maybe some travel, but when that happens, you get time off during the week."

Time off. Allie hadn't had *that* in forever. I felt myself smile. "What about benefits?"

He pointed to the sheet. "You saw 'em."

Had I? I'd been so focused on the description and the salary that I hadn't noticed much else. Again, I looked to the sheet. "Full medical? And vacation time, too?"

Holy hell. This was Allie's dream job. And she'd be terrific at it. I was absolutely certain.

I looked to Jax. "Did you mean it when you said this wasn't a pity job?" Before he could even think to respond, I added, "I mean, it's a real job, and you want a real candidate." I swallowed. "Someone really good. Right?"

He looked at me for a long, silent moment before saying in a carefully neutral tone, "If I didn't, there'd be no offer."

I hesitated. "What's wrong?"

He frowned. "I know what you're gonna say. And I don't wanna hear it."

I shook my head. "But you can't know."

"Yeah? Try me."

I gave a nervous laugh. "Shouldn't *you* be telling *me* if you're the one who's reading my mind?"

"Fair enough." Looking decidedly unenthused, he said, "You want me to hire your friend."

I sat back. "Oh." *Go figure.* Apparently, he *was* a mind-reader.

And now, I had to convince him.

CHAPTER 32

Before he could stop me, I launched into an impromptu sales pitch. "Okay, you're right. I do, but only because Allie's a perfect fit. And she's *really* terrific."

Across from me, Jax looked anything but convinced. "Uh-huh."

"And she doesn't *always* steal trucks." I paused. "I mean, borrow trucks."

"Uh-huh."

I bit my lip. That was the second "uh-huh" in a row. I wasn't a master negotiator, but even *I* realized that this wasn't a terrific sign.

I had to remind myself that of course he'd need a *little* convincing. He'd known Allie for how long now? An hour?

This might've been fine, except for the fact that during that hour, she'd cussed up a storm, trashed at least one bedroom, and led the police straight to his front door for grand theft, well, truck, I guess.

"Look," I said, "I know you probably don't believe me – and I can totally see why – but she really is wonderful. She's smart and capable, and really super loyal." My voice picked up steam. "And she's experienced, too."

On the other side of the desk, Jax's only response was a long, steady look.

Was that better than another "uh-huh"?

I wasn't sure.

So I kept on going. "And she's always wanted to live near the beach. Plus, she's an Army brat, meaning her dad was in the military, and they moved all the time, so it's not like Nashville is her hometown or anything. Her parents, they live in Alaska now, and Allie hates the cold, so she could live anywhere, like Florida, it's the perfect place."

I gave him my most encouraging smile. "If you'd just give her a chance, you wouldn't be sorry. I promise."

From the look on his face, he was already sorry.

Okay, I knew I was being obnoxious. And yes, I was asking way more than I should. Already, Jax had done me a ton of favors, and here I was, asking for another.

But if he just picked Allie for the job, he'd see that I was doing *him* a favor, too, even if he didn't yet realize it.

He sat in grim silence while I extolled the virtues of her work ethic, her creativity, and her terrific people skills.

This got me a raised eyebrow.

I cleared my throat. "Okay, so she gets a little riled up sometimes, but she only did that today because she was worried. Normally, she's really super nice." I gave Jax a pleading look. "I mean, who else but someone really wonderful would steal a truck to rescue a friend?"

At this, he looked *almost* ready to smile. "Steal, huh?"

I waved away the distinction. "Oh, you know what I mean. And she *was* only borrowing it, honest."

"Uh-huh."

Damn it. That was number-three…*not* a good sign.

But I refused to be deterred. "Oh sure, there might've been a little confusion with the ex, but in Allie's defense, he used to borrow *her* vehicle all the time, and without her permission, too."

I wasn't lying. It was one of the things they used to fight about. Before the vintage pickup, Stuart had owned a motorcycle instead. Almost every single time it rained, Allie's car would turn up missing just when she needed it most.

For someone who rode a motorcycle, the guy was strangely allergic to a few raindrops, almost like he'd melt or something.

What a wuss.

I tried for another smile. "But forget that. She really is the perfect candidate." When Jax still made no reply, I continued with my sales pitch.

I kept on talking until he held up a hand, saying "Stop. Please."

I didn't want to stop, but I did anyway. Probably, that was for the best. There was, after all, such a thing as over-selling, and already, I was repeating myself.

I leaned forward, dying to hear what he'd say. I said a silent prayer. *Say yes. Say yes, say yes.*

His response – a single word – landed with a thud. "No."

CHAPTER 33

No? Just like that?

With no discussion? No reasons? No nothing?

The hope that had kindled in my heart died a slow, sputtering death. I looked to Jax. "But why not?"

He pointed to the document that I was still holding. "You see that paper?"

"Yeah. Of course."

"It's got *your* name on it, not hers."

"So?"

"So, it's non-transferrable."

"But why?" I asked. "She's a lot better candidate."

"Maybe. Maybe not. But the offer's for you. Not her."

Feeling utterly deflated, I slumped in the chair. "So it *was* a pity job."

His jaw tightened. "I never said that."

"You didn't have to." I returned the sheet of paper to the desktop. "Because if it *wasn't* some sort of pity thing, you'd want the best candidate, not someone you feel sorry for." I crossed my arms and waited for to him to deny it.

He didn't.

Instead, he sat there, studying me with that penetrating gaze of his. His hair was perfect, and his clothes – the same casual ones he'd been wearing earlier – looked way too terrific on him, even if they *were* at odds with our formal surroundings.

I met his gaze head-on, giving him the same level of scrutiny that he was giving me.

It did no good. He was a mix of contradictions, and I couldn't begin to figure him out. Even his muscles, they didn't belong on someone with his kind of money *or* this kind of house.

No, they belonged on a biker, and not the wussy, fake kind of biker either – but rather the rough-and-tumble kind, the *real* kind who'd laugh at the rain and fuck like a Trojan.

I stiffened. *Oh, my god.* Where had *that* idea come from?

In a fit of frustration, I blurted out, "What are you thinking?"

"The truth?" He leaned back in his chair. "I'm thinking, you're different."

"I'm not different," I said. "I'm just like everyone else."

But already, Jax was shaking his head. "And I'm thinking, why is it, you did such a sorry-ass job of looking out for yourself, but you're going to bat so hard and heavy for your friend."

I couldn't decide if that was a compliment or an insult. "Hey, I look out for myself just fine."

His gaze didn't waver. "Do you?"

I crossed my arms just a little bit tighter. "Definitely."

"Not the way I see it."

I felt my gaze narrow. "Is that so?"

"Yeah. It is. And I'd say more, but you wouldn't want to hear it."

I gave him a stiff smile. "Oh yeah? Well go ahead, I'm sure I can handle it just fine."

And I could.

It's not like my life had been all sunshine and roses. I'd heard plenty of foul language and seen a lot of things that I shouldn't't've. Even the spectacle last night with my mom, it was pretty tame compared to some of the other stuff I'd witnessed.

True, she'd never included me in her schemes before, but she hadn't sheltered me from the sights – or sounds – of her activities either. Living with my mom, I'd had to grow up fast and learn to keep my mouth shut, if only to avoid attracting unwanted attention from her male visitors, which, let's face it, had been numerous.

And that was putting it mildly.

Jax gave me a dubious look. "Do you mean that? You want the

unvarnished truth? *That's* what you're telling me?"

"If you mean *your* version of the truth, sure, why not?"

He looked at me for a long moment, as if waiting for me to take it back. And when I didn't, he said, "Alright. But remember, you asked for it."

My only reply was an indifferent shrug. He might think otherwise, but there was nothing he could say that would shock me.

Or so I thought.

"Your mom," he said, "she's a gold-digger."

My mouth tightened. *Okay, this was probably true, but did he seriously have to rub it in?* I muttered, "Oh, really?"

"Yeah. And that's putting it nicely."

"As opposed to what?" My chin lifted. "Calling her a whore?" That word, even on my own lips, sounded so very wrong, and immediately, I wanted to take it back. But his implication had been clear enough.

And I'd *wanted* to shock him.

The only problem was, he didn't look shocked at all. He replied, "You said it. Not me."

"Oh, so you *are* calling her that?"

"You want me to be blunt?" He gave a tight shrug. "Alright. Yeah, your mom's a whore."

My mouth fell open, and I jumped to my feet. "What the hell?"

Still seated, he continued, "And I don't mean figuratively. I mean, she has sex for money."

I was glaring at him now. "You *didn't* just say that." Was I being a hypocrite? *Maybe*. But just because *I'd* said it, that didn't mean that *he* should. She wasn't *his* mom, after all.

He gave a low scoff. "What, you want me to use nicer words?"

"No," I said. "I want you to take them back entirely."

"Yeah?" he said, looking annoyingly calm in the face of my wrath. "You wanna know what *I* want?"

"No."

He continued as if I hadn't spoken. "I want you to listen, because you asked, and I'm not done." He pointed to my chair. "So have a seat. This might take a while."

"That's what *you* think," I said, "because I've heard more than enough already." I turned to go, intending to march out with my head held high.

But that didn't happen. And why? Because, like some kind of fiendish fisherman from hell, he tossed out the one piece of bait that I couldn't resist. "Ten minutes," he said. "Give me that, and I'll interview your friend."

I was halfway to the door when his words sunk in. My steps faltered, and I slowly turned to look. He was standing now, looking noticeably less civilized than he had just moments earlier.

I felt myself swallow. His cheeks were pale, and his muscles were bulging.

Once again, my thoughts turned to the bloodstained shirt from the night before. For the hundredth time, I wondered what exactly had been going on.

If I were smart, I'd leave and never look back – not because I was afraid, but because he was acting like such a jerk. And really, did I even *want* Allie to work for a guy like this? Someone who'd say something so completely awful and then refuse to take it back?

But the answer came way too fast.

Yes.

I would.

Allie's last boss had been the biggest jerk on the planet. And the money hadn't been half as good, even though the hours were absolutely insane.

I felt my gaze narrow. "When you say interview, do you mean you'll give her a fair shot?"

"As fair as she deserves."

At this, I had to scoff. "Do you mean for someone who showed up and cursed out your brother? Or for someone who tore up your house?"

I didn't even mention the truck, because for all I knew, she'd be charged with a felony, and felons weren't exactly an employer's dream.

Jax replied, "I mean for someone who comes highly recommended."

That made me pause. "You mean by me?"

"I don't see anyone else around." He pointed to his visitor's chair, the one I'd just vacated. "Ten minutes," he repeated. "You can time me if you want."

As if I wouldn't. I gave him a thin smile. "I don't have a watch."

In response, he pulled off his own wristwatch and set it on the desk – or more accurately on the typewritten job offer. He flicked his head toward the chair and said, "The timer starts when you sit."

If I were more dignified – or maybe a little less eager to repay a friend – I would've told him where he could shove his watch and the paper it was sitting on. But I didn't.

After all, Allie had driven ten hours to save my bacon. Surely, I could swallow my pride for ten lousy minutes in return. Silently, I returned to the chair and sat stiffly on the edge of the seat.

I grabbed the watch and made a note of the time. And then, I waited.

I didn't have to wait long. Already, Jax was sitting again. He leaned forward and said something I wasn't expecting. "I'm sorry."

I blinked. "For what? Calling my mom a name?"

"No. For what I'm about to tell you."

CHAPTER 34

It took him only a few minutes to relay what he thought I should know.

My mom's sugar-daddy – the guy *I* knew as Dominic Jones – owned a limo company, a string of strip clubs, and an escort service that specialized in high-end dates – the kind that *always* ended happily, for the clients anyway.

As Jax talked, I felt the flames of embarrassment licking at my face. Or who knows, maybe they were the flames of hell, because I was pretty sure I was in it. Turns out, my mom wasn't, in the old-fashioned term, a kept woman, but rather a high-end call girl.

And the way Jax talked, my mom's employer was always on the lookout for fresh talent, and so were his various employees. Apparently, there was some sort of bonus structure, almost like a pyramid scheme, where the experienced staff earned extra money by bringing in – as Jax crudely put it – fresh meat.

I knew exactly what he was implying. The meat was me – or *would've* been me last night, if only I'd been a little more accommodating to my mom's not-so-subtle suggestions.

As he spoke, I considered all of the signs that I'd conveniently overlooked – my mom's obsession with my appearance, her insistence that I be extra nice to Dominic, and of course, all of that weirdness with the dress.

Who knows? Maybe she had some sort of clothing allowance, and didn't want to waste it on something – or rather *someone* – who wasn't panning out.

Where Tabitha fit into all of this, I had no idea. But I *did* know that her views on sex were a lot different than my own.

Back in the day, my mom and Tabitha had been groupies together. I knew this, because even when I was a child, they never tired of telling me stories from their glory days, back when they'd been barely legal, or who knows, maybe not legal at all.

When Jax finished talking, I didn't know what to say. Did I believe him? I didn't *want* to believe him. But I wasn't stupid. And yes, maybe on some level, I'd already suspected much of this on my own.

After all, I'd literally run from the limo after my mom had started in with all of those weird hints and bits of advice.

Be extra nice to Dominic.

Don't forget to smile and laugh at his jokes.

Remember, he might have some friends he'd like you to meet.

Or maybe, we'll just have a private party alone.

And then, there was the kicker. *Have you ever thought of living it up for once, and making use of your God-given assets? A girl as pretty as you? Why would you want to wait tables when you could make a lot more as an entertainer.*

I gave a silent scoff. *An entertainer.*

Like a dumb-ass, I'd kept telling myself that surely, she was referring to my singing ability, which granted, was nothing special, even if I *did* win that one high school talent show with my rendition of some old Joni Mitchell song.

But last night, it wasn't just my mom's words that had me reaching for the limo door. It was the way she'd looked at me, like I was, well, meat actually.

Very juicy meat.

I shuddered at the memory.

Now, in Jax's office, I sat in stupefied silence, processing everything I'd just heard. After a long moment, I glanced down at the watch. "Wow. Seven minutes." I blew out a shaky breath. "Three minutes ahead of schedule, huh?"

When he made no immediate reply, I mumbled, "I guess I should thank you for telling me, assuming that I believe you."

He frowned. "Which you will if you're smart."

I stared at him. *Talk about arrogant.*

"And," he continued, "if you decide you *don't* believe me? Lemme know. I'll put you in touch with my sources."

His sources? I didn't even want to consider who those might be. "Regardless," I said, "I still don't like what you said about her."

"Fair enough." His voice hardened. "And *I* didn't like what she was doing."

I gave Jax a long, sullen look. Obviously, he was no angel himself, so why was *he* in a position to judge?

"Look," I said, "I don't know why she does it, but as long as it's consensual…" I sighed. "Well, I guess it's really none of my business." I paused. "Or yours either."

His expression darkened. "You think I give two shits who she fucks for cash?"

I stiffened. After everything he'd told me, his language shouldn't've been shocking, but somehow it was. I didn't appreciate it *or* his tone, for that matter.

I shot back, "Well, you obviously *do* care, or you wouldn't have brought it up."

"I care," he said, "but not because of who she's fucking or what kind of money changes hands." His gaze locked onto mine. "I care, because she tried to drag you into it – her own fucking daughter." He gave a low scoff. "I mean, what the fuck?"

As I stared at him from the other side of his desk, it suddenly struck me that he no longer seemed like the society type at all.

At this moment, I couldn't even imagine him in a tux, even though I'd seen him wearing one with my own two eyes.

No. The guy sitting across from me was ten times more primitive, and I couldn't help but think of how correct I'd been in sensing something darker lurking beneath his polished surface.

And yet, like a moth to the flame, and even in spite of my own anger, I was still undeniably drawn to him.

Yeah, me and every other girl.

Last night, I'd seen the way they'd all looked at him, like *he* was the meat, and *they* were the hungry carnivores on the prowl.

Pushing aside that disturbing thought, I said, "Then why was Dominic at your party? I mean, you obviously don't like him, so what am I missing?"

"A simple fact. It wasn't my party."

I shook my head. "So who's party was it? Your brother's?"

"No. It was Darla's."

"Darla? The 'little redhead' in the flapper costume?"

With a tight nod, Jax went on to tell me that Darla had borrowed the house for last night's event – some high-dollar charity thing to benefit a local sea-life preservation effort.

Before I could stop myself, I'd already asked, "How much were tickets?"

"Per couple?" He gave a casual shrug. "Five grand."

"Five thousand?" I swallowed. "Dollars? You're kidding, right?"

"No."

"But I didn't pay," I said.

"Right. Because you were my date."

I gave him a look. "Don't you mean girlfriend?" Just saying the word reminded me of Morgan, that *other* girl who claimed to be his girlfriend. If she hated me then, she probably wanted to murder me now.

Unless I was mistaken, I'd just been offered *her* job. And I *still* couldn't decide if I felt satisfied or guilty. But that was a dilemma for another time.

Returning to the topic at-hand, I asked, "But why would Dominic, a guy you describe as a total scumbag, be interested in saving any sea-life?"

"Because he isn't," Jax said. "What he's interested in, is trolling for new clients." His jaw clenched. "And maybe some fresh talent along the way."

I muttered, "Well, at least you didn't call me meat."

When he made no reply, I stood. "So, do you want to interview Allie *now?* Or do you need a few minutes to prepare?"

"Sit," he said. "I'm not done."

I almost groaned out loud. "What? There's more?"

He nodded.

"But earlier, you stopped talking, like you'd reached the end."

"I stopped talking," he said, "because I wanted to give you some time to process the first part before I got to the second."

My stomach lurched. Honestly, I wasn't sure how much more I could take. In desperation, I reached out and picked up the watch. Already, we were at the nine-minute mark.

Jax said, "Yeah. I've got a minute left, and I intend to use it."

Just great. Not only was he a mind-reader, he apparently had some uncanny sense of timing, too.

I had to remind myself that this was for Allie. So with a sigh, I sat back down and mentally started counting off the seconds.

I'd barely gotten to three when he said something that caught me completely off-guard. "You're very beautiful. You know that, right?"

"I, um…" *Yes. I did know.* It wasn't that I was conceited, but I wasn't blind to the fact that my mom was totally gorgeous, and I was the spitting image of her. Weakly, I managed to say, "Uh, thanks."

"So, you *do* know?"

Oh, God. He wanted me to admit it? "What am I supposed to say? Yes? That would make me kind of conceited, don't you think?"

"No," he said. "It would make you smart."

"And conceited."

"Fuck that."

Just great. More cursing. I said, "Is there a reason you're telling me this? I mean, obviously, you don't mean it as some sort of compliment, so I can't help but wonder why you chose to spend your last minute on this."

"I'll tell you why," he said, "because there's monsters in this world who'd like nothing better than to take a bite out of someone like you." A new edge crept into his voice. "And if you ever forget that, ask me. I'll remind you."

His statement was filled with so many contradictions that I didn't know where to begin. Like, why would I ask *him?* I barely knew him.

In fact, odds were pretty good that I'd never see him again. My heart clenched at the thought, even if he *was* being a total jerk at the moment.

I looked down at the watch. "Time's up."

"Wrong," he said. "I've got ten more seconds."

I crossed my arms and waited, silently counting down even as he said, "If I knew your dad, I'd beat his ass for letting you live with that woman."

Great. Now he'd insulted *both* of my parents. I gave him my snottiest smile. "Sorry, but I don't even *know* my dad, so I guess you're out of luck."

With that, I stood. "And just so you know, I'm sending Allie down in fifteen minutes. And unless you're some kind of welcher, you'll give her an honest chance."

CHAPTER 35

I was sitting in a chair just inside the front door when I spotted Jax's brother coming down the main stairway.

At the sight of me, he stopped in mid-step. "You're still here," he said, not looking too happy about it.

I gave him a stiff smile. "Yes. I'm still here."

"I know. That's what I just said."

God, did he have to be such a smart-ass? "Goodie for you," I muttered.

He was wearing jeans and a black T-shirt with a white skull on the front. I couldn't decide if he looked more like a college student or some kind of bad-ass. In truth, he looked like both, just like his brother.

Jaden asked, "So, what are you sitting there for?"

"I'm waiting."

"For what?"

I really didn't want to say. A half-hour earlier, I'd practically dragged Allie into Jax's office for the impromptu job interview.

From my current vantage point, I couldn't quite see his office door, but if things went South, I was in a good spot to catch Allie if she decided to make a break for it.

It was for her sake, not mine. She *still* didn't know about the visit from the police, because I hadn't told her.

Oh sure, I'd *wanted* to tell her, but I couldn't risk upsetting her right before the interview. I wanted Jax to see her at her best, not worried and glancing over her shoulder.

As Jaden cleared the bottom step, I mumbled something about waiting for Allie.

He made a scoffing sound. "The psycho?"

I glared up at him. "She's not a psycho."

"Could've fooled me."

"Oh yeah? Well, maybe you caught her on a bad day. You ever think of that?"

"No. I was too busy watching my nuts."

"What?"

"My nuts," he repeated. "A girl like that? She'd probably bite 'em off."

"Oh, please." I rolled my eyes. "Your nuts are totally safe. I doubt she even thought of them."

"That's what *you* think," he said. "So where's my brother?"

I hesitated. "I think he's in a meeting."

Jaden's gaze narrowed. "You think? Or you know?"

I was spared the need to reply when someone barged in through the front door without so much as a knock. It was Darla, the flapper from last night.

Today, she was dressed in tan shorts and a crisp white cotton blouse. She looked to Jaden and demanded, "Where's your brother?"

"Which one?" he said. "I've got a bunch."

For some reason, that surprised me. *So there were more than the two? Good Lord.*

"Cut the crap," Darla told him. "You know who I mean. Jax. Where the hell is he?"

Jaden grinned. "Why? What'd he do now?"

"He fired Morgan, that's what."

Jaden's smile vanished. "When?"

"Today. On the phone."

"But he can't do that," Jaden said.

"Well, he did," Darla said. "She's been crying on my couch for the last hour."

Jaden muttered, "Shit."

Darla frowned. "No kidding."

And then, in unison, both of them turned their gazes on me. Darla asked, "Who the hell are you?"

I stood and summoned up a smile. "I'm Cassidy. It's, uh, nice to meet you."

She didn't smile back. "You were at the party. Burgundy dress. Am I right?"

"Um, probably."

"What, you don't know?"

"Yeah. Of course, I know. I just mean, there was more than one person in a burgundy dress."

She gave me a dubious look. "If you say so. And why didn't you dress up?"

"Last night? I *was* dressed up."

"You weren't in a costume," she accused.

"Yeah, well…" I hesitated. "Lots of people didn't wear costumes – most of them, in fact."

Her frown deepened. "I know. Shitbags. It was like they didn't get the memo."

I bit my lip. "There was a memo?"

She waved away my question. "You know, the invitation." She made a sound of disgust. "Dumb-asses." She gave me a long, penetrating look. "So, what are you doing here *now*?"

Okay, I realized that I was just a guest, but her demeanor struck me as more than a little rude. I wanted to throw this latest question right back at her.

What are *you* doing here?

But I didn't, because I wasn't so much a guest as an interloper. I said, "I'm just waiting for a friend."

"Oh yeah?" Darla said. "Who?"

"Allie. She's, uh, from Nashville."

Why was I even telling her this? I glanced in the general direction of Jax's office. Probably, that was a mistake, because suddenly, Jaden and Darla were heading straight in that direction.

The way it looked, they were going to give Jax a dose of holy hell for firing Morgan. For all kinds of reasons, I *so* didn't want that to happen. I scrambled after them. "Wait! I think he's in a meeting."

Ignoring me, they kept on going and didn't stop until they reached his office door. Upon finding it shut, Jaden reached out and tried the knob. When it didn't budge, he hollered out, "Hey, asshole! Open up!

We need to talk."

"Yeah!" Darla echoed. "Like now."

Through the door, I heard Jax's muffled voice. "Ten minutes."

Jaden yelled back, "I'm not waiting ten fucking minutes."

Darla called out, "Yeah. Me neither!"

From behind the closed door, Jax replied, "Yeah? Well, too bad."

Darla and Jaden shared a look. Jaden muttered, "The guy's off his rocker."

Before I could stop myself, I said, "He is not."

They both turned to look. Neither one looked particularly appreciative of my opinion.

I cleared my throat. "I'm just saying, whatever he did, I'm sure he had his reasons."

Big mistake.

Darla gave me a hard look. "So what's the reason? You?"

I swallowed. "What?"

Her mouth tightened. "Are *you* Morgan's replacement?"

"I, uh..." I squared my shoulders. "No. Definitely not."

Even if I had been offered the job.

Darla turned to Jaden and said, "So who is she, anyway?"

"You mean *her*?" Jaden replied, flicking his head in my direction. "Eh, just some chick."

I felt like strangling him. *Just some chick?*

When Darla made no reply, Jaden added, "Jax picked her up last night."

"Hey!" I said. "It's not the way you make it sound."

Jaden said, "How so?"

I glared up at him. "You talk like he picked me up at some bar or something." I turned to Darla and said, "When the truth is, he gave me a ride, that's all."

Darla snorted, "Yeah, I bet."

I felt my eyes narrow to slits. "I know what you're implying, and I don't appreciate it."

"Yeah, well *I* don't appreciate *you* getting my daughter fired."

Her daughter?

Oh, crap.

CHAPTER 36

My gaze darted between Jaden and Darla. I almost didn't know what to say. *Had* I gotten Morgan – her daughter – fired?

Yes. And no.

I mean, it was pretty obvious that she'd lost her job because of her awful behavior. And yes, much of this behavior had been directed at me, but I hadn't forced her to be awful, and I certainly hadn't forced her to barge into Jax's bedroom this morning.

I lifted my chin. "If she was fired, it was her own fault."

Darla was glaring now. "*If* she was fired?" Her voice rose. "She *was* fired. You know it. I know it. And Morgan knows it. And *how* do I know this? Because she's crying on my damn couch."

Suddenly, the office door swung open, and we all turned to look. In the open doorway stood not only Jax, but Allie too. Allie looked to Darla and said, "Yeah? Well maybe your daughter's a horrible person. You ever think of that?"

Oh, boy.

Just shoot me now.

As I watched, Darla's face grew flushed with anger. "What?"

But Allie wasn't backing down. "Yeah, I said it. Because it's true. Do you know, when I called last night, she told me that my friend was whoring herself out for drinks and gas money."

My jaw almost hit the floor. Now, it was *my* turn to say, "What?"

"Yeah," Allie said, turning her gaze on me. "And just so you know, the word 'whoring' was hers, not mine."

God, how I hated that word. My gaze slid to Jax. He stood in the doorway like a quiet menace, looking like he wanted to hit something or more likely, *someone*. Who, I wasn't sure.

When I looked back to Allie, she said, "Last night, I called you right back—"

"But wait," I said. "How could you? I didn't have my phone."

"I know," she gritted out. "That's why I called the number you left that message from."

I blinked. "Oh." Finally, the pieces fell into place. Last night, I'd borrowed Morgan's phone to leave that frantic message for Allie. Apparently, Allie had called back, only to get Morgan instead of me.

Bracing myself, I asked, "What else did she say?"

Allie hesitated. "Nothing."

"No," I said. "Tell me."

She sighed. "Alright, fine." She looked away and muttered, "She said the two brothers would be sharing you."

I gulped. "And you believed her?"

"No. Of course not." Again, she hesitated. "It's not that I believed her, but there's the thing with your mom and, well, you know what I think of *her*."

Did I ever.

I couldn't help recall our terrible argument back in Nashville. In the heat of the moment, Allie had called my mom a money-grubbing liar and said that I'd be better off with no mom at all.

No doubt, she could have said worse.

It took me a moment to realize that everyone was staring – I bit my lip – at me.

Obviously, I was supposed to say something in response. What, I had no idea. I mean, what *could* I say?

Finally, it was Jaden who broke the silence, "So, were we taking turns? Or doing you at the same time?"

God, what a douchebag.

I opened my mouth to tell him so, but Jax beat me to the punch. "Say that again, and you'll be getting a fist in the face."

Jaden shrugged. "Dude, chill. It was just a question."

I looked to Jax. He looked chilled alright, but not in the way Jaden meant. His skin was white, and his muscles were tight. He turned to Darla and said, "Yeah. I fired her. And I should've fired her weeks ago."

Darla's face fell. "But—"

"But nothing," Jax said. "If you wanna do her a real favor, you'll go back and tell her that instead of crying on your couch, she should get off her ass and find a job she can handle."

Darla gave Jax a pleading look. "I'll have a talk with her, okay? Just give her another chance. She'll do better, I promise."

"No," Jax said, "she won't, and she's out of chances." His voice hardened. "You should know, I've already hired her replacement."

In spite of everything, my heart gave a little leap. "You did?"

I looked to Allie, but her expression betrayed nothing. I returned my gaze to Jax. *He did mean Allie, right?*

I wanted to ask, but I didn't dare – not in front of such a hostile audience.

Jaden said, "Don't I get a say in this?"

Jax didn't even hesitate. "No."

"And why not?" Jaden demanded.

"Because you hired the last one, and you did a shitty job."

From the sidelines, Darla said, "Hey! That's my daughter you're talking about."

Jax turned to look, and his expression softened. "I know. But I'm done. And when you have time to think about it, you'll see it's best for her, too."

But apparently Darla didn't agree. After a few choice words, she turned and stalked away, leaving a trail of profanity in her wake.

Funny, she almost reminded me of Allie – well, Allie in fifty years, anyway.

A moment later, the sound of the front door slamming echoed through the house. I was still wincing when I heard Jaden say, "Hey blondie, you never said."

Allie snapped, "I never said what?"

"With your friend," Jaden replied, "was it supposed to be a three-way? Or were we taking turns?"

I whirled back just in time to see Allie take a flying leap in his direction. I wasn't sure what she was planning, but I tackled her anyway, sending both of us sprawling onto the glossy wooden floor.

She yelled, "What the hell are you doing!"

I was still struggling to get a grip. "I'm saving you."

She tried to squirm away. "From what?"

She was wiry and strong, but I held on tight. "From making a fool of yourself, that's what."

Suddenly, she grew very still.

And so did I.

Probably, Allie and I were thinking the same thing. Rolling around on someone's floor was no way to preserve our dignity.

Allie was squashed face down, with me sprawled on top of her. If I let go now, what would she do? She seemed calmer, but was she really? Or was this only a ruse so she could make another run at Jaden the moment I let go?

From above us, Jaden said, "If they kiss, you owe me a beer."

Oh, for God's sake. I lifted my head to glare at him. "We can't kiss. We're not even facing each other."

Seriously, what a dumb-ass.

Underneath me, Allie muttered, "I'll give him something to kiss."

As I lay there on top of my friend, a horrible thought occurred to me. Even if Allie *had* been selected for the job, was it all for nothing now?

I was no employment expert, but I did know that this wasn't the best way to end a job interview.

With as much dignity as I could muster, I pushed myself up and then, standing in the quiet hall, extended a shaky hand to Allie.

Already, she'd flopped on her back and was staring up at me with accusing eyes. Her long blond hair was in a messy disarray, and the T-shirt she was wearing had twisted around her torso, making it look crooked and uneven. The hem of her shirt had crept up, revealing her tan stomach and the very bottom of the pink lacy bra she'd borrowed earlier.

Reluctantly, I looked to Jax and then to Jaden.

Jax gave me a look that I couldn't quite decipher. As for Jaden, his eyes were focused on Allie, as if he were waiting for her to sprout horns and a devil tail – or maybe just go for his nuts.

Whatever.

I looked back to Allie and nudged my hand a little closer. Finally, she took it and let me tug her up. Once on her feet, she gave me a half-wince, half-smile. In a hushed whisper, she said, "Sorry, I guess I blew it, huh?"

I turned anxious eyes to Jax.

He and his brother were staring at us like we were the most interesting specimens in the whole zoo.

Jaden looked to Allie and, "Who the hell are you, anyway?"

But it was Jax who answered, "She's Allie Brewster." His jaw tightened. "Your new assistant."

CHAPTER 37

His words hung there for a long, silent moment. I should've been thrilled. But mostly, I was confused.

Jaden's assistant?

Not Jax's?

I looked from brother to brother, wondering if I'd misheard. Or maybe Jax had misspoke? I held my breath, waiting him for him to correct the mistake.

But he didn't.

Jaden sputtered, "What the fuck?" He glared at his brother. "You're joking, right?"

As an answer, Jax looked to Allie and said, "Welcome aboard." And with that, he turned and stalked back into his office.

After a split second, Jaden and I followed after him.

As I scrambled to keep up, I called out, "Wait, I thought she'd be working for *you*."

Jaden added, "Yeah, what the hell?"

Jax stopped and turned around. He gave his brother a hard look. "I already have an assistant."

I blurted out, "You do?"

"Yes. I do." He flicked his head toward his brother. "Morgan was *his* assistant, not mine."

I stood in stunned disbelief. *Oh, crap.* Why hadn't I realized that? Stupidly, I'd just assumed that she'd be working for Jax. I felt my gaze narrow. Jax *had* to know what I'd been thinking. And yet, he'd said nothing to correct my assumption.

Jaden was telling Jax, "So? We'll switch, not a big deal."

"We *can't* switch," Jax told him. "You know it. And I know it."

I looked from brother to brother. Obviously, I was missing something, but what? I asked, "Why can't you switch?"

Jax replied, "Ask my brother. He knows."

I looked to Jaden. "Well?"

Ignoring me, he turned hard eyes on his brother. "I swear to God, I'll get you for this."

"No," Jax said. "You won't. Because this makes us even."

Jaden was still glowering. "For what?"

"For hiring Morgan in the first place."

Jaden gave a dramatic groan. "Shit, this again?"

"Hell yeah," Jax said. "I told you not to, but you did anyway."

Jaden practically yelled, "So?"

"So, it's *your* bed. *You* lie in it."

Jaden shot back, "No way. She's a fuckin' psycho."

I made a sound of annoyance. "Hey! She is not. She's perfectly lovely. And really smart, too."

In unison, the three of us turned to look at Allie. She was standing exactly where we'd left her. She hadn't even bothered to straighten her clothes, and I swear to God, her hair looked even messier than it had a moment earlier.

Damn it. Was she *trying* to sabotage this?

If so, it made no sense. Oh sure, she obviously wasn't a huge fan of Jaden, but he couldn't be worse than her last employer, could he?

I gave Allie a reassuring smile. "Go on, tell him. You'll be great at this."

But she said nothing. Instead, she reached up and scratched her bare stomach, like some drunk at a ballgame.

What the hell?

After a long, awkward silence, Jax said, "By the way, it includes a company vehicle."

I whirled to face him. *It did?* I didn't recall seeing *that* on the paperwork. "Really?"

Looking decidedly unenthused, he replied, "Really."

As for Jaden, he looked more irritated than ever. "But Morgan didn't get a vehicle."

"Yeah, well," Jax muttered, "she didn't show the same initiative."

I didn't even know what that meant. From what I could tell, Allie had shown nearly no initiative at all, at least when it came to securing this job.

Once again, I turned to look at her. Now, she wasn't even facing us. Sometime in the last few seconds, she'd turned toward the front door. As I studied her face in profile, it was easy to guess her thoughts.

Somewhere outside was *another* vehicle, one she'd borrowed without permission. She'd need to return it. But how? And when?

Poor Allie. She didn't even know the worst of it.

But I didn't want her to think about that now. She should be celebrating, not worrying. I summoned up my sunniest smile. "That's great," I said, turning back to Jax. "So what kind of vehicle is it?"

With no trace of a smile, he replied, "An old Ford pickup."

I gave a little shake of my head. "What?"

"Yeah," he said, "Jaden bought it a couple hours ago."

I hesitated. "You don't mean—"

But that *was* what he meant, which is why an hour later, Allie and I were in that very same pickup, looking for a new place to rent.

CHAPTER 38

We'd been driving for maybe fifteen minutes, and so far, she'd said nearly nothing. Obviously, she wasn't happy, and it was easy to see why.

I bit my lip. "Maybe he won't be *so* bad."

From behind the wheel, Allie didn't even glance in my direction. Instead, she kept her eyes straight on the road and said nothing in reply.

I tried again. "And now, you don't need to worry about returning the truck, so that's good, right?"

The truck was so ancient, it was a genuine classic. It wasn't cheap either. I knew this because I had a rough idea how much Stuart had paid for it just a couple of months earlier.

Given how much he loved that thing, I was half-surprised he'd sell it at all, which only fueled my curiosity. *How much had Jaden paid for it?*

Whatever the dollar-amount was, it had to be a lot. But of course, I knew how this went. The real payment hadn't been for the truck itself so much as a bribe to keep Allie out of trouble.

In spite of how much I disliked Jaden, I had to admit, he'd done Allie a huge favor today.

Then again, he probably didn't know the full story. If he'd known it was for Allie's sake, he might've torched the truck, pointed the police in her direction, and called it a day.

Pushing that distressing thought aside, I looked to Allie and said, "And the pay's pretty good, too, right?"

Her only response was a muttered curse.

The knot in my stomach grew just a little bit tighter. *God, I hated this.*

I'd known Allie for years, and our only big argument had been the one we'd had just before I moved down here.

But the way it looked, our *second* big argument was just around the corner.

I sighed. I might as well get it over with, or even better, head it off entirely. "Allie, listen," I began. "I'm really sorry–"

"Good," she snapped, "because you should be."

I couldn't help but cringe. Her reaction stung, even if I *did* deserve it. Somehow, in the last twenty-four hours, I'd managed to completely up-end her life, even if I hadn't meant to.

But in my own defense, with the whole job thing, I really *had* been thinking of *her*. Even when it came to moving to Florida, I'd been so certain that she'd see the transition as a positive thing, not as some sort of punishment.

After all, she'd spent some of her happiest years in Hawaii while her dad had been stationed there. Plus, over the past year, she'd been talking more and more about moving someplace tropical, someplace with a beach and palm trees, too.

With growing desperation, I pointed toward the side of the road. "Look, a palm tree."

She gave the tree a sullen glance, and said nothing in reply.

I forced a smile. "And get this. You know that apartment we're on our way to see? According to Jax, it's almost right on the beach. Pretty neat, huh?"

At the next corner, Allie yanked the steering wheel to the right, sending the truck careening onto a nearby side street. She swerved to the curb and slammed on the brakes.

And then, she turned to face me.

She looked as angry as I'd ever seen her, and I fought a sudden urge to run screaming from the vehicle. But I didn't, because she was the closest thing I had to a sister and besides, after everything I'd put her through, I could surely endure the ass-chewing that was coming my way.

Sure enough, she practically yelled, "What the hell were you thinking?"

I felt myself swallow. "I, uh, was trying to make it up to you."

When her only response was a tearful shake of her head, I no longer felt like running. I felt like crying.

Somehow, I managed to say, "Honest Allie, I never would've suggested you for that job if I didn't think you'd love it." I took a deep, shuddering breath. "It's just that, well, the pay was *so* good, and the job seemed so perfect, and I remembered that you were looking to make a move…"

Allie gave a sniffle, and the sound sliced through me. She never cried. But the way it looked, she was going to break down any moment now.

My own eyes had grown misty, too, and I choked back a sniffle of my own, not because of her angry words, but because I was drowning in guilt and uncertainty.

She was the best friend I'd ever had. I *thought* I knew her, and I'd been so sure the job would make her happy.

But I'd been so very wrong. Even with the best of intentions, all I'd done was make her miserable.

Blinking back tears, I said, "Listen, as far as the job, the apartment, the state, whatever, if you want to back out, I totally understand."

With an effort, I straightened in my seat. "I'll even tell Jax so you don't have to. Or Jaden or whoever. And we'll find you a job back in Nashville. I'll help. We'll pound the pavement, send out resumes, whatever, okay?"

Feeling beyond desperate now, I swallowed a giant lump in my throat. "I'm just so sorry."

Allie gave a half-laugh, half-sob. "God, will you stop saying that?"

"No. Because it's the truth. I didn't mean to mess up your life."

"You think *that's* why I'm mad? Because you 'messed up my life'?"

"Well, uh, yeah," I stammered. "I mean, why else would you be mad?"

"Because," she said, "that job was supposed to be yours. The money, the perks, everything, that was for *you*, not me." Her teary gaze met mine. "What the hell were you thinking?"

I blinked. "So *that's* why you're mad?"

"Of course that's why I'm mad. Why would you do such a thing?"

I waved away the question. "But how did you know? Jax didn't tell you, did he?"

"He didn't have to," she said. "I saw the paperwork. It had *your* name on it, not mine."

Damn it. I should've thought of that.

Allie persisted, "And seriously, why would you do that, anyway? This could've changed your whole life. Why would you throw it away?"

At this, I laughed through my tears. "I didn't throw it away. I would've sucked at that job." I gave an epic eye-roll. "Especially now that I know it's for Jaden. God, can you imagine?"

She gave me a look. "Yeah. I can actually."

"Oh. Right." I winced. "I guess you can."

"I'm not worried about that," she said. "I can handle *him* just fine." She sighed. "It's just that, well, you haven't had a lot of good things in your life, and I hate that you gave it up."

I shook my head. "You're wrong," I told her. "I *have* had good things." Suddenly, I couldn't help but smile. "You, for example."

On impulse, I reached out and gave her hand a squeeze. "And I wasn't lying. I would've been terrible at that job, even if it *had* been working for Jax." Under my breath, I added, "As opposed to his douchebag of a brother."

She was almost laughing now. "You are *such* a liar."

Again, I shook my head. "Are you kidding? That guy? Jax? He distracts the hell out of me."

"Yeah, I could tell."

"Really?" I hesitated. "Do you think *he* could?"

"No. And you wanna know why?"

"Why?"

"Because I think *you* distract *him*, too."

CHAPTER 39

Allie's words haunted me over the next few weeks as we settled into our new apartment, not to mention new routines for each of us.

As far as the apartment itself, it was everything Jax had indicated and then some. At least once a day, I thanked my lucky stars that he'd pointed us in that direction with the help of a local realtor.

The place was an eclectic two-bedroom unit that took up the whole second floor of a stately old Victorian house – the kind with all kinds of turrets plus our own private balcony. Best of all, it was located just a block from one of the prettiest beaches I'd ever seen.

By some miracle, I'd gotten a job almost immediately, working as a waitress at a beachside bar and grill located within walking distance of our new place. I didn't even need a car, which was a good thing, since I'd sold my prior car back in Nashville and couldn't yet afford a replacement.

All in all, things were surprisingly okay – for me, anyway. As far as Allie, she still felt way too guilty about the whole job fiasco and kept urging me to reconsider.

Of course, it was ridiculous. Not only would I never change my mind, I could only imagine how thrilled the brothers would be with yet another switcharoo.

Plus, I knew that Allie was surely exceeding all expectations, which granted, couldn't't've been terribly high, given the nature of that initial interview.

Still, it was pretty obvious that she liked *this* job a lot better than her last one, even if Jaden was, in Allie's own words, the most annoying person she'd ever met.

I couldn't argue with her there. *I* thought he was pretty darn annoying, too. But it wasn't thoughts of *him* that kept me awake late into the night. No. It was his brother, Jax, who'd become my dark obsession.

And I do mean dark, because thoughts of him kept creeping in while I was huddled alone in my bed. Sometimes, I wondered what he was doing and *who* he was doing it with. Other times, I imagined him doing those things with me, which made me feel slightly awkward every time I ran into him.

It was strange, too, because when I left his place on that Sunday afternoon, I never expected to see him again, in spite of Allie working for his company. After all, I never saw Allie's *previous* employers. And besides, she worked for Jaden, not Jax.

And yet, during the last few weeks, Jax had been turning up in the strangest places – outside the bar where I worked, in the coffee shop where I bought my morning latte, and once, even at the door to my own apartment, when he stopped by to drop off some paperwork that Allie had forgotten.

By now, I might've called him a friend, except my feelings for him went beyond simple friendship or even obligation, because let's face it, he'd been my own personal savior right from the beginning.

One Thursday night, I was pondering all of this with Allie in our living room when she said, "You know he likes you, right?"

I tried to smile. "Sure. I mean, he must, considering all the favors he's done for me."

She rolled her eyes. "I don't mean as a friend."

It was a happy thought, but it still made me frown. "That can't be true," I said, "because if it was, he'd make a move or something."

"What kind of move?" She gave me a wicked grin. "The naked kind?"

"No." I sank deeper into the couch. "Okay, well, maybe not at first, but he could at least ask me out or something."

Even as I said it, I marveled at my own stupidity. He was a billionaire, and I who was I? Just a waitress.

Oh sure, I'd taken a semester of community college, but I hadn't gone back, not because I didn't like learning, but rather because so many of the classes seemed completely at odds with what I'd ever use in real life.

Plus, there was the debt. My friends who'd continued were absolutely drowning in it. Some of them hadn't even finished, and yet they *still* had the debt hanging over their heads.

And the ones who *had* finished? Most of *these* friends were working jobs that paid peanuts compared to what their degrees had cost.

Even Allie – one of the smartest people I knew – had decided to skip the whole college thing in favor of jumping out into, as she called it, the real world.

Now, sitting in the nearby armchair, Allie asked, "Wanna know what *I* think?"

"What?"

She smiled. "I think he likes you *too* much."

Okay, that made zero sense. "What do you mean?"

Even though we were alone in our apartment, she lowered her voice. "Well, from what I hear at the office, he's pretty down on relationships."

Instantly, I thought of Morgan. If Jax's last relationship had been with *her*, this attitude made sense. I said, "Why? Because of a bad breakup?"

"No," Allie said, "because of the thing with his parents."

Now *that* was odd. Until now, I'd never really thought of Jax as *having* parents. And yet, unlike me, he apparently had two of them, double my total. *Go figure.*

I said to Allie, "So I take it they're not together?"

She nodded. "Exactly."

I felt my brow wrinkle in confusion. "But lots of people have divorced parents."

"Yeah, but their divorce was weird."

Was there such a thing as a *normal* divorce? I had no idea.

Allie was saying, "They don't even live in the same state."

"You mean his parents?"

"Oh yeah." She leaned forward. "And get this. Half of the family hardly talks to the other half. It's like they don't exist or something."

I gave her a perplexed look. "I'm not sure I get what you mean."

"Well," she said, "there's like *five* brothers—"

"Five?"

She gave a solemn nod. "Yeah. And really, it's six if you count the half-brother, too."

"Wow." I blew out a surprised breath. "Six? Are you sure."

"Totally," she said. "And the half-brother? He's super famous."

Now, I was *really* confused. "He can't be. If he's *that* famous, I would've found him."

Allie laughed. "Where? On the internet?"

"Maybe," I admitted.

"You've been doing some digging, haven't you?"

"Just a little. After all, I should know *something* about your employers."

From the look on Allie's face, she wasn't buying it. "So tell me," she said, "in all your snooping—"

"I wasn't snooping. I was just browsing, that's all."

But the sad truth was, I'd found shockingly little, at least when it came to anything about their extended family. Oh sure, there'd been lots of news articles about Jax and Jaden and their growing business empire. There'd even been a few articles linking the two brothers to various love interests.

I'd skipped over anything related to Jaden and focused all of my attention on Jax. From what I'd seen, almost all of the women he'd dated had been, in the words of Jane Austen, "quite accomplished." There was that cute pediatric surgeon, along with a professor of ancient literature, and even a classic pianist.

I hated them all.

Yes, it made me an awful person, but I couldn't help it.

And why? Because each and every one of them served as a sorry reminder of my own insignificance. After all, I wasn't educated *or* accomplished.

I gazed down at my lap. *No wonder he wasn't interested.*

And yet, a little voice reminded me that he'd dated Morgan, too. And *she* wasn't some kind of superwoman. *Was she?*

Allie's voice interrupted my thoughts. "Well?"

I jerked my head up and tried to remember what she'd been saying.

"Well what?"

She made a sound of frustration. "What'd you find out?"

"Nothing." I forced a laugh. "I mean, it's not like I hired a private investigator or anything. And besides, you know a ton more about them than I do."

She frowned. "Not really."

"You're kidding, right?"

"No. Why?"

Now, I was frowning, too. "Because, you got me all interested, like you were about to tell me everything about their family, and now, you're telling me nothing."

"That's not true," she protested. "I told you everything I know, well, except for the fact that the rest of the brothers live somewhere in Michigan. And so does their dad."

"But their mom lives here? In Florida?"

Allie gave a loose shrug. "I don't know."

"Okaaaay…" Now, I was *really* frustrated. "But what about the famous brother? You never said, who is he?"

Allie winced. "Sorry. I don't know. It was just something I overheard."

"And you didn't ask for details?"

"No. Because I wasn't supposed to be listening."

I couldn't decide if I should laugh or scream. "Are you *trying* to kill me?"

"Hardly," she said. "But I *do* know something."

"About what?"

"Jax." She gave me long, mischievous look. "Do you know he hates coffee?"

I blinked. "He does?"

"Sure."

"But—"

Allie smiled. "But that can't be true, because you keep seeing him at that coffee shop?"

"Uh, yeah."

She laughed. "Right. Because he only goes there to see you."

CHAPTER 40

At Allie's statement, my heart gave a funny little leap. Still, I tried to laugh it off. "Oh, come on. That's ridiculous."

"It is not," she said. "You go there around eleven, right?"

I nodded. For most people, eleven wasn't exactly breakfast-time, but for me, everything was different. Normally, I didn't get home from work until well after midnight, and by the time I took a bath and relaxed a little, it was usually past two or three, which meant that usually it took me a while to get going in the morning.

"Well," Allie continued, "he's been taking his lunch extra-early. And he comes back with scones and stuff. It's really weird. He doesn't even eat them."

"He doesn't?"

"No. He just leaves them in the break room for whoever." She leaned forward in her chair. "And that coffee shop? It's *not* the closest one to the office."

Since I didn't own a car, I wasn't terribly familiar with the local area, at least not beyond the few blocks that surrounded our apartment. "It's not?"

"No," she said. "There's this great little place like five minutes away. But the drive to *your* coffee shop takes him like twenty minutes – that's forty round-trip. And you know what else?"

Now, I was hanging on her every word. "What?"

"Technically, he doesn't *have* to leave the office at all."

"What do you mean?"

"Hello? He's loaded. And he has his own personal assistant, plus errand people, too. He could probably sit in his office for weeks and have live lobsters delivered straight to his desk, and no one would bat an eye."

I wasn't sure about *that*, but I did see what she meant. Still, I had to ask, "But how would he know my schedule? Or where I go for coffee?" And then, it hit me. "Wait, you told him, didn't you?"

She smiled. "Maybe."

From the look on her face, there was no maybe about it.

"But why?" I asked.

"Why not?"

I bit my lip. "You didn't tell him that I *expected* to see him, did you?" I could almost see it – Allie hinting that I was dying to see him again.

True or not, how pathetic would *that* be?

"Oh, come on," she said. "I'm not stupid. I told him because he asked."

"When?" I asked.

"My first week."

"What? And you just *now* thought to mention it?"

"I didn't want to make you nervous." She gave a little shrug. "Or get your hopes up. I know you're crazy about him."

I didn't bother denying it. "Did he ask anything else?"

"Actually…" She hesitated. "…a few days ago, he asked about your mom."

"Oh." This *wasn't* what I wanted to hear. "What did he want to know?"

"Mostly, if you'd been seeing her much."

"And what did you tell him?"

"Just the truth," she said, "that she's been making herself scarce and that she won't let you pick up your stuff."

At this, I groaned out loud. "Seriously? You told him that?"

"Yeah." She gave me a confused look. "What's the problem?"

There were so many problems, I didn't know where to begin. "Well, you *do* remember where I met him, right?"

"Sure. At that car crash."

"Right. A crash that *I* caused."

Allie waved away my concerns. "You weren't even driving. And besides, the car's already fixed."

"I'm not talking about the car," I said. "I just mean that every time I see him, I'm in some sort of trouble. It's actually pretty embarrassing."

"Oh, please," she said. "When's the last time you saw him?"

"Just today. At the coffee shop."

Allie gave me a smug smile. "Were you in trouble *then*?"

"Yes, actually." I felt color rise to my cheeks. "I forgot my money."

She laughed. "No way. So what happened?"

The whole thing had been beyond humiliating. There I'd been, in the coffee shop, about to pay when I discovered that I'd forgotten to tuck some cash into the pocket of my shorts.

This wouldn't've been so terribly bad – after all, I could've just dashed home for the money – except for the fact that Jax had shown up just as I was explaining my error.

And of course, he'd felt obligated to pay for my latte – *and* a scone – even though I'd assured him that I didn't mind walking back for the money I'd forgotten.

Did he believe me? I wasn't sure. Probably, he thought I *had* no money, which was only half true. I had money, just not a lot, that's all.

And then, to make matters worse, my least-favorite barista had spent the whole time ogling him like he was the tastiest treat she'd seen all morning.

As I explained all of this to Allie, I got zero sympathy. Still laughing, she said, "He probably thinks you're adorable."

"No. He probably thinks I'm an idiot.

Was it any wonder he preferred pediatricians and professors? *They* never forgot their money. I was almost sure of it.

But Allie was saying, "He probably loved it. You know, 'coming to your rescue' and all that."

No. He hadn't. In reality, he'd looked concerned more than anything.

Allie said, "So, do you want to hear the rest or not?"

Now, I wasn't so sure. "There's more?"

"Oh yeah," she said. "So when I'm telling him that you haven't seen a lot of your mom, at first, he's happy…" She paused. "Well as happy as he gets. He's kind of a brooder. You know that, right?"

I gave it some thought. *Was* he the brooding type? It was hard for me to tell since our relationship – or whatever it was – had consisted mostly of him pulling my butt out of the fire. The way *I* saw it, that was enough to make anyone kind of broody.

"Honestly," I said. "I'm not so sure."

"Oh, but he is," she insisted. "But like I said, at first he's sort of happy because your mom hasn't been coming around. But then, when I mention that you're having trouble getting your stuff, he gets all pissed off."

"Really?" I said. "What'd he do?"

"Well, he stands there for a long moment, and I swear, I can hear his teeth grinding together. And then, he just turns and walks away without so much as a 'thanks Allie for the information.'"

Funny, I could almost see it.

Allie was saying, "Pretty rude, huh?"

"I guess," I admitted. "But I still wish you hadn't told him that."

She straightened. "And *I* wish he hadn't been rude. So we're even."

That actually made sense in an Allie sort of way.

"But about my stuff," I persisted, "you *did* tell him that we're picking it up on Saturday, right? I mean, so he doesn't worry?"

Allie looked away. "Uh, yeah. About that…"

My stomach sank. "Oh, no. Don't tell me you have to back out?"

I only prayed this wasn't the case. Without a vehicle of my own, I couldn't do it without her. I couldn't even borrow the pickup, because the truck was a stick-shift, and there was no way I'd be attempting *that*, especially on only two days' notice.

When Allie made no reply, I said, "So do I? Need to reschedule, I mean?"

"No. But…" She paused. "It won't be *me* taking you."

"It won't?"

"No. It'll be Jax."

CHAPTER 41

I wasn't happy with the news and *still* wasn't happy two days later when Jax knocked on my apartment door – a half-hour early no less.

It was true that I'd been wanting to see more of him, but this wasn't what I had in-mind. In my fantasies – meaning the ones that *weren't* X-rated – we spent our time strolling along the beach or getting to know each other over drinks and dinner.

But instead, where were we going? To see the one person who made me feel like a total freak. And I just *knew* there'd be drama, because with my mom, there always was.

Still, I tried to smile when I opened the apartment door and saw Jax standing in the hallway wearing ratty jeans and a plain gray T-shirt.

My smile was a total waste.

He wasn't smiling, not even a little. All he said was, "You ready?"

I gave a nervous laugh. "As ready as I'll ever be."

The laugh was a waste, too.

Looking grimmer than ever, he said, "I've got a van out front." And then, he stepped aside, as if wanting me to go first.

Out of politeness? Or to make sure that I didn't back out? I didn't know, and I didn't want to speculate. So instead, I stepped through the open doorway and locked the door behind me. Silently, I moved past him, heading down the stairs that led outside.

Sure enough, parked in front of the house was a white van that looked oddly familiar. Momentarily perplexed, I stopped to stare.

And then, I realized where I'd seen it. Holy hell, it was the same van that Jax had sideswiped on the night we met.

I was almost sure of it.

Drivable or not, the thing looked awful. There was a long jagged dent that extended the vehicle's entire length. Plus, the dent itself was marred by streaks of red paint that matched the color of Jaden's car, the one that had collided with the van.

As I stood a few paces from the curb, I couldn't help but wonder why Jax was driving the van at all. Was he looking to make a point? Like, was this some sort of reminder of how much I'd inconvenienced him?

It seemed so out of character, and yet, I had to wonder. I *also* had to wonder why the van hadn't been repaired. If the vehicle belonged to anyone else, I'd assume they simply couldn't afford it.

But surely, this wasn't the case with Jax. Was it?

No. Definitely not.

As he strode past me to open the passenger's side door, I asked, "Is that the same van? Meaning the one you hit that night?"

He flicked his head toward the passenger's seat. "Probably."

As I climbed inside, I said, "You don't know for sure?"

"Alright. Yeah. It is." His jaw tightened. "Is that a problem?"

I stiffened. "No. Of course not."

"Good to know." And with that, he shut the van door, leaving me staring at him through the passenger's side window. More confused than ever, I watched as he circled around the vehicle's front and then silently settled himself behind the wheel.

When he fired up the engine, I said, "I guess I should give you the address, huh?"

"No. I already have it."

"Oh." I hesitated. "How?"

"Does it matter?"

Again, I hesitated. *No. And yes.* Finally, I asked, "Is something wrong?"

He gave me a look. "What do *you* think?"

I had no idea what to say. Even though the engine was still running, he'd made no move to pull the away from the curb.

Maybe that was a good thing. Suddenly, this was feeling like a giant mistake. Oh sure, I'd known it would be awful, but I hadn't known it would be awful like *this*.

Here, I'd been bracing myself for a family spectacle, only to be waylaid by something even more humiliating – the dawning realization that Jax didn't want to be here.

Already, my stomach was in knots. *Damn it.* I should've known.

In spite of Allie's claims, he obviously hadn't volunteered for this little excursion. Rather, he'd been guilted into it or something, no doubt by Allie, who probably thought she was doing me a favor.

Some favor.

What on Earth had she been thinking?

As my thoughts churned with all kinds of uncertainty, I had to remind myself that it wasn't really her fault. In a way, it was Jaden's. Like the douchebag he was, he'd decided just two days ago that she had to work today, regardless of our plans.

And Allie – no doubt with the best intentions – had convinced Jax to help me in her place.

Now, I was kicking myself for not realizing it sooner. Of course he hadn't volunteered. I mean, who would?

I gave Jax a sideways glance. Allie had called him a brooder, and now, I could totally see it, because whatever he was thinking, it was eating him alive.

I heard myself say, "You know what? On second thought, I'll just pick up my stuff later, like maybe next Saturday or something."

His gaze snapped in my direction. "The hell you will."

"Or I won't pick it up at all." I tried for a casual shrug. "Really, it's not a big deal."

"Is that so?"

"Sure. Definitely."

I tried to say it like I believed it. And maybe part of me did. I mean, sure, I'd be abandoning most of my clothes, not to mention my cheap notebook computer, along with a few other essentials.

But it wouldn't be the end of the world. And besides, I didn't truly plan on giving up. Instead, I planned on doing this on a different day, when it would be Allie in the driver's seat, and *not* the brooding billionaire who suddenly seemed like a stranger.

Jax said, "I've got a better idea."

"What?"

"You stay. *I'll* go."

Well, this was just terrific. Apparently, the way *he* saw it, the only thing worse than running this stupid errand was running this stupid errand together.

Was my company *that* terrible?

If so, it made no sense. I'd seen Jax at the coffee shop twice earlier in the week. He'd been fine with my company *then*. In fact, both times he'd lingered longer than I might've expected. And we'd had a great time. Or at least, I'd *thought* we did.

Now, I asked, "Is that a hint?"

"I don't hint," he replied. "I'm telling you straight up, you should stay here."

"Oh yeah?" I made a scoffing sound. "Why?"

"Because I don't want you near those people."

Well, that was unexpected.

"Those people?" I said. "Who do you mean? My mom?"

"Yeah. Her. And that Tabitha chick. And what about Dominic?"

"What about him?"

"You shouldn't be in the same room with that fucker." His mouth twisted. "Especially alone."

What exactly was he implying? I scoffed, "Like I'd even *want* to."

"You always get what you want?"

"No."

"Exactly."

I stared at him for another long moment. "Is *that* why you're in a bad mood? Because you think I'm planning to be alone with Dominic?"

If I weren't so stressed, I might've laughed. "I'm not interested in him, if that's what you're thinking."

Jax frowned. "You think I don't know that?"

"Honestly, I don't know what to think."

"Alright," he said. "Answer me this. Is *he* interested in *you*?"

It was something I didn't want to contemplate. Still, the answer was embarrassingly obvious. *Yes.* He *was* interested, whether for himself or –

I stifled a shudder – his clients. Either way, it was more than a little creepy.

Still, I lifted my chin to say, "It doesn't matter. He's not even gonna be there."

"Damn right, he's not."

I felt like I was missing something. "Sorry, what?"

"I'm just saying, you shouldn't take any chances."

"I wasn't planning on it."

"You sure about that?"

I gave a sigh of frustration. "I don't even know what you mean."

"It means, I'll get your stuff. Not a problem."

I almost laughed in his face. "Not a problem? Are you serious?"

"Do I look like I'm joking?"

No. He didn't.

But it didn't matter. I'd had just about enough. "Well, obviously it's *some* sort of problem, because you've been crabby ever since you showed up."

For the briefest instant, he looked like he just might smile. "Crabby, huh?"

"Yes. Crabby."

"Alright. You wanna know why?"

"I *know* why," I said. "It's because Allie talked you into helping me, and…" I let my words trail off. *And what?* With another sigh, I finished by saying, "Listen, I don't blame you if you'd rather not. I just wish that you'd told me, that's all. You could've saved yourself a trip."

And then, there was the thing I didn't say. *And I could've saved myself a world of humiliation.*

Jax said. "You wanna know what *I* wish?"

"What?"

"I wish you'd be more careful."

"I *am* careful."

"No. You're not. You *know* you can't go alone, right?"

"Well, obviously, since I don't own a car." *And how embarrassing was that?*

"Or," he continued, "with a stranger."

I stared in confusion. "I don't even know what you mean."

"Don't you?"

"No, I…" And then it hit me. I sank back in the seat. "Oh."

CHAPTER 42

As I sat in the passenger's seat of that beat-up van, it became glaringly obvious that Jax knew a lot more than I'd realized.

An hour ago, in a momentary burst of panic, I'd called Allie at the office and begged her to tell Jax that I didn't need his help after all.

When she'd asked what I'd been planning to do instead, I'd mentioned the possibility of doing the whole ride-share thing.

I could still recall what I'd told her. "Cheaper than a taxi and more flexible, right?"

Allie's response *hadn't* been enthusiastic. In fact, she'd berated me – and quite loudly, too – for even thinking of going alone.

"But I won't be going *completely* alone," I'd told her. "I'll just pay the driver to wait or something."

Okay, it's not that *I* was in love with the idea either, but the way I saw it, it still would've better than watching Jax get drooled on by my mom.

I liked him. A lot. And even if my mom *didn't* try to molest him, I still hated the idea of dragging him through needless drama.

His voice, quieter now, broke into my thoughts. "You wanna know why I came early?"

I turned to look at him. "Why?"

"Because I'm walking by Allie's office, and I hear her telling *somebody* that going alone is a bad idea. And I stop, because I'm thinking, 'She can't be talking to Cassidy.' But then, after some yelling back and forth—"

"Hey, *I* wasn't yelling."

After only the briefest pause, he continued. "*After* the yelling, I hear Allie say, 'You can't do that. He's already on his way.'"

"Wait, so you *hadn't* already left? Did Allie know that?"

He shrugged. "Don't know, don't care."

"Why not?"

"Because she did the right thing."

I almost didn't know what to say. I felt like I'd been ganged up on – and even worse, outsmarted. And yet, the whole thing was obnoxiously sweet as much as I hated to admit it. Still, I couldn't help but mutter, "No wonder she was talking so loud."

"Good thing, too." His gaze locked on mine. "Because let's get one thing straight. You are *not* going alone."

His eyes were dark and intense, and I couldn't help but wonder what he might've done if I *had* gone alone. From the look in his eyes, I almost didn't want to speculate.

But I *was* caught off guard. In truth, his reaction was so utterly foreign that I didn't know what to say. Finally, I settled on, "That's a little bossy, don't you think?"

He didn't even hesitate. "No."

"Oh, come on. You can't be serious."

"Wanna bet? Hell, if I had *my* way, you wouldn't be going at all."

"What do you mean?" I asked.

"Trust me, I can get a lot 'bossier' than this."

I still couldn't decide if I was flattered or exasperated. Either way, I felt an embarrassing thrill at the realization that he cared enough to look out for me, even when I hadn't asked.

But didn't he get it? I'd been looking out for *him*, too. I said, "Well, maybe I was trying to spare you."

"Or maybe," he replied, "you were risking your ass for no good reason."

I straightened in my seat. "Hey, my ass is just fine, thank you very much."

His eyes filled with mischief. "Yeah?"

Oh, crap. That *had* sounded pretty stupid. Suddenly flustered, I tried again. "I just mean that, well, it *would've been* fine, meaning the situation, not anything else."

Jax gave me a long, amused look. "I'm not gonna comment on your fine ass—"

"Good. Because *I'm* not gonna either."

At least not anymore.

Damn it.

Eager to change the subject, I said, "So tell me, do you *always* eavesdrop on your employees?"

His eyebrows lifted. "I *did* mention she was yelling, right?"

"Well, yeah, but what if she'd been whispering? Would've you *still* listened in?"

He didn't hesitate. "Hell yeah."

All I could do was stare. The guy was utterly shameless.

His voice softened. "You're important to me. You know that, right?"

I felt myself swallow. "Actually, I'm not sure what I know." My own voice grew softer, too. "Like just a minute ago, you're all crabby, and now you're all…" I gave a distracted flutter of my hands. "…different."

His reply was barely a whisper. "I know."

"You do?"

He shoved a hand through his hair. "Listen, I'm sorry I was a dick, but yeah, I was pissed. And you want the truth?"

I felt myself nod.

He gave something like a smile. "I'm still pissed."

The smile, as subtle as it was, caught me off guard. "But why? I mean, surely you've got better things to do than deal with my mom."

"Yeah. I do." His gaze warmed. "And you do, too."

I felt my eyebrows furrow in confusion. "Sorry, what?"

He leaned closer. "Lemme make it up to you."

At this, I had to laugh. "Make what up to me? Because I'm pretty sure in the big scheme of things, it's *me* who still owes you." I rolled my eyes. "Times a million."

"Yeah? Then do me a favor."

"What?"

"Stay here, just like I asked."

"Oh, please. That's no favor, for *you* I mean. If anything, it's another favor for me."

"Not the way I see it."

"And besides," I added, "you can't go alone. You don't even know what's mine."

"So I'll figure it out. Not a big deal."

That's what *he* thought. With my mom, it was always a big deal.

Sitting in the van, we went back and forth a few more times before he finally accepted that I wasn't going to give in.

I couldn't. As much as I appreciated his offer, I'd never let him take on such an unpleasant task by himself.

I wasn't a coward, and I hated the idea of me sitting blissfully at home while he waded into the muck that was my life. And I just knew that given half a chance, my mom would rip off her clothes and jump into his arms.

But as it turned out, *this* worry was for nothing. And why? Because when we finally arrived, my mom wasn't even there.

CHAPTER 43

Standing in the hall just outside my mom's apartment, I gave Jax a worried look. "Do you think I should knock *again*?"

Already, I'd knocked like five times and even tried the doorknob too, for all the good it did.

Jax said, "You got a key?"

"Sure," I said with a half-hearted laugh. "*Inside* the apartment."

"But you *did* have one?"

"Yeah. Of course."

"But…?"

"But the last time I left the apartment, I was with my mom. And she had *her* key, so…" I didn't bother finishing the sentence. In hindsight, it had been incredibly stupid to trust my mom with something even as small as a key to the place where we'd both been living.

When I didn't elaborate, Jax said, "Lemme ask you something. If I wanted to replace your stuff, would you let me?"

The question caught me off guard. "Why would you *want* to?"

He shrugged. "For the fun of it."

Was he joking? He didn't *look* like he was joking. And, judging from the tightness of his mouth, it didn't look like he'd find it particularly fun either. Or maybe he was just irritated with my mom for standing me up.

If so, that made two of us.

But it didn't matter. I'd never accept such an offer, anyway. I glanced down and was suddenly embarrassed to realize that I was wearing one of the T-shirts that he'd loaned me several weeks earlier.

Damn it. While getting dressed today, why hadn't I paid more attention?

Then again, he *had* arrived a half-hour early, so it's not like I'd had a lot of time to obsess over my appearance.

This was probably for the best. Over the last few weeks, while my mom had been giving me the runaround, I'd been seriously short of clothes. Mostly, I'd made due with the stuff I'd originally borrowed from Jax, along with some castoffs from Allie.

Unlike *me*, she'd gotten *her* things within days, mostly because her new job had apparently included full relocation – not that I'd seen that on the paperwork.

Regardless, just a few days after she'd accepted the offer, like magic, a moving truck had shown up with all of her things, professionally packed and delivered straight to our doorstep.

Cripes, they'd even unpacked it.

As far as our *old* apartment, Allie's cousin had assumed the lease and promptly gotten a new roommate, which meant that Allie was here for the long-term. She'd even changed her driver's license.

But me? I wasn't nearly as settled.

My job was fine enough, but it didn't pay half as well as Allie's. And even though she'd insisted on paying more than her share of the rent, it's not like I had a ton of money to spare, especially since I'd been forced to replace a whole bunch of things that I'd previously taken for granted.

Already, I'd spent a small fortune on undergarments, shoes, and even makeup. It was just the basics, but they added up. And I'd only had one paycheck since starting my new job.

Thank goodness for tips.

Maybe I should've skipped the lattes, but they really *were* my one luxury, and I hated the idea of giving them up, especially now that I kept running into Jax at the coffee shop.

I was still mulling all of this over when he said, "If you want, we can do it now."

I was so lost in my thoughts that it took me a moment to realize that he was talking about his offer to replace my things.

I gave the shirt another worried glance. "Technically, I still owe you for the stuff I borrowed at your house."

"No," he said. "You don't. Keep it, just like I said."

He *had* said that, but it still felt strange. Even the shirt I was wearing now, I didn't even know who it belonged to. I mean, it obviously wasn't his, so whose was it?

I didn't know, and probably I didn't *want* to know.

But I still felt funny about it. What if I ran into this person? Would they accuse me of swiping their clothes?

Oh, God. What if the shirt belonged to Morgan? I could only imagine what she'd say – or do.

It would be a flat-out spectacle. And how humiliating would *that* be? It was almost enough to make me want to rip off the shirt and torch it before any such thing could happen.

Right. Because nothing says, "I hate spectacles" like ripping off your clothes and burning them in the hallway.

Jax said, "What is it?"

I blinked. "Sorry, what?"

He frowned. "Something's wrong."

"No. Not really." Again, I looked to the shirt. "It's just that, well, I'm kind of curious...whose shirt is this?"

"Yours, just like I said."

"C'mon, you know what I mean " I bit my lip. "It's not Morgan's, is it?"

He looked at me for a long moment. "You think I'd give you her clothes?"

"Well, you gave me *somebody's* clothes." I forced a laugh. "Unless you got them from Goodwill or something, *somebody's* missing them."

I reached up to rub my temples. What on Earth was wrong with me? It was one stupid shirt. Why was I obsessing over it, when I had a whole bunch of shirts on just the other side of that door?

I still hadn't answered his question. "About your offer," I said, "that's really nice of you, but I can't let you do that."

"Why not?"

"Because you've done too much already." Again, I looked toward the door. "And besides, I'm sure I'll get my stuff eventually."

"Any chance you'll change your mind?"

I shook my head. I hadn't been lying. As wonderful as his offer was, that wasn't me. That was my mom, and I refused to follow in her dangerous footsteps.

"Alright," Jax said. "Then lemme ask you…you wanna wait in the van? Or come with me?"

"What do you mean?" I asked. "Where are you going?"

He pointed to my mom's door. "Into the apartment."

"But it's locked."

"Yeah, but not for long."

CHAPTER 44

Twenty minutes later, we were already in and out.

I'd even changed my shirt, swapping out the borrowed one for a shirt of my own. Was it silly? Probably. But I didn't care. For the first time in weeks, I was wearing my own clothes, and I had the rest of my things within easy reach.

Best of all, I had Jax in the driver's seat, pulling away from the curb all casual-like, as if we *hadn't* just done the unthinkable, for me, anyway.

During the last twenty minutes, I'd been incredibly tense, looking over my shoulder non-stop as Jax and I worked to gather up my things.

It went a lot faster than I might've expected, mostly because Jax had stocked the van with a nice supply of moving boxes, along with rolls of packing tape, too.

I had to give him credit. He'd thought of everything.

In hindsight, even his choice of vehicles had been pure perfection. No one had given us a second glance, even as we made several trips back and forth while loading up the stuff.

And now that we were finished, I almost felt like laughing. "I can't believe we broke in."

"We didn't break in." He smiled as he pulled into traffic. "You had a key, remember?"

"Well, yeah. But I didn't have it on me."

"But you do now, right?"

Yes. I did. But only because Jax had insisted. If I'd been alone, I probably would've left the key where I'd originally left it – atop the nightstand in my mom's spare bedroom.

I couldn't even call it *my* bedroom, considering that I'd slept there for barely a week.

In answer to Jax's question, I raised the key out in front of me and twisted the keyring around my finger. "Yeah, I've got it, but I doubt I'll be needing it. I mean, it's not like I'll ever be living there again."

"Good." His voice hardened. "And if you change your mind, let me know."

"Why?"

"So I can talk you out of it."

Funny, he didn't look like much "talking" would be involved. Mostly, he looked like he'd tie me to a chair if I ever suggested such a thing – not that I would after this latest fiasco.

Still, I had to ask, "So then why would I need a key?"

At the next stoplight, he turned and gave me a serious look. "The key's how you got in."

Serious or not, I couldn't help but tease, "Oh really? So you *didn't* pick the lock?"

"Me? Hell no." He gave me the ghost of a smile. "I'm an angel."

He was obviously joking, but I couldn't ignore the truth of his words. He might not realize it, but during the last few weeks, he'd been my own personal guardian angel, coming to my rescue just when I needed him most.

And he was still doing it.

As the light turned green, he added, "And remember, don't delete the texts."

I knew which texts he meant. He was referring to the texts between me and my mom, where she'd informed me of the day and time I could pick up my things.

I saw his logic. Combined with the key, those messages would make it doubly hard for my mom to cause trouble. Still, I doubted that she would. "Honestly," I said, "I don't think it matters. Probably, she'll just be glad to have the bedroom back."

He gave me a sideways glance. "No. What she'll be is ticked off that the stuff's gone."

"What makes you say that?"

"She was giving you the runaround, right?"

"A little," I admitted.

"A little, huh?"

"Oh, alright. A lot."

"Right. And you wanna know why?"

"Why?"

"Because your things were the bait."

I wasn't following. "The bait?"

"Yeah." He frowned. "To lure you back."

I hated that he was frowning. For one thing, I didn't anticipate my mom "luring" me anywhere. And for another, our trip had been a raging success, all thanks to him.

I was happy. And I wanted him to be happy, too.

Looking to lighten his mood, I said with a laugh, "Oh sure, because I'm such a juicy catch."

When he gave me an inscrutable glance, I suddenly realized how ridiculous that sounded. *Juicy? Seriously?*

Once again, I'd managed to say something incredibly absurd without thinking. I didn't normally do that, but with Jax, I found myself saying – and thinking – all kinds of crazy things.

Like right now, I was thinking how much simpler life would be if only he were just a regular guy – someone I met at the beach or maybe at work.

I gave him a long sideways look. He didn't look like a billionaire, not now, sitting behind the wheel of this beat-up van. Rather, in his plain T-shirt and ratty jeans, he looked like the sexiest working stiff I'd ever seen.

I almost sighed out loud. *If only that were the case.*

If only he moved boxes or swung a hammer for a living. Then, it wouldn't be so hard to imagine us together, to dream that our friendship might blossom into something more, or to believe that he wasn't helping me out of pity or obligation.

But he *wasn't* just a regular guy, and I wasn't naïve.

Now, I did sigh. I was no pediatrician. Or professor. Hell, I wasn't even a college graduate, which meant that he was so far above me on a social scale, I'd need a ladder just to lick his boots.

I gave a little shudder. *Lick his boots?* At least, I hadn't said *that* out loud.

Trying to rein in my thoughts, I turned my head to gaze out through the passenger's side window. Outside, it was a beautiful sunny day with hours of daylight remaining.

In anticipation of today's errand, I'd taken the whole day off work, which meant that I had hours of freedom ahead of me. I had no idea what I'd be doing, but I *did* know that I was in serious danger.

Of what?

Falling for my guardian angel.

Or maybe I already had.

Damn it.

I was still looking out the window when the truck slowed and pulled off to the side. Confused, I glanced around, but saw nothing of any particular interest – just average houses on an average residential street.

When I turned to give Jax a questioning look, he said, "I need a favor."

I summoned up a smile. "Sure."

He didn't smile back. "Don't say yes 'til you know what it is."

At this, I had to laugh. "It doesn't matter what it is. I'm pretty sure I owe you like a million favors after all you've done for me."

His jaw tightened. "Make that *two* favors."

I studied his face. For whatever reason, my comment had rubbed him the wrong way. Cautiously, I said, "Okay, what?"

"Favor one," he said. "I want you to forget I've done anything."

CHAPTER 45

I felt my brow wrinkle in new confusion. He wanted me to forget everything he'd done for me? Was he serious?

I said, "But why would I?" And then, I realized. "Oh. Are you worried you'll get in trouble, like for the lock thing?"

At this, he looked almost amused. "I'm not afraid of trouble."

Now *that* I could believe. Whether in a tux or T-shirt, the guy was absolutely fearless.

Still, I had to ask, "So what am I missing?"

"Nothing," he said. "I'm just saying you don't owe me. So forget it. That's the favor."

I gave him a dubious look. "That doesn't sound like much of a favor to me."

"Trust me, it is."

I wasn't so sure. "So what's the second favor?"

He smiled. "Say yes to the first, and I'll tell you."

Damn it. He was so devious that I couldn't resist smiling back. "Oh, so you're bribing me?"

"If that's what it takes."

I gave it some thought. "If I promise to *try*, does that count?"

He shook his head. "Sorry."

Funny, he didn't *look* sorry. He looked cool and determined.

"Oh come on," I said. "I can't control what I think. And besides, I really *am* thankful."

"Good," he said. "So do me the favor."

Talk about circular reasoning.

I protested, "But that doesn't make any sense. And besides, don't you think I'd be an awful person if I just forgot it all, like none of it mattered?"

"No," he said. "I think you'd be doing me a favor, just like I asked." His gaze met mine. "So say yes, and forget it."

I wanted to say yes. Really, I did. But it would be a lie.

Growing up, my mom had lied a lot – pretty little lies that made life easier in the short term and harder in the end. But me? I wasn't like that. I didn't *want* to be like that, especially with Jax, who was growing more important to me with every passing moment.

So I did the only thing I *could* do. I looked straight into his eyes and said exactly what I was thinking. "I *could* promise, but it wouldn't be true. I *can't* forget, and…" My voice grew quiet. "…I guess I can't help how I feel."

As I said it, I realized how accurate this was on multiple levels. After all, it wasn't just gratitude filling my heart. It was something else, something he'd never return in a million years.

But then, *his* voice grew quieter, too. "I know the feeling."

I wasn't quite sure what he meant, but there was something there, something in his tone, or maybe in his look – whatever it was, it made my heart give that familiar little flutter.

I asked, "What do you mean?"

He leaned a fraction closer. "Promise me, and I'll tell you *that*, too."

Oh. My. God. Now, I was dying to know what he'd say. "Really?"

His gaze dipped to my lips. "Really."

Feeling nearly breathless now, I joked, "Will you take a kidney instead?"

Slowly, he shook his head.

I gave him a hopeful smile. "*Two* kidneys?"

"Sorry." He smiled back. "I like your kidneys where they are."

"But you haven't even seen them."

"Remind me sometime. I'll take a look."

As we bantered back and forth, it wasn't lost on me that somehow, we were no longer discussing that strange favor. What we *were* discussing, I wasn't quite sure.

But I liked it.

I liked the look in his eyes and the fact that he was right here, almost within reach. Still, we could've been a whole lot closer, and I fought an impulsive urge to lean toward him and see what might happen.

Who knows? Maybe nothing would happen. Maybe I'd just look like an idiot. After all, he wasn't my boyfriend or even my date.

In reality, I wasn't quite sure *what* he was.

A friend? Definitely.

Something more? Possibly.

From the look in his eyes, it sure seemed that way. Desperate for clues, I said, "At least tell me this. Is the *second* favor any easier?"

His smile disappeared. "No."

And just like that, the spell was broken.

Damn it.

I studied his face. "So what is it? You might as well tell me, or I'll just drive you crazy asking."

"Alright." His gaze hardened. "When she calls, don't answer the phone."

"Who? My mom?" I almost laughed. "Don't worry. I doubt she'll be calling."

"Doubt all you want," he said, "but she *will* call, and probably sooner than you think."

"Seriously, I don't think you need to worry."

"Good," he said. "So promise me, alright?"

I didn't want to promise. I wasn't even sure I could. "Is that *really* the favor?"

"That's it," he said. "And if I only get one, that's the one I want."

As far as favors went, it was huge and tiny all at the same time. I blew out a nervous breath. "Wanna hear something funny? I've been living here for how long? A few weeks, right? Do you know, I haven't even seen her since the night you and I met?"

His expression didn't change. "Good."

Was it?

Yes.

And no.

I mumbled, "I dunno. I guess."

I looked toward the center console, where I'd placed my cellphone. In spite of what Jax might think, the odds of my mom calling – at least any time soon – were very slim.

I knew this from experience. Even back in high school, when I'd moved out for the very first time, she didn't call me for weeks even though I was technically a minor.

I'd been staying with a friend, but she didn't know that. Funny, she never even asked.

Hell, I could've been dead in a ditch for all she knew.

Still, I had to be honest. I looked back to Jax and said, "I can't promise to never talk to her. I mean, she *is* my mom."

He said nothing. But he didn't need to. His reply was written all over his face. *Wrong answer.*

I sighed. "Look, it's not like I want to be best buddies with her or anything. You want the truth? Sometimes, I'm not even sure that I *like* her, but…" I paused to collect my thoughts. "…she's the only family I have. Even Aunt Tabitha, she's not really my aunt."

"Good," he said for what felt like the millionth time.

I gave him a look. "You say that a lot."

"Only when I mean it."

That much was obvious. But *I* meant it, too, which totally sucked.

Today, he'd asked me for two favors, but I couldn't give him either one.

And whether foolish or not, I couldn't lie about them either, even though it would've been a ton easier – short-term, anyway – than sitting here, letting the silence fester between us.

I tried to smile. "I don't suppose you'll reconsider that kidney thing?"

He frowned. "No."

My heart sank. I wasn't *really* offering him a kidney, just like he wasn't really saying no to some impromptu organ donation.

Sadly, this "no" was bigger, and it felt like a door slamming between us. I hated that, but not enough to change who I was.

I gave a hopeless shrug. "I guess it's settled then, huh?" I forced a weak little laugh. "No kidney for you."

With a slow shake of his head, he turned forward in his seat. He stared out in front of us, even though there was nothing interesting to see – just a basic road on a basic street.

I figured that would be it. That he'd just hit the gas, and we'd be on our way.

But then, he said something that made me pause. "How about half a favor?"

I hesitated. "What does that mean?"

"The favors – both of them – how about just for tonight?"

"You mean, like there's an expiration date or something?"

He was still looking ahead. "Right. Forget what you think you owe me – and forget that woman is your mom." His mouth tightened. "Which means no calls, no visits, nothing."

That didn't seem *so* hard. "Just for tonight?" I repeated.

Once again, he turned to face me. "If that's the best I can get."

A combination of relief and guilt coursed through me. In reality, his request was nearly nothing. Even the thing with my mom would require zero effort on my part, since the odds of her calling were slim to none.

I had to admit, "That's a pretty small favor."

"Good," he said yet again.

"Why is that good?"

"It means it'll be easy to keep, right?"

I nodded. "Yeah, sure. Probably, *too* easy in a way." I tried to think. "I guess I'll have to owe you something else, huh?"

Finally, he gave me a smile, a *real* smile. "Nah. Let's call it even."

My shoulders relaxed, and suddenly, I was smiling, too. "Next time, I'll try to be more reasonable."

Suddenly, he was looking intrigued. "Yeah?"

"Definitely."

"If I ask you to dinner, does that count?"

And just like that, the fluttery feeling was back. Still, I had to say, "But that's hardly a favor."

"Good to know." His gaze met mine. "So, you got any plans?"

"For when?"

"Tonight."

CHAPTER 46

I was still getting ready when my cellphone rang for the third time in ten minutes. At the sound of it, I literally cringed.

I knew the ring, and I wasn't happy to hear it, which is why I'd left the cellphone on the kitchen counter instead of bringing it with me into the bedroom as I considered what to wear.

From the kitchen, Allie called out, "It's her again."

As if I didn't know. I replied with a half-hearted thanks and tried to focus on a cheerier dilemma. He said to dress up. But what exactly did that mean? Obviously, I'd need to wear a dress. But how dressy of a dress?

Unless I wanted to risk answering the door in my undergarments, I'd need to figure it out fast.

Just two hours earlier, after that tense discussion in the van, Jax had driven me home and helped me haul my stuff up into the apartment. He'd even offered to help me unpack, not that I'd accepted his offer, as thoughtful as it was.

But the way I saw it, he'd done more than enough already. Plus – I smiled at the thought – I had a date to get ready for.

Yes. It was officially a date.

I glanced at the clock, and my smile faded. He'd be arriving in just thirty minutes. And that was assuming he didn't show up early.

I was dying to see him, but not in my underpants, at least not yet.

Trying to focus, I gazed down at the three dresses that I'd laid out across my bed. There was my one-and-only cocktail dress plus my two favorite sundresses.

The cocktail dress was several years old. The sundresses were newer, but not terribly formal. None of the dresses were expensive.

Would this matter? I sure hoped not, considering that I had no time to shop – or money to burn even if I did.

I recalled the dress I'd been wearing on the night of the crash. *That* dress was nice. And expensive.

It was funny to think that I still had it. But there was no way on Earth I'd ever wear the thing, especially in front of Jax, who'd seen my mom wearing an exact replica.

Jax hated my mom. That much was obvious. Considering how we'd met, I couldn't exactly blame him.

But I didn't want to conjure up any funky memories either, which meant that the pricey dress was definitely off limits. This was probably for the best. Even after a good dry-cleaning, it still hadn't recovered from my little beach adventure.

Again, I glanced at the clock. Twenty-seven minutes. *Yikes.*

I would've been ready an hour ago, if only I hadn't lost track of time chatting with Allie, who'd arrived home just minutes after Jax's departure.

Eager for girl-talk, I hadn't been able to resist sinking down on the sofa and telling her everything that had happened. I didn't leave anything out either, which turned out to be a mixed bag. By the end, our conversation had strayed pretty far off course, especially when it came to my mom – as usual.

Allie *hated* my mom, possibly even more than Jax did. And she wasn't shy about telling me so.

Of course, it hadn't helped that my mom had called three times since then.

I hadn't answered, and not only because I'd made that promise to Jax. Oh sure, I was big on keeping promises, but even without *this* one, I realized the folly of talking to her now.

I knew why she was calling. Obviously, she'd noticed the missing stuff and wasn't happy.

But seriously, what did she expect? I'd been on her doorstep at the exact time we'd agreed on. Plus, after packing up my things, I'd even left a note, thanking her for not throwing anything out.

Jax had just *loved* that.

But in my own defense, the note wasn't due to politeness or even affection. Mostly, I just didn't want my mom to think she'd been robbed or something.

I didn't need the drama, and neither did Jax, whether he realized it or not.

I was down to twenty minutes when the phone rang yet again. It was still ringing when Allie appeared in the doorway to my bedroom. With my phone in-hand, she said, "You know what you should do, right?"

From the look on her face, I was afraid to guess. One time, Allie had suggested that I take my mom on a cruise and then toss her overboard. But that had obviously been a joke.

I mean, it's not like I could afford a cruise.

Now, Allie was saying, "You should block her number."

"Why? She never calls."

Allie lifted the phone, which of course, was still ringing. "Oh yeah?"

"Well, she doesn't *normally* call." I gave my phone a quick glance. "You don't think it's an emergency, do you?"

"Hell no," Allie said. "If it were an emergency, she'd leave a message."

When the phone stopped ringing, I listened, waiting for the beep. There was none. *No message.* That was good, right?

Allie said, "Wanna know what I think?"

I tried to laugh. "Probably not."

"Sure you do," she said. "What *I* think is that she knows you're going out, and she wants to ruin it."

"Oh, please. She's not a psychic."

"Yeah, but she's a psycho, so there's that."

I gave Allie a look. "Gee, where have I heard *that* before?"

"I'm serious," she said. "You really *should* block it. Do you really want to be nagged all night?"

I bit my lip. *No. I didn't.* But the odds of this were slim. "She won't be calling *all* night," I said. "Probably, that was her last try."

The words had barely left my lips when the phone rang yet again.

Damn it.

Allie chirped. "Told ya."

By now, the sound was like a jackhammer to my ears – maybe not as loud, but ten times as annoying.

Allie said, "Alright, how about this? Go ahead and answer, but tell her to fuck off."

I'd heard this suggestion before and refused to be rattled. "I can't." I gave Allie my sweetest smile. "I promised, remember?"

"You mean that promise to Jax?" She gave me a smile of her own. "I'm sure he'd make an exception for *that*."

No doubt, he would.

Allie said, "I don't get it. Why wouldn't you just block her number and be done with it?"

As if it were so easy.

Emotional baggage aside, my phone wasn't that fancy. Oh sure, on *some* models you could block any number with the simple press of a button. But my phone? It was older and not terribly advanced.

To block *any* number at all, I'd need to sign into my cell phone account and set it up manually. And then, tomorrow, I'd have to go through the whole process again to unblock it.

When I explained all of this to Allie, she said, "So keep it blocked, and call it good."

"You know who you sound like?" I said. "Jax."

"Good."

Good? The word was eerily familiar. "Now, you *really* sound like him."

"Good," she repeated. "It shows he's looking out for you."

"You're just biased because you agree."

"Damn straight."

When the phone rang again, I wanted to throw up. I looked to Allie and said, "Maybe it *is* an emergency. I mean, she's never like this."

"She is, too," Allie shot back. "You remember how she was when she was begging you to move down here. That one Sunday, she called you like a dozen times in a row."

Well, there was that.

But even then, the repeated calls had been completely out of character, which is one reason I'd stupidly thought my mom might've changed.

As if.

If I were smart, maybe I *would* tell her to fuck off. After all, my life had been a whole lot simpler when she'd been outright ignoring me.

When the phone stopped ringing, I couldn't even breathe a sigh of relief, because I just *knew* it wasn't over. Sure enough, the phone rang again almost immediately.

I muttered, "Shit."

"How about this?" Allie said. "*I'll* answer it, so you don't need to."

"Nice try," I said with a laugh. "I'm trying to *avoid* drama, not generate more of it."

Allie frowned. "What's that supposed to mean?"

"It means," I said, "that you'll cuss her out, and she'll be calling all night."

Looking decidedly disgruntled, Allie said, "Hey, I can be nice."'

"To my mom?" I made a scoffing sound. "Yeah, right."

"I can," Allie insisted. "And besides, you *do* want to keep your promise to Jax, right?"

Yes. I did. Plus, I didn't want to spend my night worrying. Finally, I gave in. "But remember," I said, "be nice. I *really* don't want any drama."

To my infinite surprise, Allie took my words to heart. Sounding obnoxiously cheerful, she answered with a perky, "Cassidy's phone. How may I help you?"

If I weren't so stressed, I might've laughed.

Instead, I watched with amazement as Allie smiled into the phone. "Uh-huh." She paused. "Oh really? No kidding? Wow. Uh-huh. Oh sure, I'll tell her when she gets back."

She paused again. "Yup, I sure will. Alrighty. Bye-bye now."

By the time she disconnected, I was staring. Allie *never* sounded like that, especially when dealing with my mom.

"Well?" I said.

Allie shrugged. "She said that Dominic's in the hospital and she wanted you to know."

"Really? Did she say for what?"

Allie gave a breezy wave of her hands. "Some fight or something."

"Seriously?" I'd only met him a few times, but he didn't seem like the fighting type. For one thing, he wasn't in terrific shape. "Did she say with who?"

Allie gave another shrug. "I didn't ask."

In truth, Allie hadn't asked anything. Mostly she'd just listened. Finally, I felt my shoulders relax. "Did she say anything else?"

Allie gave a cheerful nod. "Oh yeah. She said lots of things about Dominic. But mostly, she wants you to call her when you get a chance."

Would I? Maybe. Maybe not. Regardless, it wouldn't be tonight. I looked to the bed, where the dresses were still laid out.

Allie said, "If you're trying to choose, I vote for the cocktail dress."

"Really?"

"Oh yeah," she said. "He won't be able to keep his eyes off you."

As it turned out, she was right.

CHAPTER 47

"So," Jax was saying, "you got a number in mind?"

For the last hour, he'd been eyeing me with an expression that I couldn't quite decipher. He'd been asking lots of questions, too. Some were easy.

What did I think of Florida?
Did I like my job?
What kind of music did I like?

But other questions? They were tough, especially this latest one, which I hadn't yet answered.

The whole time, he'd been piercing me with that penetrating gaze of his, like he was determined to figure me out.

I couldn't imagine why. I mean, I wasn't *that* complicated, at least not compared to him.

We were sitting in a posh restaurant overlooking the water. We even had a window seat, and the setting sun was the perfect backdrop for what should've been a relaxing dinner.

But I *wasn't* relaxed.

I was flustered beyond all reason. There he was, sitting across from me in a tailored suit – open collar with no tie. And here *I* was, in my best cocktail dress – hell, my *only* cocktail dress, plus high heels and the only decent jewelry I had, which of course, was nothing spectacular.

But Jax? He looked good enough to eat, and I wasn't the only one who thought so. Even as we'd been walking in, every female head had turned in his direction. Their looks had been long and lingering, like they wouldn't mind taking a nibble if the opportunity presented itself.

It wouldn't.

Not if *I* had a say in the matter.

And yet, I couldn't blame them *too* much. His stride was confident. His clothes fit like they were tailor-made. His hair was dark and lush. And his eyes were so compelling that even now, I couldn't bring myself to look away.

Silently, I was comparing *this* Jax to the Jax who'd been driving that beat-up van just a few hours earlier. *That* Jax was rough and tumble – hard and sexy, with a distinct edge. But *this* Jax? The guy sitting across from me? He was smooth and sophisticated, the kind of guy who'd grown up with servants and a silver spoon.

Both versions scared me. *A lot.*

It's not that I was scared of *him* exactly, but rather, my feelings were just a little bit terrifying, especially now when he was asking all of these intriguing questions.

He leaned back in his chair and repeated the gist of the latest one. "So, how many?"

I blinked. "Sorry, what?"

"Kids," he said. "You got a number in mind?"

"Oh. Three or four." I tried to laugh. "Or maybe ten."

He smiled. "Ten, huh?"

I straightened. "Or *three*. You heard that part, right?"

"Big difference between ten and three."

I loved kids. But would I *truly* have ten? *Doubtful.* For one thing, kids were expensive – as my mom had reminded me nonstop when I'd been growing up.

Going for a joke, I said, "Well maybe there's three sets of triplets." I did the math and hesitated. "Plus one extra."

Carry the one, right?

"Yeah?" Jax said, looking oddly intrigued. "This extra kid, does he have a name?"

His eyes were so compelling, I could hardly think. Absently, I murmured, "Jax." I gave a little gasp.

I *so* hadn't meant to say that.

And now, that name – *his* name – hung there like an accidental burp.

Oops.

Quickly I added, "I mean, well, it's a nice name."

He grinned. "Yeah?"

"Definitely. And um, you could be its uncle or something."

Uncle?

Good Lord.

His eyebrows lifted. "So who's the dad? Jaden?"

"What?" I forced a laugh. "God, no. Why would you say *that*?" And then it hit me. Of course, in order for Jax to be the uncle, I'd have to create this fictional baby with his brother.

Yikes.

What I needed now was a muzzle.

For myself.

I said, "You know what? Forget I said that."

"I guess I'd better," Jax said, looking highly amused, "unless you *want* me to kick Jaden's ass."

I was flattered and flustered all at the same time. Now, I laughed for real. "I was thinking you'd be more of an *honorary* uncle."

He was still giving me that look. "But just an uncle, huh?"

Or something more.

But there was no way on Earth I'd be saying *that*, especially on our first official date. And besides, I wasn't even going to *think* about kids without marriage first.

My mom had plenty of faults, but there was a reason I cut her too much slack. I'd seen firsthand, it hadn't been easy raising a kid alone with no dad in sight.

Now, looking at Jax, I didn't know what to say. Finally, I settled on, "Well, we're just joking, right?"

His gaze didn't waver. "I'm not. Are you?"

Oh, God. I hadn't expected him to say that. "Honestly, I'm not sure. I mean, I haven't given it a ton of thought."

This was actually true. Thoughts were a lot like dreams, and I was determined to live within my budget. I'd been doing that my whole life – keeping my dreams small so I didn't end up disappointed.

Across from me, Jax said, "Go ahead. Think about it. I'll wait."

I stared at him. "What do you mean?"

"I mean, I'm curious."

I gave him a look. "Yeah, me, too."

"Meaning?"

"Meaning..." I hesitated. "How about you? Have *you* thought of kids?" Trying not to make a fool of myself, I added, "Probably not, huh?"

Looking completely at ease, he said, "If I didn't think about it, I wouldn't've brought it up."

Once again, his reply surprised me. "So," I persisted, "how many?"

"It depends on the girl. I'm assuming she'd get a vote."

Something in his tone made me feel warm and wonderful all over, but I wasn't going to let him off the hook. "Oh come on," I protested, "that's a pretty vague answer."

"Alright. How about this?" He smiled. "Somewhere between three and ten."

Oh, boy. Talk about a loaded answer.

I did my best Jax imitation. "Big difference between three and ten."

He lifted his glass in a mock-toast. "Good point," he said before taking a drink.

I almost giggled. "Oh sure, just because *you* said it first."

"Exactly."

Slowly, it was dawning one me that I wasn't nearly as nervous as I'd been just fifteen minutes earlier. It wasn't even because of the wine. I'd ordered only one glass, and it was still mostly full.

Maybe it was because the sun had dipped past the horizon, leaving us basking in the warm glow of candlelight. Or maybe, it was the fact that Jax was showing more interest than I'd ever seen.

During all those days at the coffee shop, there'd been a definite spark and lots of laughs, too. But suddenly, things were seeming a lot more serious.

As I watched, he set down his glass and said, "So tell me, what's your story?"

I blinked. "My story? I don't have a story."

He cocked an eyebrow. "Could've fooled me."

"If you're talking my life story, trust me…" I looked heavenward. "You *don't* want to hear it."

Smiling, he leaned forward and said in a low, seductive voice, "I'll tell you mine if you tell me yours."

Wow. That sounded so sexy.

It *shouldn't've* sounded sexy. We were, after all, only discussing the exchange of information. I said, "Tit for tat, huh?"

His eyes filled with amusement. "If that's what you wanna call it."

But already, I was wishing I'd said that differently.

Tit? Seriously?

Where was that muzzle when I needed it?

Jax said, "Ladies first."

Absently, I said, "What?"

"You tell me. And then I'll tell you."

I might've argued, except my own story was nothing spectacular, and I figured I might get it out of the way. Still, I didn't want to give in too easily, so I said, "Only if I get a bonus question."

"A bonus question, huh?"

"Yes. A bonus question." I smiled. "In advance, like a down payment."

The corners of his mouth lifted. "You're a tough negotiator."

Hardly. But I wasn't going to let the opportunity pass. I smiled. "Then you should probably take the offer, before it expires or something."

"Nice," Jax said with a slow nod of approval. "So what's the question?"

There were a million things I might've asked, but there was something specific I was dying to know – something that had been nagging at me for a while now.

Eager to put it to rest, I said, "The night we met, *was* that blood on your shirt?"

The question got me another raised eyebrow. "Blood?"

"Well, I don't mean a lot, like there was an ax-murder or something. But after you returned from that errand, or wherever you went, I noticed these little spots on your shirt. They weren't there when you left, but they *were* there when you got back. And I was just wondering, you know, out of curiosity."

I gave a nervous laugh. "I know it probably wasn't blood, but it just made me wonder." I bit my lip. "So was it?"

He looked at me for a long moment. And then, he answered with a single word. "Yes."

CHAPTER 48

Against all reason, his answer caught me off guard. Over the last few weeks, I'd been telling myself that those little droplets surely had been something else.

What specifically, I wasn't sure.

Wine? Brandy? Cherry soda?

Apparently not.

And now, I didn't know what to say. I reached for my wine glass and took a little sip, followed by another. Maybe if I sipped long enough, he'd expand on the single-word answer.

But he didn't. And soon, my glass was half empty.

Slowly, I set it down. "Well, whose was it? I mean, it couldn't have been yours, because you looked fine, unless..." I gave him a hopeful look. "You cut yourself shaving?"

Yes, the idea was ridiculous. Still, stranger things had happened, right?

But already, Jax was shaking his head.

And that's when I knew. "The blood wasn't yours, was it?"

"No."

I swallowed. "So whose was it?"

"My brother's."

Finally, my shoulders relaxed. "Oh."

Maybe it shouldn't've been such a relief, but it was. After all, this was a lot better than hearing he'd tussled with a random stranger. Plus, Jaden *was* infinitely annoying. It was pretty easy to imagine them fighting. On that first night, I'd almost wanted to hit Jaden myself, not that I ever would.

I said, "So you and Jaden got in a fight?"

"No."

Okay, now I was really confused. "But you just said—"

His gaze remained on mine. "It wasn't Jaden."

"Oh." *Of course.* He had more than one brother. Allie had mentioned such a thing. I tried to recall the specifics. Were there five brothers? Or was it six?

I asked, "How many brothers do you have?"

"Four." He paused as if thinking. "And a half."

Rounding up, that meant there were six brothers total. I couldn't even imagine so many of them. Just the two I'd met personally were overwhelming enough.

I asked, "So, which one did you fight with?"

He smiled. "Who says I fought anyone?"

I gave him a look. "Well, there *was* blood involved."

"That?" He gave something like a laugh. "You haven't seen real blood 'til you bust a guy's nose."

I almost recoiled. "No thanks."

Jax grinned. "Don't like blood, huh?"

"Heck no." I paused. "Do you?"

"Eh, I don't mind it – not that I love it. But sometimes, stuff happens."

"What kind of stuff?"

"It depends."

"On what?"

He shrugged. "Whatever."

I just had to ask, "Do you guys fight a lot?"

He paused as if thinking. Finally, he replied, "No."

I studied his face. "I feel like I'm missing something."

Looking almost amused now, he said, "Wanna know what *I* think?"

"What?"

"I think it's *your* turn to talk."

"Huh?"

"You're supposed to be telling me *your* story, not the other way around."

I gave a sheepish laugh. *Busted.*

This time, I didn't bother protesting that I didn't have a story. After all, he'd been a pretty good sport about the blood thing. So instead, I said, "What do you want to know?"

"Everything."

I studied his face. He looked like he meant it. And the funny thing was, I *wanted* to tell him.

How strange was *that?*

CHAPTER 49

A half-hour later, I was still talking. And to my surprise, Jax was still listening.

"And so," I finished with a half-hearted laugh, "my mom got stuck with me anyway."

On the other side of the table, Jax *wasn't* laughing. "Stuck with you."

"Well, yeah," I said. "It's just a figure of speech. And really, it's kind of funny, don't you think?"

From the look on his face, he didn't agree, not that I could blame him. I'd just told him the reason I'd been born.

Twenty-some years earlier, my mom had gotten pregnant after a month-long fling with Roland Cassidy, one of the biggest rock stars on the planet. Thinking she'd just hit the jackpot, she'd begun planning for the baby – *and* the huge windfall that would surely follow. Money. Marriage. Possibly both.

Unlike me, my mom tended to think big.

Unfortunately for her, multiple paternity tests proved that I wasn't Roland Cassidy's child at all, which put a serious kink in her plans.

Across from me, Jax said, "But you were still named after him?"

"Well, yeah," I said. "She named me right after I was born – just the first name, not the last. Good thing, huh? Can you imagine how silly that would sound?" I rolled my eyes. "'Hi. I'm Cassidy Cassidy.'"

Jax still wasn't smiling.

Under the weight of his gaze, I started babbling. "Still, I'm almost surprised she didn't change it – the first name, I mean. After the tests came back negative, she was *so* mad." I paused. "Or at least that's what

I hear."

Now, Jax was frowning. "You heard it from who? Her?"

"Well, her and Tabitha."

"The chick who's *not* your aunt."

"Right." Already, I'd explained how my mom and Tabitha had been groupies together and how they'd both *loved* the idea of my mom being Mrs. Roland Cassidy.

Decades later, they probably *still* blamed me for not being the kid of some famous guy I'd never met. The whole story was hilarious and horrible all at the same time. And now, I'd shared it with Jax.

Had that been a mistake?

Maybe.

But he'd known from the beginning that my life wasn't all sweetness and apple pie. Plus, telling him what happened seemed important somehow, and not only because he'd asked.

I couldn't deny that I was falling for him. Probably, I'd begun falling on that very first night. And tonight, he'd been showing some serious interest – the kind of interest I never imagined even a couple of weeks ago.

If – heaven forbid – my family history was going to make him turn tail and run, I wanted him to do it now, and not later, when I'd be risking a broken heart.

Or maybe, the risk was already there.

After a long silence, he asked the question I'd been dreading. "So, who was the dad?"

"The real dad?" I bit my lip. "I don't know."

Again, he frowned. "She never told you?"

"Oh, she told me." I shrugged. "What she knew, anyway."

I went on to tell Jax that, as best my mom could recall, my real dad was some hot roadie who'd charmed the pants off her, literally.

Jax said, "This roadie? You ever get a name?"

I shook my head. "Nope."

"Why not?"

"Well, um…" I cleared my throat "…because my mom didn't ask."

Yup, that's me, the product of a quick coupling in the back of some semi.

But I wouldn't be sharing *that* detail with Jax. In fact, I was kind of sorry I'd heard it myself.

He gave me a serious look. "And your mom kept you?"

"As opposed to what?" I said. "Leaving me on the side of the road?"

"No," he said. "As opposed to adopting you out to a regular family."

I couldn't even imagine a regular family. My mom was an only child, and her parents were long dead. Apparently, my grandmother had been pretty wild herself. And as far as my grandfather, he hadn't been the kind to stick around.

I sighed. "Yeah, well, there were complications with the birth."

"So?"

"So my mom can't have any more kids, meaning it was me or nothing."

"Yeah?" His voice hardened. "Well maybe it should've been nothing."

I drew back. "What?"

"I'm just saying, she should've found you a better family."

"Hey, it wasn't *that* bad."

Jax gave me a look, but said nothing.

I so wanted him to understand. "I'm not saying it was all wonderful, but there were times she was really fun, and besides, even adoption is a crapshoot, right? I mean, there's no guarantee of happiness with that either."

As I spoke, I studied his face, searching for clues as to how he was taking this.

He wasn't happy. That much was obvious.

But I couldn't decide if he was unhappy because he felt sorry for me or because the whole story made him want to run for the hills.

When I couldn't stand the suspense any longer, I said, "So, are you horrified or what?"

He was still frowning. "I've heard worse."

"Really?"

He nodded. "Hell, I've *seen* worse. But that doesn't mean I like it."

"Oh." My shoulders slumped. "Yeah. Who would, right?"

With his gaze glued to mine, he leaned forward and said in a low voice, "You wanna know *why* I don't like it?"

"Why?"

"Because you deserve better." He reached out and covered my hand with his own. "And, I wanna make sure you get it."

I didn't know what to say. But as it turned out, I didn't need to say anything. After his surprising statement, he deliberately changed the subject, as if he were determined to put all of the ugliness behind us.

And yet, his words haunted me all the way through dessert, even as we discussed things that were a lot less intense – like our favorite foods, local landmarks, and places we'd like to visit.

When I asked him to tell me *his* story in return, he gave me the briefest rundown of details that I already knew.

Maybe that's all there was. Or maybe – and this was my best theory – he'd decided that we'd already had enough serious talk for one evening.

Thinking about it, I actually agreed. And yet, I made a mental note to ask him for more details the next time I saw him, which looked likely to be soon.

After dinner, we spent a couple of hours strolling along the nearby pier, listening to the waves lapping at the shoreline below.

That's when he kissed me for the very first time.

He was a great kisser, and I practically fell into him, savoring the feel of his arms around my back, and later, the sensation of his hands in my hair as his mouth moved against my own.

Yes, it was only a kiss, but it was enough to make my breath hitch and my knees turn to jelly.

All in all, our date was pure perfection, until the moment we pulled up to my apartment.

That's when things went seriously south.

CHAPTER 50

The car had barely rolled to a stop when I noticed a taxi parked out front. But that wasn't the thing that made me frown. It was the sight of my mom, leaning against the taxi, with a giant suitcase at her side.

I gave Jax a nervous glance. Sitting in the driver's seat, he was looking straight ahead, watching my mom with cold, unforgiving eyes.

I returned my attention to the taxi and was horrified to see that my mom was already hustling toward us, lugging the giant suitcase behind her.

Quickly, I turned to Jax and said, "Would you mind waiting while I talk to her?"

Technically, our date was finished, well, unless I invited him inside, that is. I was seriously tempted, in spite of the fact that I wasn't quite ready to get naked with him, as delicious as that sounded.

For the last hour, I'd had to remind myself repeatedly to take it slow, because I fully understood – mostly from watching the mistakes of my mom – how dangerous it could be to jump in the sack too soon.

But that didn't rule out hot chocolate or a nightcap, did it?

I didn't know. And now, I didn't have time to think – not with a crazy woman rushing toward us.

And she did look crazy.

Oh sure, she was still dressed to the nines in a short red dress and matching high heels. But her hair was a lot messier than I'd ever seen it, and she was yanking at the suitcase like it had done her a personal wrong.

I zoomed in on her face, and felt my eyebrows furrow. Had she been crying? It sure looked like it.

Without waiting for Jax's reply, I jumped out of the car and slammed the door behind me. I rushed forward, meeting my mom just a few paces away, where I asked, "What's wrong?"

She gave a loud sniffle. "You *know* what's wrong."

I shook my head. "No. I don't."

She looked at me like *I* was the crazy one. And then, she practically wailed, "Dominic's in the hospital!"

Oh. Right. Over the last few hours, I'd hardly given the guy a moment's thought. Worse, I didn't even feel guilty.

I barely knew him, and what I *did* know, I didn't like.

Still, for the sake of my mom, I said, "Yeah. I was really sorry to hear that."

"So," she said, "why didn't you come?"

"To where? The hospital?" I didn't get it. *What was I supposed to do? Bring the guy flowers or something?*

My mom was saying, "You were supposed to pick me up."

I was? "You mean from the hospital?"

She made a sound of frustration. "Forget the hospital."

Funny, I already had – well, until she showed up to remind me, that is.

I held up a hand. "Okay, back up. *Where* was I supposed to pick you up?"

"From my place." She gave another sniffle. "So I could stay with you."

"You *do* know, I don't have a car—" And then, I froze as the rest of her statement caught up with me. "Wait, what? You wanna stay with me?"

"Well, I can't stay at *my* place."

I had no idea what she meant. Beyond confused, I glanced at her suitcase. It was very big. That wasn't a good sign. Still, hoping for the best, I said, "You mean just overnight?"

"No," she said. "I mean 'til I find a new place."

Obviously, I was missing something. "But what's wrong with *your* place?"

"I already told you, it's not safe." Her voice rose. "I was robbed, remember?"

Oh. Finally, I understood.

I almost laughed with relief. "You weren't robbed. I just came by to get my things. You *did* see the note, right?"

She gave a hard sigh. "I don't mean *that* robbery. I mean what happened outside."

Stupidly, I said, "Outside where?"

"The penthouse. Didn't you get my message?"

"What message?"

"The one I left with your roommate. I talked to her and everything."

"You mean Allie?" *As if I had another roommate.*

"Yes, I mean Allie," she snapped. "What, she didn't tell you?"

I recalled Allie's cheerful little conversation with my mom. "How many times did you talk to her?"

"Just once."

And now, I understood. *Damn it.* I should've known.

Obviously, Allie's side of the conversation had been a lot more cheerful than my mom's. Still, I felt compelled to double-check. "Just the one time? Are you sure? I mean, you didn't talk to her again later?"

"How could I?" she demanded. "When I called back, you didn't even answer."

Right. Because I'd turned off my phone – at Allie's suggestion, no less.

And now, my mom was saying, "I waited at the penthouse, but you never came."

Again with the penthouse?

I was tempted to inform her that the place was just an apartment, but at the moment, I had bigger problems than annoying terminology. I pointed vaguely toward the taxi. "Well, obviously, you weren't waiting at your place the *whole* time."

"No kidding," she said. "I finally remembered that you don't have a car – I still don't know what *that's* about – so I called a cab, and here I am."

Yes. Here she was.

And *she* was the reason I didn't have a car, but that was beside the point.

She was still complaining. "And just so you know, we've been waiting here for two hours."

I gave her a confused look. "We?"

"Yes. Me and the driver."

I winced. "Two whole hours? Are you sure?"

I'd only taken a taxi like five times in my whole life, but even *I* knew, they didn't wait for free.

"Maybe even longer," she said. "And I'll need money for the fare."

Of course, she would.

She'd pulled a similar stunt when I'd moved down here. I'd barely unpacked the first box when she'd informed me that she needed money for last month's electric bill, the pool membership, and something called a parking allowance.

I didn't even know what that was. But like a dumb-ass, I'd actually given her the funds, which partly explained why my own finances were so pathetic.

She was still talking. "And I promised the driver a big tip to wait, so I hope you have cash."

I had *some* cash, but not a lot. I gave the taxi a nervous glance. Somewhere inside that thing, the meter was ticking. And the ticking sounded an awful lot like dollar bills going up in flames.

But that wasn't even my biggest problem. It was the fact I had to tell her something that she *wouldn't* want to hear.

She couldn't stay with me.

For starters, I didn't believe that whole robbery story. My mom loved drama and exaggerated like crazy. Plus, I knew firsthand that she lived in a pretty nice neighborhood.

I tried to think. This *had* to be a ploy. But for what?

And even if she *was* truly scared, she still couldn't stay with me. For one thing, Allie might murder her in her sleep.

Now, *that* was scary.

Crap. I *hated* drama.

I hated it with a white hot passion.

My mom knew this, which is probably why she was putting on such a show. *Anything to get her way, right?*

She said, "Well? Aren't you gonna say something?"

"Yes. I am." I looked her straight in the eye and just said it. "You can't stay."

She blinked. "What? Why not?"

"For all kinds of reasons. Just trust me, you can't."

"But why?" she repeated.

"Well, for one thing, because I have a roommate."

"So?"

"So it's her place, too."

"I don't care," she said. "*I'm* staying."

From behind me, a familiar male voice, low and steady, replied on my behalf. "The hell you are."

It was Jax. *Of course.*

I almost groaned out loud.

So much for no drama.

CHAPTER 51

I didn't turn to look. I didn't need to. I could feel his presence, like a wall behind me, a big, protective wall that I could lean against if I wanted to.

I was sorely tempted. But this wasn't his problem. It was mine.

I tried to think. *Maybe if I loaned her money for a hotel?*

But of course, it wouldn't *really* be a loan, because I'd never see the money again. Unfortunately, I didn't have a lot to spare.

My mom was glaring at Jax. "You're not the boss of her."

From behind me, he replied in that same steady voice, "Yeah? And neither are you."

I turned to give him a pleading look. "I can handle this, okay?"

His jaw tightened. "No."

"Sorry, what?"

"It's not okay."

I shook my head. "What do you mean?"

"I mean," he said, "you don't have to take this shit."

Already, my mom was sputtering, "Shit? You mean me?" She made a scoffing sound. "Well, this is just terrific."

I whirled back to her and said, "He wasn't talking about you. He was talking about the situation."

"He was not!" she said. "He hates me."

Gee, I wonder why.

Still, I said, "Oh come on. He doesn't even know you."

From behind me, Jax said, "I know plenty."

"Hey!" my mom barked. "What's that supposed to mean?"

God, what a nightmare. I couldn't help but recall the last time the three of us had been standing along some roadside. *That* time, she'd been turning on the charm. Now, she was totally unhinged.

I wanted to scream in frustration. Surely, there *had* to be a middle ground *somewhere* between humping his leg and screaming like a banshee.

Then again, she'd never been great at moderation.

Of course, it didn't help that Jax was shoveling fuel onto the fire.

My mom looked to me and demanded, "Well?"

"Well what?"

"What did he mean by that?"

"I don't know," I said through gritted teeth, "but I'm sure it wasn't as bad as you think."

From behind me, Jax said, "Wanna bet?"

Damn it. I hated this. To think, it had been such a wonderful evening, and now, it was going to hell in a handbasket. And the longer this went on, the worse it would get. I just knew it.

I *so* didn't want that to happen.

I turned and gave Jax an apologetic look. "Listen, if you want to go, I totally understand."

From behind me, my mom called out, "Yeah! And that's a hint in case you didn't get it."

I cringed. Technically, her statement was true. It *had* been a hint, but not in the way she made it sound. Yes, I wanted him to leave, but not because I didn't want his company. Mostly, I wanted to spare him from drama overload.

Plus, this was all too embarrassing for words.

I turned and I told my mom, "I wasn't *telling* him to leave. I was just letting him know he *could* leave if he wanted to."

From behind me, Jax said, "Good."

I turned to stare up at him. "What?"

"Good," he repeated, "because I'm not going anywhere."

Shit. "Why not?"

He glanced toward my mom. "You gotta ask?"

My heart was racing, and my palms were sweaty. I had no idea what to do. But then, like magic, the most wonderful idea presented itself. I whirled back to my mom and forced a smile. "I know. What about Tabitha?"

She stiffened. "What about her?"

"You could stay at *her* place."

"No. I can't," she replied. "I'm on her shit-list." She looked to Jax and said, "Thanks to *you*."

"But wait," I said, "what does he have to do with it?"

She glared past me to tell Jax, "Not that *you* care, but your security goon broke her arm." She looked back to me and said, "She's been pissed at me ever since."

I froze. "Tabitha broke her arm?"

"No," my mom said. "The *goon* broke her arm. Didn't you hear me?"

I *had* heard, but I didn't really believe it. And yet, I couldn't help but recall Jax threatening such a thing when Tabitha had balked at leaving the party.

I turned back to Jax and asked, "Is that true?"

From behind me, my mom snapped, "Of course it's true. I just told you."

I was still looking at Jax. His expression was unreadable as he stared down at me.

I bit my lip. "Is it?"

He fixed me with a piercing gaze. "Is that a serious question?"

Was it? Obviously, I'd offended him just by asking. And yet, I *did* need an answer. "Well, it would be nice to know."

He looked at me for another long moment before saying in a tight voice, "Alright. The answer's no."

My shoulders sagged in relief.

But then, he added, "Sprained, maybe. But not broke."

I blinked. "What?"

From behind me, my mom said, "Yeah, but she still had to wear a sling."

I turned back to my mom. "So it *wasn't* broken?"

She straightened. "Actually, it was worse."

Huh? Unless the so-called goon had ripped off the arm entirely and beat Tabitha with it, I couldn't imagine what my mom meant. I asked, "How could it be worse?"

"It was *almost* broken," she said, "which meant she didn't even get a cast out of the deal."

Oh, for God's sake. "But isn't that a good thing?"

"No, it's not good." She gave a snort of derision. "Seriously, who wants to sign a sling?" She shuddered. "It was *so* ugly, too. She was totally screwed."

All I could do was stare. *Was she serious? She looked serious.*

"And then today," my mom continued, "Dominic was mugged right outside the penthouse, so I *can't* go back. It's not safe."

"Wait a minute," I said, "so *Dominic* was robbed, not you?"

"Well, I was *with* him," she said. "It was terrifying. There we are, standing right outside the penthouse door, and these guys come out of nowhere and drag him off like he was nothing."

Okay, *that* sounded pretty far-fetched. "You're kidding."

"No," she insisted. "He's yelling. I'm yelling. No one's helping at all. And fifteen minutes later, where do I find him? Bleeding in the bushes. He's in the hospital, you know."

"Yes," I said through clenched teeth. "I know. But did they catch the guys who did it?"

Her lips formed a pout. "No."

My gaze narrowed. "How many guys?"

"Two." Her voice picked up steam. "But maybe a lot more."

"Okaaaaaay." I reached up to rub the back of my neck. "These two guys, what did they look like?"

"How should I know?" she said. "They were wearing masks."

Well, this just got better and better. "What kind of masks?"

"I dunno, ski masks or something."

"And *when* did this happen?"

"Today, like I said. So you see why I can't go home, right?"

I tried to think. The whole story sounded like a load of bunk. And yet, it wasn't *completely* impossible. After all, Dominic wasn't an average Joe.

But let's say I *did* believe her. *What then?*

Yes, it would be awful to have your — well, whatever Dominic was — dragged off your doorstep. But I also knew that Dominic wasn't exactly an upstanding guy.

Assuming the story was true, maybe there was a reason he'd been dragged away. He was in a risky line of work. Probably, he had plenty of enemies. For all *I* knew, he got dragged off once a month.

Was I being callous? Maybe. But somehow, this whole Florida adventure had me seeing things differently, at least when it came to my mom.

She and I were still going back and forth when Jax strode past us, heading toward the cab. I felt my brow wrinkle in confusion.

He wasn't leaving, was he?

CHAPTER 52

No. He *couldn't* be leaving. If he were planning to leave, he'd simply hop in his own car and drive off.

In truth, I was surprised he hadn't already.

And yet, I *was* curious. Apparently, so was my mom. Together, we watched as he rapped on the cab's driver's side window. When it slid down, he exchanged a few inaudible words with the driver and then strode back to where my mom and I were standing.

He looked to my mom and said, "There's a room at the Plaza in your name. The driver knows where to drop you."

She frowned. "You're just trying to get rid of me."

"Damn straight," he said.

"Well forget it," she shot back. "I'm not going anywhere. I see what you're doing, you know."

"Yeah? What's that?"

"You're trying to turn my own daughter against me."

He gazed down at her with obvious contempt. "Seems to me you've done that yourself."

"What do you mean?" she demanded.

"I mean," he said, "what kind of woman whores out her own fucking daughter?"

I gasped.

And so did my mom. She sputtered, "It wasn't like that!"

"No?" he said. "Then tell me. How was it?"

"It's just a dating service," she said. "You don't *always* have to sleep with them."

He grimaced. "Is that so?"

"Of course," she said. "It's like any other date. It doesn't always end with sex." She flicked her head in my direction and said, "And even if it did, Lord knows she could use the experience."

Oh, for God's sake. I practically yelled, "Just stop, okay?"

My mom turned back to me and said, "Oh come on. You know it's true."

Okay, so I hadn't been with a ton of guys, but only because I knew where that road led, and it *wasn't* good. Still, I took a deep breath and forced some calm into my voice. "I'm not discussing this." *Especially now, in front of a guy I'm so crazy about it.*

But it was too late. My mom was on a roll. "And, do you *seriously* want to marry the first person you fuck?"

No. What I *wanted* to do was dig a hole and throw myself into it. Or hell, maybe I'd just toss in my mom and call it good.

Through gritted teeth, I said, "I'm not a virgin if that's what you're implying."

She gave me a thin smile. "Yeah, well, you might as well be. When *I* was your age, I had tons of experience." She looked back to Jax and said, "And I don't see why *you're* on such a high horse. There's nothing wrong with wanting a pretty girl on your arm."

"Yeah?" he said. "How about paying one to ride your cock?"

At the image, I felt a rush of heat – some good, but mostly bad.

The good? It happened to be Jax's cock I was thinking of, and the image of us together sent a bolt of heat straight to my core.

And the bad? I was obviously losing my mind. I mean, seriously, why on Earth was I thinking of this *now?*

After all, I had a hole to dig and no shovel.

Damn it.

When my mom's only reply was a loose shrug, Jax persisted, "Do you see anything wrong with *that?*" His tone grew harder and colder, and just a little bit scary. "And what if the girl's your own daughter?" He shook his head. "What the hell's the matter with you?"

Listening, I couldn't help but flinch. He made everything sound so terrible, which, sadly, it was.

But my mom wasn't flinching. "Oh, please," she said. "Let's all be honest here. You wouldn't even be fucking her if she was ugly."

I yelled, "Will you just shut up!" I wasn't even sure who I was yelling at. *Her? Him? Both?*

My mom turned to me and said, "No. I will not shut up. I'm saying this for your own good."

I gave a bitter laugh. "Oh, please. You've never done anything for *my* good."

"That's not true!" she said. "I've done lots of things."

"Really?" I crossed my arms. "Like what?"

"Well, I *had* you for one thing."

"Yeah. And you only did *that* to snag a rock star."

Her mouth opened, but she made no reply. It suddenly struck me that this was the first time I'd actually come out and accused her of having me just to trap some rich, famous guy.

But she shouldn't've been surprised. After all, I'd heard the story straight from her. And Tabitha, too. Repeatedly.

Especially on my birthdays.

My mom whirled to Jax. "You made her say that!"

I yelled, "He did not!"

Unlike us, Jax wasn't yelling. With a long, cold look, he told my mom, "Let's get one thing straight. I don't 'make' her do anything. And I'm not gonna either."

"Well, goodie for you," my mom muttered. She turned back to me and said, "So, you're turning me out on the street? Is that it?"

"No." I made a sound of frustration. "But I do think a hotel *would* be better."

Her mouth tightened. "Oh yeah? So who's paying?"

Before I could reply, Jax said, "Me."

I cringed. I didn't want him to pay. He'd already paid enough. I looked to my mom and said, "No. He's not. But if you don't have the money, *I'll* pay."

How, I wasn't sure. Maybe I could get a loan from Allie? Was she even home? I doubted it. I didn't see her truck, and besides, if she *were* home, she'd probably be down here already.

Hell, she could join the neighbors who were openly gawking from their porches.

Jax's voice cut through the noise. "It's already paid for. And so's the cab." He looked to my mom and said, "But the offer expires in one minute. So take it while you can."

My mom turned and gave the cab a long, speculative look. "What about the tip?"

I blurted out, "I'll get it."

"No," Jax said in a deceptively calm voice, "you won't, because I already took care of it."

My mom was still looking at the taxi. "How many nights at the Plaza?"

I wanted to slap her. "Just one. Jeez, what do you think?"

Her chin lifted. "I think it's not enough."

Jax said, "It's paid for a week. After that, you're on your own."

My mom gave it some thought. "My room, it's an ocean-view, right?"

In a tight voice, Jax replied, "They're *all* ocean-view."

Now, she was giving him the squinty eye. "What floor is it on? Is it on the top floor?"

I snapped, "Does it matter?"

"It might," she said. "You know, for safety and all that."

Jax told her, "The longer you stay, the lower it gets. Keep it up, and you'll be in the basement."

And that's what did it.

Thirty seconds later, she and her suitcase were settled back inside the cab. I watched in mortified silence as it pulled away, leaving us staring after it.

When it finally disappeared, I took a nervous look around. Almost every porch was occupied with people I didn't even know. But they knew me. *Now*, anyway.

I felt like running, or at the very least, hiding. But soon, I didn't need to, because Jax wrapped me in his arms and pulled me close. His voice was quiet in my hair. "You alright?"

I sighed against him. "Shouldn't I be asking *you* that?"

"Hell no."

I leaned back to gaze up at him. "But aren't you tired of my drama?" *Heaven knows, I was.*

"It's not *your* drama," he said, "so forget it."

I gave a weak laugh. "Easy for you to say." I took another quick look around. My apartment windows were dark, and I still saw no sign of Allie's truck.

I leaned back into him and pressed my cheek against his shirt. "Do you want to come up? Like for a drink or something?"

His grip tightened, and I felt his lips brush against my hair. His voice was quiet. "Yeah. I do." But then, he let go and took a step back. "But I'm not gonna."

Suddenly, the night felt very cold. "Why not?"

"Because you're not thinking straight."

"What do you mean?"

He looked toward his car. "I should go."

It felt like a brush-off. *Was it?*

And if so, was it any wonder? He'd done so much for me. And all he'd gotten in return was trouble. No wonder he wanted to leave.

I blew out a long, unsteady breath. "Listen, I want to tell you something…"

He held up a hand. "Don't."

"Don't what?"

"Don't tell me."

"Why not?" I asked.

"Because I know what you're gonna say, and I don't wanna hear it."

I hesitated. "What do you think I'm gonna say?"

I knew what *other* girls would say. They'd be begging him to come upstairs, and not just for drinks.

Even now, I was sorely tempted. And who could blame me? In the dim light of the streetlamp, he looked like every girl's fantasy.

He was tall and strong, with a face to die for. And if that weren't enough, just a few paces away, his pricey car was just another reminder that he was rich beyond all reason.

But these weren't the things that had me longing to see him upstairs. Rather, it was something *inside* him – the person he was regardless of where he lived or what he drove. And he'd just come to my rescue yet again.

I hadn't asked him to, but he had.

Now, I owed him. Cripes, even *before* tonight, I owed him more than I could ever possibly repay.

Desperate to let him know that I wasn't blind to everything he'd done, I looked deep into his eyes and said, "But I owe you—"

"Stop." His expression darkened. "You remember the deal, right?"

"What deal?"

"You were supposed to forget all that."

"Yeah, and I'm trying. I mean, I did." I gave a nervous laugh. "But now I owe you again."

His jaw clenched. "You don't."

"Oh come on," I said. "You're paying for my mom's hotel room."

"Yeah. And I did it for myself, not you. So like I said, forget it."

His words made no sense. I asked, "But why would it be for you?"

"I've got my reasons."

"What reasons?" I persisted.

Again, he looked to his car. "I should go."

And yet, he still wasn't moving. Was that a *good* sign? It had to be, right?

I edged closer and lowered my voice. "At least let me say it." I tried to smile. "Thank you."

He muttered, "Fuck."

Startled, I drew back. "What?"

"Nothing. Just forget it, alright?"

I stiffened. "Forget what, exactly?"

When he made no reply, I thought back to our dinner, when he'd been so warm and wonderful. And then, there'd been that kiss on the pier.

Tonight, I'd felt the beating of his heart. I'd heard something new in his voice when he said my name. And even before that kiss, I'd seen something in his eyes, something that looked an awful lot like love.

But of course, that was crazy, just like it was crazy to think that I might love him, too. After watching my mom fall in and out of love for so many years, I wasn't even sure I believed in love, at least not this quickly.

When the silence stretched out, I asked, "Are you gonna tell me what's wrong? Or do I need to guess?"

"Alright. You wanna know what's wrong?"

From the look on his face, I wasn't so sure. Still, I nodded and then braced myself for whatever he meant to say.

But when he spoke, his words – just four of them – made no sense at all.

CHAPTER 53

Allie was still staring. "Were those his *exact* words?"

I nodded. "Swear to God."

"You're too fucking beautiful?" She frowned. "What does that even mean?"

At the memory of those four maddening words, I sank deeper into the sofa. "Got me."

"And then, he just left?"

"Yup."

Sitting in the nearby armchair, she asked, "Did he at least kiss you goodbye?"

At the memory of him striding to his car and driving off into the night, I almost wanted to cry. "Nope."

She hesitated. "How about a hug?"

"Cripes, I barely got a 'see you later'."

She was still frowning. "What an asshole."

I couldn't quite agree, not after everything he'd done. Still, I wasn't thrilled. It was the morning after our date, and I'd just spent the last hour telling Allie everything that had happened.

There was only one detail I'd glossed over, and that had to do with Allie herself. But I did need to address it.

As if reading something in my expression, she said, "Go ahead. Get it over with."

"Get what over with?"

"The yelling. Or whatever you're gonna do."

"Well…" I sighed. "If you're talking about the thing with my mom's message, I guess I *am* a little curious."

She made a scoffing sound. "You are not."

"What?"

"You *know* why I did it, so you can't be curious. If anything, you're just ticked off." She paused. "On second thought, you're not even that."

I gave her a look. "Oh, really?"

"Really," she said. "You just feel like you should be."

"Yeah, because you lied to me."

"I did not," she replied. "Name *one* thing I said that wasn't true."

I tried to recall exactly what she'd relayed after talking to my mom. Only two details came to mind. Dominic was in the hospital, and my mom wanted me to call her. Technically, both of these things were true, but that was hardly the point.

"Okay," I said, "so maybe you didn't lie-lie, but there was still a ton you left out."

She looked entirely unrepentant. "Yeah. No kidding."

I tried again. "I'm just saying, it didn't really help, not in the long run, anyway."

"Why?" Allie laughed. "Because your mom caused a big ol' scene?"

"Yes, actually."

"Trust me, she would've done that anyway."

"Oh come on," I said. "You don't know that."

"Wanna bet?" Allie said. "The only difference was, she caused it *after* the date instead of before." She smiled. "So you're welcome."

Against all logic, I wanted to smile back. *And* I wanted to argue. In the end, I settled on muttering, "Oh, shut up."

But Allie wasn't done. "Wanna know the only thing I regret?"

I was almost afraid to ask. "What?"

"That I didn't realize that she'd just show up like that." Allie gave me an evil grin. "Because if I had, I would've slashed her tires."

Surely, she was joking.

But the joke was on her. I gave her a smug smile. "She doesn't *have* tires. She took a cab, remember?"

"Fine, whatever. I would've slashed the cab's tires."

Whether it was a joke or not, I was determined to make my point. "Look, I know you *think* you were doing me a favor—"

"I *was* doing you a favor."

"Yeah, I know you think that. But all I'm saying is, I can handle it on my own."

She practically snorted, "Oh yeah?"

"Yes. Definitely."

"That's such a crock," she said. "If you could 'handle' your mom, we wouldn't be living in this stupid place at all."

I sat back, surprised by her words. I wasn't even sure what she meant. I paused for a long moment before saying, "What, you don't like it here?"

Her only answer was a loose shrug.

My stomach sank. So she *didn't* like it? If so, that was news to me. I tried to think. What, specifically, didn't she like?

The apartment?

The city?

The state?

What?

I honestly didn't get it.

She adored the apartment. I'd seen the look on her face when we'd first gone through it. Regardless of what she was saying now, she loved it as much as I did.

As far as the city, she'd mentioned more than once how much she enjoyed living near the water. And, she'd been having a blast discovering a new town – or so I'd thought.

As far as the state, just last week she'd mentioned that she was trying to lure her parents down here from Alaska, and not just for a visit.

You didn't do that when you hated a place, did you?

Allie still hadn't answered, and for the first time, I noticed the dark circles under her eyes. Last night, I'd heard her come in, but I'd stayed in my room, mostly because I hadn't wanted to burden her with my sob story just before bed.

Now, I was wondering what I'd missed.

And she *still* hadn't answered my question.

I studied her face. "Do you? Hate it, I mean?"

She frowned. "Well, I hate *him*. Does that count?"

"Who? Jaden?"

Her only answer was another shrug.

I felt my gaze narrow. "What did he do?"

"Nothing."

Oh, it was something, alright. I could see it all over her face. And now, I was kicking myself for not noticing it sooner.

Desperate for some clue, I said, "He's not as bad as your last boss, is he?"

"I dunno." Now, she looked almost ready to cry. "It's just different, that's all."

My heart clenched, and I felt awful for yapping so long about myself when Allie had problems of her own, serious problems the way it looked. "Tell me," I said, "what did he do?"

"Nothing," she repeated. "He's just an ass, that's all."

"Well, he had to do *something* if you're about to cry."

She stiffened. "I'm not about to cry. I'm just mad, that's all."

It was a lie, and a big one, too. This was Allie. She might yell, but she almost never cried.

Wondering if she needed a hug, I made a move to get off the couch. "Allie, seriously—"

She held up her hands. "Sit. I'm fine, okay? The guy's just a jackass, like I said."

"Yeah, I know. But can you give me an example?"

She gave a shaky laugh. "I dunno...like he's always stealing my pens."

I paused. Yes, that would be irritating, but it was nothing to cry over. *Was it?* Still, I said, "That *does* sound pretty annoying."

"And he's totally rude."

I tried to laugh. "Now, *that* I can believe."

"Do you know," she said, "he's always leaving stuff on my desk?"

"Like what?" I asked.

"I dunno." She sighed. "Snack wrappers, socks..."

"Socks? Seriously?"

"Oh yeah," she said. "And do you wanna know what it was last night?"

So *that's* where she'd been last night? *Working?* No wonder she was tired. More concerned than ever, I asked, "What?"

"A freaking ski mask. Can you believe it?"

I froze.

No. I couldn't believe it.

Not at first.

But then, when I thought about it – *seriously* thought about it – everything made a lot more sense.

And this is why nine hours later, I was heading to a certain beachfront mansion, intending to get some answers – or kill someone trying.

CHAPTER 54

I said to the driver, "It's coming up on the left."

"I know," he said, sounding slightly peeved. "I've got a GPS."

Right. He *had* said that. And even from the back seat, I could see the display with my own two eyes. "I know. I'm just giving you a heads-up."

"Well, don't," he said. "It's distracting."

Back in Nashville, I knew lots of people who used ride-sharing services. I almost never did. And why? Because I had the worst luck with drivers.

All the time, my friends would be telling me about getting drivers that were perfectly nice and normal. But me? I was totally cursed.

Of course, today I might've cursed myself by looking like a bum or maybe even a bag lady. Probably, the guy was worried I wouldn't pay him. He definitely thought I was crazy.

On this, he wasn't wrong. Obviously, I *had* lost my mind. But seriously, was it any wonder?

Today had totally sucked, and the worst part hadn't even happened yet.

After that ski mask comment, I'd tried like heck to pretend that everything was fine, which of course, it wasn't.

Still, I'd been determined to not upset Allie further, which meant that I'd stewed silently all morning and then all afternoon while waiting for her to leave so I could make this little trip on my own.

No matter what happened, I vowed, I wasn't going to drag her further into my drama. Hell, I'd already dragged her halfway across the country. That was bad enough.

Finally, a couple of hours before nightfall, she'd left to run a few errands. And that's when I'd gone into action.

I'd thrown on shabby sweatpants and a paint-splattered T-shirt. I didn't even bother with the makeup. As far as my hair, I'd washed it, but that's about it.

And now, here I was, almost at my destination.

I gave the GPS a nervous glance. Was the driver even watching? Apparently not, because he passed the house without even slowing down.

I said, "You missed it."

"I didn't miss it," he said. "I'm just looking for a place to park."

"You don't *need* to park. They have a driveway."

"I don't *do* driveways.

Good Lord.

Finally, he stopped like five houses away and pulled off to the side. "That'll be nineteen dollars," he said.

"But wait," I protested, "I'm not even at the house."

He made a sound of annoyance. "What, you want me to back up?"

"Yes," I told him. "And you promised to wait."

"Waiting's extra."

"I know," I said through gritted teeth. "You already told me."

"And I'll need the money now," he said, "in case you don't come out."

"Oh, I'm coming out."

He turned to look at me. "Yeah. In a police car."

I was glaring at him, now. "What's that supposed to mean?"

"Look around," he said. "This is a fancy-ass neighborhood. If you think they're not calling the cops, you're nuts."

I gritted out, "They're not calling the cops."

Or, at least, I sure hoped not.

Ignoring me, the guy said, "And remember, I'll need the waiting money, too."

"Fine," I snapped, digging out the bills and tossing them over the seat. "And don't bother backing up. I'll just walk."

He made a scoffing sound. "Yeah, good luck with *that*."

Okay, so I was wearing flip-flops. But people walked in flip-flops all the time. They *were* shoes, after all.

As I shoved open my car door, I reminded the guy, "I'll be back in an hour, maybe less."

When he grunted out some sort of acknowledgement, I grabbed my plastic grocery-bag full of clothes, got out of the car, and slammed the door behind me.

And then, I started walking.

It was still light outside, but just barely, and I felt incredibly self-conscious as I strode – making flip-floppity noises all the way – toward the front door of that all-too familiar mansion.

Today was Sunday, and it was nearly nightfall. I was almost certain that he'd be here. If not, I vowed, I'd just wait on his front steps like any other crazy person.

No matter what, I was determined to see him. Unfortunately, there was one thing I hadn't counted on – seeing someone else first. And *who* was that someone?

It was Morgan, that psychotic ex-girlfriend I'd met at his party.

I stopped in mid-flop. I'd been walking with my head down and didn't even see her until I was nearly in the driveway.

From what I could tell, she'd just come out of the front door. Or maybe, or she'd been ringing the doorbell and had just given up. Either way, she wasn't facing the house. She was facing *away* from it.

And she was staring.

At me.

Of course.

CHAPTER 55

Our gazes locked, and I felt myself swallow. *Damn it.* It was too late to run, and I had nowhere to hide. The driveway was empty, and there was only a single car parked out front – hers, apparently.

Of all the things I'd planned for, this *wasn't* on the list. I'd been planning to see Jax. I'd even been prepared to see Jaden, if only to give him a piece of my mind for whatever he'd done to Allie.

But nowhere in my half-baked plans, had I ever envisioned showing up to find Morgan lying in wait, like some kind of redheaded spider.

Yes, I *did* realize that she wasn't waiting for *me*. But that didn't make it any easier when a slow, evil smile spread across her face.

I knew exactly why she was smiling.

I looked like absolute crap.

And *she* didn't.

She was wearing a lacy black mini-skirt and a cropped white T-shirt. The skirt was very short and showed off her long, tanned legs. As for the shirt, it was cropped obnoxiously high, revealing a taut stomach and a shocking amount of under-boob.

Obviously, she'd skipped the bra entirely. Even from a distance, I could see the outlines of her nipples – perky little bastards – poking up against the thin cotton of her shirt.

Comparing *her* outfit to mine, the only thing we had in common was the fact that we both wore sandals unsuitable for running.

But where *my* sandals were cheap and flat, and yes, too darn floppy, *hers* were high and sexy, with chunky heels and little white straps that wrapped around her ankles.

As I stared stupidly from the sidewalk, I asked myself the obvious question. *What on Earth had I been thinking?* When getting ready for this little adventure, I'd been looking to make a point, but not to Morgan.

Cripes, if I'd known *she* was here, I wouldn't've come at all.

I still hadn't moved. And neither had she. But I couldn't exactly turn back now, so instead, I squared my shoulders and marched forward, well, as much as I *could* march in flip-flops anyway.

Soon, she was moving, too, striding straight toward me. We met in the middle, somewhere on the private walkway that led to the front door.

She gave my clothes a long, derisive look. "Well, don't you look precious."

I gave her a look right back. "Not as precious as you." I glanced down. "By the way, your boob popped out."

She gave me a smug smile. "It's *supposed* to look like that."

I hesitated. "Actually, I don't think so."

Finally, she looked down. "Oh."

I hadn't been kidding. While striding along, her shirt had hiked up on the left side, exposing a lot more than she probably intended.

As she yanked the shirt back in place, I looked toward the house and tried to think. *What now?*

Morgan said, "He's not home, you know."

Obviously, she meant Jax, but I'd be a fool to believe her. "I'll check for myself, thanks."

"Check all you want," she said, "but no one's gonna answer the door."

"Fine. In that case, I'll leave a note."

It was a stupid thing to say. I had no pen. I had no paper. Mostly, I was just stalling in hopes that she'd just leave already.

But she didn't.

Instead, when I sidestepped around her, she turned and followed after me as I headed toward the front door. When I reached it, she was still on my heels, even as I rang the bell.

From behind me, she said, "I already told you, he's not home."

I ignored her and rang the bell again.

No one answered.

Morgan said, "Told ya." She edged closer until she was standing right beside me. She was so close, I could smell her perfume – something floral with a hint of musk.

I gave her an irritated glance. The way it looked, she wasn't going anywhere.

Well, this was just great.

How humiliating was this? Let's say Jax pulled up right now. What would he see? Not just one girl, but *two*.

One of those girls looked like sex on the beach.

And then there was me.

What did *I* look like? *Diving in dumpsters?*

Probably.

While getting ready, I'd been in the worst mood, especially after pretending for so many hours that everything was fine. I hadn't *planned* to dress like this, not at first. But then, I'd been so exasperated – not only by the thing with the ski mask, but also because of Jax's odd comment from the previous night.

Too fucking beautiful?

Seriously?

Oh, I'd show him beautiful alright. And maybe, if I goaded him, he'd tell me exactly what he meant – *after* I confronted him about that robbery.

I needed an explanation, but not in front an audience. I looked to Morgan and said, "Don't you have someplace to be?"

"Sure." She smiled. "And I'm already here."

Yes. She was.

I tried to think. What if I left now and came back in an hour? By then, it would be surely dark. Would that be better? Or worse?

And what if Morgan didn't leave? If Jax returned while I was gone, what on Earth would she tell him?

I could only imagine. So with a sigh, I sank down on the top step to wait.

To my infinite frustration, Morgan did the exact same thing. And then, she stretched out her long legs in front of her, as if determined to show them off to their best advantage.

Ignoring her, I pulled out my phone and checked the time. I'd left the car exactly fifteen minutes ago. Assuming that the driver was still waiting, and I only prayed he was, I had only forty-five minutes until I'd need to run back with more cash – cash I could hardly spare.

We sat in silence for several minutes before Morgan said, "Hey, do you wanna hear why we broke up?"

The question caught me off guard. *Yes. I did.*

But I didn't trust her one bit, so I gave a tight shrug and made no reply.

"Get this," she said. "He told me I wasn't 'wife material.' Can you freaking believe it?"

No. I couldn't.

Slowly, I turned to study her face. She didn't *look* like she was lying. But then again, how would I know? "And you're telling me this, why?"

With a little smirk, she eyed me up and down. "Because you're not either."

I stiffened. In spite of my best efforts, the comment got under my skin.

Probably, it was because I saw the truth of her statement. And it had nothing to do with my attire. Mostly, it was because Jax and I were from two totally different worlds, worlds that would never mesh, not long-term, anyway.

If he were just an average Joe, it might be different. But he wasn't average, not in any conceivable way. I loved everything about him, and yet, I couldn't help hating what that meant for us.

It's not that I was shopping for a husband. It's just that, well, I wasn't shopping for a fling. And this left me where, exactly?

Out in the cold, that's where.

When I made no reply, Morgan said, "I mean, sure you cleaned up nice for the party and all, but if *this* is your everyday look..." She gave a little shudder and said, "...well, I'm just saying, he's not gonna marry a slob."

If I cared one iota what she thought of me, I might've pointed out that I wasn't *always* a slob. But all I said was, "Maybe he won't marry anyone. Maybe he's not even the marrying type."

"Oh, he is," she said. "A few months ago, I heard him talking to Jaden, telling him to stop whoring around unless he wanted his dick to fall off."

Well, that was an image I didn't need.

Still, I managed to reply, "Just because he doesn't want Jaden to be a man-whore, that doesn't mean he's looking to settle down."

"Wanna bet?" she said. "He's got this checklist and everything."

That made me pause. "What kind of checklist?"

"It's not a *real* checklist. I'm just saying he's got criteria, you know." She raised a hand and started counting off on her fingers. "Educated, smart. Not too pretty."

I frowned. "Wait, what?"

"Yeah," she said. "I mean, don't get me wrong – he's not into trolls or anything. But he doesn't go for the knockouts." She gave a dramatic sigh. "That's probably why he dumped me."

I was staring now. "Are you serious?"

"Sure." She glanced down. "I mean, look at me. I'm a knockout, right?"

Yes. She was. But the rest of her story was too unbelievable for words. And besides, her own attire was proof enough that she was lying.

Now, I looked *her* up and down. "Good thing you're hiding your light under a bushel."

She looked around. "What bushel?"

I tried again. "I'm just saying, if he truly had something against pretty girls, you wouldn't be dressed so…" *How to put this?*

She smiled. "Slutty?"

"Um…"

"That's on purpose," she said. "I'm not going for *Jax* anymore."

"Oh?"

"Oh yeah. He's a lost cause. I'm going for Jaden. He likes 'em slutty." *Good grief.*

I was still debating what to say in response when a familiar sports car pulled into the drive. It was the same car Jax had been driving during our date last night.

And yet, I wasn't positive it was him. After all, the brothers did have a history of borrowing each other's vehicles.

I held my breath as I stared at the car. Who would be getting out? *Jax? Or Jaden?*

Turns out, it was both.

CHAPTER 56

I was already on my feet, and so was Morgan. But where *she* scampered forward, I stood still, watching awkwardly as both guys stopped to stare – not at Morgan, but at me.

It was easy to guess what *Jaden* was thinking, because it was written all over his face. *What the hell is that psycho on the steps wearing?*

As for Jax, his gaze was guarded, like he wasn't quite sure what he was seeing at his own front door. But then, a split-second later, he was striding forward, even as Morgan, with a happy squeal, launched herself into Jaden's arms.

Whether his arms closed around her or not, I couldn't say, because already, I'd returned my full attention to Jax, who, with long, steady strides, was rapidly closing the distance between us.

Soon, he was up the steps and at my side. In a low voice, he asked, "You okay?"

Heat flooded my face. "Of course, I'm okay."

He looked down at my clothes, and his eyebrows furrowed. "You sure?"

Damn it. None of this was going how I envisioned. "Yeah, I'm fine. It's just, I dunno…" *How to put this?*

With obvious concern, he studied my face. "Tell me."

Crap. I hated this. I hadn't come to make him concerned. I'd come to make a point – and to get some answers. I sighed. "We need to talk."

He frowned. "About what?"

Good Lord, did I *really* need to explain? Even if I *hadn't* heard about that stupid ski mask, I'd surely have *something* to say about how our date ended last night.

But just like always, everything was so terribly complicated because I owed him. Even now, he was paying for my mom's hotel room. With an effort, I reminded myself that no such room would be needed if it weren't for that masked mugging.

And I wasn't naive. This was Florida, not Alaska. The weather was hot and humid. No one needed a ski mask – not for anything good. And just how many people in the city owned ski gear at all?

Nearly none. I'd bet my life on it.

I crossed my arms. "Do you want to talk *here*? Or inside?"

He turned to scan the street. "How'd you get here?"

The question felt like an accusation, and suddenly, I couldn't help but wonder if he *liked* the fact that I had no car. After all, girls with no cars seldom made pesky little visits like this.

I lifted my chin. "I got a ride."

His expression darkened. "From who?"

I really didn't want to say. It was, after all, pretty pathetic that I'd had to bribe a stranger to bring me here. On top of *that*, I had only twenty more minutes until the guy left me stranded – assuming that he hadn't ditched me already.

I tried to think positive. While sitting on the steps, I'd been keeping an eye on the street. I hadn't seen the guy drive by, so that was good, right?

When Jax repeated his question, I finally said, "I did the ride-share thing, that's all."

His frown deepened. "You mean with some stranger?"

Yes. Actually. But not the way Jax made it sound.

"Oh come on," I said. "It's not 'some stranger.' The guy's a professional." *Even if he hadn't really acted like it.*

"From now on," Jax said, "if you need a ride, you call *me*, alright?"

I stared up at him. "Why would I call you?"

He stiffened. "Why wouldn't you?"

I gave a bark of laughter. "You *do* remember how last night ended, right?"

And then, you didn't call.

It's not that he *had* to call, but after the way he'd stormed off, it would've been nice to get *some* sort of explanation.

When he made no reply, I made a sigh of impatience. "You remember what you said, right?"

"I remember."

When he didn't elaborate, I figured, what the heck, I'd dressed this way for a reason. I might as well make the point and be done with it.

I lifted my arms and said, "Well, I'm not 'beautiful' now. So, what do you think of that?"

He looked at me for a long moment. "I think you're wrong."

I dropped my arms. "What?"

"You *are* beautiful." His voice hardened. "And if you don't believe me, look in a mirror."

I had no mirror, and yet I couldn't resist looking down to study my clothes. My sweatpants were lime-green, and my flip flops were pink. My shirt was all kinds of crazy colors, but only because I'd worn the thing when Allie and I had repainted our last apartment.

None of the clothes even fit, not great, anyway, and I'd barely bothered to comb my hair. Even the driver had been suitably repulsed. So what was I missing?

I looked up to study Jax's face. As our gazes locked, I couldn't help but recall Morgan's words from a half-hour earlier. She'd claimed that Jax was looking for someone who wasn't, as she'd put it, "too pretty."

For the first time, I seriously considered that she might've been telling me the truth.

If so, it made no sense.

If Jax were any other guy, I might've chalked it up to insecurity. But he wasn't insecure. That much was obvious. He exuded raw confidence – not just with me, but with everyone I'd seen him interacting with.

Now, standing on his doorstep, I quickly considered – and then just as quickly discarded – all kinds of crazy theories. None of them made a lick of sense.

And unfortunately, the clock was still ticking.

Finally, I said, "You know what? Never mind. That's not even the reason I'm here." I glanced toward his front door. "And you never said, do you want to talk out here? Or inside?"

This was an obvious cue for him to invite me in.

But he didn't.

Instead, he replied, "What I want, and what I'm gonna do are two different things."

I stared up at him. "What do you mean?"

"I mean," he said, "if I invite you in, you're gonna regret it."

More confused than ever, I turned to look at his front door. As I did, an awful thought occurred to me. Was someone inside, right now, waiting for him? Maybe in the pool? Or, heaven forbid, up in his bed?

My stomach roiled at the mere thought. And yet, if that was the case, I wanted to know. I *needed* to know. In the calmest voice I could muster, I asked, "Why would I regret it?"

He loomed closer. "Alright, you wanna know why?"

Probably not. Still, I forced a single nod.

His voice grew very quiet. "Because I can't promise to keep my hands off you."

I blinked. Of all the answers I'd been anticipating, this one hadn't been on the list. I mumbled, "What?"

"You heard me."

As I studied his face, I couldn't decide if I was thrilled or angry. It took me less than a second to decide that it wasn't anger making my knees tremble. And yet, I *was* irritated, because the mixed signals were giving me a serious case of mental whiplash.

Again, I looked to his door. What was he saying? That if we went inside, we'd be getting naked? I *liked* the thought of getting naked with him, but not with such a cloud of uncertainty hanging over our heads.

And certainly not when he was acting so strange.

And besides, that *wasn't* why I was here, so I stiffened my spine and said, "There's something I need to know." I waited. And when he offered no encouragement, I finally just blurted it out. "Yesterday, were *you* the one who robbed Dominic?"

CHAPTER 57

For the longest time, the question hung there, unanswered and unacknowledged.

Still, I waited, determined to get a reply, one way or another.

Around us, the daylight was fading to night. Near the curb, a streetlight flickered to life. In the driveway, Jaden's car was slowly backing out, even as Morgan's car squealed off to parts unknown.

But here on the steps, Jax had grown very still. I searched his face, trying like crazy to figure out what emotion I was seeing. But the longer I searched, the less I knew. It was like a mask -- and perversely, *not* a ski mask - had fallen over his face, hiding his thoughts from my probing eyes.

Finally, he gave me an answer. "No."

I stiffened. *That's it?*

The answer was way too short for such a long delay. I waited, certain that he'd say something more. But he never did.

I didn't bother to hide my irritation. "So, you didn't rob him? That's what you're saying."

"Yeah. That's what I'm saying."

"Oh come on," I said. "I *know* what I know."

Of course, I couldn't tell him *everything* I knew – not without causing trouble for Allie. Already, she was having a terrible time at work, and I could only imagine how thrilled both brothers would be to learn that she'd been the cause of this little visit.

In front of me, Jax said, "So you think I'm lying."

I didn't want to call him a liar, but I didn't want to be a sap either. "I don't know," I said. "Are you?"

His mouth tightened. "I don't lie."

If this weren't so pathetic, I might've laughed. "Oh, really?"

"Yes. Really." He wasn't looking away. "And I'll do you one better. I'll never lie to you."

He made it sound like he'd have the chance, like we'd have years and years to share nothing but the truth. It was a lovely sentiment, and I might've believed in the possibility, except for one thing.

I was fairly certain he was lying to me now.

This morning, after Allie had made that comment about the ski mask, I'd casually requested more details. She'd offered none, except to say that she'd discovered the mask last night when stopping by the office for something she'd forgotten.

I also recalled that story from my mom. She'd claimed that two guys had dragged Dominic into the bushes. At the time, I hadn't quite believed her. But in hindsight, the details were impossible to ignore.

Two guys.

Two brothers.

Jax and Jaden.

Who else could it be, especially with the whole mask thing?

Why Jaden would leave *his* mask on Allie's desk, I had no idea. Maybe it was simply to annoy her. Maybe he hadn't considered the fact that we were roommates. Or maybe, he *had* considered, and he was hoping to cause trouble between me and Jax.

If *that* was the goal, he'd succeeded wonderfully.

I still hadn't responded to Jax's claim that he'd never lie to me. But what *could* I say? Nothing good. So instead, I tossed him another question. "What about Jaden?"

"What about him?"

As if he didn't know. "Did *he* rob Dominic?"

"No."

Now, I couldn't help but scoff. "Oh, then I suppose he didn't drag him into the bushes either, huh?"

"That's right."

The denial stung, because I just knew he was giving me a load of crap. *So much for that whole, "I'll never lie to you" routine.*

Beyond frustrated, I turned away, intending to stomp back to the car. But then, Jax added, "It was me."

Startled, I turned back. "What?"

"I did the dragging, not Jaden."

I was staring now. "But I thought you weren't there."

"I never said that."

"You did, too."

"No," Jax said in a tone that was annoyingly reasonable. What I *said* was, I didn't rob him." He gave a tight shrug. "Which I didn't."

What the hell? "But that's a distinction without a difference."

"Not to me."

"Oh, please," I said. "So who robbed him? Jaden?"

"No."

I gave Jax a look. "You know what? I've got like two minutes to get back to the car, so if your plan is to keep giving me the runaround, you'll have to do it another time."

As if there'd *be* another time.

His gaze shifted to the street. "What car?"

"The car that's waiting."

He looked back to me and asked, "Where?"

I flicked my head in the general direction of where I'd been let off. "Up the street." *In theory, anyway.*

His jaw tightened. "If you wanna leave, *I'll* drive you."

I wanted to scream in frustration. "Forget the car. Didn't you hear anything I just said?"

"I heard."

My eyebrows lifted. "So….?"

"So, if you want the story, you'll be getting in *my* car, not his."

This whole conversation was beyond ridiculous. "What is that? A bribe?"

He shrugged. "If that's the way you want to look at it."

I held up a hand. "So just to clarify, you're saying that you'll *only* tell me if I do what you want?"

"No. What I'm *saying* is, I don't want you getting in some stranger's car."

This again? "In case you didn't notice, I got here just fine."

I wasn't even sure why I was arguing. The driver was a giant douchebag. For all I knew, he'd already ditched me. And yet, I hated the thought of Jax driving me home just because he felt he *had* to, and not because he wanted to.

Plus, I wanted answers, not a ride in his car. And I was about to tell him so when he turned away, heading down the front steps.

I called out after him. "Wait, where are you going?"

Over his shoulder, he said, "Hang on. I'll be back in a minute."

I didn't *have* a minute. I scampered after him, arguing the whole way, even as he reached the sidewalk and then turned in the direction of where I'd pointed.

Oh, God, he wasn't seriously heading to that guy's car, was he?

But yup, he sure was.

Not that it mattered.

The guy was gone.

How humiliating was this?

CHAPTER 58

Together, Jax and I stood on the darkened sidewalk, facing the spot where the car *should've* been. I muttered, "Well, he *was* here."

The douchebag.

Beyond annoyed, I turned to Jax and said, "I suppose *you're* happy."

He frowned. "Hell yeah."

Just great. Another mixed message. I glared up at him. "And what were you gonna do, anyway?"

"Depends on the guy."

That was hardly comforting. "You know you're acting crazy, right?"

His only reply was a long, drawn-out look, starting at the top of my messy hair and ending at the tips of my pink flip flops.

I didn't appreciate it one bit. "Hey, what's that supposed to mean?"

He shrugged. "What?"

"That look. It meant something."

"No kidding."

"Well?" I said. "What?"

"It means I'm not the only crazy one here."

"Aha!" I said. "So you admit you're acting crazy."

He shoved a hand through his hair and muttered, "Shit."

"And what does *that* mean?"

"It means," he said, "I've been crazy for a month."

That made me pause. "Really? Why?"

His gaze met mine, and something in his expression changed. "You *know* why."

As I stared up at him, I fought a sudden urge to smile.

It was stupid, really. My ride had just ditched me, and my dream-guy had just called me crazy – maybe not directly, but the implication had been clear enough.

Then again, I *was* dressed like a bag lady, which reminded me… "Oh, crap." I looked toward his house. "My bag."

"What bag?"

"The bag of clothes," I said. "I must've left it on your porch."

"Good."

"Why is that good?"

"Because it means you'll be coming back."

It was a funny thing to say, considering that he'd refused to let me in. "To where?" I tried to laugh. "Your front porch?"

"Meaning?"

"Meaning, I don't even know what you're getting at half the time. It's like you're sending me all these crazy mixed-up messages."

His voice grew quiet. "I know."

"Well, if you know, why don't you stop?"

"I will," he said, "if *you* stop being so fucking thankful."

I drew back. "What?"

"I don't want your gratitude."

"Then what *do* you want?"

Something in his gaze warmed. "You."

The simple, solitary word sent a swarm of butterflies straight into my stomach. Stupidly, I mumbled, "Me?"

"Yes. You." He reached for my hand. "And I don't mean for just a night."

Suddenly, I was feeling just a little bit breathless. "Then what *do* you mean?"

"That's what I wanna figure out." He gave my hand a tender squeeze. "But I want *you* to figure it out, too, *without* complications."

I didn't get it. "What *kind* of complications?"

"For starters, that hang-up you've got with your mom."

"What hang-up?"

"Do you know, I want to spoil you like crazy?"

His hand felt warm and wonderful, and I fought a sudden urge to fall into his arms. "You don't *have* to spoil me," I said. "I mean, jeez, you've spoiled me enough already."

His hand stiffened in mine. "And *that's* what I'm talking about."

"What do you mean?"

"I want to do things for you…buy you things, take you places." His gaze grew intense. "Hell I'd do more if you let me. But then, you get this look, like I'm buying you for the night—"

"I do not," I protested.

"Wanna bet?"

I stopped to think. *Did I?*

I was still thinking when he continued. "And then, I think, 'shit, give it another day, another week, another month.' But then, something happens, and…" He shook his head and looked away.

"Something happens?" I prompted. "Like what?"

He looked back and said, "Everything. Your mom, your apartment, whatever. And it's like the clock starts over." He shook his head. "And I fucking hate it."

"I can see where you would." I gave a nervous laugh. "I mean, who needs the drama, right?"

"I don't give a shit about that," he said. "You wanna see drama? Ask me about my own life sometime."

I gave him a look. "I *have* asked you, not that you've ever answered, not really."

He gave our surroundings a quick glance. "Let's just say, I didn't grow up in a place like *this*."

I couldn't decide if I was surprised or not. "Where *did* you grow up?"

"Ask me later," he said. "I'll tell you all about it."

"Why not now?"

"Because there's something I else wanna tell you, and it can't wait."

"What?"

He gave my hand another squeeze. "I love you."

CHAPTER 59

As I stared up at him, I swear, the world stopped spinning. And then, like an idiot, I blurted out the first thing that popped into my head. "You can't."

"Yeah?" He gave a low laugh. "Tell me about it."

That seemed an odd response. "What?"

"I *know* what you wanna say."

Did he?

I *wanted* to say that I loved him, too. It sure *felt* like I loved him. But that was crazy. We weren't even a couple, not officially. In fact, all we'd shared was a single kiss.

At the memory, I felt my tongue dart out between my lips. "I, um…"

"See?"

I shook my head. "See what?"

"I know what you're thinking."

Now, I had to laugh. "Oh, really? What?"

"It's the same thing you wanna say."

I was dying of curiosity. "Okay… what am I thinking?"

"You're thinking that it makes no sense, that we're not even together, stuff like that." His tone grew teasing. "But you're thinking something else, too."

Now, I could hardly breathe. "What?"

He moved closer. "You're thinking….that you love me, too."

I swallowed. *Yes. I did.* Or least, it sure *felt* like I did. But the whole idea was beyond crazy. Another nervous laugh escaped my lips. "Oh, am I?"

His gaze met mine. "Hell yeah."

Now, I almost wanted to giggle. "Well, aren't *you* confident?"

"I know what I know."

Yes. He did.

But I knew what *I* knew, too. We lived in very different worlds. Choosing my words very carefully, I said, "Well, it *feels* like I love you. I mean, I think about you all the time."

He grinned. "I know."

And just like that, I was laughing again. "Oh, I see how it is."

"No. You don't. But you're gonna."

"What do you mean by that?"

"I mean," he said, "I'm tired of the bull, so here's the deal. You're gonna let me spoil you, and you're not gonna say one word about owing me or anything like that."

This truly *was* ridiculous. "Is that so?"

"Yeah. It is. Starting..." After a long, dramatic pause, he gave me another smile. "...now."

"Why now?"

"Because I'm tired of waiting. And so are you."

He was right. I *was* tired of waiting. And wondering. And obsessing. I couldn't help but recall the very first time I'd seen him, standing in the shadows after that crash.

Even then, I'd wanted him. Was it lust? It might've been. But now, it was something else. Something more. And – oh, boy – the lust was still there.

Still, I wasn't quite sure what was going on. Just fifteen minutes earlier, he'd been refusing to let me into his house. And now, he was confessing love?

I felt compelled to ask, "Is this a sudden thing?"

"How I feel? No." His gaze met mine. "But how I'm gonna deal with it? Yeah. But like I said, I'm tired of waiting."

I knew the feeling. I was tired too. I was tired of longing for him, thinking of him, obsessing over him, and so much more.

I bit my lip. "So, where do we go from here?" I glanced toward his house. "Like, does that mean you want me to come inside?"

"No."

"No?" I gave a confused shake of my head. "Why not?"

"Because I'm taking you out."

"Where?"

"Shopping."

Was he joking? He had to be. "For what?"

He gave it some thought. "For starters, a car."

My jaw dropped. "What?"

He gave a slow nod. "Yeah. A car. What's your favorite color?"

"Um, purple, I guess."

He gave another nod. "A challenge. I like it."

"But you're not serious."

"The hell I'm not."

"But why would you buy me a car. I mean, you've already—"

Suddenly, he leaned forward and pressed his lips to mine, smothering my objections with a kiss that sent a bolt of heat straight to my core. I sagged against him, loving the feel of his hard body as he pulled me close.

He wanted me. And if I couldn't tell from the kiss alone, the hardness pressing into my hip was proof enough.

Our tongues met, and I reached up, linking my fingers behind his neck. In the back of my mind, I knew we had to be making a spectacle of ourselves – or at least, it *would* be a spectacle if not for the fact we were cast in shadows.

But then, he pulled back and said, "You remember the deal, right?"

After that kiss? I was too giddy to remember anything. "Deal?" I breathed. "What deal?"

"I'm gonna spoil you, and you're not gonna say squat about it."

"But—"

He held up a finger. "Wrong answer."

I laughed. "But you didn't even ask me a question."

"The question was implied." He reached for my hand. "Now c'mon."

CHAPTER 60

Allie's mouth was still hanging open. "But it's a Sunday night."

I blew out a long, unsteady breath. "Yeah, I know."

Together, we were standing outside the apartment, staring at the new car, a cute little compact in the perfect shade of purple.

He'd wanted to buy me something more expensive, but I'd absolutely refused. Instead, I'd zoomed in on the cheapest model they had – which was *still* a lot pricier than anything I could've bought on my own.

And yet, I felt incredibly awkward that he'd purchased the car at all. It was crazy and wonderful and more than a little unsettling. In my own mind, I was considering the money a loan, even if I had no idea how I'd ever repay him.

Next to me, Allie was saying, "So, what happened? Did a dealership open up just for you or something?"

"Pretty much."

She gave a low whistle. "Wow."

"Yeah. No kidding."

"Sooooo…" She gave me a sideways glance. "Did you guys…"

"No." I sighed. "Not even close."

She turned to stare. "You're kidding."

"I wish."

"Well, that's weird."

It was. And it wasn't. But Jax had been adamant, telling me that he'd rather wait than give me some messed-up impression that he was buying me for the night.

And yet, he *had* wanted me. I could tell.

And *I* wanted *him.*

So damned bad.

With an effort, I pushed aside thoughts of his naked body and said, "Get this. He said the car was for *him*, not me."

"Oh. So it's like a loaner or something?"

"Not like *that*," I said. "What I mean is, he tells me that he wants to buy me a car, and I tell *him*, 'Thanks, but no freaking way.' And we go back and forth and argue like crazy about it, and *then*, he tells me that it's for *his* sake, not mine, so I should just do him the favor and be done with it."

Allie's eyebrows furrowed. "A favor? For *his* sake? You mean so he doesn't have to drive you around or something?"

"No." I forced a laugh. "So he doesn't end up – in his words – 'beating some driver's ass.'"

Her brow wrinkled in obvious confusion. "What driver?"

"Not any driver in particular," I explained. "Just in general." As she listened, I went on to tell her how Jax had reacted after learning that I'd taken a ride-share to his house.

Allie frowned. "You didn't seriously?"

"Do what? Take a ride-share? Yeah. I mean, people do it all the time, right?"

"Sure," she said. "But *you* shouldn't, not here, anyway."

"Why not?"

"Because your mom's pimp—"

"He's not a pimp."

"Fine," she said. "Your mom's 'boyfriend' is big into that sort of thing. He's got that limo company, the taxi service, and he's a partial owner in that local ride-share, too."

"He is?"

"Yeah. You didn't know?"

"No. I didn't." In truth, I didn't know a lot about my mom's activities, but that was no accident. I'd learned a long time ago that it was best to not think too much about whatever she was doing, or *who* she was doing it with.

Allie said, "And that guy, Dominic, he's bad news, especially for you."

"Why me?" I asked.

"Hello?" she said. "He was trying to recruit you."

"Technically," I said, "my mom was trying to recruit me." Hearing this, even from my own lips, I almost shuddered. *Getting "recruited" by your mom wasn't exactly an improvement.*

Allie gave me a serious look. "Yeah, well, *she* probably asked you a lot nicer than *he* would've."

Recalling that argument in the limo, I mumbled, "Actually, she wasn't *that* nice."

"Gee, that's a shocker," Allie said. "So tell me, did Jax totally flip out when he learned how you got to his house?"

"No." I paused. "Okay, maybe a little. But really, he didn't need to. The service was national, not local."

Allie looked at me like I was nuts. "So?"

"So Dominic had nothing to do with it."

"Yeah, well, a lot of national names are locally owned. What, you've never heard of franchising?"

"Yes. I *have* heard. But it was totally fine."

She made a scoffing sound. "I doubt *that*."

"What do you mean?"

"With *your* luck in drivers?" she said. "I'm surprised the guy wasn't drunk or belligerent or something."

I cleared my throat. "Yeah, well...for your information, he was perfectly sober."

And yes, just a little bit belligerent.

But there was no way I wanted to admit *that,* so I launched into a side story about how Jax and Jaden were the ones who mugged Dominic outside my mom's apartment.

I finished by saying, "Except they didn't really mug him, because they didn't steal anything."

Allie frowned. "Well, that's unfortunate."

"Oh, so you *wanted* him robbed?"

"Definitely," she said. "And roughed up, too."

I gave her a look. "Well, he *is* in the hospital, remember?"

She brightened considerably. "Oh yeah. I almost forgot."

I had to laugh. "Well, aren't *you* blood-thirsty."

"Hey, he had it coming," she said. "But back to Jax, did he say *why* they did it?"

Yes. He did. And it all boiled down to one simple thing. "He said he didn't want that guy near me."

Allie gave a slow nod. "Good." She glanced toward the apartment. "But come on, tell me the rest."

A few minutes later, sitting in our living room, I filled her in on the rest of the story. Apparently, the night before Jax and I were scheduled to pick up my things, he'd driven by my mom's place to get familiar with the layout.

While checking out the exterior, he'd seen my mom walking Dominic to his car and overheard them talking about me coming out there the next day.

The way it sounded, Dominic was planning – in Jax's words – a nice little sales pitch just for me. And my mom was doing nothing to discourage him.

Allie said, "Wait, *where* was Jax when he overheard this?"

"In the van, supposedly."

"Supposedly?" she repeated. "You don't believe him?"

I recalled what Jax had said, that he'd never lie to me. But sometimes, as I'd learned firsthand, he wasn't always terribly forthcoming.

Still, I *did* believe him, and I told Allie so, adding, "but it's so strange. I mean, why would he do that?"

"I'll tell you why. He's crazy." She said this like it was a good thing. But then, her tone grew wistful. "Love makes you do crazy things."

I could definitely relate. I'd been feeling crazy for weeks now.

I went on to tell Allie that the two brothers had gotten together and decided to have an anonymous talk with Dominic before *he* could have a talk with *me*.

I concluded the story by saying, "And apparently, the talk didn't go too terrific, because it ended with Dominic in the bushes."

"And?'

"That's it."

"I know that's the *end* of the story," she said, "but you left out a whole bunch of stuff in the middle."

"Yeah, so did Jax."

"What do you mean?"

"I mean," I said, "he wasn't big on those details."

"And you didn't ask?"

"Sure, I asked."

"And…?"

"And he said it was better if I didn't know."

She shook her head. "And you let him get away with that?"

"No. Not really. I mean, I told him I wanted to know everything."

"And what did he say?"

"He said – and I quote – 'Too bad.'"

"Too bad? That's it?"

"Yeah. And then, when I pressed him on it, he tells me, the guy's lucky he only ended up in the bushes."

"As opposed to what?"

I winced. "Honestly? I didn't ask."

But the very next weekend, I *was* asking questions, and none of them were about Dominic.

CHAPTER 61

"But what were you fighting about?" I asked.

Jax gave a low laugh. "Trust me. You don't want to know."

It was a beautiful Saturday afternoon, and we were lying beside his pool in an oversized chaise lounge. The pool, along with the rest of the patio, was surrounded on three sides by the house, leaving the fourth side open for a magnificent view of the ocean.

I snuggled closer to him and gave a happy sigh. I felt like I was on vacation – *or* living in one of the prettiest postcards I'd ever seen, complete with my own personal dream-guy lying right next to me.

We'd already gone for a swim and were now drying off in the open air.

I gave him a playful poke in the ribs. "No fair. I told *you* about my fight with Allie."

I meant, of course, the huge argument we'd had back in Nashville.

I'd just given Jax a blow-by-blow of the whole thing, beginning with my announcement that I was moving in with my mom, and ending with Allie showing up at Jax's front door to rescue me from his evil clutches.

Next to me, Jax said, "First, tell me something. Who was yelling louder? Her or you?"

"Why would you wanna know *that*?"

"So I know what to expect when you get pissed."

I laughed. "You've seen me mad. I don't yell." Under my breath, I added, "Most of the time, anyway."

This was true. I wasn't a yeller, and I loathed drama. And yet, that argument with Allie had included a fair bit of both.

With a smile in his voice, he said, "You sure about that?"

I tried to think. I didn't *recall* ever yelling at him. *But had I?*

I considered the question for like two whole seconds before I pulled back to say, "Hey, you're changing the subject, aren't you?"

"Me?" He flashed me a wicked grin. "Never."

I rolled my eyes. "Oh, I forgot, you're *such* an angel."

In spite of my teasing, he *was* being an angel in the worst possible way. Here we were, lying around in hardly no clothes at all, and yet he'd been perfectly behaved.

Damn it.

I'd been trying not to stare, but sometimes, I could hardly help it. Whenever I let my gaze slip just a little, I could see the water droplets easing down his abs, following the same contours that I was dying to trace with my fingers.

Even now, I was sorely tempted. And yet, I wasn't quite brazen enough to make the first move, especially now, when I'd hardly seen him over the past week.

And besides, *he* was controlling *himself* just fine. *Unfortunately.*

This was in spite of the fact that I'd worn my skimpiest bikini – a little black thing that covered next to nothing. *And*, I'd been dropping subtle hints ever since I'd arrived an hour ago.

Was I trying to seduce him?

Definitely.

If only I were a little bolder, I would've ripped off my bikini fifty-nine minutes ago and pounced on him like the man morsel he was.

I felt my eyebrows furrow.

Man morsel?

Good Lord.

I shifted in the lounge, and the side of my thigh rubbed up against his leg. The leg was lean and muscular, just like the rest of his body – as I'd seen oh-so clearly today for the very first time.

Oh sure, I'd seen hints before now, but here, with very little clothing and just enough water to accent every line and ridge of his physique, I'd seen everything in all of its magnificent glory.

Or, at least, I'd seen *almost* everything.

Some parts were frustratingly hidden.

During the last week, I'd seen him only twice, and both times had been at the coffee shop, where we'd been seriously limited in terms of privacy and time.

In a perverse twist of fate, he'd been out of town for most of the week, and I'd had to work both nights that he *had* been in town. This left me no opportunity for all of the things that I'd been fantasizing about – and not just naked things, either.

There were so many things I wanted to know, including the question that he hadn't yet answered. Pulling my mind out of the gutter, I said, "Soooooo… Are you gonna tell me or not?"

He turned on his side and leaned close to nuzzle my hair. In a voice filled with sin, he said, "Tell you what?"

My breath caught. It was a totally innocent phrase, and yet, he'd made it sound like he'd just said the filthiest thing imaginable. I heard myself murmur, "Huh?"

A low chuckle sounded in my ear. "I missed you."

I felt myself smile. "I missed you, too." And then, seeing this for the distraction it was, I gave his ankle a playful kick. "But you *still* have to answer the question."

He lifted a single eyebrow. "Aren't you bossy?"

I laughed. "I'm not half as bossy as you are."

"How about this?" he said. "I'll tell you if you promise me something."

"What?"

"That you won't run off."

"Why would I run off?" I asked.

"Because it was damned embarrassing."

Now, I was *really* intrigued. Lying on my back, I gazed up at him. "Oh come on. It can't be any more embarrassing than all the stuff *you've* seen with my mom."

"Wanna bet?"

I smiled. "I'd love to."

Now, *he* was looking intrigued. "So, what kind of stakes are we talking?"

For some reason, I wanted to giggle. "Wait a minute, are we talking about a real bet?"

He shrugged. "Why not?"

"Well, for starters," I said, "I can't think of anything I have that you'd actually want."

His gaze dipped to my bikini. "You think, huh?"

Something in his voice made my pulse jump. "I, uh…" Suddenly lost for words, I felt my tongue dart out between my lips for just an instant before I somehow managed to say, "Well, I *do* have my swimsuit."

He gave a slow nod. "It's a nice one."

Good Lord. How could a simple nod be so sexy?

"Well…" I was feeling so stupidly breathless. "…it's all yours if you win."

He reached out and ran a single finger underneath the nearest bikini string, one of two that held up my top. "And what if I lose?"

His touch was electric, and I longed for his finger to dip lower, to trace the outline of my nipple and maybe even take it into his mouth. The air wasn't cold exactly, but there was a cool breeze coming off the water, making both of my nipples stand at attention and long to be warmed with the heat of his mouth.

The thought alone was almost too much. In a breathless rush, I blurted, "You win."

A slow smile spread across his lips. "I know.'

"Wait, how do you know?"

"I'm with *you*, aren't I?"

I wanted him so very much. I met his gaze. "If we go upstairs, you *could* be."

"Upstairs, huh?" He looked around. "What's wrong with here?"

I sucked in a breath. Here would be amazing, and yet, way too risky. "We can't do anything *here*." And yet, I felt myself swallow. "I mean someone might see, right?"

But Jax looked entirely unconcerned. "Like who?"

"Well, Jaden for starters."

He ran his finger just a little bit lower. The movement, as small as it was, made the fabric of my damp bikini shift maddeningly against my hardened nipple.

I stifled a moan. That shouldn't've been so exciting. It was, after all, just a finger – *and* just a nipple. Cripes, the finger and nipple weren't even touching.

But that finger happened to be attached to the hottest guy I'd ever met. And more than that, it was a guy I loved, a guy I'd been fantasizing about for weeks.

He gave the string a playful tug. "Out of town."

So Jaden wasn't even here? That was good. *Really* good. With growing excitement, I asked, "What about your cleaning people?"

"Came yesterday."

My breath was growing more unsteady with every passing moment. "Does anyone else have a key? To the house, I mean?"

"Nope."

"Are you sure?"

"Trust me." His gaze smoldered into mine. "No one – and I mean *no one* – is gonna look at you, but me."

Oh, boy. He was looking at me *now*, and I was looking at *him*. My gaze dipped lower and stopped at the proof of his arousal. Earlier, his swimsuit had been on the loose side.

It wasn't loose now.

In fact, it looked way too small to contain him. Like someone in a trance, I reached out and ran my hand over the massive bulge. My breath caught when it pulsed beneath my touch. He was so incredibly hard, and already, I could myself growing hot and wet under the cool fabric of my bikini bottoms.

Suddenly, upstairs seemed too far away.

He leaned his head close to mine. "Say yes."

Already, I was almost too breathless to speak. "Yes."

A million times yes.

CHAPTER 62

His voice was low in my ear. "That's my girl."

I *was* his girl. Probably, I'd been his right from the start, when I'd first seen him on that darkened street.

Funny, too. I wasn't one to believe in immediate connections, in love at first sight, or whatever else that people used to justify all kinds of crazy decisions.

But this didn't feel crazy. Or maybe it was just the right kind of crazy.

I loved him.

And he loved me, too.

Even without the words, I would've known. Already, I'd seen it in his eyes and felt it in his touch – his hand on mine, his finger tracing the contours of my face, his arms pulling me close as he kissed me on the sidewalk.

But all of that – the hand-holding, the kissing, everything – it was all a wonderful a prelude to this, the thing that I'd been craving for way too long.

Now, under the string of my bikini, his finger was inching higher, heading toward my collar bone. I stifled a whimper of frustration. It was going in the wrong direction. I wanted him to go lower, eventually *much* lower. Over his swimsuit, my hand was still on his erection, and I gave it a squeeze of pure longing.

His swimsuit was damp from our time in the pool, and yet, even through the cool fabric, I could feel his heat raging underneath. He was so hard. And I was so wet – and not with pool water either.

Good Lord. How could I be so ready so soon?

And why wasn't his finger heading lower? My nipple was aching for his touch. Other places were aching, too.

Soon, the answer to my silent question became stupidly obvious.

Of course.

With agile fingers, he undid the knot holding up my bikini. With me on my back, the bikini stayed in place, with only the strings falling aside.

His voice was a low caress. "Cold?"

"No," I breathed. "I mean, yes. I, um, well, it depends on what you're asking." Quickly, I added, "I don't want to go inside though, if that's what you mean."

He gave a low chuckle. "I'll go wherever you want."

I looked down toward my torso. From this angle, I could see my nipples protruding against the damp fabric. With a breathless laugh, I said, "I guess parts of me are a *little* cold."

"Yeah?" He lowered his head and pressed his lips to the spot where his finger had been inching along just moments earlier. And then, he slowly moved lower, leaving a trail of kisses that led straight to the damp fabric still covering my breasts.

On the side closest to him, he nudged the fabric aside and trailed his lips lower still. Soon, his warm mouth covered my cool nipple, and I felt my eyelids flutter shut. *Yes.* When his tongue danced around the tip, I gave a soft moan of pure bliss.

Soon, his hand was on the other side, gently nudging down that fabric, too. His fingers captured the nipple and gave it a tender squeeze, even as his mouth worked pure magic on the other one.

This was almost too much, and yet not nearly enough. Beyond eager, I fumbled for the waistband of his swimsuit and nudged it downward, freeing him from the damp fabric.

With as eager as I was, I wanted to rip the swimsuit right off him. But even in my desperation, I realized the impossibility of such a thing, so instead, I urged, "Your swimsuit, you should take it off." I was finding it so hard to breathe. "Or better yet, let me…"

I made a move to lift myself up, but Jax wasn't budging. Against my skin, he whispered, "Not yet."

"Why not?"

"Because this." His teeth grazed along my nipple, sending little prickles of pure pleasure straight through me.

"Oh," I murmured with a little laugh. "Good reason."

I was still touching him, squeezing him, rubbing him. With every pulse in my hand and every murmur against my skin, I felt new waves of excitement building deep in my core.

In my hand, he was so massively hard, and I couldn't help but wonder what it would feel like to have him fully inside me.

Soon.

Or at least, it had *better* be soon, or I'd go absolutely insane.

I whispered, "I want you."

"I know."

I almost laughed. "Well then…"

"And you're gonna want me a lot more before I'm through."

What on Earth did that mean?

But soon, I didn't have to wonder, because his hand was heading lower, sliding down my torso until it reached the intersection of my thighs. Already, my hips were rising, and I said a silent prayer that the lounge was as sturdy as it felt, because if not, I was pretty sure we'd both be tumbling onto the patio by the time we were done.

And if that happened?

It would be *so* worth it.

He nudged aside the crotch of my bikini bottoms and ran a finger along my wetness. He sucked in a quiet breath before saying, "I wanted you, you know."

I was so distracted, I could hardly think. "Oh yeah?"

"When I saw you. So fucking beautiful." With a smile in his voice, he added. "And sweet." As he said this last word, he slipped a long finger inside me, and I lifted my hips, wanting more.

Somehow, I managed to murmur, "I wasn't that sweet."

"Yeah?"

"Yeah. Because I wanted you, too."

His tone grew playful. "And if I'd asked…?"

I paused. "Well, I would've been tempted…" My words trailed off as I felt another finger slide inside me. It felt so amazingly good.

"How tempted?"

Oh, man. What was he doing with his thumb? Whatever it was, it felt incredible. My clit was aching now, just like my nipples had been aching for more of his touch.

In fact, all of me was aching with raw need.

In a teasing tone, Jax said, "Tell me."

"What?" I gave a shaky laugh. "Oh, yeah. How tempted? Well, the thing is…"

Oh, my. That felt *so* good. With everything he was doing, how was I supposed to think, much less form a coherent sentence?

In a leading voice, he said, "The thing is…?"

"Well, I didn't know you all that well, and I didn't think there'd ever be anything between us." As his fingers worked their magic, I gave a muffled moan. "Just like now, I don't want anything between us."

I wasn't even sure if I was making any sense. I was definitely rambling. But seriously, how was I supposed to think straight when he was doing all of these wonderful things to my body?

I heard myself say, "Like my swimsuit. And your swimsuit, too. They shouldn't be between us."

His fingers were moving slowly in and out, driving me to distraction. I was so warm now, and I could feel the slickness between my thighs building with every delicious motion.

My eyes had been mostly shut, but now I opened them, wanting desperately to see him. When I did, I was surprised to discover that he was looking straight at my face, like I was the most fascinating person he'd ever seen.

As if.

No. He was the fascinating one, not me. And this felt like a dream, complete with the endless ocean and the sky above – but most of all, Jax.

He said, "I'm never gonna let you go. You know that right?"

I would've loved to know such a thing, but even in my blissful state, I knew there were no guarantees in this world, especially with a guy like him, who could have any girl he wanted.

But I *did* know one thing for sure. I wanted him. And the thought of waiting a moment longer was too unbearable to consider. I whispered, "Then maybe you should get closer."

It had to be now, because already, I was on the verge of losing it, and I wanted him inside me when it happened.

Finally, when I thought I'd go absolutely insane, he pulled back and nudged down my bikini bottoms. Desperate to have him inside me, I tugged at his swimsuit, pushing it past his hips until his body was completely free.

At last, we were both naked, and he was above me, looking down with the same desire that I felt coursing through my entire being. I reached between us, and positioned his length at my opening.

Finally, in one slow, steady motion, he slid into me, filling me so completely, I could hardly think. I could hardly breathe.

I was trying to be quiet. We were, after all, technically outdoors. And yet, I couldn't stop myself nearly as much as I wanted as he drove into me like there was no tomorrow.

I wrapped my legs around his hips and my arms around his back. We were so very close, and it felt like all my very best fantasies come to life.

Almost immediately, I felt the telltale contracting of my muscles and the fluttering in my stomach. His lips closed on mine as we continued to move, and I fell into sweet oblivion, too lost to even wonder if the chair would hold us or if anyone would hear.

But the lounge did hold, and if the neighbors heard, they didn't complain – thank goodness.

When Jax shuddered against me, I felt happy and sated in a way I'd never imagined. Who knows, maybe this *was* a fantasy, because things like this simply didn't happen in real life.

Did they?

Afterwards, we lay together for a long, blissful moment, listening to the waves against the shore and the wind rustling the nearby trees.

I gave a sigh of pure contentment. And then, a sudden giggle escaped my lips. "You still need to tell me, you know."

He reached up and brushed a lock of hair that fallen over my eye. "Tell you what?"

I'd meant the story of that fight, or whatever had happened, on the night of that party. But that wasn't *all* I wanted to know. So I answered with one breathless word. "Everything."

With a smile in his voice, he said, "How about this?" His tone grew utterly sincere. "I love you."

The words warmed my heart, and I gave another giggle. "I love you, too, but you've *still* gotta tell me what happened."

And so, after a little more prodding on my part, he did an hour later when we returned to the patio.

CHAPTER 63

"My brother's a dick."

We were sitting in separate chairs facing the ocean. I gave Jax a confused look. It was an odd way to start a story, and I wasn't quite sure how to respond.

Jaden *was* a dick, but should I really agree?

He wasn't *my* brother, after all.

Trying to be tactful, I said, "Yeah, well, I guess he is sometimes, but he's um…" *Damn it.* I was trying to think of something *nice* to say, but nothing came to mind.

Allie hated him.

And I *had* to hate him, because he'd been so awful to Allie.

Now, the way it sounded, Jax hated a few things about him, too.

Lamely, I finished by saying, "…a good swimmer."

Jax lifted a single eyebrow. "A swimmer, huh?"

I cleared my throat. "Well, Allie mentioned that he swims in the ocean sometimes, so he *must* be a good swimmer, right?"

Already, I could feel the blush creeping up my cheeks. Sex – that *had* to explain it. Normally, I didn't sound quite so ridiculous. But in my own defense, the sex had been *very* good, fabulous actually. No wonder my brain was mushy.

Eager to move along, I said, "So, what'd he do? You said he was being a…" I *still* didn't want to say it. It really *did* seem rude.

Jax grinned. "A dick? You can say it, you know."

"I know. I just don't want to. I mean, he's not *just* your brother. He's also Allie's boss."

"No," Jax said. "He's not."

My stomach sank. *Oh, no.* "You don't mean he fired her?"

I'd been worried about such a thing. I'd *also* been worried that she might flat-out quit. I didn't know what was going on at work, but I knew that it couldn't be good.

Was *that* the reason Allie had been so quiet last night?

Jax said, "Don't worry. I'm not talking about Jaden."

"Oh. So, which brother did you mean?"

He frowned. "My oldest."

I tried to think. I didn't even know which one *was* the oldest, but that wasn't my fault. Jax had been very tight-lipped when it came to his family. "So, what's his name, again?"

"Jake."

Something in his tone suggested a distinct lack of brotherly love. I recalled what Jax had told me earlier, that the story was embarrassing. But from the look on his face, he wasn't embarrassed. He was ticked off.

I asked, "So, what'd he do?"

"Alright, lemme back up," Jax said. "It's the night of the party, right? And for the last few months, Jake's been threatening to come pick up this car."

"Wait, what do you mean by threatening?"

"I'm just saying, we didn't invite him."

"Oh." I still wasn't quite sure what that meant. "What car do you mean?"

"The way *he* sees it? His car."

"But it's not?"

Jax made a waffling gesture with his hand. "Depends on who you talk to."

"So what's *your* version?" I smiled. "From the beginning, okay?"

"Alright. A few years ago, Jaden and I borrow this car—"

"Wait. How *many* years ago?"

Jax gave it some thought. "I dunno...fifteen I guess."

I shook my head. That was *a lot* of years, too many, in fact. "But that can't be right."

"Why not?"

"Well, because you're twenty-nine years old."

"Yeah, so?"

"So, that means you'd be fourteen at the time." I did the math. "And Jaden would be what, twelve?"

"Close. He'd just turned thirteen." Jax got this faraway look as he added, "I remember, because we did this birthday cake thing in the car. It was just a vending machine snack, but..." He paused. "Eh, that's not important."

It was to me.

I wasn't a huge fan of Jaden, but the image struck me as just a little bit sad. "But you weren't alone, right?"

"No."

I breathed a sigh of relief.

Jax grinned. "There was Jaden, too. Remember?"

"Oh, come on," I protested. "You know what I meant."

He was still grinning. "Did I?"

Now, I couldn't help but smile back. "I *know* you did."

He shrugged. "Yeah, well..."

"So?" I prompted. "Fifteen years ago, you and Jaden 'borrow' this car and...?"

"And Jake's been wanting it back."

I gave a snort of laughter. "After fifteen years? I'm sure he does. So, why didn't he just get it already?"

"Because," Jax said, "we wouldn't give it up."

"For fifteen whole years?"

"Hey, we paid him."

"How much?" I asked.

"Five-hundred bucks."

My mouth fell open. "That's all?"

"Why not? That's what *he* paid."

Even fifteen years ago, five hundred dollars would've been incredibly cheap for a car. I murmured, "He must've gotten *some* deal."

"Nah. The car's a hunk of junk."

"So why didn't you give it back?"

"Because we didn't want to."

Well, that was informative. "Why not?" I asked.

"Because we paid him. It's ours."

Obviously, there was a lot more to this story. "But you have like a dozen cars already. And so does Jaden."

"Hey, it's not a dozen."

I gave him a look. "It is between the two of you." I hadn't seen all of the cars, but thanks to Allie, I knew they stored most of them in a warehouse near their corporate headquarters. "So, why'd you want to keep this one?"

Jax turned to gaze out over the horizon. "Because he's a dick, just like I said."

That hardly seemed like a good reason. Plus, I couldn't quite understand why any of them wanted the car if it was so terrible. Searching for some clue, I said, "Is he short of money or something? I mean, if the car's *that* awful, he must've been pretty desperate to want it back."

"He's not desperate," Jax said. "It's just a power-play, something to piss us off. He's good at that."

"So *that's* why you got in a fight?"

Jax shook his head. "I didn't fight him."

"So, who did? Jaden?"

Jax turned again to face me, and his gaze warmed. "Before it all happened, we're at this party. And I'm dancing with this incredible girl…"

I felt a silly smile spread across my face. "Really?"

"Really. And one of my security guys comes up to tell me that my dick of a brother has picked that night to show up and try to lift the car."

"Lift?"

"Steal, whatever."

"Do you think he picked that night on purpose? Like he knew you were tied up?"

"Knowing him? Probably. So Jaden and I take off, thinking we're gonna be gone maybe an hour, just long enough to tell our brother to fuck off, but by the time we get there, Jake's gotten to the security guy."

That sounded bad. Bracing myself, I asked, "You mean, like he hurt him?"

"No." Jax gave a humorless laugh. "He's driven the guy nuts."

Huh? "Sorry, I'm not following."

"You'd have to know Jake," he said. "The way it looked, he'd been pushing the guy's buttons, messing with him, getting under his skin. He used to have this saying, that he could make a priest hit him."

"Could he?"

"Hell yeah."

"So...?" I prompted. "What happened?"

"He bit him."

I sucked in a breath. "Seriously? Jake *bit* your security guy?"

"No. The guy bit Jake."

I paused for a long moment. "You're kidding."

"I wish. But anyway, we show up, and Cooper – that's the security guy – is latched onto Jake like a mongoose on a snake. And there's blood all over the place, and Cooper looks like he'd be foaming at the mouth, except he's not gonna let go."

"And what's Jake doing?"

"The fucker's laughing."

I shook my head. "No."

Jax nodded. "Yeah. He is. And this guy who works for him, he's filming it, like the whole thing's one big joke."

"So, what did you do?"

"So I get the fire extinguisher, and I turn it on Cooper."

"The security guy? And what does *he* do?"

"Well, at first he's mostly gagging. But then, he finally lets go."

"Uh, well, that's good."

"But now, Jaden's pissed. He and Cooper, they hang out sometimes–"

"But wait," I said. "Shouldn't Jaden be mad at Cooper? I mean, he's the one who did the biting."

"Trust me," Jax said. "You'd wanna bite Jake too if he started messing with you."

I forced a laugh. "Sorry, I don't think I'd ever be that hungry."

"That's what you think," he said. "But anyway, Jaden's so pissed that he grabs a gas can, and get this. He douses the car."

I stifled a gasp. "You don't mean Jake's car?"

"No. I mean *our* car. We paid for it, remember?"

I didn't want to quibble. "So, what'd Jaden do *then*?"

"What do you think? He torches it."

"In the warehouse? Isn't that dangerous?"

"Hell yeah, it's dangerous. He almost took out the Bentley and a few other cars, too. They were parked in the same section, *with* full tanks of gas."

I shuddered to think. "And what about the warehouse?"

"It's got a sprinkler system – a good thing, too, since I'd blown the extinguisher on Cooper. Anyway, the water comes pouring down, dousing all of us, and the car, too."

"You mean the five-hundred dollar one?"

"That's the one."

"So what happened then?"

"So, we've got this mess to clean up, and Jake, I drag *his* ass to the doctor for stitches."

I almost didn't know what to say. I mumbled, "Well, that was nice of you."

"It wasn't 'nice,'" Jax said. "Mostly, I didn't want his wife to give me grief."

That made me pause. "He's married? Seriously?"

"Hard to believe, huh?"

"Uh, yeah. His wife – do you know her well?"

"No."

"So when's the last time you saw her?"

"A few weeks ago, when she stopped by the house."

"With Jake?"

"No. With the other wives."

"You mean your brothers' wives?"

Jax nodded. "They've got this crazy idea that we should all make up, be a regular family." He gave a low scoff. "Like that's gonna happen."

I gave a nervous laugh. "Well, it definitely won't happen if you go around biting each other."

"Hey, *we* weren't the ones who did the biting, remember?"

I gave him a look. "What about torching each other's cars?"

He paused. "Well, there is that."

I was still trying to process everything I'd just heard. "So *that's* why you were so late getting back? To the party, I mean?"

"That's the reason."

"Have you guys talked since?"

"Who? Me and Jake?" He shook his head. "No."

"Why not?"

"You've gotta ask?"

"Well, you have to make up *sometime*, right?"

A ghost of a smile crossed his features. "It's nice that you think so."

"But don't *you*?"

"No."

"But—"

"What *I* think is that *you* need dinner."

It was an obvious change of topic, and I was tempted to argue. But I'd already pried enough for one day, and besides, we had the rest of the evening to revisit the subject.

But as it turned out, talking wasn't the primary thing on either of our minds, and I couldn't say I regretted it – not even the next day when I returned home half-asleep, only to learn that I'd had an unwanted visitor of my own.

CHAPTER 64

When I walked in through the apartment door, Allie gave me a sly smile. "Well, *someone* had a good time."

She was right. I did. With Jaden out of town, Jax and I had the whole place to ourselves, and I'd enjoyed every inch of it.

I stifled a giggle. I'd enjoyed every inch of *him*, too – multiple times.

Allie laughed. "You're blushing."

Probably, I was, but it wasn't due to embarrassment. It was the heat of the memories combined with simple happiness. I felt like I was living in a dream – a dream that I never wanted to wake from.

It was late Sunday afternoon, and tomorrow, I'd be seeing Jax again. Already, I could hardly wait.

But tonight, I had to work.

As I got ready, I told Allie all about my time with Jax. Leaving nearly nothing to her imagination, I even told her the story of what had happened between Jake and the bitey security guy.

When I mentioned the part about Jaden torching the car, she said, "God, he's such a tool."

I wasn't going to argue. *Poor Allie.* To think, she actually worked for the guy. I swear, there were times I wondered whether I'd done her a favor at all by pushing her into that job.

I was just debating asking her when she said, "Hey, guess who stopped by last night."

From the look on her face, I didn't need to guess. "Don't tell me." I cringed. "It was my mom, wasn't it?"

"Nope."

"Really?" I couldn't imagine who else it could be. "So who was it?"

"Tabitha."

"You're kidding."

I'd known Tabitha my whole life. During all those years, she'd never stopped by to simply say hello, at least not to me. I asked, "What did she want?"

"Oh, you're gonna love this," Allie said. "She came by to gripe that *she* didn't get a hotel room."

I gave a confused shake of my head. "What?"

"Yeah," Allie said. "She heard about the thing with your mom, and she's all ticked off, wondering why no one put *her* up in a fancy hotel."

I was staring now. "*Please* tell me you're joking."

"Hardly," Allie said. "The way it sounds, your mom's been rubbing it in pretty good."

"What do you mean?"

"Apparently, your mom's been ordering steak and lobster from room service. And then, she's been calling Tabitha to tell her all about it."

As I listened, Allie launched into an overblown imitation of my mom. "Guess where I am. Guess what I'm eating. Ooopsie, room service is here. Gotta run."

Funny, I could practically hear it. But this *wasn't* good. "So who's paying for all of this?"

"Not her, that's for sure."

At this, I literally groaned. This could only mean that Jax was paying for it. *Did he know?* He *had* to know, right?

Now, I *was* embarrassed. It was bad enough that he was paying for the hotel. Now, he was paying for room service, too?

Allie was saying, "And it gets better."

Almost afraid to ask, I said, "By better, do you mean better-better? Or worse better?"

"Worse better."

Damn it. "I knew it."

"Apparently," Allie said, "she's been getting loads of spa treatments, too."

Spa treatments? That sounded expensive. With renewed dread, I asked,

"Like what?"

"Facials, massages, pedicures, you name it, she's getting it."

I'd never had a pedicure in my whole life. Come to think of it, I'd never had a facial either. And as far as massages, I'd never had a professional one, that's for sure.

I bit my lip. If Jax didn't know about this already, he'd surely be finding out soon. *Would it be better if I called to warn him?*

Probably.

And yet, I dreaded the thought.

What on Earth would he think?

Nothing good.

I sighed. "So *that's* why she stopped by? To complain about my mom?"

"*And* to gripe about her injury."

"What do you mean?"

"Well, after she got done complaining about her 'missing' hotel room, she launched into this big boo-hoo story about her arm." Allie laughed. "Get this. It's still in a sling."

Okay, I wasn't terribly fond of Tabitha – and that was putting it mildly – but it did seem a bit cruel to laugh about it. I asked, "Am I missing some sort of joke here?"

"Oh yeah," Allie said. "She's a big ol' faker."

"Well…" I hesitated. "I guess I wouldn't put it past her."

"You don't *have* to guess," she said. "I'm telling you, she's totally faking."

"How do you know?"

"Because, she's standing in the doorway, blathering on about how awful she's got it, and what a rotten niece you are—"

"I'm not *really* her niece."

"Yeah. I know. But she's milking that cow for all it's worth."

Well, that was an image I didn't need.

Allie was still talking. "According to *her*, you're totally breaking her heart."

Sure I was. I muttered, "As if she had one."

"No kidding," Allie said. "But anyway, I go to slam the door in her face—"

"Seriously?"

"Well, yeah," Allie said. "I mean, there's only so much Tabitha I can take."

I knew the feeling. Still, I had to say, "Yeah, but didn't you feel at least a *little* bad about her arm?"

"Hell no. Because like I said, she's totally faking."

"Yeah, but—"

Allie held up a hand. "Just lemme finish, okay? So I go to slam the door, and quick as anything, she grabs it..." Allie grinned. "...*with* the arm that's supposedly hurt."

"Are you sure?"

"Of course I'm sure. She's wearing the sling remember?"

I *did* remember, but the whole thing still bothered me. "Yeah, I know." I grimaced. "But I still wish that security guy hadn't done that."

Allie gave a decisive shake of her head. "It wasn't a guy."

"It wasn't?"

"No. It was a woman. You didn't know?"

"Actually, I didn't ask." Probably, I should've, but it was a subject I'd been studiously avoiding.

"And besides," Allie said, "even if the arm *was* hurt, it was Tabitha's own fault.'

"Why? For not leaving?"

"No." Allie paused. "Well, yes. That too. But what I mean is that she fell on her arm when she took a flying leap for Rosie."

I shook my head. "Rosie?"

"Yeah. The so-called goon." Allie gave a distracted flutter of her hands. "But you didn't let me finish. So last night, I tell Tabitha that she's a giant faker, and she flips out."

I frowned. "What'd she do?"

"Well, first, she rips off the sling and throws it on the floor, and then..." Allie gave a dramatic pause. "She yells, 'Where's my fucking lobster!'"

I stared at Allie for a long moment. I wanted to snicker. "Okay, now I *know* you're joking."

"Alright, fine," Allie muttered. "She didn't say the lobster thing, but she *was* pretty mad. And she *did* rip off the sling."

Now, *that* I could see.

I gave Allie a sympathetic look. "I'm really sorry you got stuck dealing with her."

"Don't be. I'm not."

"Really?"

"Oh yeah. You would've been way too nice."

"Hey, I wasn't too nice at the party. You remember, right?" Allie hadn't been there, but I *had* told her all about it.

"Yeah, but knowing you, you were still nicer than she deserved."

I wasn't sure I agreed, but that wasn't terribly important in the big scheme of things. I asked, "Anything else?"

"Oh yeah. She said you'd better call her." Allie rolled her eyes. "Or else."

"Or else what?"

"Who knows, who cares? If it were me, I wouldn't call her at all."

That sounded like a perfect plan to me. After everything she'd done, Tabitha didn't deserve a call back.

See? I wasn't nearly as nice as Allie thought.

Besides, I had a different call to make. That call was to Jax, who definitely deserved a warning about my mom's hotel charges.

But as it turned out, he already knew.

Into the phone, I said, "Really? When did you find out?"

"Tuesday."

"And you never said anything? Why?"

"Because it's not a big deal."

"It is to me," I said. "I mean, don't you feel cheated?"

"Hell no."

"But—"

"Hey, today's the last day, so forget it."

It took me a moment to realize what he meant. A whole week had passed since that ugly scene with my mom. This meant that her stay was officially over.

I asked, "But what if she doesn't leave?"

"Then I'll deal with it. So don't worry, alright?"

I promised to try, but I wasn't sure that I'd be able to.

Sure enough, worry haunted me for the rest of the evening.

And it might have haunted me a lot longer, if it weren't for something crazy that Jax did later that same night.

CHAPTER 65

I was gripping the sheet with clenched fingers. "Oh, God, don't stop."

"I wasn't planning on it," he said, driving into me hard and fast. Both of us were naked in the penthouse suite of The Plaza – the very same hotel where my mom had been staying until earlier today.

This was *so* wrong, but it felt so right.

I reached up and gripped his ass with both hands. His tight muscles shifted in time with his movements, and I yanked him closer again and again.

On the floor surrounding the bed, my clothes – my work uniform actually – was lying in tatters with the buttons scattered who-knows-where. The uniform had been lying there for a while now, after Jax had literally ripped the thing off me.

I'd need to replace it. I did, after all, have only two. But at the moment, I was too far gone to care. I was way too distracted by how wonderful Jax felt and how many orgasms I'd had already.

Was it three? If so, I was hurtling fast toward number four.

By now, I knew a little something about the way Jax operated. He was a tease in the best possible way. I'd been naked a long time before he was, and I'd been pure putty in his hands.

And under his lips.

Oh boy, his lips. And his tongue. So freaking talented.

By the time he'd actually let me remove *his* clothes, I'd been a sweaty, begging mess. Even now, my hair was sticking to my forehead, and I could feel the dampness dripping down my chest.

But I could hardly care.

If I weren't so far gone, I might've laughed out loud. Instead, all I could do was breathe, "You're a monster, you know that?"

This time, I *wasn't* referring to the size of his cock, which yes, was definitely monster-sized.

He gave me a long deliberate thrust. "Yeah. And don't you forget it."

I wouldn't.

In fact, I wouldn't forget anything about tonight, because all of it had been way too unexpected and surreal.

Even now, my eyelids kept fluttering open and shut, torn between the desire to get fully lost in the sensations filling me to the brink *and* the need to look at him – to gaze into his eyes, and to admire the muscles of his shoulders and chest as they shifted and moved above me.

But soon, I couldn't keep my eyelids open another moment, because all of the sensations were simply too much, and I was falling fast into sweet oblivion. And just like that, I was tingling all over, from my toes to my fingertips and everywhere in between.

When he climaxed against me, I took another deep, shuddering breath. Somehow, I managed to say, "I meant it, you know."

His lips were very close to my ear. His tone was rough and teasing. "You meant what? You're crazy about me?"

I giggled. "Yes. I did mean that."

"And you love me?"

Oh, boy. Did I ever. I took another long trembling breath. "Yes."

"That's my girl."

I liked it when he said that. In fact, I liked all of this. I *loved* it, actually. Still, I had to protest, "But that's not what I meant."

"I know."

"You do?" I laughed against him. "So you admit you're a monster?"

"Hell yeah." He lifted his head and met my gaze for a long moment before turning to glance at the silver tray sitting on a stand near the bed. "More lobster?"

And just like that, I was giggling again. I almost never giggled. I shouldn't be giggling now. And yet, I couldn't seem to help it.

Over my protests, he'd long ago ordered a whole slew of finger food, including these amazing little lobster roll appetizers and peppered steak-bites. He'd fed me with his own fingers in little nibbles as he'd slowly teased and tempted my body.

And now, I was sated in every possible way.

I'd never been in a penthouse suite before, and I was still surprised at how big it was. Even the bed was enormous, at least compared to what I had at home.

Although this was the same hotel where my mom had been staying earlier, it *wasn't* the same room, thank goodness. According to Jax, she'd been staying lower, in a room that was nice, but not like this.

As I caught my breath, I glanced around. The suite – as luxurious as it was – couldn't begin to compare to the place that Jax called home.

I said, "So I guess Jaden's back, huh?"

"What makes you say that?"

"Well, we're here, aren't we?"

Jax pulled away, and nestled himself beside me. "He's still gone, but that's not a factor."

"Oh?"

He gave a low laugh. "What, you think him being around would've stopped me?"

"It wouldn't?"

"Hell no. It's a big house, remember?"

I smiled. From last night, I *did* remember. But if privacy wasn't an issue, why was he splurging on a hotel room? I wanted to know, but wasn't quite sure how to ask. "So...."

"Why are we here?"

"Well, I *am* sort of curious."

He turned and brushed a lock of damp hair away from my eyes. "We're here, because you're gonna kiss that worry goodbye. Remember?"

He meant worry about my mom's thoughtless extravagance. I knew this, because he'd said so earlier, when he'd surprised me in the parking lot of the restaurant where I worked. By some miracle, I'd been sent home early, and like magic, he'd been right there in his car, waiting.

I smiled at the memory. And yet, I had to admit, "I'm not sure I'll be able to. I mean, I still hate that you got stuck with the bill."

"I didn't get stuck," he said. "It was my idea."

"But—"

He leaned over and silenced me with a kiss. One thing led to another and soon, worry was the last thing on my mind.

It wasn't until early the next morning when I realized something funny. With an embarrassed laugh, I said, "I don't know what I'm gonna wear home."

We'd just gotten out of the shower and were sitting in white hotel bathrobes on the balcony overlooking the ocean. I gestured vaguely toward the suite's interior, where my tattered clothes were still scattered about. "I mean, I can't wear my uniform, at least not without making a spectacle of myself."

He smiled. "Who says you're going anywhere?"

I loved the idea of staying, but that simply wasn't possible. At noon, I had to work.

Originally, this hadn't been the case, but after being informed last night that I was being sent home early, I'd talked one of my co-workers into giving up her shift the next day – today, in fact.

If only I'd known that I'd be spending the night with Jax, I might've taken the day off regardless. But I *hadn't* known, which was probably for the best.

After all, I did need the money.

When I mentioned the noon shift to Jax, he said, "So, blow it off."

"I can't just 'blow it off,'" I told him. "I practically begged Pam to give me the hours." I smiled. "And besides, you've probably got work to do yourself, right?"

"Nothing I can't postpone."

"Yeah, because you're the boss." I gave a playful eye-roll. "But me? I'm just a lowly waitress."

He reached out and tugged me onto his lap. Into my hair, he said, "You're not a lowly anything."

"I know. It's just a figure of speech, but I really *do* have to work." I gave a nervous laugh. "So, what do you think? Will I be able to make it out without giving everyone a show?"

"No one's getting a show but me." He pulled back and flicked his head toward the suite's interior. "Don't worry. I brought you some clothes."

"You did?" I gave him the squinty-eye. "So you *knew* you'd be destroying my uniform?"

"A guy can dream, right?"

He hadn't just dreamed. He made it a reality. And I sure as heck *wasn't* complaining.

But I *was* wondering. "So, whose clothes are they? I know you didn't bring any of mine, because Allie would've told me."

"I grabbed them from my place," he said. "From the same stash as before."

Obviously, he was referring to the clothes that he'd loaned me on that very first night.

"You know," I said, resting my head against his shoulder, "you never did tell me whose clothes they were."

"So, you wanna know?"

I nodded against him.

"They're Chloe's."

I tried not to stiffen at the unfamiliar name. "So, who's Chloe?" I pulled back to study his face. "An ex-girlfriend?"

"Why?" He grinned. "You jealous?"

I forced a little laugh. "Do I look jealous?"

"A little."

"Well, I'm not." Under my breath, I added, "Much."

Jax laughed. "Don't be. She's my brother's wife."

Now, *that* was unexpected. "Which brother? Jake?"

"Nah. My half-brother. Lawton."

For some reason, the name sounded vaguely familiar. *Lawton and Chloe.* And then it hit me, "Oh, my God. You don't mean Lawton Rastor?"

"Yeah, I do."

"He's your brother? I had no idea."

A few years earlier, I'd actually seen their crazy wedding proposal on the internet. Hell, me and a few bazillion other people. The guy was beyond famous, and Chloe had become semi-famous herself as a result of that video.

Jax was saying, "Yeah, but we don't like to publicize it."

"Why not?" I asked.

"Because I like to keep a low profile."

I could see that. Even though Jax had a ton of money, he could go out in public almost like a normal person. I doubted that would be the case for someone as famous as Lawton Rastor, or his wife, for that matter.

I was still processing what I'd just learned. "I was wearing *her* underwear? Seriously?"

"No."

"No?"

"Everything was new," he said. "I figured you wouldn't take them any other way."

This was true – and very sweet. "I know. I'm just saying, *she* bought them?"

"Her or Lawton. They were here a couple of months ago, and that's the room they stay in when they visit."

I was pretty sure he meant the same room that Allie had trashed. If only she knew. "So what happened?" I asked. "Did they forget some of their stuff when they left?"

"No. They keep some things at the house, to save on packing."

I couldn't imagine being so wealthy that I could afford to leave a bunch of clothing behind. Still, I *was* happy for them – and insanely relieved to hear that the items belonged to a relative as opposed to an ex.

It shouldn't have mattered, but for some reason, it did.

But this did pose another question. "So, you get along with him? Lawton, I mean?"

"Does that surprise you?"

"Sort of," I admitted. "I mean, the way you talk, it's like you don't get along with any of them, well, except for Jaden, anyway."

Jax was quiet for a long moment before saying, "Yeah. And there's a reason for that."

"What is it?" I asked.

"Ask me later, and I'll tell you."

"Why later?"

He smiled. "Because – as someone just told me – we're short on time. And hell if we're gonna spend it on anything dealing with my crazy-ass family."

I might've argued, except the way we spent our remaining time at The Plaza was nothing to complain about it. And besides, once I did hear the full story, it was easy to see why he hadn't wanted to share it.

It wasn't pretty. That was for sure.

CHAPTER 66

It was a Thursday night, and we were having drinks out on his patio – beer for him and wine for me. We'd been seeing each other exclusively for over a month, and I still knew very little about his family.

Obviously, it was a sore subject, so I'd been waiting for the right time to bring it up. But just now, Jax had mentioned something about cars, and it seemed like the perfect opening.

"Speaking of cars," I said, "you never *did* tell me why you took that car of Jake's."

"Hey, it was there."

"And...?"

"And I needed it."

"For what?"

He took a long pull of his beer. "To get to Florida."

This didn't tell me a whole lot, considering that we were in Florida now. "From where?" I asked.

"Michigan."

I almost dropped my glass. "You're kidding, right?"

"Nope."

"But that's like what? A twenty-hour drive?"

"Give or take."

I was staring now. "But you were fourteen years old."

"Yeah, so?"

"So that's not *nearly* old enough to drive, not legally anyway."

A few weeks ago, when he'd first mentioned the incident, I'd been shocked enough. But now, after learning that the drive had been cross-country, I was utterly flabbergasted.

From the chair beside me, Jax was saying, "Then it's a good thing we weren't stopped, huh?"

Obviously, he meant by the police, but he was missing the point. "So let me get this straight," I said. "You and Jaden stole—"

"Borrowed."

I gave him a look. Allie had made a similar claim when she'd "borrowed" her ex-boyfriend's truck. But in Allie's case, she'd had at least *some* plan to give it back.

I asked, "What does that mean? You were planning to return it?"

"I dunno," Jax said. "We didn't give it much thought."

It was a funny thing to say. I'd known Jax for months now. He was smart and almost never left anything to chance. I could hardly reconcile the guy I knew today with the kid he'd been.

"But why'd you do it?" I asked. "Were you going someplace in particular?" I tried to laugh. "I mean, *please* don't tell me you were just heading to the beach or something."

"We had a beach back home, didn't need a car for *that*."

I already knew that he'd been born in Michigan, so the statement made at least a little sense. His home-state was nearly surrounded by some of the biggest lakes in the world. No doubt, there *were* plenty of beaches.

"So...." I said, "if you weren't looking for a beach, what *were* you looking for?"

Jax turned forward to stare out over the horizon, where the moon was shimmering across the water. He was quiet for a long moment before saying, "My mom."

My breath caught. "What?"

"I was looking for my mom."

Up until now, he'd never mentioned his mom. Oh, sure, I realized that he had one, but on the rare times we even broached the topic of his family, he'd only mentioned his dad and a bunch of brothers.

Speaking more softly now, I said, "And she was in Florida?"

Jax was still gazing out over the horizon. After the briefest pause, he gave a tight nod.

His whole demeanor was making me nervous. "So, did you find her?"

"Yeah. We did."

I felt like I was treading on dangerous ground, but I loved him. For both of our sakes, I wanted to know. Still, I asked, "Would you rather not talk about it?"

He gave a tight shrug. "There's not much to say."

That couldn't be true. I tried to keep my tone light. "I'm not sure I believe *that*. Two teenagers? Cross-country? And a parent waiting? I bet there's a lot to tell."

Jax gave a bitter laugh. "She wasn't waiting."

"Oh." Now, I wanted to kick myself for my own stupid assumption. After all, I knew firsthand that being a mom and *acting* like a mom weren't always the same thing. "I'm really sorry."

"Don't be. It's not a big deal."

It was an obvious lie, and I dreaded calling him on it. But to let him stew alone in his pain – or whatever this was – seemed impossibly cruel.

I reached for his hand and gave it a squeeze. In a very soft voice, I said, "It seems like a big deal to me."

His hand closed around mine, and he turned to meet my gaze. "Back then, yeah, it felt like a big deal. But now? I don't think about it."

Cautiously, I said, "Do you want to tell me what happened?"

"Not much to tell," he said. "Life at home sucked. My mom left when I was thirteen. We always figured she'd come back, you know. She used to do that sometimes, take off for a few weeks, a few months. But she always came back."

I bit my lip. "But this time, she didn't?"

"No. She didn't." His mouth tightened. "I should've known. She'd been gone a long-ass time, almost a year. And us kids, we're all wondering if she's dead or something – even though my dad keeps telling us to shut up, she's not dead, she's just fucking around."

I gave a stunned shake of my head. "He didn't really say that?'

"Why not? It was the truth." Jax gave a low scoff. "But me and Jaden, we don't believe it. We start thinking, you know what, we'll bring her back."

At the image, I didn't know whether to smile or cry. "But how'd you know where she was?"

"My grandma – her mom – she lived a few blocks away."

"So *she* told you?"

"Not exactly," he said. "But it wasn't hard to figure out."

"How?" I asked.

"For starters, she never had any money, but then all of a sudden, she's driving a new car, putting new shutters on the house, things like that. It didn't make sense." His voice hardened. "And I just knew it had something to do with mom."

"So what'd you do?"

"Well, me and Jaden, we start lifting her mail."

"You mean your grandma's?"

Jax nodded. "Every day. Check it out, put it back. Sure enough, my mom's been sending checks from this address down in Florida. And so Jaden and I, we figure she must've gotten a job down there or something."

"So you decided to see for yourselves?"

"Right. Jake has this car, a total beater, but I'd driven the thing before, and Jaden and I get to thinking, 'What the fuck?' We'll go get her, tell her she's gotta come home."

At the image, I felt my eyes grow misty. "So, did you find her?"

"Oh yeah. We found her alright." He gave a bitter laugh. "You wanna hear something funny?"

Whatever it was, I was nearly certain that it wouldn't be funny at all. Bracing myself, I asked, "What?"

"When we get there, the skank is pregnant."

I stifled a gasp. I wasn't even sure if it was because he'd just called his mom a skank or because the image was such a surprise. Now, I had no idea what to say. Lamely, I murmured, "Wow."

Jax gave a low scoff. "Wow is right. I mean, there we are – me and Jaden – standing on her doorstep. And this doorstep, it's really fucking nice."

"How nice?" I asked.

"Nicer than our whole house back home. And the rest of the place, it's like a palace. And my mom's standing there in the doorway, looking at us like we're a couple of insurance salesmen that she's gotta get rid of."

I sucked in a horrified breath. "No."

"Oh yeah."

"So, what did you do?" I asked.

"Well, Jaden – the dumb-ass that he is – he starts asking, 'When are you coming home?' And she tells him, 'I *am* home. You didn't get the letter?'"

"Oh, my God." My stomach sank at the mere thought. "So she wrote you a letter, telling you she wasn't coming back?"

Jax gave another laugh, just as bitter as the one before. "Shit, she didn't write the letter. She got her husband's lawyer to write it."

I stared at him. "What?"

"Yeah," Jax said. "Turns out, she'd divorced my dad the year before, and neither one of them bothered to tell us."

"But wait a minute. How could they hide it? I mean, that's kind of hard, right?"

"Not for them. They fought all the time anyway."

I winced. "That bad, huh?"

"Eh, you get used to it," he said. "Funny though, they'd been yelling about divorce my whole life. Only sometime the year before, they went and did it." He paused. "Or more accurately, she got the ball rolling."

"So *she* divorced *him*? How do you know?"

"A few years ago, I had someone look into it."

"But didn't she at least want to see you?"

"Me and Jaden? Hell no."

"But why not?"

"Because she'd traded up, probably didn't want the complication."

It was so cold, I stifled a shiver. "Wow." At the sound of my own voice, I winced. "I guess I already said that, huh?"

Jax gave a half shrug. "What else can you say?"

"So what happened after you showed up there?" I asked. "I mean, I bet your dad was pretty worried, right?"

"Doubt it."

"What do you mean?"

"I mean, it's not like he came looking for us."

"Oh." I hesitated. "But what did he say when you got back home?"

"We didn't go back home."

"Not ever?"

"Nope."

"So, what did you do?"

"So we're a few miles from my mom's new place, and we're sitting there in the car, with no gas and no money – actually slept in the car a night or two. And this lady knocks on the car window and asks if we're okay. And we say 'Yeah, fuck off.'"

In spite of everything, I almost laughed. "You didn't."

Jax smiled. "We did."

"And what did she say?"

"She told us to 'fuck off' right back. And then, she tells us she's just made lasagna, and that we should get our asses inside before it gets cold."

"Inside where?"

"Her house."

"So, did you? Go inside, I mean?"

Jax shrugged. "Well, it *had* been a couple of days."

"And then what happened?"

"Nothing," he said.

"What do you mean nothing?"

"I mean, we never left."

I sat, stunned, for a long moment. Finally, I said, "And this lady, it's Darla, isn't it?"

"Good guess."

It wasn't *that* good, considering how obvious it should've been. This explained so much, but it also reminded of something I'd overheard on the night we'd first met.

"On the night of that party," I said, "Jaden threatened to tell Darla what you did last October. What was it?"

"Nothing, but it would still tick her off."

"Yeah, but what was it?" I persisted.

"The short story is, we paid off her house."

"And she didn't know it was you?"

"Technically, it was me and Jaden. And no, she doesn't know." He gave a rueful laugh. "I'd been wanting to do it for years, but she always got so ticked."

"So, how'd you manage it?"

"Some sweepstakes thing."

"What kind?"

"The kind you don't enter."

I smiled. "So you arranged for her to win a fake contest?"

"Pretty much."

I was glad. I'd only seen Darla a few times, and it was pretty obvious that she didn't like me. But I knew why and tried not to take it personally – at least not yet.

I said, "That must've been pretty awkward, with you dating her daughter."

"You're telling me," Jax said. "Dumbest thing I ever did." His voice softened. "But she's not all bad. You know, she's not Darla's natural kid any more than I am?"

"Really?"

"Really."

"How'd that happen?" I asked.

"The same way it happened with us – except it was a couple of years earlier."

I wanted to ask more, but wasn't sure that I should pry, at least not about Morgan, since they'd once been an item. And besides, there was something else that I was more desperate to know.

"Back to your brothers," I said, "is that why you guys don't get along? Because you never went back home?"

"That's part of it," Jax said. "But the other part is, well, Jake said some things that I didn't wanna hear."

"Like what?"

"For one thing, he called our mom a whore."

I tensed. "To her face?"

"Knowing him? Probably. But that's not what I meant. I meant, that's what he told me when he showed up in Florida."

"So he came looking for you?"

Jax gave a hard scoff. "No. He came looking for his car."

"Oh, come on," I said. "That couldn't've been the only reason he showed up."

"Wanna bet?" Jax said. "Shit, he even told me."

The more I learned, the more my heart went out to him. "But there's something I don't get," I said. "You said that Jake called your mom, well, something not very nice, and you said you didn't like it, but…" I wasn't quite sure how to put this.

"But I called her a skank?" He shrugged. "I guess I'm no angel either."

"You're wrong," I said. "You are."

I couldn't help but recall our conversation about *my* mom a couple of months earlier. At the time, it had seemed so out of character, but now, I thought I understood.

Obviously, he was dealing with family issues of his own. When another minute passed in silence, I leaned closer to him and said, "You've been *my* angel, anyway."

At this, he looked almost horrified. "Angel, huh?"

"Well, I mean, you've been really wonderful—"

He stood. "That's it."

I stared up at him. He didn't look angry. In fact, he looked almost amused. Or maybe that was just bravado.

Either way, I asked, "What do you mean?"

"I mean, I wanna show you something."

"Really? What?"

His gaze met mine. "That I'm no angel."

It took me a moment to realize what he meant. But when I did, I felt a weight lift from my shoulders. Maybe I didn't know exactly what to say, but I did know what I wanted to do – and that was to love him with every ounce of my being.

So that's what I did. And he loved me back – not just on that night, but on countless nights as the weeks slid by in blissful ignorance of something secret he'd been doing on the side.

No. He wasn't cheating – thank God. But it *was* something that sent me spiraling into all kinds of uncertainty.

CHAPTER 67

It was a sunny afternoon, and I had the day off. In fact, I'd had lots of days off lately. Probably, I should've been worried, but I wasn't.

The last few months had flown by in a flurry of sex and fun, with only the barest amount of work. It wasn't that I *wanted* to be a bum, but somehow, I always ended up with the shortest shifts and very few weekend shifts at all.

And, on the rare times I *was* scheduled to work on a weekend, it never failed that someone begged to take my place. In a way, I could see why. Weekend shifts were, by far, the most profitable because that's when the tips really stacked up.

Normally, I'd hate to give up so much money, but for once in my life, I was barely thinking about it at all.

The reason for that was obvious. In the last few months, my expenses had fallen to nearly nothing. I rarely needed groceries, because Jax was always taking me out. I never needed new clothes, because he was constantly taking me on surprise shopping trips. I wasn't even buying my own lattes anymore, because Jax was constantly surprising me with gift cards to my favorite little coffee shop.

This particular afternoon, I'd just used one of those cards for my daily latte when Kimmie, my favorite barista said, "Oh come on, lemme see it."

She was talking about my new driver's license, which I'd just gotten that day. After months of putting it off, I'd finally given up my Tennessee license, and was officially a Florida resident.

I laughed at Kimmie's request. "No way. It's like the worst picture ever."

"It can't be worse than mine." As proof, she reached under the counter and dug through her purse. A moment later, she handed me her license and said, "See?"

I gave it a quick look. It *was* bad, but not quite as bad as mine. "You're on," I said, handing back her license and digging out my own.

When I handed it over, she studied it for a long silent moment before saying, "Wow. That *is* bad."

She was right, of course. In the picture, my skin had this weird greenish hue, like I was from outer space or something. The only thing missing were the antennas.

Kimmie was still looking at my license. "Hey, you wanna hear something funny?"

"What?"

"You're living in my cousin's old place."

"No kidding?"

"Oh yeah." She pointed to the license. "I recognize the address. Man, she loved that apartment – hated to give it up though."

"Then why did she?" I asked.

"It was the rent," Kimmie said. "Three grand a month?" She gave a low whistle. "Hard to afford *that* on a bookkeeper's salary."

I paused. "Wait, three thousand? Are you sure?" She had to be mistaken. Allie and I were paying less than half that amount.

"Oh yeah," Kimmie said. "I told her she was biting off more than she could chew, but she was insistent, said she'd get a roommate or something. She even asked me, but there was no way I could afford *that*, or rather, half-that, I guess, since we'd be splitting it."

I was so confused, I didn't know what to say.

Kimmie paused to study my face. "What's wrong?"

"Nothing." I summoned up a smile. "It's just that, well, that's not what *we* pay."

"Oh, I believe *that*," she said. "Rent's been going up all over." She looked toward the window. "It's because of the beach. The closer it is, the pricier things get."

She looked back me and sighed. "And one thing about waterfront, they're not making any more of it, that's for sure."

I nodded, even as my mind whirled. Why was my rent less? Rent never went down. *Did it?*

Kimmie was still talking. "Just between you and me, even the coffee shop was having trouble."

"Trouble with what?" I asked.

"The rent," she said. "Just like everywhere."

"But they got it all sorted out?"

"Yeah, but only because a new company bought the property."

"Oh, so you're under new management?"

Kimmie shook her head. "No. It's just that a different company owns the building, and they're charging us less for rent."

So rent *did* go down, at least sometimes. Still, something about the whole situation seemed not quite right, and I couldn't stop thinking about it.

So later that afternoon, I did a little research, and what I learned made me feel more than a little funny.

CHAPTER 68

Allie had just walked into the apartment when I said, "I've got a question. Double J – does that mean anything to you?"

She shut the door behind her and dropped her purse onto the nearby side table. "Yeah, why?"

"Well?" I said. "What does it mean?"

She looked at me like I was crazy. "You know what it means. *You're* the one who got me the job."

I groaned. "So it *is* them?"

"If you mean Jax and Jaden, yeah. What, you didn't know?"

"No. I didn't. I mean, I knew their initials, and I knew the name of their regular company, but I didn't know they had that whole other side thing going."

"You mean the real estate?"

"Yeah. It's like they own half the city."

"Not just *this* city," she said. "They've got property all over."

I was frowning now. "Yeah. Including *this* place."

Allie stared at me for a long moment. "No." And then, she glanced around the apartment. "They don't, do they? Are you sure?"

"Definitely. And get this, they *also* own the restaurant where I work."

"Oh. Um, no kidding?"

I felt my gaze narrow. "You knew?"

"Me?"

Allie was a terrible liar. I gave her a serious look. "Yes. You."

She winced. "If I did, is that bad?"

"Yes," I said. "It's bad. *Very* bad."

"Why?"

"Oh come on," I said. "You didn't tell me. What does *that* tell you?"

"Huh?"

"I'm just saying, you *had* to know it was bad, or you would've mentioned it."

"Alright, fine," she said. "I knew. But I figured you'd feel funny if you found out."

"Of course, I feel funny," I said. "I work for my freaking boyfriend."

She gave me a tentative smile. "Well, technically you don't *really* work for him. I mean, he's not the manager or anything."

I made a scoffing sound. "Yeah, because it's worse. He's the manager's manager with a whole bunch of people in-between." In a flash, I suddenly realized something that I should've considered hours ago. "Oh, my God. I bet *that's* why I never work weekends."

"Oh, stop," Allie said. "Now, you're just being paranoid."

"I am not," I said. "Do you know how rare it is for a waitress to get weekends off?"

"Yeah, but you've worked weekends."

"Not lately," I said. "And get this, if I ever *am* scheduled for a weekend, someone always begs to take my place."

"Well, maybe they need the money. You did say those shifts were the best, right?"

"Sure, but don't you think that's odd? I mean, to be asked every single time to switch?"

"Maybe a little," she admitted. "But hey, they've gotta make their rent somehow, right?"

At this, I gave a hard scoff.

Allie hesitated. "What now?"

"Rent," I said. "How much do we pay a month?"

"Twelve-hundred, as if you didn't know."

"Yeah. Twelve-hundred. Wanna know what the *last* people paid?"

"I dunno. A thousand?"

I gave another scoff.

"You should probably stop that," she said, "or you're gonna hork up a lung or something."

I gave her a look. "Ha ha. Now, guess again."

She gave it some thought. "Nine hundred?"

I shook my head. "You're going in the wrong direction."

"Sorry, what?"

"The last person – or who knows, maybe a few persons ago – they paid more."

Allie paused. "How much more?"

"A lot."

"How much is a lot?"

"Eighteen hundred."

Her surprise was obvious. "Wait a minute, so they paid eighteen hundred for this place?"

"No, it's worse. They paid three thousand. I meant the *difference* was eighteen-hundred."

Now Allie was staring. "No."

"Yes."

Silently, she took a slow look around. As she did, I could practically read her thoughts, because they were same as mine just a couple of hours earlier. The place was nice and only a block from the beach.

From the first moment we'd seen it, we couldn't believe our good luck. Now, it was beyond obvious that luck had nothing to do with it.

Allie murmured, "But I write the checks. They go to that realtor."

"Yeah," I said. "A realtor who manages the property – on *their* behalf."

"Are you sure?"

"Oh yeah."

"And you learned all of this, how?"

In reply, I told her about my conversation with Kimmie and then went on to say, "So it got me thinking. And I made some calls, did a little digging on the internet, too. But trust me, the information's good."

Allie blew out a long breath. "Wow." And then, like someone in a dream, she walked to the nearest chair and fell back into it. "Shit."

I sank down in the chair opposite her. "Is that good or bad?"

"I don't know."

"Should I say something? To Jax, I mean?"

"I don't know," she repeated.

I sighed. "I can't just pretend to not know."

I'd already done the math. Allie and I had been living here for over four months. During that timeframe, we'd underpaid our rent by more than seven thousand dollars.

And counting.

That was a lot of money.

I thought back to the last few months, when I'd been living the high life on someone else's dime. Slowly, I sat back in the chair. "Oh, my God."

"What?"

Suddenly, I was feeling sick to my stomach. "I'm turning into my mom."

CHAPTER 69

It had been several days since I'd last seen him, and I'd been missing him like crazy. And yet, I kept on avoiding him, mostly because I still didn't know what to do about everything I'd learned.

On one hand, I was beyond thankful for all of his help. But at the same time, I knew exactly where this road led. And if I ever forgot, a nice visit with my mom would be the perfect reminder.

Funny, I couldn't even do *that*, because she and Tabitha were off on some extended trip to California, supposedly to visit some of their old haunts. By now, they'd been away for so long, I started to wonder if they were gone for good.

The timing *would* be about right. After all, they did have that habit of moving from place to place in search of new thrills and the guys who'd be paying for them.

As for myself, I wasn't seeking any thrills at all as I tried to focus on regular things, like earning money for whatever might happen next.

It was a Thursday night, and I was just leaving work when Becka, a fellow waitress, called out, "Hey Cassidy, wait up, will ya?"

When I stopped and turned around, she scurried forward and said, "I'm looking for extra hours. Wanna give up tomorrow's shift?"

Tomorrow was the first Friday I'd been scheduled to work in forever. A week ago, I would've jumped at Becka's offer.

Not anymore.

I shook my head. "Thanks, but I'd better keep this one."

Her face fell. "Are you sure?"

"Yeah. Sorry."

"Are you *really* sure?"

"Uh, yeah." I gave a shaky laugh. "Gotta pay the rent, right?"

She bit her lip. "So....you're not gonna change your mind?"

No. I wasn't. And her persistence was rubbing me the wrong way. Still, I summoned up a smile. "Maybe you should ask Tori."

Becka frowned. "Why *her*?"

"Because she sounds like she's coming down with a cold. I bet she'd love tomorrow off."

Becka was still frowning. "Yeah, but I'd rather switch with you."

Okaaaaay. That was a bit strange. "Why me?"

She shrugged. "Why not?"

I felt my gaze narrow. "Is there something I should know?"

At first, she denied it. But then, after a good deal of nagging – plus a bribe, if you can believe it – I finally had the whole story.

And I wasn't happy.

Ten minutes later, I was walking through the parking lot with my head down and my thoughts churning like a jumbled crazy mess. I was flattered. And angry. And very, very confused.

I was so lost in my thoughts that it took me a moment to notice Jax leaning up against his car – or rather, one of his cars. Cripes, the guy had so many, I could hardly keep track.

I stopped in mid-step and stared at him from across the distance. His gaze met mine, and he smiled like he always did when he was happy to see me. I tried to smile back, but my lips wouldn't cooperate.

His smile faded, and he strode forward, meeting me more than halfway, between a long row of cars. In a low voice, he asked, "Baby, what's wrong?"

We were standing very close, and I couldn't decide if I wanted to fall into his arms or run in the opposite direction. "Nothing."

His gaze probed mine. "Tell me."

I *so* didn't want to do this, to play the old, "nothing" game and make him guess over and over. But honestly, I wasn't sure that anything *was* wrong. I mean, I should be thankful, right?

In a way, I was.

And yet, this wasn't where I wanted my life to go. I didn't know how to explain or where to begin. But I *did* know that a parking lot – *this* parking lot in particular – was no place for this discussion.

I sighed. "I don't want to talk about it, at least not here."

He looked at me for a long moment before saying, "Alright. You wanna grab dinner or something?"

Probably, this was the wrong question, because it only fueled my suspicions. I'd been scheduled to work until much later, but the restaurant had been slow, and like so many other nights, I'd been the one selected to leave early.

I stared up at Jax. "How'd you know I was leaving?"

"What do you mean?"

"I mean," I said, "I was supposed to work 'til ten."

"Yeah, so?"

"So it's not even eight."

"And…?"

"And you had my schedule," I said, "so why are you here?"

He frowned. "Am I not supposed to be?"

This should've been hilarious. I tried to laugh, but the sound came out wrong. "Sure you are. I mean, you *do* own the place, right?"

At this, he grew very still. In a carefully neutral tone, he said, "Is that a problem?"

"Well, it would've been nice to know."

"Yeah? Why's that?"

"Because it's weird that I didn't."

"Not to me."

I made a sound of frustration. "But it's weird to *me*. The whole situation is. Doesn't that count for something?"

"You know it does."

"So….?"

"So maybe you were better off not knowing."

I made a scoffing sound. "Well, that's rich. So tell me, what else don't I know?"

As he gazed down at me, I could practically see the wheels turning. Probably, he was wondering exactly what I knew.

I knew a lot, but at that moment, I had to wonder, was there anything else?

There couldn't be, right?

But as it turned out, I was wrong.

CHAPTER 70

In front of me, Jax still hadn't answered.

I gave him a stiff smile. "Would you like to hear what I know already? Would *that* help?"

He paused to study my face. "I doubt it."

What was that? Sarcasm? I felt my teeth clench, even as I said, "I *know* that you own the place where I work." I kept the smile plastered in place as I continued. "But I've already mentioned that, so let's move on, shall we?"

See? I can do sarcasm, too.

When he made no reply, I kept on going. "You own the place where I live. You own the car that I drive. You–"

"The car, it's yours, just like I said."

"It can't be mine," I pointed out. "I haven't paid you for it."

"You don't have to. It's a gift."

Yes. And it was incredibly thoughtful. I realized this. But my mom had received plenty of gifts, too – including a car from that auto executive she'd dated a few years back.

As far as my car, the one from Jax, I loved it. Truly, I did. But I didn't love it nearly as much as the guy who'd bought it.

And now, like some sort of ingrate, I was giving him a hard time.

Right on cue, there it was – that familiar whiplash between gratitude and fear, contentment and panic, love and obligation. It was too much, and suddenly, I almost felt like crying.

Jax reached out, as if to pull me into his arms. I held up my hands, palm-out. "Don't distract me, okay?"

He stiffened. "I wasn't trying to."

On some level, I knew that I was being unreasonable, but I couldn't seem to make myself stop. Oh sure, it would've been so easy to fall into his arms and pretend that everything was okay.

And maybe it *should've* been okay. Hell, my mom would've been delighted to be in my shoes. In a way, I *was* delighted.

I loved him so very much.

And I knew he loved me.

But this road, it was so dangerous, because I knew exactly where it ended.

I took a deep breath and tried to smile. "Just let me finish, okay?"

His mouth tightened, but said nothing.

Deliberately I softened my tone. "I know you've been bribing people."

His face was unreadable. "Yeah? Who?"

"Well, my co-workers, and probably the manager, too."

I waited for him to deny it. But he didn't. Instead, he looked away and muttered, "Fuck."

"So, you were?"

He returned his gaze to mine and said, "Maybe I didn't see it that way."

"Oh yeah? So, how did you see it?"

"A win-win," he said. "Trust me, they weren't complaining."

No doubt, they weren't. I recalled what Becka had told me. Through some weird arrangement with the manager, she'd been getting a fifty dollar bonus – in cash, no less – for every weekend shift she worked in my place.

Obviously, she hadn't been the only one. Already, I could think of two other waitresses who'd been begging for my shifts.

I looked to Jax and asked, "So why'd you do it?"

His gaze met mine. "You know why."

"To spend time with me?"

"That's part of it."

"And the other part?"

"You were happier when you didn't work."

I almost laughed. "Yeah. Everyone is. But that doesn't mean you should go around bribing people."

"I don't care about 'everyone.'" His voice softened. "I care about you."

His words were so sweet, and he obviously meant them. Still, he hadn't answered my earlier question, and I felt compelled to ask it again. "So tell me, what else have you been doing?"

When his only reply was a tight shrug, I said, "I'll find out eventually, you know."

He was silent for a long moment. And then, he asked, "And what happens when you do?"

"What do you mean?"

"Let's say you do find something else. What then?"

"I don't know," I admitted. "I hardly know what to do already."

"And why's that?"

I wanted to explain, but I hardly knew where to begin. Just then, a noisy group of customers emerged from the restaurant and began heading in our direction. I bit my lip and waited, praying they'd pass quickly.

Jax watched them for only an instant before saying, "Come on. We can talk at my place."

I didn't want to talk at his place. It was too darn distracting, and the thought of running into Jaden was more than I could stomach. I shook my head. "How about mine?" I gave a humorless laugh. "Or should I say yours? You know, since you own it and all."

His voice was quiet. "Forget that."

"I can't. I shouldn't. I mean, I know I should be paying a lot more in rent."

He shook his head. "If I had *my* way, you'd be paying nothing."

I believed him, too. Probably, the only reason we paid rent at all was to keep us from getting suspicious.

Too late for that.

When I said nothing in response, he gestured to his car. "C'mon. I'll drive us."

"Where?"

"To your place, like you said."

I glanced toward his car and hesitated. "Actually, would you mind if I walked instead?"

He glanced in the general direction of my apartment. "Why?"

"Because I want time to think, and I always think better when I'm walking." This was true, but it wasn't my only reason. Knowing Jax, he'd coax me out to dinner, or maybe to his place, and I'd lose control over everything.

"Alright," he said. "But I'm walking with you."

"Why?"

"Because you're upset, and I don't want you going alone."

I sighed. "I'm not upset. I'm confused."

"You're both." He gave me the ghost of a smile. "And I'm coming with you, so deal with it."

In spite of everything, I almost laughed. This was vintage Jax, and I loved him all the more for it.

I even loved how he wasn't mentioning that my own car was parked just a few car lengths away, making my decision to walk sound doubly stupid.

I couldn't help but smile. "Actually, that would be really nice."

And it *was*, especially when he started telling me some things that I *didn't* know – even if I should've.

CHAPTER 71

Our walk began in silence, with each of us lost in our own thoughts, or maybe that was just me.

We were halfway to my place when Jax said, "I saw you, you know."

I wasn't sure what he was talking about. "You mean in the parking lot?"

"No. On the street, the night we met. I saw *you* before you saw *me*."

I gave an embarrassed laugh. "Well, obviously, since I was playing in traffic."

"No." His voice was quiet. "You were running. And you were scared."

"I wasn't *really* running," I tried to make a joke of it. "High heels and all."

"Yeah. But you bolted anyway."

This was true, but only because I'd been so desperate. Between my mom and the limo driver, I'd felt incredibly trapped and yes, maybe a little frightened, especially when the driver had refused to pull over. In the end, feigning sickness was all I had.

At the memory, I stifled a shiver. "That was quite a night, huh?"

"Best night of my life."

At this, I stopped walking. And so did Jax.

I turned to face him and said, "It couldn't've been *that* good, with the accident and all."

He gave a slow shake of his head. "It was no accident."

"Sorry, what?"

"The crash," he said. "It wasn't by accident."

This made no sense. "So, what was it?"

"You want the whole story?"

Wordlessly, I nodded.

"That night," he began, "I'm sitting in Jaden's car, waiting at one of our warehouses for him to catch up, and I see this limo fly by and then veer off to the side. The thing screeches to a stop, and the back door opens. A split-second later, I see the most beautiful girl bolt out, like she's making a break for it."

Listening, I felt a rush of heat, but I couldn't tell if it was due to embarrassment or something in his voice, something incredibly tender. Whatever it was, it was making me feel warm all over.

Jax continued. "And this girl, she looks scared, and I'm thinking, I don't want her to be scared. And I sure as hell don't want anything bad to happen. And I'm just about to head over there when I see the driver's door fly open."

I blinked. "Did it really? *I* didn't see it."

"Yeah, because you were looking the other way. But the driver leans out, and something in his look, well, I didn't like it."

I didn't like the look either. Oh sure, I hadn't seen it *that* time, but I *had* seen his expression in the rear-view mirror when I'd slid aside the glass to tell him that I was about to be sick.

He'd been annoyed, and not just a little.

Now, Jax was saying, "But I'm a long ways off, on foot anyway."

Listening to him, I was utterly mesmerized. I knew how the story ended, but the beginning was something new. When he said nothing more, I asked, "So, what did you do?"

"You saw what I did." He gave me a rueful smile. "I floored it."

At the simple explanation, I almost laughed out loud. I couldn't resist teasing him, at least a little. "You were awful close."

"To you? Nah. Sure, I cut it closer than I liked, but I'll tell you one thing, the driver was back inside before he knew what hit him." Jax paused. "Or, almost hit him, if you wanna get technical."

Now, I did laugh. But the laughter didn't last, because I suddenly recalled what happened afterward. "But then you crashed. I felt so bad. I still do." I searched his gaze. "And you could've been hurt."

"Nah. I was ready. 'Cause like I said, it was no accident."

"So what are you saying? You crashed on purpose? Why would you do that?"

"Why not?" he said. "It worked, right?"

"But the car—"

"…is just a car," he said. "And we owned the van, so…" He gave a loose shrug and didn't bother finishing the sentence.

I tried to think. "But when you came up to talk to us, you were so calm."

"Yeah, because I didn't want to scare you. And you want the truth?"

I felt myself nod.

"You were so fucking beautiful, it took my breath away."

I smiled. It was such a lovely thing to say, and I really *did* appreciate it. And yet, I couldn't help but recall what Morgan had told me on his front doorstep. "Thanks. That's really nice, but…"

"But what?"

I forced a laugh. "Well, I'm no pediatrician."

"And that matters, why?"

"Well, I know that you like women who are…" I made little air quotes. "…'accomplished', I guess."

"And you're not?"

"Hardly. I'm just a waitress."

He reached for my hand. "You're not 'just' anything. You're the most incredible person I've ever met."

"Oh come on," I said. "That can't be true."

"Yeah? Why not?"

"It's just not. That's all."

"Listen," he said, "I've known a shit-ton of people in my life, people who've had it a lot easier than you, and turned out a lot worse."

"But—"

"But nothing. Just hear me out, alright?"

Again, I nodded.

"My dad? He married the most beautiful girl he'd ever seen. And you know what it got him? A load of grief." Jax shook his head. "That wasn't gonna be me, lost in a pretty face or a hot body." He gave my hand a tender squeeze. "You won't always look like this, you know."

I looked down. He was right, of course. In fifty years, I'd look totally different. And so would he. But I'd still love him, well, assuming that by some miracle, we were still together.

He smiled down at me. "I called you beautiful. And you are. But that's not why I love you. It's not even the first thing I liked."

"Really? What was?"

"You."

"But—"

"On the inside," he clarified. "There you were, up to your neck in who-knows-what, and you're worried about me, the car, everyone but yourself. You took a lot of shit from your mom that night, but you got really riled when she started in on me. And I thought, 'Man, I bet she'd make a great mom.'"

I stifled a sudden giggle. "You didn't."

"I did." His voice grew softer. "And, before that, a great wife. A partner. Someone to grow old with."

I sucked in a breath. "Oh, c'mon. You didn't really."

"Why not?" he said. "I'm not one to mess around."

This was true. Jaden might mess around, but Jax wasn't like that. Now, I didn't know what to say. I was almost too overwhelmed to speak.

Into my silence, he said, "But this girl – the girl I love – she won't let me do a damn thing for her." He gave me a crooked smile. "So yeah, maybe I've gotta get creative, but the way I see it, she deserves to be spoiled, even if I've gotta hide it once in a while."

I was still smiling. "Once in a while? Oh, please. You've been hiding everything."

He grinned. "I know. Including this." As he spoke, he reached into his pocket and pulled out a little black box. A moment later, he sank to one knee right there on the sidewalk.

My breath caught.

This wasn't happening.

It couldn't be.

But then, he said, "I love you. And you know what I'm gonna ask."

My tongue was in knots, and my eyes were growing misty. "I, um…"

He smiled. "And you're gonna say yes. You know that, right?"

I *did* know that. I loved him. And I could think of nothing better in this whole world than to spend the rest of my life with him. I felt myself nod.

He whispered, "That's my girl." And then, he said it. "Cassidy…"

I could hardly breathe. "Yeah?"

"Will you marry me?"

A choked laugh escaped my lips. "Yes."

EPILOGUE

I almost tackled him right then and there. Probably, the only thing that stopped me was the realization that getting both of us banged up on the sidewalk would be a horrible waste, considering what I desperately wanted to do next.

So instead, I reached out and tugged him to his feet, giving him nearly no time at all to slip the ring on my finger. But when he did, I realized something – something I should've known all along.

I wasn't my mom. I couldn't be, even if I tried. Oh sure, on the outside, we might've been twins. But on the inside, we were two different people entirely.

I loved Jax – and for all the right reasons. I would've loved him just the same if he drove a van or moved boxes for a living.

Maybe I was funny that way. But how could I help it? He was, well, simply amazing.

Almost in a dream, we walked hand-in-hand, heading toward the apartment. Allie had just left for a week-long trip out of town, which meant that Jax and I could celebrate in style, and I didn't mean with a fancy dinner or public display.

As we walked, we swapped secrets back and forth. He admitted everything that I'd suspected him of doing. And me? Well, I admitted that I loved all of it, even if I felt a little funny sometimes.

We practically burst through the apartment door, working at our buttons as we moved. I'd missed him so very much, and we had some serious making up to do.

Funny though, we never got the chance, at least not in my apartment, because we'd barely reached the sofa when a thump sounded from the rear of the apartment.

I froze. And so did Jax.

Unless I was mistaken, the sound had come from Allie's bedroom. I stifled a giggle. "Oh, crap."

Jax flashed me a grin and murmured, "No kidding."

I whispered, "But her flight left at six." Or at least, I'd *thought* it was leaving at six. *Maybe it was delayed?*

I glanced at the side table near the door. Sure enough, her purse was right there where she usually dropped it.

Still, I refused to see this as a totally bad thing.

I wanted Jax so bad I could taste it, but the thought of telling Allie was impossible to resist. I whispered, "Would you mind waiting just a second? I'd really like to tell her."

He smiled. "Hey, you're worth the wait. I'll tell ya what. Remember that suite at The Plaza?"

I gave a happy nod.

He reached for my hand. "Let's go back."

I couldn't help but snicker. "Only if there's lobster, and plenty of it."

He grinned. "Well, aren't you getting spoiled."

"I hope not."

"Yeah? Well, I hope *so*. In fact, you just wait. I'm gonna guarantee it."

It was a wonderful thing to say, but the way I saw it, I was *already* spoiled, and I told him so with a long, lingering kiss.

And then, laughing, I bounded away, heading toward Allie's room. After only a single knock, I barged in, only to stop in stunned disbelief.

She wasn't alone. She wasn't even clothed. And neither was the guy with her. And just who *was* that guy?

My future brother-in-law.

Jaden Bishop.

What the hell?

THE END

Other Books in the Bishop Brothers World
(Listed by Couple)

Jaden & Allie
One Bad Idea

Lawton & Chloe
Unbelonging (Unbelonging, Book 1)
Rebelonging (Unbelonging, Book 2)
Lawton (Lawton Rastor, Book 1)
Rastor (Lawton Rastor, Book 2)

Bishop & Selena
Illegal Fortunes

Jake & Luna
Jaked (Jaked Book 1)
Jake Me (Jaked, Book 2)
Jake Forever (Jaked, Book 3)

Joel & Melody
Something Tattered (Joel Bishop, Book 1)
Something True (Joel Bishop, Book 2)

ABOUT THE AUTHOR

Sabrina Stark writes edgy romances featuring plucky girls and the bad boys who capture their hearts.

She's worked as a fortune-teller, barista, and media writer in the aerospace industry. She has a journalism degree from Central Michigan University and is married with one son and a pack of obnoxiously spoiled kittens. She currently makes her home in Northern Alabama.

ON THE WEB

Learn About New Releases & Exclusive Offers
www.SabrinaStark.com

Made in the USA
Monee, IL
30 November 2025

36882887R00218